GOLD *of* KINGS

**Center Point
Large Print**

Also by Davis Bunn
Available from Center Point Large Print:

Winner Take All
Elixir
The Lazarus Trap
Imposter
Full Circle

**This Large Print Book carries the
Seal of Approval of N.A.V.H.**

GOLD *of* KINGS

Davis Bunn

CENTER POINT PUBLISHING
THORNDIKE, MAINE

This Center Point Large Print edition
is published in the year 2009 by arrangement with
Howard Books and Touchstone Books,
a division of Simon & Schuster, Inc.

The text of this Large Print edition is unabridged.
In other aspects, this book may vary
from the original edition.
Printed in the United States of America.
Set in 16-point Times New Roman type.

ISBN: 978-1-60285-542-7

Library of Congress Cataloging-in-Publication Data

Bunn, T. Davis, 1952-
  Gold of kings / Davis Bunn.
     p. cm.
  ISBN 978-1-60285-542-7 (library binding : alk. paper)
  1. Large type books. I. Title.

PS3552.U4718G66 2009b
813'.54--dc22

2009012513

TO PAUL AND MARION FIDDES
Your wisdom and example have enlarged our vision more than you will ever know.

ACKNOWLEDGMENTS

Researching this story has been the work of dreams, and the people who helped shape the tale include a number of new friends. Among them is Jane A. Levine, formerly the assistant federal prosecutor of New York, now vice president of compliance at Sotheby's. The importance of Jane's input cannot be overstated. Also helping with research on the international trade in art and treasures was Judy Oppel, director of the Palm Beach Art and Antiquities Fair, and her assistant, Caitland MacEntyre. My thanks also to James Sheeran, Publisher of *Palm Beach Society* magazine. And a very special note of gratitude to Herbert Horsley, proprietor of the Trafalgar Square antiques shop in Vero Beach, and one of the nation's leading collectors of fore-edged books. Thanks must also go to my mother, Becky Bunn, an expert in the American Jacobean movement, for instilling in me a love of all things old and rare and beautiful.

Debbie Bernstein, a former CIA operative now with DOD intel, has helped immensely in shaping today's Washington scene and Interpol's connection. Brian Hunter, former AF special ops, has aided considerably in getting the feel as well as the vision of our most highly trained hunters. Thanks also to James P. Wynne, special agent with the FBI.

Bob Marx is one of the world's most highly acclaimed treasure hunters. His help was invaluable, and his tales a treasure trove. His wife, Jennifer, is a renowned expert in the molecular sourcing of ancient gold artifacts. Mel Fisher's entire organization went out of their way to assist in structuring a true-to-life overview of the modern treasure salvage business. Thanks also to Dr. Alan Marumoto, a radiologist whose weekend passion is aiding in finding underwater wrecks, and to Tom Morrisey, editor of *Sport Diver* magazine.

Roberta Harris-Eckstein is chief librarian at the Leo Baeck College. Her assistance was vital in several areas, especially in the accurate portrayal of early Judaic history, the contents of the Copper Scroll, and Josephus' description of the Second Temple.

There was considerable difficulty in knowing which names to use for cities in what is now Turkish Cyprus. Even the locals seemed to switch back and forth between the former Greek names and the newer Turkish ones. The older the inhabitant, the more he tended to rely on the Greek. In most cases, I have stuck to the modern Turkish renditions. But in one case, Kyrenia, I have avoided the Turkish name of Girne. The reason is simply that almost all the locals I spoke with kept to the Greek name. Like everything else attached to the island's current tragic state, any such decision is going to raise the hackles of some people somewhere. I can only say that no offense was intended. Cyprus was one of the most breathtakingly beautiful places I have ever visited. Wherever I went, I was met with a hospitality that humbled me. The very earth seemed to breathe history, as though the past four thousand years walked alongside me. I have tried to instill in this story a bit of the wonder I discovered while visiting that amazing land.

I am deeply indebted to Dave Lambert, for his gentle skills as editor and guide through the publishing process. I am also most grateful to others within Simon & Schuster who have contributed so much, particularly John Howard, Denny Boultinghouse, and Mark Gompertz.

And to my wife, Isabella, who has encouraged me through yet another mystery quest, I can only offer my heartfelt thanks and love.

ONE

THE RAIN PELTING SEVENTH AVENUE tasted of diesel and big-city friction. Sean Syrrell stared out the limo's open window and let the day weep for him.

Sean gripped his chest with one hand, trying to compress his heart back into shape. His granddaughter managed to make the end of the block only because her aunt supported her. They turned the corner without a backward glance. Not till they were lost from view did Sean roll up his window.

Storm's survival demanded that she be cut loose. He had fired her because it was the only way he could protect her. Sean knew the enemy was closing in. He had felt the killer's breath for days. Storm was his last remaining hope for achieving his lifelong dream, and establishing his legacy.

But the knowledge he had been right to fire her did little to ease the knife-edged pain that shredded his heart.

The driver asked, "Everything okay, Mr. Syrrell?"

Sean glanced at the young man behind the wheel. The driver was new, but the company was the only one he used ever since the danger had been revealed. If the enemy wanted a way to monitor his movements in New York, he'd handed it to them on a platter. "Why don't you go for a coffee or something. I'd like a moment."

11

"No can do, sir. I leave the wheel, they pull my license."

Sean stared blindly at the rain-streaked side window. He could only hope that one day Storm would understand, and tell Claudia, and the pair of them would forgive him.

Unless, of course, he was wrong and the threat did not exist.

But he wasn't wrong.

"Mr. Syrrell?"

Sean opened his door and rose from the car. "Drop my bags off at the hotel. We're done for the day."

Sean passed the Steinway showroom's main entrance, turned the corner, pressed the buzzer beside the painted steel elevator doors, and gave his name. A white-suited apprentice grinned a hello and led him downstairs. Sean greeted the technicians, most of whom he knew by name. He chatted about recent acquisitions and listened as they spoke of their charges. The ladies in black. Always feminine. Always moody and temperamental. Always in need of a firm but gentle hand.

Among professional pianists, the Steinway showroom's basement was a place of myth. The long room was clad in whitewashed concrete. Beneath exposed pipes and brutal fluorescent lights stood Steinway's most valuable asset: their collection of concert pianos.

All but one were black. The exception had been

finished in white as a personal favor to Billy Joel. Otherwise they looked identical. But each instrument was unique. The Steinway basement had been a place of pilgrimage for over a hundred years. Leonard Bernstein, Vladimir Horowitz, Sergei Rachmaninoff, Leon Fleisher, Elton John, Glenn Gould, Alfred Brendel, Mitsuko Uchida. They all came. An invitation to the Steinway basement meant entry to one of the world's most exclusive musical circles.

Sean Syrrell had not been granted access because of his talent. As a pianist, he was mechanical. He did not play the keys so much as box with the music. He lacked the finesse required for greatness. But fifteen years ago, he had done Steinway a great favor. He had located and salvaged the grand that had graced the White Palace, summer home to the Russian czars.

After the Trotsky rebellion, the piano had vanished. For years the world believed that Stalin had placed it in his dacha, then in a drunken rage had chopped it up for firewood. But Sean had found it in a Krakow junk shop the year after the Berlin Wall fell, just one more bit of communist flotsam. He had smuggled it west, where Germany's finest restorer had spent a year returning it to its original pristine state. It was now housed in the Steinway family's private collection.

The basement was overseen by Steinway's chief technician. He and an assistant were "juicing" the hammers of a new concert grand. Sean spent a few minutes listening and discussing the piano's raw tones. Then he moved to his favorite. CD-18 was more or less retired from service after 109 years of touring. Occasionally it was brought out as a favor to a special Steinway client. The last time had been for a voice-piano duet—Lang Lang and Pavarotti. For fifteen years, Van Cliburn had begged Steinway to sell him the instrument. Yet here it remained.

Sean seated himself and ran through a trio of exercises. His hands were too stubby for concert-quality play, his manner at the keys too brusque. Added to that were his failing ears, which had lost a great deal of their higher-range tonality. And his strength, which these days was far more bluster than muscle. And his heart, which still thudded painfully from firing Storm.

This time, it took a great deal longer than usual to leave the world behind. He hovered, he drifted, yet he was not transported. The tragic elements of his unfolding fate held him down.

When peace finally entered his internal realm, Sean switched to an étude by Chopin. It was a courtly dance, even when thumped out by his bricklayer's hands. The instrument was bell-like, a radiant sound that caused even his antiquated frame to resonate.

Between the first and second movement, his playing transported him away from the realm of business and debt and his own multitude of failings. He knew others believed he harbored an old man's fantasy of playing on the concert stage. But that was rubbish. He was here because twice each year, for a few treasured moments, an instrument brought him as close to divinity as Sean Syrrell would ever come. At least, so long as he was chained to this traumatic ordeal called life.

Sean detected a subtle shift in the chamber's atmosphere. He was well aware of what it probably meant. He shut his eyes and turned to his favorite composer. Brahms was so very right for the moment, if indeed he was correct in thinking the moment had arrived.

Brahms above all composers had managed to form prayer into a series of notes. Yet Brahms had always been the hardest for Sean to play. Brahms required gentle eloquence. Normally Sean Syrrell played with all the gentleness of a drummer.

Today, however, Sean found himself able to perform the melody as it should be performed, as a supplicant with a lover's heart.

Then Sean heard a different sound. A quiet hiss, accompanied by a puff of air on his cheek.

Sean opened his eyes in time to see a hand reflected in the piano's mirrored surface, moving away from his face. It held a small crystal vial.

Sean's cry of alarm was stifled by what felt like a hammer crashing into his chest. He doubled over the instrument, and his forehead slammed into the keyboard. But he heard none of it.

His entire being resonated with a single clarity of purpose, as strong as a funeral bell. He had been right all along.

Sean did not halt his playing. Even when his fingers slipped from the keys, still he played on.

His final thought was of Storm, which was only fitting. She was, after all, his one remaining earthbound hope.

He was carried along with notes that rose and rose until they joined in celestial perfection, transporting him into the realm he had prayed might find room for him. Even him.

TWO

FOR HIS THIRTY-NINTH BIRTHDAY, HARRY Bennett received a year and a day of unexpected freedom.

The present didn't come gift wrapped. Bows and bangles were in short supply within the Barbados prison system. Harry did not mind. In fact, he had no idea he'd received anything at all. Harry had not even had a visitor in eleven months, since the last time his rotten lawyer had stopped by to inform him that his High Court appeal had been turned down. The same day Harry's bank balance had finally reached zero. His lawyer had actually smiled at Harry. As though milking Harry Bennett had been his goal from the beginning.

The Barbados prison operated on what Harry

called the uncertainty principle: don't tell the inmates a thing. The first hint Harry had of coming change was when the guards called him from his cell. Which in itself was a major cause for celebration after three weeks of lockdown. There had been no reason for the lockdown, either. It had happened once before, when half of the guards had come down with gut rot and the prison director simply shut the prisoners in their cells until his staff was back to full strength.

The guards knew all about what lockdown did to a prisoner, sitting in a concrete box and watching the walls close in. So two of them came to fetch Harry. But Harry was in no mood to make trouble. They watched him silently count the steps. Two, three, four. Then hesitate. Even though there was no wall to force him to turn around, still he had to take a breath to break through the invisible barrier. One of the guards actually laughed.

They took him through the rattling cell-block doors and watched as he glanced down the long hall to the glass doors at the end. Through those doors were the induction office and the visitors' center and the street. Prisoners always looked in that direction before taking the stairs up to the director's office, where Harry assumed he was headed. Which was not a good thing. A visit with the prison director almost always ended up with time in the hole. Only today Harry was steered toward the guards' station.

A packet wrapped in brown paper and tied with twine rested on top of the counter. Harry's name and prisoner number and date of release were scrawled across the top.

Harry stared at the bundle.

"What's the matter, treasure man? You don't want it?"

Harry just kept staring at the bundle and the date written on the top. The day after his *fortieth* birthday. Three hundred and sixty-six days from now.

"Harry's having such a fine time here with us, he don't want to leave. Ain't that right?" The guard shoved the bundle closer. "Go on, mon," he said. "This be your getting-out day."

Harry stripped there at the counter and dressed in the poplin suit his rotten lawyer had bought for Harry's court date, since Harry had been arrested wearing nothing but a pair of cutoffs and boat shoes. The arrest had come in what Harry knew for a fact were international waters, three miles beyond Barbados territory. But the Barbados government had wanted Harry's treasure ship for itself. And the easiest way to keep from paying Harry Bennett his rightful commission was to arrest him for piracy.

Of course, there was also the matter of diving permits.

Which Harry Bennett did not have. Since he'd never entered Barbados waters.

Allegedly.

Once dressed, Harry did not let himself take a second look down to where freedom's sunlight splashed hard against the glass doors. Even when the guards gripped him by the elbows and started down that long corridor, Harry kept his eyes on the concrete floor. The guards grew bored in lockdown. Dressing up Harry Bennett for his birthday and then apologizing for getting it wrong was just their sort of ticket. They'd be laughing about this for weeks.

But when they reached the bullet-proof door, the buzzer sounded. One guard pushed it open while the other slapped a pink release form in Harry's hand. "You know the way from here."

Harry crossed the yard in a sunlit daze.

The guard who operated the outer gate was as black as the hole Harry Bennett had come to know all too well. His grin was probably good-natured. But Harry had known guards who laughed when they beat the prisoners. The guard said, "Don't say the island never gave you nothing, Harry."

Harry stared at the street beyond the gates. "No, indeed."

The guard held out a pale-palmed hand for Harry's release form. He registered the number in his book and asked, "Will I be seeing you again, Harry?"

"Not a chance in this whole wide world."

"That's the answer I want to be hearing from

you." The guard waved his hand in the languid island manner. The guardhouse rang the buzzer and opened the gates. "You be good, now."

Harry stepped outside. He turned right because it was toward the sun. The light was so bright he could not see where he was going. Harry squinted and kept moving down the empty street. And counted his steps.

The Barbados prison was located in the old fortress down on the bad side of Bridgetown. The yard was a postage stamp thirty-three paces wide. When Harry reached step thirty-four, he was shaking so hard he had to lean against the wall. It was the longest straight line he had walked in seventeen months.

"I say, would you happen to be Harry Bennett?"

Harry focused on a skinny black gnome seated in the rear of a powder-puff blue car. "That's a fifty-six Buick."

"Fifty-five, actually." The gnome opened his door. He shooed the hustling driver away and eased himself out in elderly stages. He wore a dark pin-striped suit that could have held two of him, and peered up at Harry. "It is you, is it not?"

"That depends."

"Well, of course. How could I expect you to respond willingly to questions from a perfect stranger. Particularly given what you've just managed to survive." He offered Harry a gnarled hand. "Wilberforce Lincoln Pawltwell, at your service. I apologize for keeping you waiting, good sir. But I was led to believe you would not be released until tomorrow. I dread to think what would have happened had my contact in the director's office not bothered to phone."

Harry gripped the man's hand like he would ancient crystal. "Should I know you?"

"We share a mutual friend, Mr. Bennett. Or rather, we did. But first let's make ourselves comfortable." He waved toward his car. "Please allow me to offer you a ride."

"First tell me why."

The gnome lowered his voice and said, "Sean Syrrell's dying request was that I come to your aid."

The sun dimmed somewhat. "Old Sean's gone?"

"He is indeed. But not before he phoned on your behalf. And now, dear sir. Do join me."

Harry waited until he was in the car to ask, "When did Sean die?"

"Three days ago." Pawltwell leaned forward. "The airport, Jimmy. This gentleman's plane leaves in less than three hours."

"I'm not going anywhere."

"But you must, Mr. Bennett. Sean distinctly—"

"The Barbados government owes me one quarter of two point six million dollars. I heard from the guards that's the take from my wreck."

"That would be a most injudicious attitude to take, sir. The courts have declared that you have no claim whatsoever."

21

"You're a lawyer?"

"Called to the bar sixty years ago next week."

"I hate lawyers."

"Yes, well. Given your choice of defense attorneys, I can understand the sentiment." Pawltwell's hands had the frail quality of a child's, wrapped in skin like burnt parchment. He gathered them on the head of his cane. "Harry . . . may I call you Harry? I speak with six decades' experience when I say your case is unwinnable."

"I never entered Barbados waters—"

"I took it upon myself to make enquiries. I immediately received a visit from a most unpleasant individual. A simply horrid soul, sir. Representing an arm of my government I did not even know existed."

The Buick smelled of sweat and age and mothballs. "I think his cousins work as guards inside.

"No doubt every nation on earth has its share of such dark souls. This particular ogre informed me that were I to pursue my enquiries, I would join you inside a place without windows. I believe you know the place of which I speak."

Harry shut his eyes.

"My dear Harry, we are all a hairsbreadth from eternity. Your recent experiences have no doubt driven that fact home in brutal detail. Were you to take this exceptionally unwise course, my visitor assured me you would join the living dead." Pawltwell shuddered delicately. "To hear him describe your fate left me quaking in my brogans."

Harry did not say anything more until they pulled into the airport's forecourt. Barbados palms rustled and waved a salt-scented farewell in the afternoon sea breeze. "Where am I headed?"

"London." Pawltwell handed over a shiny new briefcase, so packed the sides bulged. "In the side pocket you will find a passport, a ticket, a receipt for two nights' prepaid stay at the Heathrow Sheraton, a file, and traveling funds. The file contains Sean's dying request. Two, actually."

"Which are?"

"First, go and see a certain gentleman in London. His name and rather elaborate contact details are in the file. It's all a bit cloak-and-dagger for my taste, but Sean obviously thought it important."

"After that?"

"Protect Storm Syrrell, his granddaughter. A remarkable woman, by all accounts." The old man pointed Harry toward the airport and the waiting plane. "Balance your loss against your remarkable good fortune, that's my advice. And don't give another thought to what you will never recover."

Harry felt a prisoner's helpless rage. "Easy for you to say. You're just a hired gun."

Pawltwell tapped the head of his cane. Once, twice, three times. A silent admonition. He did not glance over as Harry climbed out. "Sean also instructed me to tell you the rewards could be great, but the risks are even greater. But you are well versed in living with danger, are you not?" The old man signaled to the driver and dismissed Harry, all in one wave. "Come, Jimmy. Let us leave this gentleman to choose his fate."

THREE

WHEN THE CORONER FINALLY RELEASED Sean's body, Storm and her aunt Claudia drove from New York back to Alexandria. The rental car tires hissed through a late-season slush, while overhead loomed a sky that reflected Storm's own future. Every sweep of the wipers revealed the hearse, throwing grit and tears back upon them like the shadow bringer himself.

After helping Claudia see to the funeral arrangements, Storm drove to Dulles and caught the last flight to Palm Beach. When she arrived home, she dumped her luggage and stayed in the shower until all the hot water was gone. Her bones ached, more from failure than fatigue. She dressed in a Dolphins T-shirt, crawled into bed, hugged her pillow, and wondered why the tears still refused to come.

After her first night's sleep in three days, Storm woke to sunlight streaming through her window, unhindered by drapes she had not bothered to close. She made coffee and half listened to her messages as she dressed. A few friends in the trade phoned to express their condolences. Others called seeking either bargains or news. The only odd note came from her pastor, Richard Ellis, who had phoned six times. Storm carried her recharged mug through the apartment, the litany of voices following her every step. Richard had been Sean's friend, not hers. Friendship with a pastor suggested a comfort level with faith that Storm did not possess. But when Sean had been in town, he and the pastor had often talked long into the night. Storm assumed Richard was phoning about funeral details and mentally added his name to the list of things that would never get done.

When the call from Claudia finally came, Storm was as ready as she would ever be. "I'm here."

"How was your night?"

"I actually slept."

"Glad one of us did." Claudia Syrrell was normally as polished and gentle as Storm's grandfather had been brutal. Today, her voice carried the discord of a cracked bell. "I've just finished with the lawyers."

Storm seated herself at the desk that had once belonged to Sean. "Tell me."

"The reading of Sean's will was all empty gestures and worried looks. As in, there is no chance the company will survive. The meeting with the accountant was nightmarish. I knew Sean had eaten into his assets, keeping us afloat. But . . ."

Claudia drew a ragged breath. "It's gone. All of it. There's nothing left."

"Did he even mention me in the will?"

"No, honey. He didn't."

Claudia's regretful pause gave Storm time for flight through painful memories. Sean Syrrell had disowned Storm's father before Storm had been born. She had not even met her grandfather until two weeks after her twenty-first birthday. Sean had neither offered a glimmer of apology for the lost years, nor even suggested they mattered to him. Even so, working at Syrrell's had been all Storm ever wanted, even long before she'd met her grandfather.

At thirteen she had befriended her aunt Claudia and started visiting their Palm Beach office. She had chosen her university and her major on Claudia's advice: accounting with a minor in art history. With that background, Storm had realized months ago that Syrrell's was in dire straights.

Claudia changed the subject. "When are the packers coming to set you up at the convention center?"

The Palm Beach Art and Treasures Fair was one of the largest in the country, with over a quarter of a million visitors. Booths were offered by invitation only. As much as a billion dollars in merchandise would trade hands.

Storm struggled to maintain a steady tone. "Three days."

"Have them clear out the office and the apartment while they're there. Get it done and over with."

Storm winced at the thought of all those snide faces watching her public flameout. "I can't handle the exhibition."

"Consider it your last duty for Syrrell's. Don't tell anyone the shop is closing. Not yet."

"Everybody will know, Claudia."

"Just don't make it official."

Storm knew her aunt was trying for professional. But it came across as cruel. "Can't we—"

"Use the exhibition to unload everything you possibly can. Cash only." Claudia's voice broke for the first time. "Try to find yourself another job."

THE COURTYARD CONTAINING THEIR PALM beach shop had been built in the thirties by a Creole merchant and possessed a fanciful touch of old Orleans. The pastel buildings were rimmed by a single gallery, segmented by wrought-iron screens that matched the balcony railings and two circular staircases. Originally the square had contained a tailor, a shoemaker, and a Catalan butcher whose home-smoked chorizo sausage had spiced all of Worth Avenue. In those early days, the merchants had lived above their shops. Sean had torn out the interior walls and formed an L-shaped living-dining area with high ceilings, Florida mahogany floors, and an office area rimmed by four teak pillars. Sean had fashioned it for himself as a second home, away from the frantic pace of Alexandria and their home office. He had seemed genuinely pleased when Storm had asked to rent it from him. The apartment was the first place Storm had ever cared for enough to call home.

Storm went downstairs, switched off the alarm system, and took a slow stroll around the shop's two rooms. Every item was mentally emblazoned with stories that meant more than her own life's recollections. This passion fueled her ability to sell both the artwork and the fable of ownership. Storm Syrrell was very good at her job. And look where it had brought her.

Storm had no idea how long she'd stood there before the front door chimed and a woman's voice asked, "Ms. Syrrell?"

"The shop is closed." Storm's throat was clenched so tight the last word could not emerge. She coughed and said, "Sorry. Dust. We're not open today."

"Are you Storm Syrrell?"

"Yes."

"My name is Emma Webb. I'm an attorney with Baxter and Bow. I'm here at the behest of your grandfather. Could you please take a walk with me?"

"Today is not a good day, Ms. . . ."

"Emma Webb. I understand. But this can't wait."

"It has to."

"Ms. Syrrell, I've been by three times a day since your grandfather's demise. I was specifically ordered not to phone. His instructions were, 'Only in person.' And 'Do this *immediately*.'"

Digesting this information took Storm through several long breaths. "Sean told you to contact me after he died?"

Emma Webb backed out the door. "Can we go, please? Now?"

The attorney waited in the courtyard as Storm locked the shop and reset the alarm. "I was ordered to make contact the moment notice came of his demise. And not before. Mr. Syrrell did everything but tattoo his instructions on my arm."

"That sounds like Sean."

Emma Webb pointed them east along Worth Avenue, toward the ocean. The woman was perhaps a decade older than Storm's twenty-five years and moved like a tennis pro. Strong tanned legs stretched the fabric of her skirt with each stride. "I'm sorry for your loss. I should have started with that. But to be honest, I'm a little shook being here at all."

"How long ago did my grandfather contact you?"

"Fifteen days."

Storm stalled in midstride. "Sean came to you two weeks ago and said, if I die, do this?"

"Can we keep walking, please?"

Storm remained planted on the pavement. "Did that sound the *least* bit suspicious to you?"

"Of course it did. And to answer your next question, Mr. Syrrell's exact instructions were, 'Don't bother with the cops.'" She tugged on Storm's arm. Hard. "Ms. Syrrell, your grandfather told me this was *extremely* urgent."

The Worth Avenue Bank predated the arrival of serious money. The building anchored a block containing a Hermès emporium, Storm's largest competitor, and a jeweler whose principal address was the Place Vendôme. The bank specialized in clients who used other people's fingers to count their loot. Storm said, "We operate through First American."

"I know." Emma Webb approached a guard stationed by a central stairway and said, "We have business in the safety-deposit vault."

Downstairs, Emma Webb set a bank card on a waist-high counter manned by yet another uniformed officer. "This is as far as I go."

"I don't understand any of this."

"That makes two of us. My law firm has never represented Syrrell. Do you have any idea why your grandfather would come to us now?"

"No. But my grandfather was notorious for being secretive."

The security guard checked the card's number on his computer, then swiveled a logbook around.

"Show the guard your ID, Ms. Syrrell." When Storm had done so, Emma Webb reached into her shoulder bag and came up with a manila folder.

She said to the officer, "Would you witness this handover, please?"

"No problem."

The attorney slapped the file onto the marble counter. "These are ownership documents for a safety-deposit box. The fee for this box is paid through the next five years. This card acts as your key. Don't lose it. And your grandfather instructed me to give you this."

The folder contained a medical fitness report for Sean Syrrell, dated three weeks earlier. Storm leafed through the pages. "Did you read this?"

"Basically, it states that your grandfather was in perfect health." The attorney gave Storm a tight look. "Ms. Syrrell, do you have legal representation?"

She had trouble dragging her gaze from the pages. "No."

"Your grandfather obviously had concerns about a number of things. Including the legal group that normally represents your company's interests." Emma Webb flipped the pages over to a form imprinted with her firm's name. "The items you'll find in the vault were deeded to you two weeks ago. Do you understand what this means? They don't appear in his will because legally, at the time of his death, they did not belong to him. Sign here and here, please."

Storm had difficulty making her fingers obey.

"Your signature confirms that you have received

the items Mr. Syrrell left in our care and that we have performed our duties as per his instructions. My card is stapled to the front of the folder. I would urge you to get in touch if you need anything. Anything at all."

STORM AND THE GUARD ENTERED the safety deposit vault through a revolving steel-barred drum. The guard led her through an area as large as the bank's main hall. Every surface was covered in tan carpet and possessed a crypt's ability to suck away sound.

"If you want privacy, use one of the side alcoves. You fasten the curtain, stay as long as you like." The guard pointed her to a rear wall lined with vaults the size of narrow broom closets. "Okay, this one is yours. You want to open it?"

"I guess so."

"Slip your card in this slot." Her evident confusion melted his gruff attitude a trifle. "Caught you by surprise, all this."

"Absolutely."

"Well, all I can tell you is, vaults this size cost more than the rent on my apartment." His key ring zipped back to the metal brace on his belt. "You need anything, just holler."

Storm waited until the guard departed before opening the door. Which proved to be a good thing. Because the cupboard's contents proved the day's undoing.

FOUR

HARRY BENNETT TOOK THE EXPRESS train from Heathrow Airport to Paddington Station. He stopped by a department store for a dark sweater and slate grey trousers: clothes that would blend with the rain-swept day and the workers in their purgatory uniforms. He took the Circle Line tube to the Barbican Station, then walked a street shaped like an asphalt gorge to his destination.

At first glance, the Guildhall resembled a Gothic mockery of a Grecian temple. Harry stepped into an alcove across the street from the Guildhall's front entrance and scoped the terrain.

Right on time, Harry's contact appeared at the top of the Guildhall steps. He looked exactly as the Barbados lawyer's file described: a slender bearded man carrying a red umbrella.

Harry left his alcove, passed through a curtain of rain, climbed the hall's sweeping stairs, and asked, "You Philip?"

The rain had turned the young man's hair translucent. "I prefer to be addressed as Dr. Pinter."

Harry spotted a guard watching them from just inside the tall bronze doors. He drew Philip around a pillar. "You got something to show me?"

"I don't even know your *name*."

33

"That's right, Phil. Did Sean's lawyer tell you my name? No, he did not. But he said I'd be coming. And part of your deal with Sean was you'd show his contact whatever it is you've dug up."

"It's not that simple anymore. Mr. Syrrell assured me I would be placed in no danger by this association." Dr. Philip Pinter was delicate in the manner of someone who had never picked up anything heavier than a parchment scroll. His patchy beard trembled as he sought to keep his voice steady. "I'm fairly certain I'm being watched."

"Where, here at work?"

"Here, on the bus home, at the shops. I've seen the same man in different spots. Or think I have. Perhaps I've been imagining things. Mr. Syrrell's demise came as quite a shock." He removed frameless spectacles and used a poorly knotted tie to dry the lenses. "I don't see why you need to see the document yourself. I made careful notes. All this could have been taken care of at a much more agreeable location."

Harry had a serious problem with weakness, and his time in prison had only heightened that aversion. Weak people were dangerous people. They weaseled and ratted and squealed and backstabbed and stole. "Phil, look at me."

"I specifically asked that you call me Dr. Pinter."

"Who else did you tell?"

The scraggly beard draped around his mouth like

moss hanging about a cave. "Whatever gave you that idea?"

"Phil, you just said someone's been following you. Which means one of three things. Either the opposition has ESP, which is unlikely. Or Sean ratted on us, which is impossible. Or you got greedy. I'm standing here watching you shake, Phil. And my money's on greed."

The young man swallowed hard. "You don't know, you can't possibly *imagine,* how hard it is to make tenure these days. My professional *life* is on the line."

"Tell me who else knows, Phil."

"I might have mentioned the fact in passing to a colleague at the Royal Society. But only in the strictest confidence." Pinter fumbled in his jacket pocket and came out with a clip-on badge marked with a large blue V. He handed it over without meeting Harry's gaze. "If anyone asks, you're a visiting scholar. Where should I say you're from?"

"Barbados."

"No, no, that's ridiculous. Houston. You're on the faculty of Rice University."

"Whatever. Slow down, Phil. People are watching. We're going to take it easy. What happens when other people bring in first timers? They get a tour, right?" Harry kept his voice to an easy drone that echoed off the stone walls and high-vaulted ceiling. "So that's what we'll do. Tell me what it is I'm seeing."

"We're passing through the Guildhall's main chamber. Ten centuries ago, Britain was ruled by a triad of powers. Balanced against the crown and its knights were the dual forces of the church and the guilds. The church was ruled from Rome, through the mouthpiece of the Archbishop of Canterbury. The guilds were governed by a Council of Masters, who met here. Five hundred years later, Henry the Eighth ended Roman rule over the British church. Slowly, reluctantly, the old guild system also gave way to a new form of power. One that promised a voice to the smallest and weakest of England's citizens. This new form of earthly power was called Parliament. But in the ninth century, when it came to commerce in the British empire, the guilds ruled supreme."

This guy was born to lecture. Harry studied the flag-draped hall, sixty yards wide and ninety long, flanked by Corinthian columns thick as redwoods. Each stone pillar supported a huge banner depicting the royal emblem of a medieval guild—goldsmiths, silversmiths, blacksmiths, butchers, wooliers, on and on down both sides of a hall that was only a few degrees warmer than outside.

"Nine years ago, work was begun to shore up the Guildhall's crumbling foundations. To the restorers' astonishment, they discovered that this massive structure was built upon the ruins of the original Roman Coliseum, lost now for almost two thousand years. The arena's ruins are pockmarked by caverns apparently dating from the Guildhall's earliest days. When the restorers inspected the tombs, they discovered a trove of records and documents which we had long assumed were lost forever."

Harry counted six guards strolling the premises. And twice that number of cameras. Harry did the tourist thing, linking his hands behind his back and ogling in every direction. If the alarms went, the only way out of here would be in the back of a police van.

Pinter led them toward a narrow set of stairs. The guard studied their badges and opened the barrier. Pinter's voice echoed as they descended the curved staircase. "The guild masters are a crusty, hypersensitive lot. They live in a past where their strength rivaled the crown. They hoard their treasures and have slowed the examination of these newly discovered documents to a snail's pace."

At the foot of the stairs, Harry noticed electronic steel gates poised overhead, ready to slam down at the press of a buzzer. He entered a long room that had clearly served as an underground chapel. The chamber was sectioned off by shoulder-high partitions forming individual workspaces. Almost every cubicle was taken. The atmosphere was intense, the conversation a soft background murmur. As Harry followed Pinter down the central aisle, he counted eighteen cameras monitoring their progress: one in each ceiling corner, four more down the length of the room, ten more scoping the alcoves.

When they were seated in Pinter's work space, Harry said, "Walk me through what Sean had you checking out."

Pinter opened his laptop and scrolled through hundreds of photographs and microscope slides and illuminated manuscripts. "Here. This is a letter from a knight of whom we have no official record. One Sir Reginald Furrow, or Furlough, or Furrwelle, depending on how one . . ." Pinter caught the look Harry gave him. He nervously cleared his throat and resumed. "Sir Reginald thanks the guild masters for backing his endeavors in the Holy Land. Which is utterly fascinating, you see."

"No, Phil. I don't."

"Clearly this crusading knight was financed by the guild masters. Sir Furrow is offering the guild two gold chalices, and in exchange he declares that his debt is paid in full. And we have a drawing of the items here, as you see." Pinter scrolled down to the charred lower edge, where part of a shallow dish emerged from what looked like burn marks. "Sir Reginald reminds his backers that King Richard the Lionhearted, who conquered Jerusalem in the eleventh century, had ordered him to hunt down temple treasures. We must assume he is speaking of the Second Temple, rebuilt by

Herod the Great and destroyed by the Romans in AD 72. Which means we're speaking of a treasure smuggled out of Jerusalem before the Romans broke through the city walls. This is utterly fascinating, because rumors have swirled for centuries that the Romans only found a small fragment of the temple treasures. I suppose you've heard of the Copper Scroll?"

"The name, sure." But what Harry thought was, *Whoa.*

Sean had played around with the legends of Jerusalem's temples for as long as Harry had known him. Not the first one, built by Solomon. The second, started by Judeans returning from the Babylonian diaspora and finished by Herod the Great. All of which Harry knew only because Sean had told him. Not that Sean had said all that much, seeing as how Sean was a miser with words. But every treasure dog Harry knew fixated on some legendary hoard that sparked their late-night musings. It was all part of the game. Harry had spent six years tracking down what most of the treasure world had called a myth, and had been rewarded for his troubles with seventeen months in a Barbados jail.

And look where Sean's search had got him.

Pinter was saying, "If the Copper Scroll actually lists treasures from the Second Temple, which is disputed by some experts, it means that there was some cache which the Romans never found. We know what the Romans took away after destroying Jerusalem, because they inscribed their war booty on a triumphant arch that still stands in Rome." Pinter waved an impatient hand, as though Harry Bennett had voiced an objection Pinter had heard innumerable times before. "Oh, all right, for centuries tales have abounded about some hoard located by the Knights Templar and subsequently lost. But this letter is suggesting the Templars arrived ten centuries too late!"

"I need to see the original." Harry rose from his chair. "Where do they keep this thing?"

"In the tombs."

"Come on, you're going to walk your colleague back and show him what he needs to see, then we'll be done."

Pinter led him down the central aisle and across the nave. He nervously told the guard, "My colleague wishes to see the document I've been examining."

The guard noted the numbers on their tags, then motioned them through a steel door set in an ancient stone frame. Pinter scurried down the catacombs' central aisle, through another cramped doorway, and into a second chamber even smaller than the first. The carved recesses where the masters had formerly been laid were now filled with supersized filing drawers. From the third on the right, Pinter pulled a document wrapped in clear plastic sheeting. He moved to the far wall and drew out a fold-down shelf. "I can't possibly imagine what good will come from this."

"Come stand beside me, Phil." Harry had not seen an audio feed. Which was not any guarantee, but he thought the system was video only. He traced a finger down the document's edge. The plastic cover was cool. The parchment beneath was yellowed and scarred. "Tell me what you see here at the bottom."

"The lower four inches of the document are lost, we suspect from fires that swept through the medieval city. Thankfully the document was stacked in a pile, so tightly compressed the fire didn't eat any farther inside. But this leading edge is gone."

Harry pointed at the reason he had come in here. A narrow drawing ran along the bottom right corner and disappeared into the document's charred edge. "Tell me about this."

"This?" Pinter squinted. "It looks like a river, or a shoreline with waves breaking on it. I have no idea. It could very well be nothing more than a stain from the fire."

"Who else has seen this thing?"

"So far as I know, I'm the only person who's realized what we have here. But it can't stay secret forever, if that's what you're asking."

"Which is why you felt like it was okay to mention what you'd discovered to the folks at the academy, right, Phil?" Harry bent closer still. It wasn't a stain and it wasn't a river. It was a treasure hunter's dream come true. "Give me your pen."

"My . . . what?"

"That thing in your pocket. Give it to me. Okay, now I want you to take three steps back. That's it. Turn to your right. No, Phil. Your other right. Pull out that drawer there. Good. Now take out something and pretend to read. Ten seconds and we'll be out of here."

Harry moved fast. Pinter's position blocked the overhead camera from seeing Harry's hands. If the guards were alert, they'd already be moving.

Harry peeled away the plastic sheeting. He held the sheeting aloft with his teeth, uncapped the pen, pressed the document hard into the shelf, and began blacking out the drawing.

A horrified voice hissed over his shoulder, "What are you *doing*?"

Harry bore down hard enough to ensure that not even X-rays would show what had been scripted there.

"*Stop that this instant.*"

Harry went over the entire segment a second time, then a third. He released the sheeting and flattened it over the document. Sweat from his hand streaked the plastic.

"You have *desecrated*—"

Harry hissed one word. "Guard." He spun around and blocked the guard now slipping through the narrow entrance. "A most interesting find. Utterly fascinating. Well. I suppose I'm done here. What about you, Phil?"

"I . . . that is . . ."

"Swell." Harry slipped the document back into the open tray and slid the drawer shut. "Why don't we call it a day."

Harry submitted to the search, climbed the stairs, returned his badge, and followed Pinter back down the flag-draped hall.

At the exit Pinter stopped. "I never want to lay eyes on you again."

"Step outside with me a second." Harry stepped around to the patio's far corner. Pinter slowly approached, squinting against more than the swirling mist. "You need to take a vacation, Phil."

But Pinter's mind was still encased in what had happened downstairs. "You have destroyed a *crucial* bit of historical evidence."

"Listen to what I'm saying. If you hadn't blabbed, this would be the end of it. Nobody else would ever know. But they do know, Phil. And it's your fault."

"You can't be certain of that!"

"I know Sean is dead, Phil. Somebody might already be looking for this thing. And you're the key. You hear what I'm saying? Maybe this bogeyman you think is following you really exists. You're married, right? You got kids?" The way the color drained from Pinter's face was all the answer Harry needed. "Take a vacation. Don't tell anybody where you're going. Do it now."

"H-how long?"

"Couple of weeks should do. By that time, one way or the other, this will be over and done. You can publish then, Phil. Tell the world everything." As Pinter turned away, Harry added, "Don't return back downstairs. Go straight home. Pack up your family. Now. Today."

Harry turned and trotted down the Guildhall stairs. He crossed the street, half a pace below a jog, scoping the street for a threat. Jail-honed senses told him danger was still there. Not back down in the realm of guards and cameras. Here with him now. This very instant.

On the other side of the street a shop-front window provided Harry with a rain-swept reflection. In the glass he saw Pinter clutch his chest and collapse against a pillar.

Harry raced back across the street. Pinter watched Harry leap up the stairs, his beard framing a mouth unable to scream.

Harry arrived just in time to catch Pinter when his grip on the pillar gave way. *"Help!"*

He searched for the attacker, but saw no one except for a little tan figure, just another wispy academic. The man was hunched against the rain, clutching a lumpish briefcase to his chest. Pinter gripped Harry's soaked jacket and dragged his attention back around. Pinter's face and neck were clenched in the rictus of a heart attack.

"HELP!"

As two guards punched through the Guildhall's main doors, the little tan man slipped into a taxi and was gone.

FIVE

THE NEXT MORNING, AN UNCOMMON wind blew off the Atlantic. Florida springs normally arrived drenched with the fragrant weight of the tropics. But today was desert dry, the sky overhead a pewter bowl. After a dawn run, Storm unlocked the shop and set on the counter the only item she had taken from the the bank's vault. It had a zippered binding of red Moroccan leather. At least it had been red, forty years and a million deals ago.

Storm prowled the shop, always returning to the same place. She reached out several times, tracing a finger over the binding. There were a thousand things that needed doing. In two days, the movers would arrive to strip the shop and the apartment and her lifetime dreams. The day after began the Palm Beach Art and Treasures Fair. Storm still had several items to select and carry through the exhibition's vetting process. And she knew that Claudia was right; she should be putting out feelers, looking for a job.

Instead, Storm wheeled a padded leather stool over to where the leather binder rested upon the countertop. Her grandfather's notebook was famous within the industry. The one time she had asked him about it, Sean had referred to it as his greatest asset. What she now held for the very first time contained her grandfather's secret contact list, developed and distilled over fifty-two years in the trade. Buyers, sellers, experts; who owned what, who could be trusted, whom to avoid at all costs. A lifetime of wisdom. Now hers.

But as she unzipped the binding, the phone rang. She lifted the receiver and said, "Syrrell's."

"This is Detective Mallory of Scotland Yard. With whom am I speaking, please?"

"Is this some kind of joke?"

"Officers of Her Majesty's police forces are not known for their sense of humor, miss. Might I have your name?"

"Storm Syrrell."

"Ah. Excellent. Ms. Syrrell, we have a gentleman in custody who claims he is in this country doing research on your behalf. His name is Harry Bennett."

Storm was launching into denial when her eye fell upon the still unopened notebook.

"Hold just a moment, please. I'll be right with you." Storm set down the phone and took a deep breath. She was surprised her fingers didn't burn from the act of opening the tattered cover.

Harry Bennett's name was starred. She had no idea what that meant, except that it was the only one on that page to be so adorned.

Storm picked up the phone. "Has Mr. Bennett done something wrong?"

"I am not at liberty to say, miss. Can you please confirm that he is in your employ?"

She touched the star by his name. "Mr. Bennett is a business associate."

"Can you say what he is working on?"

Storm very much wanted to know the same thing. The problem was, the lines beneath Harry's name were blank. All the other names on that page had notations about items, last contact, possible values. For Harry Bennett there was not even an address.

Which could only mean one thing. "Treasure."

"Ah. And what precisely is the nature of your business, Ms. Syrrell?"

"We are dealers in art and antiques."

"I see. Should we require further details, will you be reachable at this number?"

Storm swallowed a sudden lump. "For another three days."

She was still staring at the notebook's page when the phone rang twenty minutes later. A man said, "I owe you one, Ms. Syrrell."

"Mind telling me how you got my name?"

"Sean told me to get in touch. Who got to him in the end?"

"He had a heart attack."

Harry Bennett huffed what might have been a laugh. "Old Sean didn't just happen to drop down and play like fertilizer."

Hearing this stranger express her own thoughts with such confidence left Storm wanting to share her discoveries. Instead, she asked, "Who *are* you?"

"I'm the guy who'll be in touch," Harry said.

The line went dead.

SIX

O N THE FLIGHT FROM LONDON to Miami later that day, Harry Bennett tried to decide if his future involved Sean's granddaughter. Sean had been Harry's backer and best friend, almost but not quite to the end. But how far did Harry want to go for a woman he'd never met?

Then again, there was the little matter of treasure.

On the one hand, the Second Temple hoard had managed to remain lost for almost two thousand years. If it existed at all.

On the other, old Sean had apparently discovered something interesting enough to get himself seriously dead.

Harry took a taxi to one of Miami's original South Beach hotels. In the high season, New York wiseguys still drank espresso in the downstairs café while their honeys decorated the poolside. But now the late spring doldrums had set in, and the hotel lobby was full of old women with big jewels and bigger mouths, all of them complaining at once. Harry showered and slept, then bought beachwear in the downstairs boutique and took off.

The sidewalks were full of young people doing happy things. He walked the nighttime streets to a steak place he remembered. Harry let himself be guided to a table by the side wall, away from the patio crowded with laughter and shiny eyes. Glances slid off him, just another loner relegated to the sidelines. Harry felt like the last two years had stained his skin.

He finished dinner, then flagged another taxi and took it to Overland, two miles and a universe removed from South Beach. Overland was where Miami riots began. Cops patrolled in flank formation. Salsa music and ganja smoke drifted through Harry's open window. Harry paid the driver to wait, because there was no way he'd find another taxi in Overland after dark. Harry entered a place he remembered and bought a Browning pistol so decrepit he'd have about as much chance of doing serious damage if he threw the bullets. But it was the best the guy had, and after the situation in London Harry wanted to travel armed.

The next morning Harry checked out of his hotel, rented a car, and took the turnpike north.

Beyond the Miami confines, the highway opened up and Harry found real pleasure in the drive and the sky's tropical stain. Wind blasted through all four open windows. The concrete ribbon was empty enough to let him sort through the London data, the researcher's heart attack, Sean's similar demise, the cold English rain, the locked cubicle at Scotland Yard, the hard questions and harder cop gazes. Like all treasure hounds, Harry Bennett had several places he couldn't go back to. But it had always taken more than a day and a half for a country to pull up the welcome mat.

ON MOVING MORNING, STORM DRESSED with fastidious care. She selected an outfit neither grey nor black, an in-between dress too somber for her normal moods, which tended toward a state of perpetual excitement. Even on her worst days, she could still remind herself that she held the position of her dreams, living above the shop where her life had really started, doing the work she'd been born to do. But today required a dress she could drop into a Dumpster with the packing lint and the unrequited dreams.

The movers were due at ten. Storm was outside the bank when it opened at nine. Downstairs she had the guard open Sean's vault, revealing Sean's mysteries.

She spent an hour making a careful inspection and listing the vault's contents but came up with no clear answers. She left Sean's notebook in the vault and carried her list and her questions back to the shop.

The movers were impersonal and efficient. Syrrell's used the same bonded company for the transport of every major piece. The team included three security officers and three white-uniformed loaders. One guard camped inside the shop, another remained by the truck, and the third moved back and forth with the movers. They stripped the walls and emptied the display cases with the stealth of professional pallbearers.

When the distress began eating at her insides, Storm left the shop and locked herself in the upstairs bathroom. She washed her face and mashed the towel hard against her features until the sorrow was tamped down. Then she pulled out the sheet of paper listing the vault's contents.

Her list was twelve items long.

There were seven paintings, all from her grandfather's personal collection. Four had hung in her grandfather's office and three in his apartment above the Alexandria shop. There had been no separation between Sean's work and his private life after the death of his wife when Storm was two, the same year Storm lost her mother. Storm had not learned of her grandmother's death until Claudia told her, twelve years later. Nowadays Storm referred to that period as the lost years.

The seven paintings were all religious, reflecting

her grandfather's intensely spiritual bent. One was Spanish, two French, four English. All by midtier artists, the sort of canvasses that might interest an informed collector or a provincial museum. Total value: four hundred thousand dollars. On an extremely good day.

But still.

Next was a shallow gold dish, possibly a chalice, definitely ancient, possibly intended for temple incense. Storm had never seen it before, which was strange. Sean had sold off almost all his personal treasures and used the funds to try and save the company. The dish was oval and stood fourteen inches. The gold base was hollow and filled with wax, often done to strengthen ancient items shaped from raw gold. The dish had no markings that she could find. Normally anything as valuable as a gold dish would have been ornately decorated.

Then came an illuminated manuscript, yet another item Storm had never seen before. Sean had never shown any interest in antique texts, and Syrrell's rarely carried such items.

Next on the list was Sean's old Bible.

Sean's notebook.

And finally, his briefcase. And the briefcase's contents.

Forty-three thousand dollars. Cash.

This from a guy whose company was entering bankruptcy. And who had not even mentioned her in his will.

Storm lifted the sheet of paper and held it next to her face. She said to her reflection in the bathroom mirror, "Sean gave you all he had. You have a *future*."

PALM BEACH ISLAND HAD ALWAYS struck Harry as a Disneyland for billionaires. The superrich could cross the causeway, get their ticket stamped, and play pretend at life. Everything was safe here, orderly, manicured. The only people who smiled were the schmoes hustling for tips or for women or both. Harry parked off Worth Avenue and walked the last three blocks to the shop.

A truck from the bonded movers Sean used was parked directly in front of the passage leading back to Syrrell's. Harry stood on Worth Avenue and checked out the security guard eyeing the foot traffic from behind mirrored shades. Harry fitted coins into a slot and bought his first paper since getting outside. The headlines shouted news that only made him feel more excluded. Harry tucked the paper under his arm and strolled across the avenue, just another tourist wishing he could afford to belong.

The passage leading to Sean's shop had been redone in the Mizner style. Mizner was the architect whose Spanish Renaissance gave Palm Beach much of its unique style. The corridor's beamed ceiling was lined by carved Spanish arches. Nowadays a Mizner private estate went for upward of twenty mil and seldom actually hit the market. The passage opened into a broad court-yard, paved in rough-cut marble with a sparkling fountain in the middle.

Harry claimed a table at the upscale Caribbean café opposite Sean's shop and watched white-uniformed movers haul out the old man's treasures. The movers were not there to take away some recently sold item. They were stripping the cupboard bare.

Harry stretched his coffee out over a couple of hours but spotted no one who might have been Sean's kin. When the security guard started giving him the eye, Harry refolded his paper and fol-lowed his nose to a sidewalk eatery. When he returned with his steak sandwich, the moving truck still flanked the passage entrance but the movers were gone. A lone security joe leaned in the truck's shadow. The guard's expression said being bored at twenty bucks an hour was fine by him. Harry had met a lot of guys like that inside, and more still in the navy, guys to whom ambition was as foreign as Arabic. Personally, he couldn't understand the mentality. A few hours of that job and the truck's shadow would become just another cage, every paycheck just another iron bar. Harry wondered if the guard had done time, he was that good at killing hours in the heat.

Harry took up station on a bench just down Worth Avenue across from the courtyard passage.

That corridor was the only way in or out, another reason Sean had liked the location. Harry was wiping steak sauce off his chin when the cop passed.

The cop was wearing a beige suit and trailing a distinctly female scent. But there was no doubt in Harry's mind.

She wore shoulder-length dark blond hair clenched by clips above her ears. Her open suit jacket flapped away from a very shapely frame. She came close to being extremely attractive, except for the expression cops liked to call their game face. Wraparound shades could not mask the compressed tightness to her features.

The cop cast a single glance in Harry's direction, enough to freeze him solid. Harry had no doubt the lady could now describe him right down to the toenails. She swept into the passage and vanished.

Harry unlocked his chest. Maybe someday he'd manage to take an easy breath around cops.

He raised the sandwich. His belly wasn't much interested in food anymore. But prison reflexes pushed him to eat while he had the chance.

The wax paper masked the lower half of his face just as the little tan man appeared.

As in, the same guy Harry had last seen slipping into a taxi on a rain-swept London street.

The man stepped out of the passage leading to Sean's shop. He turned away from Harry, slipped past the security joe, and vanished around the front of the moving truck. There and gone in the space of two heartbeats.

"STORM? MS. SYRRELL?" THE AFTERNOON light fashioned a stylish silhouette of the woman standing in the doorway. Emma Webb lifted the bag she was carrying. "I assumed you would forget your need for food."

"I'm really not hungry."

"I can imagine." Emma Webb walked over and set her satchel on the countertop. "But as legal counsel, I advise you to give food a chance."

Before Storm could frame a response, Richard Ellis entered the shop. The pastor of Sean's old church hugged Storm, shook Emma's hand, then traced his way around the empty rooms. Richard wore a pastor's collar over a black shirt and black pants. He was a traditionalist only when it suited him, which meant that he was either coming from some official event or felt like he should treat this visit as a funereal occasion. Richard watched the movers carry Sean's desk out the door and asked, "You have somewhere to go tonight?"

"They're leaving me a mattress and my clothes. The exhibition starts tomorrow."

"That's not what I meant." As the movers packed the contents of the last display cabinet, Richard stepped around the counter. Blocking her vision and ensuring she heard him. "Why didn't you call me back?"

She shifted her position enough to watch the movers fold a ruby-studded chain into a moving blanket. The gold chain had been lifted from a treasure hulk off Manila Bay. The knowledge that no one would ever appreciate those items like she did left her speechless.

Richard said, "I lead a group tonight. It's called Fresh Start. I want you to come." When she shook her head in silent protest, Richard touched her wrist. His fingers probed like a doctor's, down where the pain lurked just beneath the surface. "Storm, I was not making a request."

The pastor turned to Emma and asked, "Are you a friend?"

Storm managed to say, "She's a lawyer. She represented Sean."

"Did she now. Represented him in what?"

"I'm not allowed to discuss that," Emma replied.

"Well, you certainly have the look of strength about you. Storm needs that just now."

The crew's supervisor walked over, clipboard in hand. "We're all done. You want to check?"

Storm reached for the forms. "I'll take your word for it."

When she had signed, he tore off her copy, watched her stow it away unread, and said, "Me and the boys, we just want to say, you know, sorry."

"Thank you."

"This town will be poorer tomorrow."

When the movers had left, Richard said to Emma, "I want Storm to come to a class I'm giving. It begins in just under an hour. Will you bring her?"

"Where is it?"

He nodded as though everything was settled. "Storm knows." He patted her hand once more. At the door Richard turned back and said, "When it's over, we really need to talk."

SEVEN

AFTERNOON SHADOWS CLOAKED HARRY'S return to the courtyard. Harry chose his seat so the fountain's waterfall partly blocked the shop entrance. The courtyard café was filling up now, the after-work crew winding down with over-priced drinks and chatter that reminded him of South Beach. The movers were long gone. The pastor from Sean's church had stopped by and left carrying the same sorrow that lurked around Harry's gut. Harry sipped a drink he didn't want and argued with the empty seat across the table. Something had caused Sean Syrrell, the most professional dealer Harry had ever met, to pursue a treasure unto death. There only was one thing Sean Syrrell had valued more than his trade and his allies. Harry thought of the pastor and knew for certain Sean had been after more than old gold.

As soon as the ladies came out, Harry knew the younger woman belonged to Sean Syrrell. She had Sean's incredible power, only in a distinctly female form.

The word that came to Harry was *smoking.*

Storm Syrrell wore a rumpled suit of dark grey silk and a day's worth of dusty smudges. No jewelry, not even a watch. Long fingers and strong hands, golden tan set off by raven hair. She was into something seriously athletic, Harry was certain of that. The lady cop was maybe ten years older and carried a world of grim experience, but Harry figured Storm might still take her in a pinch. Storm had a rangy strength, like somebody comfortable with testing her limits, over and over and over. Harry put Storm's age at midtwenties and her station as completely out of his range.

The cop was intent on saying something to Storm through the doorway. Harry gave the cop another inspection, which was easy duty. Storm locked the door and keyed the remote for the store's alarm system. She slipped the keys and the alarm remote back into her purse. Then Storm stood and stared at the awning with the name in Gothic gilt, SYRRELL'S. Storm looked bereaved. Harry was tempted to walk over and introduce himself. Then he thought again of the man who had vanished before his eyes. Harry stayed where he was. Off the radar screen. Watching.

The ladies walked to the cop's car. Harry dogged them until the cop chirped off her alarm. He then hoofed it back to where his wheels baked in the late afternoon sun. The vinyl seat threatened to blister his back. He floored out of the space, gunned through the stop sign, and took the turn overwide. He missed an oncoming Caddy and a plumber's van by inches, and left a chorus of horns in his wake.

He was afraid he'd lost them. But when he came to the first major intersection, Harry spotted the cop caught by a traffic light. When the light turned green, Harry crawled forward, two cars removed from the cop and Storm. As far as Harry was concerned, people in Florida drove like they were swimming through congealed grits.

Harry hung back when they turned into the parking lot of Sean's church. The last time Harry had been here, he and Sean had argued. It was the only argument Harry had ever had with Sean, and things had gotten out of hand. The next day, Harry had left for the Caribbean. It was the last time he had ever spoken with his late best friend. Harry had spent a lot of time in prison reflecting on their quarrel. Three times he had started to write Sean and apologize. But he'd never finished the letter. Other times he wished he had clocked the arrogant bugger. One good punch. Boom. Out and gone.

The church was another of those Mizner structures, a Palm Beach landmark set in acres of immaculate gardens. Sean had once told him it was modeled after some cathedral in Spain, mammoth grey stone and neo-Gothic and flanked by royal palms. The ladies left their car and joined others heading for smaller buildings clustered behind the church. The crowd was an odd mix for a town this well groomed. Some of the people climbing the stairs with Storm bore the subtle stain of living rough. Harry joined the next crowd of arrivals and entered a hall that was neither full nor empty. He saw a lot of smiles and an equal number of hard cases, but Storm and the cop had vanished. Harry settled into an alcove by a glass-fronted office. The corridor gradually went quiet. The place obviously saw duty as a school, because the walls were lined with paintings of sunshine and boats and fishermen and happy houses.

Because Harry was studying the artwork, he almost missed the flitting shape.

A small man slipped past, wearing clothes that matched his complexion, one shade darker than beige. The guy was *fast*. Harry remained in his alcove for a tick, not longer than a few accelerated heartbeats. But when he emerged, the corridor was empty.

STORM FELT LIKE SHE WAS stuck in the business equivalent of an AA meeting. Richard's class was filled with human refuse ground down by the corporate garbage disposal. She glanced around the room and wondered how many of those gathered were hooked on failure like her father, open to any excuse that let them float on a tide of prescription drugs. Storm's childhood home in the West Palm Beach artists' colony had been a haven for cynics and druggies who'd sought out every possible reason to waste a life. Storm made no attempt to pay attention as Richard wrote a passage from Galatians on the board: "Bear ye one another's burdens." The day had left her stuffed in a cocoon fashioned from the mover's padding. Richard had tried to speak with her before class, but she had brushed him off. Enduring his concerned sympathy risked crushing her resolve.

Emma glanced over, but did not speak. Storm sighed and sank lower in her chair. She definitely should not have come.

HARRY WORKED HIS WAY DOWN the hall. The classroom doors had windows inset at face level. He studied each room in turn—a choir, bell ringers, people sorting donated clothing, a library, a trio of colorful classrooms with child minders. He was about ready to decide that he was the victim of a hyperactive imagination when he turned the corner and saw the woman.

Harry's first thought was, *Streetwalker.* Somebody whose survival had once depended on judging the safety of whoever sat behind the wheel of the car she approached. She was attractive in a brutal sort of way, with the flattened features of a South American Indian. The woman was plastered against the wall. She stared down an empty corridor and clawed the whitewashed concrete blocks.

Harry whispered, "Where is he?"

She used her chin to point. A single classroom door stood between them and the side exit. Taped to the wall beside the class was a handwritten sign, *Fresh Start*.

Now that someone else had sensed the same thing, Harry's heart surged to redline. He scouted through the glass, then opened the door.

"Welcome, friend. There are some seats up front."

Harry waved at the grey-haired man by the lectern and scouted the room. He let his glance sweep over where Storm and the cop were seated by the far wall. The little tan man was nowhere to be found.

Harry leaned against the rear wall, near where Storm sat in the next-to-last row with her pal. The pastor talked about letting the past go and making room for life's next stage. Probably something Harry could have used. But not just then. His brain was too busy playing tricks. He wondered whether he was chasing down one of those shape-shifters the Barbadians loved to talk about after lights-out. Harry had always put it down to the locals playing with the poor white man's mind. Until now.

The class broke up. As the two ladies departed, the cop gave him a hard stare. Just his luck, to meet a cop so good at her job she recalled him from a three-second glance. Harry ducked his head and played with his button, like he was still pondering whatever it was he hadn't heard. The pastor, penned up near the blackboard by a trio of parishioners, frowned as Storm walked out the door.

Harry followed the two ladies into the corridor and hung back. Whenever someone glanced his way, Harry did the prison deal of inspecting the ground at his feet. Some of the hard timers, they'd do you for looking at them straight in the eye. Harry did his best to disappear in plain sight.

The hallway was packed. The hooker was nowhere to be seen.

Outlaw rush. Harry almost said the words aloud. He'd heard the term a hundred thousand times. Barbadians hunkered on the floor after lights-out, dark features lit by the glow of ganja smuggled in by the guards. Laughing in that slow, deep way that was almost music, almost a dirge. Talking with the smoke about how they'd gotten caught, why they'd done what they did. Outlaw rush, mon.

Which was exactly what Harry felt the instant he spotted the tan man.

The little man was leaning against the railing at the bottom of the exit stairs. Just some loser watching the bats chasing bugs in the parking-lot lights. Maybe searching for solace in the twilight. Face almost hidden by the railing shadows. Harry's entire system was full-on screaming menace as he pushed his way through the crowd by the exit doors. The people were still in church mode, too polite to do more than glare in his direction.

Ahead of him, Storm followed the lady cop through the glass doors and started down the stairs.

Harry shoved harder.

Somebody huffed, "Watch it there!"

The man waiting at the bottom of the outside stairs was in his early to midforties. Slender, almost frail looking. His dark brown hair was so thin Harry could see the skull glinting in the street-lights. His skin was sallow, almost yellow. He wore shapeless beige clothes, everything chosen to go unnoticed.

The guy reached into his pocket.

Harry's brain shouted, *Knife!*

He vaulted through the doors and used the shoulder of a hefty guy to launch himself over the railing.

The little man was totally focused on moving toward Storm. His hand emerged from the pocket holding a glass vial with his finger hooked over a top like a perfume sprayer. Harry slapped the man's arm, not even trying for a grip. Harry landed and rolled and came up facing a different guy entirely.

The little man reached into his pocket again, and this time it *was* a knife. He snarled something Harry didn't need to understand, and pounced.

The guy could not possibly have jumped as high as he did. He bared his teeth and swept the blade in a hissing arc *down* on Harry.

Harry ducked and rolled a second time. Only he didn't finish his roll. He stayed on the ground, taking all his weight on his shoulders, and kicked. Hard.

The knife went spinning.

The man roared in a voice ten times the size of his body. He stomped on where Harry should have been.

But Harry was already on his feet and charging. There was only one way to handle a guy like this. Fast and hard. Get him before he brought the *next* thing out of his pocket.

Only the little man was faster.

Harry felt the punch before he actually saw the guy move. The man's hands were just two blurs. One to the solar plexus, and the other should have been to his neck, a killing strike to the jugular. But Harry got his chin down in time to take the blow on the top of his head.

Harry saw stars.

Poleaxed by a waif of a man using his open hand.

Only then did Harry realize that he couldn't breathe. And that he was on the ground again. On all fours.

The church grounds were in total bedlam. The last thing Harry heard clearly was a woman's voice shouting, *"Federal agent! You're under arrest!"*

Not exactly what Harry would have classed as a welcome bedtime melody.

Until now.

EIGHT

THE LOCAL POLICE INTERVIEWED HARRY in the outpatient wing of Good Samaritan, the mainland hospital just off the northern Palm Beach causeway. By that time Harry had learned that the woman with Storm was named Emma Webb. Emma hung back while Palm Beach's finest did their business. If she flashed them a badge, Harry didn't see it. But Harry remained fuzzy about a lot of things between the tan man's second punch and the hospital.

Because of the police, the hospital had put him in a room with a real door. Harry lay on a paper sheet on a narrow examination bed. Storm stood between the wall and his bed, from where she shot Emma Webb looks of tight suspicion.

Emma Webb shut the door behind the departing cops, leaned against it, and said to Harry, "I have the distinct impression you held something back from the police."

Storm said, "Oh, please."

Emma asked, "What didn't you want to tell the officers, Mr. Bennett?"

Storm said, "You're saying *he's* not being completely honest?"

"I did what I was ordered to." Emma kept her gaze on Harry. "I've put in a call to my superiors. Soon as I report in, I'll be able to talk. I hope."

Storm crossed her arms. "Whatever."

Storm was standing beside the bed. Whenever she shifted in anger or impatience she brushed Harry's shoulder. Harry liked the feel of her being that close. Not from any possible his-and-her thing. His brains hadn't been rattled that bad.

Storm said, "I'm still trying to get this straight. You've been operating under false pretenses ever since you walked into my shop?"

"Everything I told you was the truth."

"Oh. Right." She switched her aim to Harry. "And just exactly how long have you been on my case?"

"All day."

"All day. When were you planning on introducing yourself?"

He stuck out his hand. "Harry Bennett."

Storm kept her arms linked across her middle. "Very funny."

Harry dropped his hand and said to Emma, "What you said about holding back. You were right. I've seen that guy before."

"Who, the assailant? You're sure?"

Harry nodded. "Twice."

The doctor came in as Harry was finishing his tale about the London researcher. The doctor repeated his inspection of Harry's reflexes, and pronounced him bruised but intact, nothing broken, possibly a light concussion, see his doctor if his vision went blurry. When the doctor left, Harry swung his feet to the floor and sat up, then had to wait for the world to stop spinning. Storm placed a steadying hand on his shoulder. Harry liked that too.

Emma pressed, "You saw the attacker earlier today?"

Harry shut his eyes against the world's slight tilt and regretted his refusal of pain pills. "Just after you spotted me on the bench. You went in, he went out."

Storm said, "Can we get out of here?"

"In a minute," Emma said. "I made you, but not him."

"I was in plain view," Harry said. "This guy wasn't."

"I have trouble accepting that he and I were in the courtyard together and I didn't make him."

"You were five feet from him on the church stairs. Did you notice him before he attacked?"

Emma inspected the linoleum at her feet.

"This guy isn't just fast. He's pretty much invisible."

"A pro," Emma said.

"You find whatever it was he dropped?"

"I'm on it. Can you tell me why Sean Syrrell contacted you?"

"Sean and I go way back."

"So he just called and said, 'Go see this researcher, then watch after Storm, and—'" She was halted by the chirping of her phone. She pulled it from her pocket, checked the readout, opened it, and said, "Webb."

Whatever she heard tightened her features even further. She slipped from the room and shut the door.

Storm gave it a minute, then walked over and checked the hall. "She's gone."

"Maybe we should leave too."

"I can't believe she lied to me like that."

Harry shrugged. Cops.

Storm asked him, "Do you have a place to stay?"

"Tell the truth, I haven't looked that far ahead."

"Well, I've got a floor until Sunday."

"Works for me."

She hesitated, then asked, "Do I have to worry about you, Harry Bennett?"

He took his time replying. "Hearing your grand-father was gone dimmed the sun. He asked me to help you out. That's the only reason I'm here."

She liked that enough to say, "Let's go home."

THEY DID NOT SEE EMMA WEBB as they left the hospital, which was fine by Harry. Storm did not say a word during the taxi ride. Harry figured the lady had as many reasons as she needed for staying silent. Harry just plain didn't feel like talking. He had refused the doctor's pain pills because he wanted to stay alert. The attacker was still on the loose. But his head throbbed, his gut ached, and Harry wondered if maybe a lower rib might have a hairline fracture. As the taxi pulled up on Worth Avenue, Harry recalled the little man's speed and became slightly nauseous.

He emerged from the taxi in careful stages. "Wait here a second."

"You're not looking so good, Harry."

"I'm okay. Just hang tight there in the car." The way he felt, he wouldn't slow a pro one millisecond. Even so, Harry shuffled down the passage, scanned the empty courtyard, then returned to say, "All clear."

Harry took the wrought-iron stairs in measured doses and leaned heavily on the balustrade. He kept scouting, but the courtyard radiated a cozy feel. A night wind brushed the sky free of clouds, and the central fountain played a tropical melody. As Storm unlocked the apartment door, he said, "This place always struck me as special."

Storm reached inside and turned on the light, revealing a hollow home and a face to match. "Sean thought so."

"That's what you called him?"

"It was his name." She led him inside, locked the door, and pointed to a lonely sofa that was clearly too battered to take away. "Will that do?"

"Sure. Do you have any Advil?"

"I'll check." She came back with a glass of water and two tablets. She watched him swallow the pills and asked, "It's true, what you told Emma?"

"Always best to tell the cops the truth. They catch you lying on the small stuff, they assume you've got something bigger to hide."

She watched him intently with Sean's dark gaze. "So Sean asked you to come protect me."

Harry stumped over to the sofa. His footsteps echoed in the empty room. The sofa and two bar stools by the counter were all the remaining furniture. "More or less."

"Protect me from what?"

"He didn't say."

"And you didn't think it was a question worth asking?"

"I didn't have the chance." Harry eased himself onto the sofa. "One of Sean's buddies contacted me three days after he died. This lawyer did me a favor. A big one."

"For Sean."

"No other reason, since I'd never laid eyes on him before." Harry knew she wanted to ask what the favor was. And she deserved to know. But not now. He stretched out, adjusted the pillow, said,

"You need to call your aunt, tell her what's gone down."

"You know Claudia?"

"Like I know you, through Sean. Listen to what I'm saying. If they got Sean and tried for you, it's only natural . . ." Harry stopped talking because Storm was no longer there.

NINE

STORM WOKE HIM WITH A mug of coffee and "The bathroom is through the bedroom. We need to hurry."

In the middle of the night, Harry had awakened to find a blanket on top of him and a sofa spring digging into his hip. He had stretched the blanket on the floor, rolled himself up, and slept well. Harry was still dressed in the shorts he had purchased from the hotel boutique. He raised himself onto the sofa, sipped from the mug, and took stock. His body was sore, but nothing hurt too much. Harry drained the mug, set it aside, and pushed himself upright. When Storm reached over to help, Harry said, "I'm okay."

"Your shirt was a goner. Stained and torn and ugly to start." She handed him an oversized Gators T-shirt. "This should fit. Our first stop will be for some new clothes."

He showered and inspected his bruises and decided he would live to fight another day. He slipped the T-shirt over his head and was enveloped by a distinctly feminine fragrance, one pleasant enough to stifle the groan from raising his arms. When he came out, Storm met him with a recharged mug and a breakfast of toast and fruit. Harry downed another two Advil, sat at the counter, then ate in silence. He liked the lady's calm intensity, the way she was comfortable both with silence and his presence, giving him space, treating him like a friend.

Finally he set down his mug and said, "I was in jail."

She gave that a slow nod. "When?"

"Until four days ago. Seventeen months. Barbados. Sentenced to four years for stealing treasure out of Barbadian waters. Which I didn't do. But that's for another time."

"Sean got you out?"

"His pal did. Don't ask me how." Harry spun his mug and debated whether he should give her the other barrel, describe what Pinter had discovered.

She answered that one for him with, "Do you mind if we hold the rest of this talk for later? I've got . . . things."

Harry slipped from the stool. "What can I do to help?"

"I don't know. I mean, I don't even know . . ."

"Storm, I'll only say this once." Harry took a big breath. "I've given this a lot of thought. Sean didn't bust me out of prison because then I'd owe him one. He did it because he trusted me. He can't be here to help you. I can."

Storm just stood and stared at him with that darkly fractured gaze. "Was he murdered?"

"You want my take on it, I'd say, absolutely."

She tied her fingers in a knot, a strong and lovely woman trying hard to hold on. "I don't understand any of this."

"That's why I'm here. To help find out what we need to know."

STORM WROTE OUT THE ADDRESS where he was to meet her, and sent him off with instructions precise as military orders. Harry's first stop was the fanciest barbershop he had ever visited. The old guy was seriously displeased with Harry's state. Harry used the time to give himself a long inspection. He found a few deeper lines and some he hadn't seen before. The biggest difference was his eyes, which had gone prison flat. Something a fancy haircut couldn't disguise.

He returned to Worth Avenue and entered Saks. He bought gabardine slacks and knit shirts to match, a couple of cotton sweaters, belt, shoes, and a midnight blue Armani suit. Harry had not worn a suit since his last court appearance and could not remember the last tie he'd owned. Not to mention a dress shirt with studs and a bow tie, which Storm had insisted on. He managed the entire process without once looking at the prices.

Harry waited while they hemmed his pants, then dressed in slacks and a sports shirt. The woman rang him up on Storm's credit card.

He used Storm's key to let himself into the upstairs apartment and dropped off the purchases he wasn't wearing. Harry took a long moment to study the empty chamber. Sean's absence compressed the air. Harry said to no one in particular, "I won't let you down."

Harry took a taxi to the church and retrieved his rental car. He followed Storm's instructions across the southern causeway to the convention center, a new structure in a redone region of West Palm Beach. A huge marquee over the front entrance announced the annual art and treasures fair.

The convention center was Palm Beach elegant, with plush carpeting and walls of glass overlooking the obligatory palms and oleander borders. Chandeliers hung from a pine ceiling stained to look like teak. The people spoke in polished tones that suggested they were born to handle treasure other people sweated over. Storm had left him a merchant's badge at the front desk. A woman who managed to look casual in silk and pearls directed him down the proper aisle.

When Harry found Storm, he said, "I'll never complain again over paying you folks your cut."

Harry helped Storm unpack a variety of items from crates, all of which bore pink tags marked *Vetted*. In the terse manner of someone chewing over a lot more than the work at hand, Storm described the honor of being invited to join as one of only 212 exhibitors allowed to rent space. Other vendors passing their booth scouted the terrain like vultures hovering above an almost-dead body.

When Storm went quiet, he said softly, "The loss just keeps on growing with each breath."

She gave him what Harry could only call a look straight from Sean. Layers of meaning, intent as a drill. Storm said, "There's something I need to tell you."

Harry let her draw him to the back of the booth, where a clever little corner held a trio of chairs and an Italian Renaissance secretary, for those moments of discreet negotiation. Like now.

Harry was so touched by Storm trusting him it took a moment for her words to sink in. "Sean orders you to New York," he summarized, "where he fires you in the back of a limo, then drops dead half an hour later. Then the day after you get back, this so-called lawyer you've never met waltzes into the shop."

"Less than an hour after I opened up."

"And takes you to a bank vault where you find his *notebook*?"

Storm gave her head a tight shake. Not in denial. Tamping down on a sudden surge of grief. "Sean knew what was about to happen to him. He knew, and still he went on with it."

"I've been wondering about that very same thing."

"Why didn't he just *stop*?"

"It was important."

Her eyes glittered so bright it hurt Harry to meet her gaze. "More important than Syrrell's?"

Harry heard the real question, the one Sean's granddaughter would never ask—more important than being there for her? He saw the yearning for what the old man had probably never offered: a kind word, an embrace, an affirmation. Harry said, "Let's look at what we know. Sean cared for you enough to set you apart. You've got the tools and the space to operate. If you want to."

"What I *want*—"

"Listen to what I'm saying. Getting angry with the old man now, when he's gone, won't get you any further than while he was alive." Harry gave her time to blink, to breathe, to refocus. "Sean had something in his sights that was bigger to him than his company, than his *life*. What could that possibly have been?"

A droll voice filled the empty moment. "Storm, finally. I've been looking all over."

Storm did not look up. "Curtis, now isn't a good time."

"I won't keep you long. It's only the matter of that Grecian vase." A foppish gentleman stepped into the booth. The gold insignia on his navy blazer caught the light as he pointed. "I have a buyer, you see."

"The price is the same as last week."

"Do be reasonable. I'm offering cash on the silver palaver, as it were. Take it while you can claim it as your own, that's my advice. Next week, who knows, your money could well go straight into some banker's purse." He used his nose as a lofty pointer. "Shall we say a hundred and fifty thousand?"

"My bottom price is two-ten."

"You are a tough nut. But I do want that for my client. Two hundred even, but only if you throw in that little stand."

"This happens to be a Napoleonic commode with its original ormolu facade. The price on that is eighty thousand."

"Oh, all right. Two-twenty for the both of them."

When Emma Webb appeared at the entrance, Storm reluctantly rose to her feet. "Two-fifty for the pair. Banker's draft or cash. I'll red-tag it until tomorrow only. Don't even think of arguing, Curtis. You'll have to excuse us."

Emma slipped past the departing dealer. The federal agent wore a suit the color of desert khaki, only in silk. The short skirt revealed shapely legs in matching tights. Heels, gold Rolex and choker, diamond studs. Everything distinctly feminine except the expression. And the metallic tint to her voice. "I need to speak privately with you."

"Not a chance."

"Are you aware that Harry Bennett is a convicted felon?"

Harry said, "There's no such thing in the Barbados legal system as a felon. Besides which, I was framed."

"Oh. Excuse me. An innocent con. How novel."

Harry told Storm, "I'll go walk the halls."

Storm stopped him with a hand on his arm. "Harry Bennett is here because my grandfather asked him to come. I'm still trying to work out exactly what role you play."

Emma said, "We have a suspicious death tied directly to Harry Bennett, not to mention the attack on you."

"Which Harry foiled. And don't forget you only know about the London attack because he told you."

Harry said to Storm, "I forgot to ask. Did you call your aunt?"

"Last night."

"Excuse me, I'm talking here," Emma said. "My superiors are concerned Harry Bennett might be part of some plot."

"You're suggesting Harry had something to do with my grandfather's death? That's insane."

"Not directly, no. He couldn't have. We checked. Harry Bennett wasn't in the country when Sean Syrrell died. But we don't know who he works for. Or why precisely he's here at all."

Storm crossed her arms. "Funny. I was just going to say the same thing about you."

Emma punched a hand into her purse and came

out with a leather case. She flipped it open and held it out.

Storm inspected it carefully. "At least you didn't lie about your name."

"I told you. Everything I said was the truth."

Harry read off the badge. "Treasury?"

"On temporary assignment to a Homeland Security task force. I also act as liaison between the task force and Interpol."

Harry asked, "Interpol was investigating Sean?"

Storm said, "Sean was the most honest man I've ever known."

Harry said, "I'd give that a big ten four."

"Imagine my surprise when Sean Syrrell showed up in my law office, a setup that was supposedly top secret, and asked me to represent him."

Harry liked that one. "He broke your cover. That sounds like Sean."

"You're missing the point," Storm said, her gaze locked on Emma. "He knew there was nothing he could say to stop your investigation."

"Sean Syrrell showed up and said, 'Do this in the case of my death,'" Emma said.

Harry was nodding now. "Any warning he might have passed on would only have heightened your suspicions. But this . . ."

Storm's voice almost broke over the weight of saying, "He knew *everything*."

Harry asked, "What do you want from Storm?"

"My superior would like to have a word."

"Your Interpol guy?"

"No. Homeland Security."

"Not a chance," Storm replied. "In case you haven't noticed, we're a little busy around here."

"Fine. Give it half an hour and I'll be back with a warrant." Emma Webb stowed her badge back in her purse. "Now how do you want your eggs?"

TWO BRIDGES SPANNED THE INTRACOASTAL Waterway connecting Palm Beach Island to the real world. Nobody who worked on PBI and lived on the mainland called them causeways. They were simply the roads to work, as in, take the south road because the north is jammed with the tourist brigade. A block east of the north bridge, the road divided and broadened and slowed where the frenetic tide of mainland energy met the barrier of serious wealth. A palm-lined park split the east and west lanes. The northern side facing the park held the Palm Beach equivalent of a strip mall—Kobe-beef burger joints and beach shops selling thousand-dollar thongs. Emma led Storm into the café and stopped at a table by the rear wall. "Storm Syrrell, Jack Dauer."

Dauer was the only guy in the place wearing a suit. When he waved Storm into a chair, the motion opened his jacket so his gun and his badge gleamed in the sunlight. Storm was fairly certain he did it on purpose. "Have a seat, Ms. Syrrell."

Emma asked, "Coffee?"

"Cappuccino. Thanks."

"I don't know if our budget will stretch that far." Dauer watched Emma step to the counter. "These prices, man, I haven't seen anything like this place since I chased down a suspect in Istanbul. You know Istanbul, Ms. Syrrell?"

"No."

"You sure? Your grandfather did a lot of business around the Med." Jack Dauer was so lean as to suggest all human kindness had been leeched away. He tapped a large class ring on the back of the empty chair beside him as he inspected her. When Emma Webb returned, he said, "So you don't know about your grandfather's Istanbul dealings. What portion of his illegal activities did you handle?"

Storm sipped from her cup and licked the froth from her upper lip. She remained caught between her conversation with Harry and the thought that all this, even the guy seated across from her, worked off a script of her grandfather's making. "If you thought I actually knew about unlawful activities, we'd be having this conversation in your offices."

The guy had a lizard's way of flicking his gaze. Hard and totally without emotions of any kind. Over to Emma, back to her. "Sean Syrrell was under investigation by our offices for a variety of matters. We're not sure about you yet."

Storm met his gaze. "Just exactly which division of which government sent you here?"

"My badge says FBI, Ms. Syrrell. But Agent Webb and I are part of a multiagency taskforce."

"Investigating what?"

Emma slipped into the seat across from Storm. "We're looking for clarification on several points. Why is Syrrell's almost the only high-end dealer to handle salvaged treasure?"

"Is that what you're investigating? Stolen treasure?"

Dauer snapped, "Answer her question, Ms. Syrrell."

"Most houses have become increasingly specialized in order to survive. Sean chose salvaged treasure as one of Syrrell's main lines."

"When did this happen?"

"Ten years ago, maybe more. Sean had a passion for sunken treasure. He collected old maps and early records from past generations of salvagers. He fed them to a select group of treasure hunters."

Dauer said, "One of whom was this convicted felon, what's his name?"

Emma Webb replied, "Harry Bennett."

"Harry Bennett is a good man," Storm said.

"Misplaced loyalty can be a dangerous thing, Ms. Syrrell. What can you tell me about your grandfather's latest acquisitions?"

"I have no idea. Sean was very tight with his sources. It was one of Syrrell's trademarks. Sean built a reputation for total confidentiality. A wealthy family suddenly facing hard times often prefers to unload items without anybody knowing. If they entered the open market, people would talk. Sean was one of a few dealers able to arrange a major sale without word leaking out."

"Secret seller to secret buyer," Dauer sneered.

"Sometimes. Why are you asking me all this?"

Emma lifted a file from her shoulder bag. She glanced at her boss. Jack Dauer glowered in response. She set the file on the table between them. "I want you to look at something."

She opened the file, revealing a photograph taken of a man stepping from a limo. "Do you know this person?"

The man had the aquiline features and sleek bearing of a Mediterranean prince. "I have no idea who he is."

"You've never seen him before?"

"No."

"Does the name Selim Arkut mean anything to you?"

"No. Sorry."

Dauer snorted. "You expect her to tell you the truth?"

Emma continued, "Could you check your records and see what items have originated from him?"

"I just told you. The only record of sources was kept in Sean's head. Payments for items on commission almost always went through attorneys. Everyone working for Syrrell's had strict instructions never to look further than that."

Dauer said, "Looks like we'll just have to hold you responsible for the stolen artifacts in your possession, Ms. Syrrell."

"You do that." Storm gathered up her purse. "In the meantime, could I get a lift back to the exhibition?"

EMMA WEBB DIDN'T SAY ANYTHING until she pulled up in front of the Palm Beach convention center. When a car jockey reached for her door, she badged him. "Five minutes."

Emma took a curbside spot between a Bentley and a Maybach. She left the motor running for the AC and said, "The tests came back on the juice that guy tried to spray you with. A compound the Chinese use for rat poison. Not for sale in this country. The interesting thing about this, it's harmful only if ingested. Otherwise, nada. You can bathe in the stuff and be okay, long as you don't swallow or breathe. But inhale one whiff, we're talking massive liver failure, kidneys shut down, lungs clog up, bang and gone."

"But not heart failure."

Emma looked over. "Ms. Syrrell, dead is dead."

"I was talking about Sean. Of course, if the attacker had one killer perfume, he could have others."

Emma did not say anything.

"What about that guy in London who died in Harry's arms?"

"We're working on that. In the meantime, I'd appreciate it if you kept a close watch on Harry Bennett."

"No problem, seeing as he's sleeping in my living room." Storm climbed from the car. "Will you call me if you learn anything?"

"Ms. Syrrell, letting that con get close to you is a seriously bad idea. We ran a check. His juvie records are sealed. Which means he's been in trouble before."

"But nothing from then until this recent problem, right?"

"He joined the navy on his eighteenth birthday. My guess is the court ordered him to choose between that and hard time."

Storm leaned on the windowsill. "Sean trusted him. I trust him. And you should too."

The wraparound shades created a copper sheath to Emma's face. "He's a con. You don't know cons. I do. They will say anything to get what they want. To a con, words are just another lever."

"What was that comment Dauer made about Sean's operations in Istanbul?" When Emma shook her head, Storm pressed, "I've answered everything you wanted. Tell me, please."

Emma remained where she was, parked between two thrones of chrome and power. "We don't actually know for certain that your grandfather was doing business in Istanbul."

"Then why—"

"The trail went cold there. Jack was fishing." Emma slapped the car into gear. "You're sure you've never been?"

"No." Storm waited for the car to pull away to add, "I've never been anywhere."

TEN

THE AFTERNOON PASSED IN AGONIZING sluggishness. The aisles filled with an assortment of South Florida's snobs. Waiters circulated with canapés and champagne. A trio played show tunes in the hall's far end. Harry watched helplessly as Storm endured three hours of polite torture. A number of patrons stopped by to offer condolences. Others enquired over the future of Syrrell's and departed with snide humor in their eyes. Harry could not tell which hurt Storm more. The stench of failure, and Sean's absence, hung over their booth.

When it was over, Harry drove them back over the causeway and followed Storm's terse directions to her gym, where she told him she was going to work out and then run to the apartment. She looked as if she was waiting for him to argue. Harry recognized a good head of steam when he saw one, and didn't even bother to tell her to take care. He bought a Starbucks coffee, found himself a comfortable spot of shade, and practiced the art of waiting. Forty minutes later Storm came out wearing a sleeveless T and shorts of a very interesting length. She glared in his direction, then set off running. Harry tossed his coffee and dogged her in the car.

He parked in front of the apartment, then walked down Worth Avenue to the sandwich shop. When he returned he heard the shower running. Harry left Storm's sandwich on the kitchen counter and took his own meal down to the waterfront. The yacht club started where Worth Avenue bent to join the river road. Harry seated himself on the first empty bench and watched the waters flame through another tropical display. A couple of the moored boats were interesting—steel hulls, originally designed as oceangoing tugs, refitted as pleasure craft but retaining their ability to handle heavy seas. Harry had nothing but scorn for most of the other vessels. Overpowered palaces with silly lines, designed to cushion their owners against any hint of real life. Harry had long ago split the world into two classes: natives who worked for a living and the breed who lived to buy the flavor of the month. People like Sean, who could handle big numbers and stay focused on life's important issues, were rare indeed.

Harry returned to the apartment to find Storm seated on a counter stool, dressed in a white terry cloth robe, her hair done up in a towel. She was still pink from her run and the shower. The sandwich wrapper was open. Storm stared at the untouched meal as he entered and locked the door and walked over and sat down beside her. Up close he could smell the shampoo she had used. Storm looked about twelve years old. And so very sad.

Harry decided he might as well talk about him, since Sean was on both their minds. "I got to know your grandfather about fifteen years ago."

"Is this where I'm supposed to say you can't be that old?"

"Ouch."

"How old are you, Harry?"

"Eat all your sandwich and I might tell you." When she turned over the top bread and picked up a morsel of meat, he said, "I'm old enough to know better. But stick me in a suit and put a pretty lady on my arm, hey. Suddenly I'm open to arguments to the contrary."

"Having you here makes me feel like he's a lot closer."

He found himself swallowing sorrow solid as a brick. "Funny. I was thinking the very same thing about you."

They savored a shared silence. Then, "So you guys met."

"Yeah, back before the last ice age. I'd heard about this guy, a gallery owner who had an interest in some pieces of mine. Which was completely new. Back then, treasure dogs sold through middlemen. Gallery types wouldn't touch us with a barge pole. They took their cue from museum directors and the bureaucrats, who claimed we were all thieves. When we got together, Sean struck me as a real hard case."

"Right the first time," Storm said.

"He knew his stuff, though. And he asked questions about what he didn't know. I didn't trust him at first, and he didn't have trouble with that either. He had no idea where the boundaries were between what he could ask and what I couldn't answer. He just took what I gave. He ate information. He *devoured* it. I had no idea what to make of this guy, running a major art house, down on his hands and knees on this carpet that cost more than my boat, tracking on a hand-drawn map as I explained how we found the stern hold of my latest salvage. The stern hold, see, that's where—"

Storm took up the line. "The captain kept a strongbox in his stern cabin where his owners stored gold for the voyage home. They made two keys to the strongbox, which the captain could not open. One key locked it in the New World or the Spice Islands, the other opened it back in Europe. The richest passengers also had their cabins at the rear, many of whom traveled with their own strongboxes. The captain usually had another chest where steerage passengers could store their valuables."

"You're definitely Sean's granddaughter."

"That's right," Storm said. "I am."

"Sean refused to buy anything outright. He said he'd front me what I needed for the next voyage, and keep the rest for when I got back, minus his cut. This was . . ."

"Unheard of," Storm said. "Impossible."

"You got to understand, my profession attracts a lot of scallywags. A lot of salvagers are one notch above pirates. You can imagine what happened when word got around there was this gallery owner who was offering to handle salvaged goods for a commission."

"He got laughed at."

"Right out of the bars from Banda Ache to Jamaica. But there was something about him, I don't know."

"You trusted him," Storm said. "And you made a friend."

"A year or so later, I took him out on a salvage operation. We were working a merchant vessel that went down off the coast of Cozumel, just happened to land on a reef outcropping shallow enough for us to dive. Sean had never strapped into diving gear before. The guy was like a kid on safari. First time down, he found a gold chain. Just plucked it out of the sand. Almost blew his ventilator, shouting and dancing around."

"He kept it in his office. I never knew where it came from." She gave that a beat, then, "I don't want to go to the reception tonight."

Harry started picking meat off Storm's sand-wich. "If you're looking for somebody to talk about obligations and all that, you've come to the wrong place."

"Sean would want me to go."

"I'll tell you something about your grandfather. He'd either be your best buddy or make you want to beat him with a ball-peen hammer. Which I almost did, the last time we met." Harry ate another bite. "Go, don't go. Nobody here's gonna complain one way or the other."

THAT EVENING, AS STORM TURNED the car into the Breakers Hotel drive, Harry plucked a word right out of her head. "Memories."

She dragged up enough air to ask, "Sean brought you here?"

"For the most expensive burger I've ever tasted. A hundred bucks." They joined the line of cars waiting to divulge their glitzy loads. He inspected her in the glare of hotel lights. "You look great, by the way."

"Thanks." Storm wore a vintage Balenciaga gown she had found in a Palm Beach–style garage sale. It was fashioned in the thirties Art Deco style, of black and white silk velvet. "It was still in the dry cleaner's bag from last year."

"Same event?"

"Yes."

"With Sean?"

"He used the event to announce I was taking over the Palm Beach shop." It had also been the first time Sean had ever publicly introduced Storm as his granddaughter. She tried to offer Harry a smile. "Like you said, memories."

"Say the word, we're out of here. Until then, we'll tough it out together."

The car jockey opened her door and welcomed them to the Breakers. Storm started to rise from the car, then turned back. She inspected Harry carefully.

"What?"

She leaned forward and kissed Harry's cheek. "Thanks for being here, Harry."

Harry didn't speak. But he rubbed the spot where her lips had been and gave her a look she carried out into the night.

Harry Bennett entered the Breakers Hotel with a boxer's swagger and a total lack of guile. No matter how she might buff and shine the man, Harry would always remain a buccaneer. Wearing his midnight blue Armani and formal shirt with studs and black bow tie, Harry was handsome in the manner of a drill sergeant in full dress uniform. She gripped his arm and fed on his hard-earned confidence.

The Breakers had originally been built as an afterthought to Flagler's Royal Poinciana Hotel, which had stood three miles further inland. Guests had often requested rooms close enough to hear the surf, so a smaller inn of cedar and pine had been erected on the tip of Flagler's ten square miles of Palm Beach Island. By the dawn of the twentieth century, the demand to stay in the inn nicknamed the Breakers by its regulars was greater than at the inland palace. When the inn burned down three years later, Flagler ordered a new beachfront structure built in the style that came to be known as the Gilded Age.

The arriving guests made a stately procession down the Spanish baronial hall, beneath a cathedral ceiling adorned with royal crests. They passed through the main bar and entered the vast circular ballroom. For Storm, last year's event had swept by in a flash of elation. Her necklace had become one of the evening's most talked-over items. The emerald pendant had weighed in at sixty-one carats, the largest of twelve stones found in a stern lockbox on the *Kristinya*, a Dutch vessel sunk off Curacao in 1715. Storm had recounted the tale four times that night, until a Hollywood mogul bought it over champagne and canapés for his newest leading lady.

This year's reception was filled with cold shoulders and knowing smirks and poisoned hugs. Harry took up station a few steps back, his stone-like demeanor telling everybody he had no interest in small talk. Storm stood on the outskirts of a cluster that did not quite shut her out. When a quartet began playing Brahms, she decided she had endured more than enough.

But a male voice chose that moment to say, "This must be so very hard for you, Ms. Syrrell."

Storm made a half turn and found herself facing the man whose photograph she had just seen inside an FBI file. "Do I know you?"

"You have been pointed out to me."

Harry noticed the change and stepped forward. "Everything all right?"

Storm lifted her chin, motioning him away. Harry took a step back, but his gaze never shifted. Storm said to the gentleman, "You worked with my grandfather?"

"We did business together for many years." He sipped from his glass, revealing a gold cuff link with the largest star sapphire she had ever seen. "I have an item for sale. One I wish you to handle for me."

Selim Arkut, that was the name Emma Webb had used. Storm put him down as Persian or Turkish, late sixties, black hair laced with silver, the profile of a nobleman, the nose of a bird of prey. "Our shop is in the process of closing."

"I am not offering the item to your shop, Ms. Syrrell, but to you personally."

The night swirled around her, only now it left her untouched. "Is the item in Palm Beach?"

"Perhaps."

"How do you want—"

"It would be best if our discussion remained confidential. Most particularly in regards to your aunt."

"What do you have against Claudia?"

But the man had vanished, and her question was directed at empty air.

ELEVEN

THE NEXT MORNING, STORM LEFT Harry in charge of the booth while she went to rush several final items through the vetting process.

Harry was no monk, and his absence of physical desire for this softly vulnerable woman astonished him. He did not feel fatherly. As Harry stood in the booth's entrance and waited for the convention's starting bell, he decided there was only one way to describe how Storm made him feel.

He felt needed.

Nothing—no smiling lady crossing a smoky bar with promise in her eyes, no find uncovered in a forest of coral and old bones—nothing felt quite so fine as the kiss she had laid upon his cheek. One touch to flesh scarred by a lot more than prison, and Harry tipped a mental hat to the lost friend who had sent him here.

As soon as the gates opened, the convention center aisles became rivers of two-legged money. People strolled and shopped and greeted one another with confident tones and polished laughter. Harry made no attempt to hide Storm's cheat sheet. He was amazed at both the prices he quoted and the way people didn't even blink. An hour into the show, he had red reserve tags on two paintings, a jade sculpture, and one of the ruby amulets.

As soon as he spotted the woman in the booth's entryway, Harry knew her as Sean's daughter. Claudia Syrrell was sophisticated, refined, and statuesque and carried her fifty-plus years with the same elegance as another woman might wear pearls.

But she was not Sean.

Storm carried the old man's stamp. Claudia Syrrell merely bore the name.

Claudia searched the booth for her niece. Even her frown was graceful. Harry said, "Ms. Syrrell?"

"Yes."

"Harry Bennett. Storm got called away. She asked me to handle things for a second."

"How kind, Mr. . . ."

"Bennett." He remembered manners drilled into him by a pair of Ivy League lieutenants. How a man never offered a lady his hand, but rather waited for her to decide if she wanted to shake. Which Claudia Syrrell most definitely did not. "I was very sorry to hear about Sean."

"Did you know my father, Mr. Bennett?"

He liked the quiet sigh that inflected the name. An emotion too strong for even this stylish woman to fully disguise. "He was one of my closest friends."

She studied the vendor's badge dangling from Harry's neck. "Are you a collector?"

"I have been. Most of it's gone now."

"Sold through us, I hope." Not even her cultured tones could quite mask the question's mechanical quality. "Did you have any particular passion?"

Harry noted the delicate way she pried. Her clients weren't in the market for something. They collected. They didn't shop for an item. They had a passion. As though the extra zeros required a different lingo. Harry replied, "Gold, jade, and porcelain mostly. Some silver and pewter, not enough of either. Most recently, sixteenth-century conquistadors' booty."

"How very interesting. Three years ago, we carried quite an interesting line of Spanish gold artifacts from that same era."

Harry spotted Storm walking the aisle toward them. He saw how people paused in their shopping and their discussions. Some probably because of the shadow of loss she carried. But most of them, Harry surmised, because of the woman's aura.

He said to Claudia, "Actually, it was four years back."

She blinked. "They were yours?"

"Yes."

"You're a salvager."

"That's right."

"One of Sean's unlikely crew." She noticed Storm. "Well, hello there."

Storm kissed Claudia's cheek. "You've met Harry."

Seeing the two women standing side by side only highlighted the difference between them. No doubt Claudia had a natural ease with clients and collectors. Yet Sean's fire was missing from his daughter. The magnetism. The fierce enticement.

Everything Storm had in double portions.

Storm said, "Harry's the man I told you about on the phone. He saved my life."

Harry knew Claudia wanted to dismiss the claim as overly dramatic. But all she said was, "Would you please excuse us for a moment, Mr. Bennett?"

"No problem." He started to turn away, then added, "I'm sorry for your loss. Truly."

"Our loss," Storm softly corrected.

Harry could see Storm's aunt disliked the comment. He moved purposefully away, but as soon as Claudia returned her attention to her niece, Harry shifted behind the wall adjoining the next booth and listened.

Claudia asked, "How was the opening event?"

"Harry made it bearable. Barely."

"You took that man to the Exhibition Ball?"

"Sean trusted him."

"Sean had a soft spot when it came to such people. That man is a salvager, Storm. A treasure hound. They're all borderline insane." When

Storm did not reply, Claudia's voice rose a notch. "Take it from me. Give him one whiff of new treasure and he'd sell you to white slavers."

"I'm sorry. But you're wrong."

A young woman stepped out of the neighboring booth and asked Harry, "Can I help you with something?"

"Just looking, thanks." Harry moved down the aisle. Storm's words were nice. But what really wound his clock was the way she said it. He liked the idea that someone was so confident in him. He liked it a lot. Even when he didn't feel the same way about himself.

STORM FOUND HARRY PROWLING THE aisles, asked him to watch the booth, then joined Claudia for an early lunch. The convention center diner served cold sandwiches and soda in Palm Beach style. Tiny round tables were padded with layers of starched tablecloths. The chairs were plush and the waiters wore dinner jackets. The sandwiches were served on bone china, with little tureens of relish and Dijon mustard and a single orchid at each table.

Claudia chose a table by the aisle. The chattering throng granted them a semblance of privacy. "I'm so tired my bones ache."

Storm did not need to ask if there was any news. It was written on Claudia's face. "I didn't know you were coming down."

"I'm not here for the show." Claudia waited for the waiter to deposit her sandwich and cappuccino. She inspected the baguette wrapped in plastic. "Forty-two dollars for this?"

"Forget the sandwich. Tell me what's going on."

"I've had more meetings. We're facing unexpected debts, and we're burdened with assets we can't unload fast enough to help us through the crisis."

Every major dealer lived in terror of scandal. Syrrell's had been struck twice in the space of ten months. A Chagall had been proven to be the work of a master forger, but only after it had been sold to a regional museum. The seller had by then vanished, so Sean had bought it back with funds from his own pocket. Five months later, an even more devastating crisis erupted: a Byzantine silver plate handled through a source Sean had thought to be impeccable turned out to have been stolen. Sean had been forced to swallow that one as well. His pockets might have been deep, but few dealers could handle two such hits in a year and stay afloat.

Storm said, "Sean had no choice. He had to pay them back."

"Storm, we left blame behind a long while ago." Claudia took a single bite of her sandwich and pushed the plate to one side. "I've been living on coffee and fear."

"What aren't you telling me?"

"I've been approached by attorneys representing a buyer."

"That's great. For which item?"

"For the firm."

Storm felt her middle congeal into one frozen knot. "You can *not* be serious."

"I'm meeting their lawyers tonight. In Boca. But some important items have gone missing. Sean's book of contacts for one."

"You'd give strangers his notebook?"

"The buyer has offered a price high enough to clear our debts, and I'll try to negotiate upward. He gets what he wants. Including the remaining items in Sean's personal collection, which I also can't find."

"The buyer knows about Sean's private collection?"

"His lawyers do. According to them, Sean recently acquired two new items. An illuminated manuscript and a chalice. How they obtained this information, I have no idea. But they have told me the deal won't go forward without these items. I've searched everywhere."

"That's why you're here?" Had it not been for the news of the possible sale, Storm would have told her aunt everything. "Who wants to buy Syrrell's?"

"I am specifically ordered not to tell you."

"Why would they shut me out?"

"They say it's because you were fired."

103

"Harry says Sean fired me to protect me. Not that it worked."

That brought Claudia around. "You've told that salvager everything?"

"Listen to what I'm saying, Claudia. What if the buyer is tied into these attacks?"

"I wish *you* would listen. You are divulging secrets crucial to our company's future to a man who is little more than a pirate."

"You just told me. It's not my company anymore." Then it struck her. "Have they offered you a job?"

"Nothing's definite."

"Oh, this is sweet."

"Didn't you hear a word I just said? It's this or nothing."

But Storm was already in departure mode. "Just exactly who are you working so hard to convince?"

STORM KNEW SHE SHOULD RETURN to the booth. But she wandered the aisles, occasionally greeting people without actually seeing who spoke to her. She could not tell which disturbed her more: hearing that Claudia was talking to a buyer, or not telling her aunt about the bank vault and its contents. There had never been secrets between them. Not telling Claudia ripped another shard from her tattered world.

The first time she met Claudia, Storm had been

thirteen. An impossibly elegant woman rang their bell one afternoon, then stood in the doorway and stared at Storm and wept. Storm felt naked beneath the gaze of a woman she had never seen before, one who shed tears from the pain of just looking at her.

When the woman recovered, she wiped her eyes with an embroidered handkerchief and said, "You must be Storm."

Storm had stood there, mute from the distress on the woman's features. The stranger was beautifully refined. Her features were as cultured as her voice. Her clothes were stunning. Everything about her spoke of a world beyond Storm's reach.

The woman asked, "Do you know who I am?"

"My aunt Claudia. I've seen your picture."

"Can I come in?"

Storm hesitated out of deep shame.

Claudia said, "Joe is my brother, Storm. I know what he's like."

Storm stepped aside.

As soon as Claudia entered the house, her nose wrinkled at the odor. Dope's sweet, cloying stench permeated everywhere. Storm's shame deepened.

Claudia asked, "Where is he?"

"In his studio." At least that was what he called it. But the brushes were rock hard and the paint tubes had long become bricks. Whenever anyone visited him, the only items he showed off were his collection of bongs.

"Where is that, Storm?"

"Last door on your left."

But Claudia remained where she was. "Joe's choices are your future only if you make them so."

When Claudia started down the hallway, Storm left the house and crouched on the front steps. Claudia didn't stay inside long. When she came out she was no longer sad. Instead, she looked furious.

Claudia slammed the front door behind her. She walked down the three steps to the sidewalk. She stood staring across the street, her jaw clenched tight. Storm studied her intently. Claudia's hair was prematurely grey, matching her blue-grey silk suit. Her eyes were the same opal black Storm saw in the mirror. On the trailing edge of the scarf around her neck Storm could read the name Hermès.

Finally Claudia said, "I don't suppose I need to ask if he's like this often."

"Almost every day."

"What about you, Storm? Do you get high?"

Storm liked the woman's directness enough to reveal one of her closely guarded secrets. "When I was seven he started getting my dog stoned. He and his friends. They watched the dog and laughed. Then they tried to do it to me. Like I was just another pet, just another reason for them to laugh." Storm was breathing hard now. "I hate it."

"Good." Claudia looked at her. "If your grandfather knew I was here he would fire me. You know about your father and Sean, my father?"

"I know Daddy hates him." Raging against Sean Syrrell was another thing Storm's father liked to do when he was high.

Claudia brushed off the step beside Storm and seated herself. "Joe wanted Sean to display some of his paintings in the shop."

"Joseph," Storm corrected.

"What?"

"Daddy hates being called Joe."

Claudia looked at her a moment. "To be perfectly frank, I don't much care what *Joe* does or doesn't hate. Okay?"

"Sure."

"Sean told him he would do it on two conditions. First, Joe had to attend a proper art school and graduate. Second, he had to clean up his act and start learning discipline, start honing his gift. Otherwise Sean wouldn't hire Joe to paint his doorpost."

Storm tasted a smile. "My grandfather said that?"

"He did indeed. The next day, your father stole two items from Sean's private collection. One was a very valuable painting. The artist was Pissarro, an Impressionist painter from France—"

"I know who Pissarro is."

"The other was a medieval triptych, which is a fancy word for a carving set into three folding

107

panels. The triptych was Sean's most treasured possession. Which is no doubt why Joe took it. There was no hard evidence who the thief was, of course. But we are certain it was Joe. When the theft was discovered, Joe and Sean had a raging battle. Your grandfather disowned Joe and he moved down here. And now I'm tired of talking about your father." Claudia opened her purse and drew out a card. "Do you know our shop on Palm Beach Island?"

"Yes." It was on Worth Avenue, with a huge glass window always filled with the most beautiful things Storm had ever seen.

"Our manager has retired, and there's a problem with our lease. I've come down to find a new location for the shop and to run it until we find someone else. If you like, we could meet there on the weekends and go for a coffee and a chat. Just call and make sure I'm available."

"What would Sean say?"

"This would have to be our secret. Can I trust you with that?"

Storm wanted to hug the woman. Or cry. Which was ridiculous. Storm never revealed any emotion at all. And this woman was a complete stranger. So she hugged herself instead. "I won't ever tell."

TWELVE

THAT AFTERNOON HARRY MANAGED THE booth. Storm returned from her meeting with Claudia in a serious funk. Twice Harry approached her, once to bring coffee and another time to squeeze her shoulder. Letting the lady know she wasn't alone. He didn't see any need to ask what had happened. If Storm wanted to talk, she knew where to find him. Harry had no problem with silence between friends.

A half hour before closing, the guy appeared. Harry noticed him because if Harry had been planning a move, this was when he'd do it. The exhibition hall was winding down. The plainclothes detail was clustered by the exit, as weary as the departing clientele. All the eyes Harry could see were dulled from a very long day.

The guy definitely had his share of eastern Mediterranean blood. But his outfit was pure LA hip. Black suit, knit shirt, woven leather shoes, narrow black shades. Dark hair glossed and gelled. A thin gold chain from his left wrist.

Harry moved to intercept him in the aisle. "Help you?"

"I got some business with the lady."

Probably Turkish. Harry had met guys like this before, merchants to the world. They didn't just pick up the lingo. They got the accent down so heavy they sounded local. This guy had done some serious street time either in Chicago or Detroit. "The lady is not in."

"I mean the one right there behind you."

When the guy tried to step around him, Harry moved to block. "Take off the shades and look at me."

"Get out of my face, old man."

"Listen to what I'm saying. The lady in question is not available."

"Oh, is that so." The guy reached inside his jacket.

Or tried to, because Harry got one grip on the guy's wrist and another at the point where his jugular met his jaw. "You want to live, you bring that hand out empty."

The guy's shades fell to the carpet by his feet. His dark eyes were too surprised to be angry. "Man, what is your problem?"

Storm asked, "Harry?"

"Go get security."

"No!" The hand came out empty. "There, now will you just back off?"

Harry dropped his hands as two plainclothes jogged up. "What is going on here?"

Harry lifted his vendor's badge, his gaze not leaving the guy's hands. "I thought I recognized this man as a troublemaker. But I might have been mistaken."

"Were you ever." The guy scooped his shades off

the floor and jammed them into his pocket. "Can I reach into my jacket for something?"

"Slow and easy."

"I was told to do this quiet. And I would have. 'Cept for gung ho joe here." His hand emerged holding an envelope. "All that was gonna happen was, I give this to the lady and ask for an estimate. Nothing else."

"Sure thing," Harry said. And reached out.

The hand holding the envelope retreated. "Nothing doing, old man."

"Anything that goes to the lady goes through me."

The guy didn't like that either, but the world was watching, and the security was still poised for trouble. So he said something in Turkish that Harry didn't need a translation for and passed him the envelope.

Harry opened it to find himself looking at a gold cuff link framing an oversized star sapphire.

"Can I see?" Storm took one look and stiffened. Harry felt the change through the hand on his arm. When she spoke, all her weary funk was gone. "I can't do the appraisal here. We have to go."

"Yeah, that's exactly what shoulda gone down without fireworks." He reached for the envelope, then used it to point at Harry. "The old man stays here."

Storm slipped into her jacket. "His name is Harry and he's coming."

ONE OF THE SECURITY PLAINCLOTHESMEN escorted them outside. The Turk slipped behind the wheel of a black stretch limo, far too angry to be holding anybody's door. The guard asked Storm, "Are you sure you're all right, ma'am?"

"Yes, thank you."

The security guy said to the driver, "I'm making note of your license. And we've got you on camera."

The Turk had something to say about that, too. He gunned his limo out of the lot, swung hard into traffic, and rolled up the divider window.

The limo swept through the rush-hour traffic and took the newly opened overpass to Palm Beach International Airport. The driver had a word with the guard by the private-jet concourse, passed through the gates, and rolled up to a narrow aluminum needle with wings. A pilot saluted as he opened Storm's door. "Ms. Syrrell?"

"That's right."

He eyed Harry rising from the limo's other side. "I was told you'd be traveling alone."

"My associate comes, or I'll have the limo take me back to town."

The pilot was young and carefully ironed and trained to handle the extremely rich. "Guess I heard wrong. This way, folks."

Harry climbed the stairs and asked, "Where are we headed?"

The engines were already winding up as the pilot sealed the door and replied. "Our flight plan reads Teterboro."

But the jet had scarcely reached cruising speed before it started winding down again. The sun swung through a brilliant arc as the plane descended. Ten minutes later, they landed and wheeled over to where another limo waited, this one a white town car. When the pilot reappeared, Harry asked, "What's going on?"

"Sir, all I can tell you is we've made an unscheduled stopover at a private strip near Jupiter Beach. But we're leaving immediately for New York."

"Without us."

In response, the pilot stepped back to admit an older woman in a chauffeur's dark suit. "Ms. Syrrell?"

"That's right."

The driver offered Storm an envelope. Through the opening she saw a second star-sapphire cuff link. "I was told to give you this."

THE DRIVE FROM THE JUPITER landing strip back to Palm Beach Island took just under an hour. It was almost dark when the limo pulled up before a French provincial home surrounded by a high concrete wall. The wall's two entrances were solid steel and painted the same chalk blue as the razor wire running along the top. The driver locked the limo's doors before walking over and ringing the bell. Storm said, "We're talking serious money."

Harry continued to scout the gloom. "Funny. With the jet and the limos and all, I had kind of assumed that already."

The driver of their first limo stood just inside the perimeter wall. He offered Harry a serious stink eye as they entered. The garden was illuminated by lights planted at the base of palms and blooming wisteria. The gentleman she had last seen at the Breakers reception said, "Ms. Syrrell, how very nice of you to join me."

"This is my associate, Harry Bennett. Harry, meet Selim Arkut."

"So we are properly introduced. How very excellent." He motioned to the man smoldering in the garden. "I believe you have already met my nephew."

Harry said, "That was some roundabout journey to get here."

Selim led them back toward the house, as his nephew went back to patrolling the garden. "These days, attention is being paid to all our movements."

"Any idea who the watchers are?"

The gentleman ushered them inside with a courtly half bow. The house was an empty shell littered with packing material. Selim locked the door behind them and replied, "The wrong kind of people. The wrong kind of attention."

Harry said, "Let me guess. A small guy who likes

desert colors and vanishes before your very eyes."

Storm added, "It could also be a federal agent with darkish blond hair."

"I am familiar with Agent Webb. And I have heard of your attacker. Mediterranean in coloring. Perhaps Latino, but I personally do not think so. He appears to be very good at his job. I have never seen him before and do not yet have a name."

Mediterranean was a perfect way to describe their host, in his dark slacks and midnight blue silk pullover and Italian loafers and no socks. He wore a gold watch thin as a gigolo's moustache. His hair was oiled and immaculate, black except for the silver-fox streaks by either temple.

Harry asked, "You know most of the South Florida pros?"

"I know who I know, Mr. Bennett. This way."

The house was like the other beachside homes Storm had visited, an elegantly fortified citadel. The air was as controlled as the lighting and scented by packing dust. The walls held vague shadows of vanished artwork. Their footsteps echoed loudly through an empty house as Selim Arkut led them down a side hall, through polished double doors, and into a carpeted room that must have formerly served as his master bedroom. He entered a vast walk-in closet, slid aside a panel, and coded numbers into a keypad. The rear wall sighed open, revealing a door of fortified steel. "Follow me, please."

The vault was larger than Storm's bedroom. The chamber was almost bare. The carpet held a deep imprint where an armchair had rested before an empty easel. The wall beside the entrance held six miniature flatscreens, a bank of switches, two keypads, and a phone. When the door slid shut and the safelike wheel rolled steel bars into locking position, Storm saw Harry shudder. "Are you all right?"

"I've got a thing against cages."

"You could wait outside if you like, Mr. Bennett."

"I go where she goes."

"A trusted ally. I commend you, Ms. Syrrell." Selim worked the panel. Steel shutters rolled up the far wall, revealing a deep floor-to-ceiling alcove. The tiers of metal arms were intended to hold perhaps a dozen paintings. Now the alcove contained just one canvas. Selim released the latches and lifted the frame free. He moved to the artist's easel standing beneath a single light. "I would be grateful if you would please identify this for me, Ms. Syrrell."

A single glance was enough to say, "Identification isn't the issue, though, is it."

Harry asked, "What's the matter?"

"If it's real, it's a museum-quality piece. But I can't determine the authenticity without proper equipment and a lot more time than we have tonight. The same goes for giving a valuation."

"I am merely requesting an identification."

"You know perfectly well what this is."

Harry said, "The guy's fronted us two limos and a jet. You got to admit, it's an expensive way to waste our time."

As she approached the easel, Storm felt the exquisite, gnawing hunger that only a voracious collector ever understood. "The painting is by Albrecht Dürer, of course. Assuming it's real. This work contains many of the same elements he applied to his self-portrait of 1499, which is considered by many art historians to have created the structure of portrait painting that is still applied today."

The subject stared intensely at the viewer, his arrogance and power reaching across five hundred years to grip Storm's chest and squeeze so hard she was left breathless. "Dürer's signature is here in the upper-left section, just off center, as it is in his self-portrait. This too is an abrupt change from the norm. Dürer is declaring himself a creator who deserves full credit for his composition and his talent."

Storm shivered from pure craving. The painting was a magnet for the light. It possessed the ability to transform even this steel and concrete cave into a sanctuary. The subject was obviously a cardinal. He wore the ermine robes and red cap of office, with a massive gold crucifix dangling from his chest. This was matched by the gold beaten along the painting's borders, an eight-inch frame of pure gold leaf. Which in and of itself was another suggestion of authenticity, for no forger would dream of making such an investment, particularly since the practice hearkened back to the early Middle Ages. But Dürer's father had been a goldsmith, and the cardinal in question was clearly rich and haughty enough to have ordered such a finishing touch.

Storm took a mental step away from the painting. She asked, "You have provenance?"

Selim Arkut was unsettling, the hawk nose and the thin way his lips compressed into what could be pleasure or disapproval. Or both. "There is mention in Dürer's letters of a visiting cardinal who admired his work."

Her shivers intensified. "Where did you find this?"

"Like your grandfather, Ms. Syrrell, I have never divulged a name. Many of my clients keep their wealth a secret because the alternative is for them and their families to be erased from the scrolls of life. Your grandfather and I began working together in the chaos following the Shah's fall from the Peacock Throne. We solidified our relationship when the generals took power in Ankara. Throughout such lands and times, trust is a matter of life and death." He motioned at the canvas. "This was the first time your grandfather had used me to hunt down a work of art. But he had heard of this, and when I approached the owner, he seemed almost grateful for the chance to redeem it for cash and exit visas from Iran for his family."

Storm caught the slight hesitation and asked, "You're being hunted because of this painting?"

"No, Ms. Syrrell. I am in danger because of the other request your grandfather made. To help him identify the person seeking to destroy his reputation and his company."

"What did you learn?"

"Almost nothing. My search took me to a lawyer who specializes in shadows. Yesterday I learned the lawyer has vanished. I have decided that I must depart as well."

Harry asked, "Any mention where the bishop in this picture here was from?"

"I believe Cyprus was mentioned. Why?"

Harry shrugged. "Just curious."

Storm did not believe him, but now was not the time to be asking questions. She returned her attention to the canvas. A new find like this, if it was indeed authentic, would be headline news throughout the art world. There was no telling what the painting was worth because it had been decades since another painting by Dürer had come on the open market. Besides which, medieval artists were not presently in vogue. Even so, half a million dollars would certainly be within reach. Perhaps more.

But that was not what set Storm's heart to racing.

The bishop held his right hand in the traditional medieval form of a public blessing, two fingers touching his thumb. The other hand held a triptych.

Storm had seen that triptych before.

Selim obviously noticed Storm's intense scrutiny, for he asked, "Was there something else, Ms. Syrrell?"

Harry interrupted Storm's response with "Something's going down."

Selim glanced at where an orange light flashed in the center of the control panel. "My nephew has set off the alarm."

On the central security screen, the limo driver ran through the illuminated garden. He held a pistol in a practiced two-arm grip. Suddenly the flatscreens were lit up by a pair of brilliant flashes. Harry said, "Your man is taking fire."

Storm was amazed at Harry's sudden calm. Five minutes earlier, he'd been sweating buckets over being locked inside a steel room, and now he appeared so far beyond cool he could turn steam to sleet.

Harry walked to the door, picked up the panel phone, listened briefly, then set it back. "Line's dead. Check your cell phone."

"There is no signal inside this room."

Storm had never been good at chaos. The fact that she had been raised in it, that she'd had a fresh helping every morning with her breakfast cereal, had not improved things. Harry, though, had actually steadied in the face of danger. He asked Selim, "Do we go or do we stay?"

"My nephew is in danger." Selim moved over beside Harry and pressed one of the panel buttons. An unseen drawer slid silently out from the wall. The drawer was padded like a photographer's case and held a matte black revolver and two clips.

"Place comes equipped with everything for the modern family," Harry said. "You keep another piece?"

"Of course. A Glock." Selim slapped the clip into place and cocked the gun. "My nephew is presently firing it."

"Swell."

"You are not armed?"

"It's back in Storm's living room, where it'll do us all a lot of good."

Storm said, "You left a gun in my apartment?"

"Later, okay?" To Selim, "How do we play this?"

Selim coded the door open. The two men stepped out and listened intently. Storm thought she might have heard someone shout from outside the house. But she could not be certain.

Selim said, "Leave through the garage."

Harry asked, "Where's that?"

"Back to the hall. Go right. Leave through the steel door at the back of the garage." A shot penetrated the home's compressed silence. Then four more in rapid succession. "Two-one-five twice. You understand?"

"Another keypad," Harry said, calm as a weatherman. "The door's combo."

Selim was already moving. "Go!"

Harry remained where he was, scouting through the doorway. "You follow me, but not too close. Move when I say move. I raise my hand, you freeze. Ready?"

"Wait." Storm went back to the easel and hefted the painting. When Harry's eyes widened, she said, "He got this for Sean. It's coming with me. We can work out the details later."

Harry gave her a buccaneer's grin. "Hey. We're out of the cage, we got the loot, and somebody else is off chasing bullets. I'd call that the makings of a good day."

She followed him through the bedroom and on to where the side hall opened into a pristine garage. Two spaces were empty. The third was occupied by a sky blue Bentley. Harry crossed to the steel door. More gunfire sounded from outside the house.

"Small arms," Harry said. "What was that combo again?"

"Two-one-five, two-one-five."

"Sure hope our friends don't shoot each other." The door clicked and sighed open on a pneumatic lever. Lights flickered on automatically, revealing a long, empty tunnel. Harry peered down its length, asked, "What is this?"

"Most of these mansions have a tunnel under the beachside road. There'll be a gate at the other end."

The ocean's salty fragrance swept in with a trace of a breeze. Harry took a tentative step inside. "I don't like this."

"Why not?"

Harry raised his hand. Wait.

The garage echoed from a single great *boom*.

"Unh-unh." Harry backed from the tunnel. "No way."

"What was that?"

"Shotgun. I'd say twelve gauge." Harry stepped back into the garage. "There's got to be a better way than running down a tunnel in the dark. Unarmed. Carrying that thing. Might as well run out carrying a sign that reads, 'Here we are, shoot us now.'"

He checked the car door. It opened. Harry bent inside, came back out, and scouted the garage. Then he spotted the keys hanging from the hook by the house door. "Thank you, Selim."

"You're stealing his car?"

"You can leave the painting with me and go see if he minds." Harry took the canvas from her hands, set it on the rear seat. He slipped behind the wheel, started the car, waited for her to shut her door, said, "Grab something and hold on tight."

Harry flipped the switch by the rearview mirror and jammed the gas pedal down so hard, Storm could see his leg muscles bunch through his trousers. The garage pulsated with the engine's howl. Behind them, the garage door slid up in tandem with the outer steel barrier.

Revealing a man with a rifle.

Harry slapped the car into reverse.

The man raised the gun and fired one shot. The car was spattered with the sound of metal rain. The rear window fractured with crystal tattoos.

Storm screamed. She was pretty sure it was her. Harry's voice couldn't possibly reach that high.

The car shrilled in tandem with Storm, a hyper-charged whine from beneath the hood and another from the smoking tires. The gunner had no chance for a second shot. It was either leap aside or go down.

Harry swerved, trying to take out the gunner, but the man jumped and rolled. Harry slammed into a palm on the cul-de-sac's other side. He shifted and hit the gas. The car drilled Storm back into her seat.

Harry shouted over the sound of the racing engine, "Houston, we have liftoff!"

THIRTEEN

EMMA WEBB FINISHED INTERVIEWING THE neighbors clustered beyond the police tape and slipped her notebook back into her purse. Despite the hour, the bystanders looked pulled from a photo shoot, everybody buffed and polished and groomed. They were also caught up in shocked incredulity. They had supposedly bought their way into a safe haven. Now this.

The patrol officer standing duty by the perimeter tape glanced at the badge hanging from her waist and smirked. "So you're Treasury. Like in the secret service?"

"They're one branch, I'm another."

The cop lifted the tape. "Is that as glamorous as they make it in the movies?"

"Absolutely. Look where it's brought me. To a Palm Beach crime scene."

Emma entered Selim Arkut's private compound just as Jack Dauer appeared in the home's entrance. He called over, "Anything?"

"Several neighbors heard gunfire and called it in. Nobody saw anything worthwhile. Only one of them even knew the name of the man living here."

"I hate the rich. Give me a good old-fashioned gangland slaying any day." Dauer radiated a constant state of aggravated heat. The local cops did their best to pretend Dauer wasn't even there.

Emma envied them. "The place is stripped bare. Like your friend Syrrell tipped him off we had him under surveillance."

"You heard her say they never met—" Emma felt her phone vibrate in her pocket. She checked the readout and said, "Interesting."

"What?"

"Storm Syrrell."

Dauer stared at the night. "This just keeps getting better."

Emma walked past the policeman collecting shell casings. His clear plastic bag was half-full and glinted in the fancy lighting like poisoned gold. The house was a minifortress, the grounds perfectly manicured, the setting idyllic. That is, aside from the bullet holes punched in the house's pastel walls. "This is Webb."

"It's Harry. I thought I'd better give you a heads-up."

"You're responsible for this mess?" Emma felt her heat rise. "Storm specifically told me she'd never met Arkut."

"Which she hadn't at the time. Arkut approached her last night."

"How convenient."

"Hey. If listening is too big a problem, I'm happy to hang up."

She turned her back to Jack Dauer's glare. "Go on."

Harry fed it to her in the bullets of a pro. Terse, no

126

unnecessary details, data centered on major items.

"Selim Arkut showed you a painting he had located for Sean Syrrell?"

"Only artwork left in the house. The man was definitely on his way out. But I guess he's already told you that."

"Selim Arkut has vanished."

"What about his nephew?"

"Who?"

"A miniversion of Arkut with a major attitude problem."

"There was no one on the premises when we arrived."

"No bodies either?"

"Just a garden littered with ammunition casings and a few dozen bullet holes in the garden wall and the house's exterior." Not to mention a dozen or so highly irate and politically powerful neighbors.

"And a seriously dented palm. My bad."

"Where . . ." Emma walked out the open drive gate and flashed her light across the street. "Never mind. I see it."

"I was aiming for our guy. Missed by a frond."

"You're certain it was him?"

"Positive."

Emma had seen Harry Bennett's record. For Dauer, Harry's presence confirmed that Storm Syrrell was perpetuating a series of felonies. "Are you telling me the truth, Harry?"

"Hard to believe, I know."

"Where are you now?"

"Sean's church uses what looks like an old motor court as guest quarters. I've stayed there on occasion. It's located just behind the building where we met."

"I need to speak with Storm."

"Yeah, the pastor said the same thing when we showed up. I'm telling you what I told him. The lady was seriously shook. I put her to bed. Talk with her tomorrow."

"I could insist."

Harry sighed. "Just like a cop."

"Harry—"

But the man was gone.

EMMA RETURNED TO THE GARDEN just as Dauer snapped his phone shut and ripped a page from his notebook. She said, "That was Harry Bennett."

"All this was the pirate's work?"

"He claims they were caught in the cross fire."

Jack Dauer possessed the snort of a bilious dragon. "Don't tell me you actually believe the con."

Emma hesitated, then said, "Everything he's told us so far has checked out, sir."

"Then you're not looking hard enough. Where are they now?"

"Holed up in guest quarters at the church."

"Which one, Webb?"

"The same church where Bennett saved my life and Ms. Syrrell's, sir."

"I say we bring them both in."

Emma waited.

He shook his head, as though she had voiced her disagreement. "Something's just come over the horn. Local cops reported an incident. Think it might be tied to us. Go check it out."

"Yes sir."

"And keep your phone on. I could still order you to swing by and bring in the suspects."

EMMA DROVE EMPTY MIDNIGHT STREETS and turned into an upscale development in West Palm Beach. The security joe was as wide awake as he had ever been on this job, and directed her down an oleander boulevard to the only house where all the lights blazed. A paramedic wagon was parked nose out in the driveway. Emma stepped through the open front door and met the cool wash of air-conditioning on high. She called, "Detective Duchamp?"

"In the back."

The home's front rooms were open plan. Emma followed vague noises through the living room. Rear windows overlooked a glowing pool where a yellow inflatable chair floated in the empty water.

A woman with a gold detective badge hanging

from her jacket pocket stood in the doorway between the kitchen and the garage. She asked, "You Webb?"

"Yes."

"Badge?" The policewoman was shaped like a carbon blade—narrow, lethal, and very black. "Am I going to have trouble with you?"

"Absolutely not."

"Because I'll tell you straight up, that guy I talked with first, Dauer, is exactly why I got no time for feebs. You give me trouble, I'll eat you alive, no matter what alphabet you got there beside your name."

Emma stowed her badge back in her pocket and waited.

Duchamp asked someone Emma could not see, "How much longer?"

"All done. Okay, let's have the gurney."

Duchamp hit a switch by the doorjamb. Emma heard the garage door start open. An unseen man snapped, "How about taking a little more care with your end."

"This guy weighs a ton."

Emma entered the garage as two men fitted a stiffening body into a black sack. Duchamp noticed her grimace and asked, "You ever worked a murder scene, Agent Webb?"

"Afraid not, no. But I've been a federal agent for six years."

One of the men settling the body bag onto the

gurney drawled, "Homicide is homicide, honey. Either you is or you ain't."

The other man pushed his spectacles up his nose and grinned. "You can't be fed. Feds don't allow your sort of packaging."

Duchamp said, "Roll on out of here, Harv, before that sexist chatter finds you up on departmental charges."

He popped his gum. "Can't take the cracker outta the good ol' boy."

Duchamp waited until the wagon's rear doors slammed shut, then hit the switch. The garage door rolled down, shutting out the night. Duchamp said, "I apologize for Harv. We give coroners a lot more latitude than we probably should."

Outside, the ambo pulled away. The smell was still strong enough to fill the garage. A young woman in a white coverall worked the vic's car exterior, dusting for prints. Emma asked, "Can you tell me why I'm here?"

"Here's what we know. Randall Sykes, fifty-one, former dentist, lost his practice for drinking on the job. Currently employed as sales rep for a dental supply house. That was him in the Wagoneer."

The Jeep Cherokee was cream colored and relatively new. A bloody handprint blurred the front windshield, almost black in the fluorescents. Emma followed Duchamp around to the open passenger door. An open bottle of Russian vodka lay on the floor. The smell of spilled booze added to the mix. The driver's seat was punctured in several spots. Rust-colored stains covered the car's interior. Top to bottom.

"Far as we can tell, the perp broke in through the garage side door. We found signs of tampering. We assume to steal the bike."

Emma used that as an excuse to turn away from the car. But she could do nothing about the stench. An empty drop cloth lay stretched across the garage's other bay. "Bike?"

"New Harley Softtail. The vic brought it back from its first service yesterday. We assume the perp picked Randy up there, followed him home. Here's the interesting part. We checked with the dealer. They discovered a missing dealer's tag."

Emma cleared her throat. "So he follows the victim home, then goes back, breaks in—"

"No sign of break-in at the dealership. Probably waited for a quiet moment, slipped in and out in a flash. My guess is, the perp was hoping he'd have a few days before anyone noticed it was missing."

The crime scene investigator was Latina, in her twenties, and respectful. "Excuse me, Detective. I need to dust this area."

"Found anything yet?"

"Three partials. I'm not sure they're enough to work on even if they do belong to the perp. He cleaned up really good."

Duchamp guided Emma back toward the kitchen. "Where was I?"

"He entered to steal the bike, only the victim was seated in the Jeep. Drinking."

"I figure the perp was caught totally off guard. He planned on slipping in and out with no problem, roll the bike down the street, be gone before anybody noticed, switch plates, hide inside a biker's helmet, make himself invisible in plain sight. Only there was a problem. Randy and his wife had been fighting. The wife left to go stay with friends. Randy slipped into the garage with the bottle." Duchamp stepped into the living room and took a long look around. "What kinda guy has a place like this, goes into the garage to drink?"

Emma said, "I'm still not clear what I'm doing here, Detective."

Duchamp slipped a notepad from her jacket. "We counted sixteen stab wounds. Apparently the perp lost his cool when he found Randy out here in the garage. Once he was done, he used a cleaner Randy kept in the garage and wiped the place down. We found the rag. But not before he searched the house for witnesses. Good thing the wife was away."

The crime scene investigator emerged from the garage. "Okay if I dust the back room, Detective?"

Emma said, "Don't tell me there were kids."

"With the wife, I'm happy to say. But there's something else you need to see." Duchamp followed the CSI down the rear hall. "We got a

BOLO for a knife-wielding assailant who attacked a woman leaving Saint Anthony's."

"Actually, he attacked two people."

"So we've got ourselves somebody doing innocent people with a machete?"

"It wasn't a machete. Assuming we're talking about the same man, the assailant expected to do a quick hit and leave the country. Only we foiled his first attempt. With heightened security he didn't want to risk traveling around in a rental. So he broke in here to steal himself a bike."

"You got a name?"

"No. But we do have a solid description."

When Emma finished, the detective inspected her carefully. "Your guy sounds too lightweight for this sort of crime."

"That's part of his modus. But he's vicious."

"Loves his knife."

"Not exclusively. When he attacked the lady at the church, he was carrying a glass vial with an aerosol stopper."

"You mean, like a perfume spray?"

"Exactly like that."

"You stopped him?"

"He caught me totally by surprise. I acted like some rookie fresh out of training. We were saved by a civilian."

The detective turned pages in her book. "That wouldn't be the same Harry Bennett your guy Dauer warned me about."

"That's him."

"The guy in your office claimed Bennett's got a record, warned me to keep an eye out for him. But I ran his name through the system and came up blank."

"Bennett did time in the Caribbean."

"You're sure this isn't drug related? Dauer suggested Bennett was one step away from being arrested again."

"The intended victim and I are alive because Harry Bennett was alert when I was napping."

"Don't that just burn your toast." She motioned Emma into the room. "Mind you don't touch anything."

The room was clearly a guy's office, with leather furniture and framed posters of bikes. There was a recessed alcove behind a desk. The carpet was covered with glass. Reinforced doors were torn off their hinges.

The detective said, "Randy sure did like his toys."

The alcove held a rack of guns. Several pistols still hung from loops, several of them antiques. Four World War II vintage carbines stood on display, alongside a tommy gun with the original wooden stock.

Another check of the notebook. "According to the wife, we're missing a twelve-gauge over-and-under, two nine-mil Glocks, and a Remington hunting rifle."

"He attempted another attack tonight. This time he was armed."

"This the firefight over on the beach?"

"Yes."

The detective's eyes narrowed. Emma had the impression that Duchamp could be one mean lady in the interrogation room. "Just exactly what have you brought down on my city?"

FOURTEEN

HARRY SLEPT LIKE THE DEAD, deeper than a coma. When he woke he felt better than he had in a long time. Years.

This was no boat, but sleeping on a boat often brought that druglike state. Closing his eyes to the soft laughter of waves on the hull, rocked by the wind and the moon. Hearing quiet voices of the watch on deck, smelling the salt and diesel and the sweat of work he loved. He could shut his eyes and just leave. Harry reflected on that as he showered. He had not thought about life on board in a while. In prison, a man learned to focus on the day and the danger at hand. When he was dressed he knocked on the door to the adjoining room and wondered if maybe he was learning to leave the bad behind. Or if it was just an old adrenaline junkie sleeping off his latest fix.

"Storm?"

Through the outer screen door a voice replied, "She's long gone."

Back in the fifties the line of eighteen rooms had seen duty as a roadside motel. Now it and a neighboring apartment building both belonged to the church. They were sheltered from the main road by a stand of live oaks and bougainvillea taller than a man. Harry stepped into the morning light and found Emma Webb in a metal chair with one peaked shoe propped on the banister. "Storm said you took your coffee black."

Harry accepted the Styrofoam cup. "Thanks."

"I assume if we dusted that shot-up Bentley in the church shed, we'd find your prints all over."

Harry sipped from the cup and grunted a noncommittal reply. So much for the morning's fine mood.

"When I showed Storm a photo of Selim Arkut, I asked if she knew him. She claimed not. Next thing I know, I'm getting word about this guy's house being turned into a free-fire zone, Beirut style."

"What I told you on the phone was the dead solid truth. Storm had no idea who Selim was until you showed her that photo. She met him later that same night. He sashayed up at the Breakers' reception, gave her thirty seconds, then vanished."

Emma stripped off her shades and rubbed her face. She looked very tired. "At least you managed to keep your stories straight."

"Any word on how Arkut is doing?"

"We haven't heard a peep from the guy." Emma slipped her shades back on. "Can you give me the long version of what went down last night?"

Harry seated himself in the flaking chair next to hers and laid it all out. Started with the Turk showing up at the convention center, the jet, the second limo, the panic room, the painting room, the attack. Emma spent the entire time watching a pair of mockingbirds hunting worms in the strip of green between them and the road.

When he stopped talking, she gave it a couple of beats, then rose from her chair. "You want to take a ride?"

"I ought to go see what Storm's got planned for my day."

"I've got two junior agents dogging her steps. You've been officially turned loose for the duration."

When they got to the parking lot, Emma entered the shed, walked past the two riding mowers, and did a slow sweep around the Bentley. When she touched one of the bullet holes, Harry said, "Shotgun."

She moved on to the trunk's concave depression. Harry supplied, "Palm tree."

"Know how much a car like this costs?"

"No idea." Even with the bullet holes and the compressed trunk, the Bentley gleamed as only serious money could. "Hundred grand?"

"Try two fifty."

"Get out."

"Funny a guy would lose a car worth a quarter of a million dollars and not bother to report it missing. We're assuming for the minute Selim Arkut is alive. We picked up about a zillion rounds, but no bodies."

Harry said, "The house was empty. A tomb. Stains on the walls where he'd taken down his art. Selim was definitely on the way out. And seriously freaked over somebody being on his tail."

Emma didn't say anything further until they were in her car and she had the motor and AC running. "Storm said I should trust you."

"Yeah, she sang me that same tune about you."

Emma pulled away from the church, took the bridge to the mainland, and headed west. Taking her time, holding tight to her thoughts and the wheel. She drove like a cop, gunning the engine around slower traffic, impatient with everybody else on the road, as aggressive as an angry man. Only today there wasn't any tension between them. He sat twisted slightly in his seat, staring at her openly.

Emma was dressed in a blue suit as severe as a naval uniform. No jewelry except for a flat gold watch on an alligator band. No rings of any kind. Pale polish on her nails. Ditto for the lip gloss. A single clip keeping her hair in position.

She stopped at a light, glanced over. "What."

He just shook his head. No way was he going to tell her what he was thinking. Which was that Emma Webb was one fine-looking lady. Shame about the badge and the baggage.

Emma said, "I want you to do me a favor. Pretend we're on the same side for a while. Lay it out for me."

"I just did."

"Not last night. The whole deal. How you got here, why you're staying. Everything."

"Why should I?"

She tightened a notch, then took her mind off the verbal trigger. Harry actually saw it happen. She pointed at the front windshield and replied, "An hour that way is a little town called Clewiston. By the time we get there, I need to make a decision. Either I'm going to make you sit in the car while I go handle something, or I'm going to put my career on the line."

Harry tried to recall the last time he had gotten complete honesty from a cop and came up blank. So he used the seat controls to slide all the way back, stretched out his legs, and gave it to her straight. Starting with the moment the toffee-colored gnome sprung him from the Barbados jail, through watching the two-timing London researcher expire in his arms, to today. The whole nine yards.

A half hour beyond the Palm Beach County line, they entered the other Florida, the one big-city types liked to pretend was paved over and archived. Only those pundits were as blind as Miami condo living could make them. Because the truth was, Florida remained the third largest producer of cattle in the United States, and was second only to Kentucky for horse breeding.

The state's famous orange groves were restricted to regions with super-rich soil and unlimited fresh water. The Everglades and the state's three other swamps were rimmed by scrublands, populated by half-wild cattle and ranches that measured their size in tens of thousands of acres. Roads were often still paved with oyster shells, and folks wore stained cowboy hats and spiced their speech with a genuine cracker twang. Harry had worked with several salvagers who preferred the Florida countryside to the beachside glitz. He liked the region and the people just fine.

Lake Okeechobee was a placid silver mirror laced with sky-bound streamers from over-powered speedboats. They stopped at Clewiston's only gas station for directions, then drove to a poor segment of an impoverished town. The local grove owners, ranchers, cowhands, and airboat gunners had been overwhelmed by immigrant laborers who worked the Everglade sugar plantations. The north part of town was infested with sawdust bars selling water glasses of tequila and shanties half-hidden in the live-oak groves, where Haitian mulattas plied their trade.

They found the strip mall tucked between the highway and the earthen dike. Lake Okeechobee was forty-six miles from tip to tip and broad enough to throw twelve-foot waves in hurricane season. The flat-topped dike loomed over the dilapidated buildings. Among the dusty pickups and souped-up Japanese models was a police car and two vehicles that could only be unmarked government vehicles. Emma parked beside a black Explorer with tinted windows. "If anybody asks, you're with me."

They entered a storefront bank advertising payday loans and fund transfers. Latinos stained with sugar-cane tar and swamp muck and exhaustion crammed the front room. The workers pretended to ignore a blue-jacketed woman interviewing a nervous employee.

The woman spotted them and walked over. "Help you?"

Emma opened her badge. "Emma Webb, Treasury. I'm looking for Agent Drummond."

The woman gave Emma's ID a careful inspection, then called back, "Ross!"

"Yo."

"You in?"

"Depends."

She pointed them down the rear hallway. "He's all yours."

Ross Drummond was a heavy-set man with a brush moustache and a nylon Windbreaker that read DEA. He inspected Emma with a marbled gaze. "You Webb?"

"Yes."

"And he is?"

"An associate."

He shook hands with them both, brusque and perfunctory. "You might've made the trip for nothing."

"Won't be the first time."

"Tell me. Okay, here's what we got." He knocked on the nearest raw-pine door and pushed it open to reveal a closet-sized cubicle. Three adults occupied the chamber's only chairs. All held squirming infants. More children sat on the floor, while a young man and three women slouched against the rear wall. They faced a wide flatscreen that showed two elderly couples. The conversation halted momentarily, until the DEA agent said, " *'Sta bien.*" Soon as he shut the door, Harry heard the conversation pick up where it had left off.

Drummond said, "The nation being in what Washington likes to call a state of heightened vigilance, illegals don't dare plan a trip home. They're afraid they won't get back in. So these videoconferencing services are as close as many come to reaching out and touching the families back home. Money-transfer companies like this one have seen a fivefold increase in profits. All it takes is a similarly equipped hookup at the other end."

Emma was nodding, so far ahead of Harry, he didn't have a clue where all this was headed until she said, "DEA wired the hookups."

"Sound and light," Drummond confirmed. "Clewiston's become a major drop for incoming shipments of Mexican brown and coke. Every now and then we find ourselves staring at some real heavies."

"But not this time."

A wiry woman wearing bottle-bottom glasses and a lab tech's white one-piece stepped from a cubicle farther along the aisle. She called, "All done here, Ross."

"Find anything?"

"The place is jammed with prints. I'll sort through the IDs and get back to you."

Ross nodded and said to Emma, "Like I told you, this could be a total waste. But our office got red flagged with a high-priority request from Interpol. Attempted hit by a professional assassin, possible terrorist connections."

Harry said, "Terrorist?"

Drummond's gaze swiveled over. "Your man here is exactly who?"

"The only one who's gotten a clear look at the assailant." To Harry, she said, "We don't know who he is, Harry."

Drummond shrugged it off. "So anyway, this morning we got a flag from our regional officer. He claims he's got a match for your BOLO."

"Your local agent matches a picture off a screen to an interagency alert?"

"Actually, our man on the ground got a heads-up because of where this fellow was calling. We don't get many calls aimed at Paris, France. Matter of fact, this was the very first one. The caller's image doesn't match anybody in our files. According to the manager, this wispy fellow drifted in, waited in line with everybody else. The manager remembers him because he was the only one that shift who came in alone. He made his call, left, came back an hour later, made a second call. Our records show it was to the same number."

Emma said, "Can we see what you have?"

"Right this way." They filed into the cubicle. A young agent sat perched on the edge of a hard-backed chair pulled up close to the screen. The screen, the computer terminal, the desk, the chair arms, and the door were all liberally coated with fingerprint dust. Drummond said, "Okay, roll it."

The instant the image flashed onto the screen, Harry said, "That's him."

Drummond said, "Freeze it there." To Harry, "You're certain?"

"No question."

Drummond asked Webb, "Can you confirm that?"

"I saw him for a total of maybe half a second. Then the guy slipped away, using the crowd as a shield. But yes. I can confirm that this is our attacker."

Harry said, "I've seen him three times. And there is no question. None."

Drummond asked, "Does this have anything to do with drugs?"

Emma said, "As far as we know at this point, not at all."

"If it does, you'll return the favor, right?"

"Count on it."

Harry stared at the image. The attacker looked no more substantial frozen on the flatscreen than he had in life. Pointed little chin. Almost fragile-looking features. No lips to speak of. Copper-colored skin, eyes as dark as his close-cut thinning hair. Ears small as an infant's and mashed close to his head.

Emma asked, "Can we hear what was said?"

"Sorry, no dice. This is totally off-the-record. But what got us willing to check outside our own division was, this guy encrypted his conversation."

"You can do that?"

"Officially, no." He said to his guy crouched by the machine, "Show them."

The young man pulled an item from his pocket. "Looks like just your basic memory stick. Fits in the USB port here. There's a system developed for our agents in the field."

"Not just us," Drummond said. "CIA, DEA, Defense, all their covert agents carry one. We thought it was top-top secret. Until now."

"May I see it, please?"

The agent got the nod from Drummond and passed it over. "It only works when paired with another on the receiving end. That's the beauty of the deal. Unless you've got the matching decrypter, you haven't got a hope of ever figuring out what was sent or received."

Emma pointed at the screen. "But that picture is clear as a bell."

Drummond said to the agent, "Show them."

The agent unfroze the image. On the monitor, the assailant said, "*Je suis prêt.*"

Harry offered, "He's saying he's ready."

The attacker leaned forward. The image flashed into static.

"Bang and gone," the agent said.

Drummond led them back into the hallway just as another cubicle door opened and divulged a crowd of chattering Latinos. He walked them through the front room and out into the sun-drenched parking lot. "Who's got the lead on this?"

Emma answered very carefully. "The head of our interagency task force is Jack Dauer."

"What is he, fibbie?"

"Roger that. Agent Dauer was sent down from Washington to lead this assignment. I am assigned to be the group's liaison officer with Interpol."

"What will Dauer think of Interpol's alert bringing you a serious lead like this?"

Emma chewed the inside of one cheek and did not respond.

Drummond smirked. "You know what I think of this interagency alphabet game? A goat rope. That's an expression we brought back from our first dance in the Gulf. Tie a bunch of goats to a rope don't mean they'll go where you want them."

"I'm sure Agent Dauer would be interested in your opinion, sir." She held out her hand. "May I have the phone number in France our man contacted? As I said, I'll share with you anything we come up with."

"We ran you off his photograph as well." Drummond passed over two printed sheets. "You want my advice?"

"Absolutely."

"Washington staffers like Dauer get antsy when their people play outside the frame. You do your business with Interpol and you leave this fibbie totally out of the loop. He gets a tiny hint you've started building yourself a system of useful allies beyond the Washington playbook and he'll bury you, Webb. Warm, breathing, screaming your head off, it won't make any difference. You're gone."

FIFTEEN

STORM HAD NO IDEA WHAT the two federal agents thought of their detail, shepherding her around. She didn't want to know. Her morning was too tightly compressed.

One agent was female, lean, Storm's age, and Hispanic. The other was male, blond, crew cut, chunky. Both seemed comfortable with her silence. They moved the painting from her room to the trunk of their unmarked Crown Victoria, then the man stayed with the car while the woman followed her into the church office.

Storm sat and made notes detailing the day ahead until Richard Ellis appeared. The pastor took one look at the agent by the doorway and asked, "Are they arresting you or guarding you?"

"Guarding. For the moment."

"Let's move to my office." As they walked down the hall, he asked, "Did you get some rest?"

"A little, not much. I apologize for Harry's late-night call. He thought we'd be safe here, and to be honest I was so shook up I just followed his lead."

"He was right to call."

It was the first time Storm had been inside the man's office. The room was nice enough, wood paneled and spacious with a window that overlooked the windswept pines separating the church from the parking lot. Richard wore an open-necked shirt and brown tweed jacket. His hair was still wet from the shower. She knew he was a dedicated marathon runner because she had been approached by him to join the church's team. But Storm did not run in order to compete. Nor did she much care for what she had always considered the forced intimacy of church. She had been born with a double dose of the loner gene.

Richard asked, "How long are you staying?"

"Today is the last day of the exhibition. Tomorrow morning we fly to Dulles for Sean's funeral."

"And from there?"

Storm shook her head. She could not afford to look beyond the next few hours. She reached into her purse, drew out Sean's Bible, and opened it to the page marked by a decrepit leather bookmark. The previous night, Storm had fed off that page's comfort and the odd sense that her grandfather was studying with her. She swiveled the book toward Richard and pointed to where her grandfather's brutal script had actually torn the page. He had made angry notations all around the borders, filling the spaces with his rash demands for answers.

She pointed to the underlined passage, now almost lost beneath the smudged cellophane. "Explain that."

Richard possessed many of Sean's most volatile traits. He was adept at impatience, some would say far too talented in that department for a minister. Also like Sean, he had been widowed for some time and showed no interest in remarrying. Richard's bluntness was one reason he didn't run Saint Anthony's, but rather remained relegated to the church's peripheral activities. Another reason was Richard Ellis did not care. He bent to no political wind. He remained indifferent to parishioner disapproval. He said what he thought. No senior pastor in a heavy-wallet area like Palm Beach could get away with brutal honesty as his defining trait.

But he showed none of that impatience now. "The first time we met, Sean told me he'd once read the Bible cover to cover and found it a thoroughly dissatisfying experience. He said it was like tramping over buried treasure and being in too much of a hurry to dig. From that point on, Sean searched out passages that troubled him. Dissatisfied him. Angered him. And he *dug*. He read the commentaries and he studied the original Greek or Hebrew or Aramaic. He wrestled and he argued and he fought. And only when he was satisfied did he move on."

"That sounds like Sean."

"That page marks the last passage Sean battled over: *For to him who has, will more be given, and he will have abundance: but from him who has not, even what he has will be taken away*. If Sean ever reached peace with that one, he never said."

Storm pressed quietly, "He told you, didn't he. About the threat, and about his plans."

"He asked me to give you something, if . . ."

"If I asked."

"You are not using me to go out and get yourself killed as well."

"What did he leave me, Richard?"

"I told Sean I wouldn't do it. He said I was the only one he could trust to pass it on at the right moment. He wouldn't say what that moment was."

Storm nodded slowly. "I understand."

"Nobody could ever push my buttons like your grandfather."

Storm stared out the sun-bleached window. "You know why I started coming to church?"

"Because Sean came here. Your grandfather was no saint."

She shook her head. "Because it was everything my father wasn't. I was fourteen and rebelling against a man who burned holes into every day with his bong. Or sailed away from reality on whatever magical mystery tour he happened to find in his stash. There was nothing that would get my old man madder than to know I'd started going to the same church as Sean. The biggest, the most fashionable, the most conservative church in Palm Beach."

Richard was silent now. Which made it easier to face him and speak around the rasp that had crept into her voice. "Last night I realized Sean had left me not one choice, but several. I could go after the prize that got him killed, or use the funds to start my own business. Grow beyond my past, or not."

Richard leaned over and opened his bottom drawer and pulled out a sealed envelope. Set it on the desk. "The first time he told me of his search for the Second Temple treasures, I was the one laughing. That mystery has swirled about for two thousand years. Your grandfather insisted he had uncovered new details, and that both his quest and the goal were very real."

The letter on the desk bore Storm's name written in her grandfather's abrupt script. Keeping herself from reaching for it was about the hardest thing she had ever done. "When was this?"

"Back around the time you started coming to church." Richard stared blindly at the letter. "I warmed to the idea quickly enough. Sean's friendship had opened my eyes to the world of treasures and major new finds. I had decided that if anybody had what it took to uncover the mystery of the ages, it was Sean Syrrell. I *encouraged* him."

Storm clenched her hands together in her lap. "You didn't kill him, Richard. There's nothing you could have done that would have stopped Sean from going after that treasure."

He looked at her then, his gaze hollowed by the depth of his loss. "I'll tell you what I should have told your grandfather. A true believer doesn't need external confirmations. No historical artifact, no treasure, no new discovery, is going to make any difference. Why? Because believers either know or they don't. Down deep, at the level beyond words and earthly things, the spirit has entered and has *changed*. No discovery, no matter how incredible, can compare to the light of true faith. No matter how important the world may think this to be."

Storm rose to her feet and slipped the envelope into her pocket. "That's not the verdict we're talking about, though. Is it."

AT HER REQUEST, THE AGENTS drove Storm to her apartment. After the female officer checked the terrain, the other agent stayed with the painting and the Crown Vic while Storm followed the lady officer into the courtyard. As she passed the shuttered shop, Storm mouthed one word to her reflection in the empty window. Soon.

She left the agent in the living room, stopped by the kitchen for an item she thought she would need later, then carried Sean's letter into the bathroom. She locked the door and turned on the shower. Only then did she open the envelope. The letter was handwritten and one page long. The script was as abrupt as the man who'd written it. The letter began, *My dear Storm.*

She used a towel to stifle her sobs as she read the letter through several times. Then she showered and dressed and packed a few items for later in the day. Once back in the car she was tempted to reread the letter, but she did not want to risk ruining her makeup. Today she had to remain in absolute control.

They drove to a specialty phone shop near the exhibition center. Storm had the salesman take her purchases from the plastic wrappings and show her precisely how to make them do what she wanted. There was neither room nor time for fumbling. She had one shot to get this right. One.

They were parked in front of the convention center nine minutes before the doors opened. The imperial palms lining the front walk and the parking lot cut idyllic swaths from the morning light. The two agents sat in the car's front seat with the silence of people who where good at waiting. The car's four windows were down. The wind drifted off the ocean, tangy with salt. Traffic rumbled over the neighboring causeway. When the security detail in their gray blazers unlocked the exhibition doors, Storm said, "Let's go."

They joined the line of well-heeled stallholders rushing toward the entrance and the day ahead. There were worse ways for a girl to make an entrance than holding a museum-quality artwork flanked by two armed officers. By the time she registered the painting and received a preliminary vetting, word had spread. Storm knew this by the way heads were out and watching as she entered the hall and walked to her stand.

Storm positioned the painting upon the center of

the rear wall, where anyone walking the main aisle could not help but see it. At her request, exhibition security dragged over two brass stands and a velvet rope. Then she waited.

"Excuse me, I beg your pardon." Curtis Armitage-Goode eased his way forward. He asked Storm, "May I?"

Storm nodded to the agent standing by the makeshift barrier. "Let him approach."

"I am indeed most grateful." Curtis moved so close that his nose almost touched the canvas. He swept back and forth, up and down, then patted the pocket holding the silk scarf that matched his tie. "Drat. I left my glass behind."

"Middle drawer of the jewel stand."

"Many thanks."

The crowd grew respectfully silent. They watched Curtis use the magnifying glass to inspect several points on the canvas, remaining still and intent for minutes at a time.

A small dark-haired woman with olive skin appeared at Storm's elbow. "Ms. Syrrell—do I have that right?"

"Yes."

"I'm Chandra Suritam with *Artworld*. May I have a few words?"

"Of course."

"Do you mind if we take a few photographs?"

"No flash."

"No, naturally not."

Curtis snapped from his position by the painting, "You can ruddy well wait until I'm done."

Storm answered the journalist's questions in the curt half measures she had heard her grandfather use. Offering more mystery than anything else. Finally Curtis slipped back through the crowd and joined them. "Good morning, Chandra."

"Hello, Mr. Armitage-Goode. Is it genuine?"

In response he said to Storm, "Name your price."

A fizzing current passed through the crowd. Storm said to the reporter, "Excuse us for a moment."

"No problem." The reporter moved forward to stand beside where her photographer was setting up a tripod.

Storm pulled Curtis to one side, angled so she was both removed from the crowd yet within visual range of her booth. "Do you know the Palm Beach Bank?"

"The dinosaur on Worth Avenue. Certainly."

"Meet me downstairs in the safety-deposit vault in one hour."

"Certainly. But you really must give me some idea of the price you wish—"

Storm halted him by tapping one finger on his foulard. "Be on time."

STORM CARRIED HER SHOPPING BAG into the bank, signed into the safety-deposit vault, opened the left box, and took out her grandfather's note-book. She relocked the box and entered one of the alcoves. She was careful to seal the thick velvet curtain on both sides. Overhead an AC vent sighed softly. Otherwise there was no sound. Storm pulled out her new phone and went to work.

The next-generation Nokia had a ten-megapixel camera, Zeiss lens, and twelve gigs of memory. Storm photographed her grandfather's notebook, one shot per page. The salesman had assured her that the phone shot crystal-clear close-ups in idiot mode. She worked through the notebook in less than twenty minutes.

The alcove was completely lined in carpet the color of caramel and smelled faintly of disinfectant. The claustrophobic silence left her perspiring. She closed the notebook and followed the salesman's instructions. The phone opened like a jewel box to reveal a fold-out OLED screen. The organic light-emitting display was only microns thick and attached to a slim plastic backing. When unfolded, her viewing area was six inches by nine and astonishingly sharp. As the salesman had promised, the screen flashed the message VIEW PHOTOGRAPHS Y/N. Storm scrolled through enough to be certain her grandfather's notes were clearly legible.

She returned the notebook to the vault and retrieved the golden chalice. The beige carpeted desk proved a perfect backdrop for photographing.

There was nothing she could find that gave any hint of the dish's origin. She suspected Phoenician because of the gold's reddish hue, rich as desert sands at sunset. But she remained concerned by the absence of any carvings. Virtually all gold articles from the ancient world were richly adorned. Nowadays atomic profiling could identify gold by the region where the ore had been mined. But gold from the Fertile Crescent, if that was what she just photographed, was often melted down and recast, particularly if it was war booty. There could be a dozen different mines represented in any such artifact.

The dish was fourteen inches long, eight inches wide, and about an inch and a half deep. The base mirrored the bowl's oblong shape, too pointy at the ends to be called a true oval. She turned the chalice over and inspected the wax filling the base. Storm scraped the surface with a fingernail. Her impression from the other day was confirmed. The wax was new. She had thought long and hard about this and come up with only one reason why someone would reseal the base of a carefully stored artifact. Whatever they had discovered inside was meant to be kept secret.

She took the paring knife she had brought from her kitchen to carve away the wax, being careful not to touch the surrounding gold. The wax was pliable and came out cleanly. Three inches into her excavation, she stopped. And stared.

"Ms. Syrrell?"

She jerked. "Yes?"

The guard made no move to open the curtain. "There's a gentleman out front asking for you."

"Tell him to wait." She listened to the guard's soft footfalls, then scooped up her camera and photographed the exposed interior.

Deeply inscribed onto the interior was a set of letters. She photographed the inscription from a variety of angles. Then she lowered the camera and whispered, "Well, hello there."

She had seen that inscription before.

CURTIS ARMITAGE-GOODE WAS MANY THINGS. He was foppish, superior minded, master of the subtle put-down, a throwback to a bygone era of princelings and courtiers. His wardrobe tended toward navy blazers with foulards and matching silk pocket kerchiefs. He could send an insomniac into a total snooze with his blow-by-blow retelling of deals, as he had done to Storm on their one and only date. But his clientele was as aristocratic as he pretended to be. And while he would deal in any article that would turn a tidy profit, his personal passion was books.

Storm returned the chalice to the vault and extracted the illuminated manuscript. She carried it to the alcove and covered it with her jacket. She then walked through the vault, ensuring she was alone.

She greeted Curtis with "Thanks for coming. Show him some ID and sign in. There's something I want you to see."

"Don't tell me you have more."

Storm asked the guard, "Is it possible for you to let me know if someone else shows up and wants to enter the vault?"

Clearly this was not the first time he had been asked that. "Sure thing, Ms. Syrrell."

"Thanks. This way, Curtis."

Back in the alcove, Curtis watched her fasten the drape into place and observed, "Rather soon to be fitting me out for a coffin."

"Keep your voice down." Storm set one hand on her jacket, draped over the waist-high counter. "Here's the deal. I'll give you right of first refusal on the Dürer."

"I have a German museum curator, a major client, who is willing to make a cash offer—"

"I'm not interested in talking about the deal today."

"When?"

"I'm not sure. Three months at least. Maybe more."

"I say, you can't possibly expect my client to sit on such a pile of cash that long."

"Curtis, listen to me. You can't have it. Not now."

He turned petulant. "Then why have you dragged me away from the floor?"

"The deal is exactly what I said. When I decide to sell, you have the right to match any offer."

"In exchange for?"

"You tell me what I have here. And you keep it absolutely quiet."

He tried to pretend no interest in what lay beneath her hand and her jacket. But he could not keep his gaze from dropping, or erase the avarice gleam. "You're asking for a professional valuation?"

"I don't care what it's worth. Well, I care. Sure. But it's not for sale."

"My dear Storm. First rule of a dealer. Everything is for sale."

"You'll hold this in utter confidence?"

"Not a peep. Now do be kind enough to remove your hand."

She pulled away her jacket.

"Oh, I say." His eagerness was such that his hands shook as he pulled a pair of white cloth gloves from his pocket. Most curators and high-end dealers carried them as naturally as they did their wallets. Curtis ran his gloved hands over the leather cover.

"Tell me what you see."

"Well, obviously it's a chain book. Press here, yes, feel the holes where the spine was originally bound to an iron bar."

Chain books were named after the manner in which a palace or monastery kept its prized manuscripts from disappearing. A chain ran from the iron plate in the book's spine to a hook attached to the stone floor. The practice began in the late Dark Ages and continued until Gutenberg's printing press made books more readily available.

Curtis opened the book and breathed, "This is quite unique."

"Why?"

"It's a Gospel of John, which was all the vogue during the Middle Ages. But see here, the facing pages give the readings in Latin and in Greek. Which means it would have originated from somewhere that refused to show strict allegiance to either Rome or Constantinople. After the eighth century, when the Ottoman Saracens attacked the eastern church, such places grew increasingly rare."

"Where did it come from?"

"Hard to say, really." He turned the page. "My dear sweet word. You realize of course this was done for royalty. Such a pity monasteries refused to sign their name to these illuminated works. Claiming authorship was considered an earthly vice, approaching pride. But see here, the gold leaf was literally hammered into the vellum. And this blue, it's positively electric. Crushed sapphires, most likely."

"Curtis."

"Eh? Oh, its origins. Hard to say, really."

"Istanbul?"

He lifted his gaze. "Why on earth would you think that?"

She hesitated, then decided to entrust him with that much. "Sean was planning to travel there."

"Ah. I see. Well, if you want my opinion I'd say his journey would have been utterly futile. By the eighth century all the monasteries around Constantinople were either demolished or turned to mosques. And this quality was not known before the ninth century." His gaze dropped back to the book. He turned another page. Breathed another fascinated sigh. "Armenia, now, there's a thought. The Caucasus region had several churches that remained strictly in the Roman camp, while retaining the Greek rites . . ." He squinted over the page. "Hold on a tick."

"What's the matter?"

He traced one gloved finger down the page's outer edge. "That's not possible."

"Tell me, Curtis."

He shut the book and seemed to gather himself. Then he opened the front cover, gripped the pages by the top and bottom, and slowly, cautiously, peeled back the pages. Gradually a narrow pyramid was formed of the outer edges.

Bringing a new picture into view.

"Well, we can safely date this." His words emerged somewhat breathlessly. "The first half of the tenth century at the very earliest."

"What *is* that?"

The image cascaded down the book's outer edge, visible only when the pages were held as Curtis did now, angled and pinching them tightly together. "What we have here is a very early example of a fore-edged book. They became quite the rage in the Georgian era, late seventeen hundreds. Manuscripts as early as this have been found from time to time. But they are exceedingly rare."

The image was in black and white, an etching of remarkable clarity yet done in the two-dimensional style of medieval artistry. "I say, it appears to be the arch of Titus." Curtis leaned in closer. "Yes, I'm quite certain of it. See the menorah here? How astonishing."

"Why is that a surprise?"

"Well, traditionally a holy text would have a biblical scene for a fore-edged decoration. This is quite the opposite. Titus built this triumphant arch in Rome to signify his destruction of Jerusalem and the crushing of the Jewish revolt. You've heard of this, surely."

"Of course." She lifted the camera. "Turn the image toward me."

Curtis did as she instructed. "In AD 66 the Jews revolted against their Roman masters. They had several resounding victories. They even managed to rule Jerusalem for a time. Then Vespasian and his son Titus arrived, along with the African legions, and crushed the revolt in a most brutal fashion. Eventually Vespasian returned to Rome to be crowned Caesar, leaving his son to finish the siege of Jerusalem. Titus destroyed every structure in the city, stone from stone, then salted the earth.

"So to have a fore-edged illustration of the arch . . ."

"Quite unheard of. If I had not seen it for myself I would call it a fraud. You can now safely rule out Armenia as a source. They did no fore-edged illustrations. Somewhere in the Mediterranean basin is my guess." He stiffened. "Wait a tic."

"What is it now?"

"I just want to check something." He closed the book and turned it over. "Occasionally a text will have a second image etched into the reverse edge. Only the most valuable books, mind, which this most certainly is."

He carefully tilted the pages, and another illustration of an arch came into view. "How decidedly odd."

His movements became swifter as he shut the book, reversed directions, and again fanned the image into view. "Yes, I'm quite certain. This first one is the Titus arch. Whenever a general marched in triumphant entry into Rome, their last prize was always the vanquished nation's temple gods. But the Jewish temple had no such image, of course. So instead the Titus arch shows a soldier carrying the Torah scrolls. See here, the menorah, the fire basin, these carvings are a record of the treasures

Titus stole from the temple and brought back to dedicate to the temple of his own Roman god, Jupiter. A more horrid desecration the Jews could not have imagined."

Curtis reversed the book once more. "Now here . . ."

"No scrolls." Storm leaned in tight. "Different images."

"I am at a complete and utter loss."

"A second arch?"

"I am quite certain there has never been any mention of such." He released his hold on the pages and set a proprietary glove on the cover. "You really must let me have this book."

"Sorry, it's not for sale."

"Oh, fiddle. I know perfectly well what you're up to. It's how I made my own start. You intend to take over Syrrell's defunct Palm Beach office and use the painting to establish your name." He prodded the leather cover with a gloved finger. "But one painting, no matter how glorious, does not make a collection. You need *capital*. However much you're earning from the sale of that Dürer, it won't be enough."

"Hold the edges so I can photograph this second image."

When she finished, she found Curtis staring at her oddly. "Was Sean killed over this?"

"I'm trying to find that out. Remember what you promised."

"Not a whisper. I wouldn't want to have a hand in your demise." He watched her shut the book and wrap her jacket around it. "You will take care, won't you? At least until I have my hands on these exquisite articles."

SIXTEEN

THE CROWDS CLOGGED STORM'S BOOTH until the final bell. The same stallholders who had dismissed her with smirks and snide sympathy stopped by, purchased items, and invited her to closing receptions reserved for insiders only. They discussed the coming season of art shows—New York, Basel, Munich, Paris, Stockholm, Santa Barbara. They spoke of future alliances with this young woman who had endured the phoenix flames and now rose on wings as brilliant as Dürer's brushstrokes.

If Storm had not still been facing the day's hardest task, she might even have enjoyed the attention.

The same bonded shippers she had used to clear out the shop packed all her remaining items except one. She departed the instant they finished. Every dealer and employee within range stopped what they were doing and watched her carry the painting down the side passage and out the main doors. Were she faced with anything other than the chore ahead, she would have counted it as a fine hour indeed.

The bank was closed for the day, but the manager was there to greet her. He personally led her downstairs, where the guard gave her an overtime smile, accepted her key, and unlocked the safety-deposit box. Storm stowed the painting and took a moment to survey her grandfather's parting legacy. She slipped six bound bundles of cash in her purse beside Sean's tattered Bible, shut and locked the vault, then returned upstairs.

The female agent was stationed by the bank's entrance, as impassive as she had been all day long. Storm steeled herself against what loomed ahead and said, "I need to make one more stop."

While much of western Palm Beach County slithered into gangland chaos, Lake Osborne remained a stubborn enclave of middle-class stability. Generations of New England plumbers and shopkeepers slipped in unnoticed by the barrier-island rich. They lived the same lives here as farther north—quiet, respectable, conservative, fanatic about safety, active in their adopted community. The lake itself was rimmed by parks and fifty-year-old palms. A new generation of grey heads walked their dogs and played chess in the cooling dusk. But the fiercely stubborn calm remained. As a young girl, Storm had felt frozen inside someone else's idea of a good time. Now she would have admired them, were it any other hour than this.

The artists' colony had been formed a century

earlier, when Flagler's castle had dominated the eastern skyline. The clapboard cottages formed a bizarre New England enclave surrounded by bougainvillea. The roads twisted upon themselves, designed to maintain an isolated decorum.

Storm had spent a sleepless night planning this moment. But when the unkempt lawn at the end of the cul-de-sac came into view, she knew she would never be truly prepared. "Would you turn on your siren?"

The stocky agent slowed the car and swiveled in his seat. "Excuse me?"

"I need . . ." Storm's swallow sounded choked in her ears. "Just do it. Please."

The driver glanced at the agent seated beside him. She shrugged her reply.

Storm added, "And your lights."

They traversed the final half mile at the pace and volume of a marching band. When they pulled up in front of the house and the sound faded, Storm rolled down her window and listened.

The female agent asked, "Are you intending to go inside?"

"I have to."

"Is there a crime in progress?"

"I don't . . ." Then she heard the faint grinding noise. Storm opened her door. "I'll be right back."

"I need to check the place out before you—"

"Wait here!"

Storm stalled momentarily where the cobblestone lip of the drive met the road. She had not been back since the day she had started work for Syrrell's. The day her father had thrown her out of the house, accusing her of making disownment a family trait.

Thunderclouds clogged the eastern sky and rumbled a traditional Florida greeting as she hurried up the drive. Dark trailers streamed over the intracoastal waters. The humidity and heat made a drenching mix. She climbed the front steps and recalled steaming August days seated where she now stood, dreaming of life in some frigid mountainous land. At twelve she had started a correspondence course in Norwegian and filled out online au pair applications, inflating her age by half. The next year she met Claudia and everything changed. She had not thought of Norway in years.

She used her key and opened the door. The sweet stench of old smoke burned her throat. The grinding sound was much louder now.

Storm raced down the central corridor. The house had two safes. The massive lockbox in the garage held her father's stash. Her father liked to claim that he did not deal drugs. He merely shared the wealth with a few close friends. Storm entered her father's bedroom with its quasi-Moroccan motif and flung back the carpet. She pried loose the floor tile, revealing the second safe, the one she wasn't supposed to know about. Her heart skipped a frantic beat as she spun the dial. If he had changed the combination all was lost.

The safe popped open. Storm clawed through the jumbled contents, mostly his collection of antique North African bongs. She froze when her fingers touched the worn silver picture frame, the reason she had often returned to this safe as a child. The frame held the only photograph she had ever seen of her mother, who had died when Storm was two years old. She fought off a sudden craving to take the picture with her. She had argued over this all night long. But the photograph was not hers. And what she sought was definitely not her father's. In the middle of the restless night, her logic had carried a lot more force than now. But there was not time for further argument. She pushed the photograph to one side and dug further.

When her hand touched the old velvet pouch nestled at the bottom of the safe, she groaned aloud.

Storm pulled out the pouch and forced her trembling fingers to untie the leather drawstring. She had to be certain her memory was correct. She drew out the contents, opened the opposing sleeves, and groaned a second time.

The word *triptych* came from Greek, meaning threefold. The artform was based on the ancient Roman writing tablet, which had two hinged panels flanking a central display. Triptychs varied in size, from pendant jewelry to giant altar pieces.

In this case, the three interlocking panels were each the size of her hand, peaked at the top like arabesque doors, and carved from ivory.

The triptych was the one her father had stolen from Sean.

It was also the one in Dürer's portrait.

Storm traced the central panel's carved face, marveling at the mystery unfolding before her eyes.

Then the grinding noise abruptly stopped.

Storm locked the safe, slipped the tile back into place, straightened the carpet, stowed the triptych in her purse, and raced back to the living room.

Her voice was breathlessly fractured as she called, "It's only me, Dad. Everything's cool."

The garage door opened and her father stepped into view. "You brought the cops here?"

"They're my escort."

"They're not here for me?"

"No, Dad. We've had some trouble . . . at the office. They're just watching out for me."

Joseph Syrrell wore a heavily embroidered caftan belted at the waist, which was good for another bitter memory. For years Joseph and his artist friends had talked of buying a house in Marrakech. They had made it as far as a meeting with international Realtors in Miami before everything dissolved into their usual squabbling.

When Joseph waved his arms, the caftan's sleeves flapped like empty wings. "I just dropped five hundred tabs of Cotton down the drain!"

For a woman who had never taken anything stronger than aspirin, Storm was amazingly mindful of drug lingo. Cotton was slang for oxycontin, a synthetic morphine. Also known as Oxy. Big O. Or the one she loved most. Killer. "I'm sorry, Dad."

He stared at the rear door. Next to the garage lockbox was a sink with an industrial-strength garbage disposal. "That stuff cost me two thousand bucks."

In three years Joseph Syrrell had put on forty pounds. His beard only partly hid the flesh creasing his jaw and neck. When he faced her full on, his jaw melted into the hair rising from the caftan's opening. He turned and studied her. Storm wore a pinstripe Lanvin suit she had bought on sale at Off Fifth. He smirked. "The old man's sure got his claws in deep."

"I came to tell you that Sean is dead."

Her father actually smirked. "This is supposed to mean something to me?"

She turned for the door, her duty here done. "The funeral is tomorrow. We're flying up in the morning. If you want to come, I'll pay for your ticket."

Storm shut the front door on her father demanding, "Why should I care what's happened to that old man?"

174

SEVENTEEN

THE NEXT MORNING, HARRY'S SLEEP ended with a razor-sharp break. He flashed to awareness, rolled off the bed, and moved to the window in a crouch. The predawn hour was a faint grey splash, the church buildings and surrounding gardens utterly still. But Harry's internal alarms were shrieking. He swiped at his face and rose from the bed. One look out the window was enough to tell him what was wrong.

He crossed the room and knocked on the connecting door. "Storm?"

When he had gone to bed she had still been hard at it, seated at the pastor's desk, hammering away at the computer. The lady agent stationed in a chair opposite Storm had looked beyond weary. Storm had been terse with him, her attitude a closed door. He'd told them both good night and gotten nothing but the tapping of keys in reply.

Only now the federal agents were gone.

Harry rapped on the door a second time. Through the paper-thin walls Harry heard a muffled groan. He opened the door and said, "Get up."

"What time is it?" Storm's hand emerged from the covers, fumbled around the bedside table, found her watch, pulled it back under the pillow. "Our plane's not until nine."

He returned to his own bed, slipped his hand

under the mattress, and came out with his Browning. The previous evening he'd asked Emma to drive him by the apartment. The day's events had left Harry's hand aching for the comfort of a serrated grip.

He walked to Storm's window and pulled the curtain back a fraction. The day remained utterly still. "What happened to your two watchers?"

Her muffled voice replied, "They said they'd be on duty all night."

"Their car's gone."

"Maybe they moved it." She remained lost beneath the covers. "Or somebody's come and taken their place."

Harry doubted that. If he couldn't see their car, they couldn't see Storm's room. He walked to Storm's bed and ratcheted a bullet into the chamber.

Storm's tousled head emerged. Soon as she focused on the gun in Harry's hand, her eyes went from sleepy squint to round-eyed alarm. "What's wrong?"

Harry said, "You've got ninety seconds. What you can't pack in that time, you leave."

Harry returned to his room, dressed, and threw his gear into the nylon duffel. "Storm!"

"I'm ready."

He liked that. A lot. The lady had the makings of a pro. "We're taking the Bentley. You remember where it's parked?"

"I . . ."

"The shed for the mowers. Back left side of the lot. I need you to carry my duffel." He moved to the door, checked the window a final time. "I open, you bolt. Don't run in a straight line. Okay, *go!*"

Harry let her set the pace. He ran one step behind and to the left. He did not stop to reconnoiter. If the attacker was there, he'd be positioned where he could observe and remain utterly hidden. Harry wanted to show light, action, awareness, moving targets. He held the pistol in his right hand, the car keys in his left. If the guy took a shot, Harry's plan was to fire, tap her rear foot and trip her, fire, fall on top of her, fire. Standard ops.

The palms were silent silhouettes cut from the yellow streetlights and the early dawn. Despite her carrying both their bags, Storm accelerated to where she almost pulled away from him. She checked her forward thrust by bouncing off a parked SUV, twisted like a ballplayer searching out the empty pocket, and jinked to her left. If Harry had not been so worried he'd have laughed out loud.

The mowing shed smelled of gas and oil and cut grass. He pressed the key fob and the Bentley's lights blinked in response. Storm slipped on the oily concrete and almost went down, but Harry gripped her arm and flung her toward the passenger door. He scrambled over the hood, jammed the pistol into his belt, gunned the motor, slapped the gearshift into reverse, and hammered the pedal. The wheels spun on the oily concrete, twisting the car around to where it scraped Harry's side on the shed door. Harry spun the car through a tight circle, rammed the car into drive, and burned rubber out of the parking lot.

TO STORM'S SLEEP-ADDLED BRAIN, HARRY carried a charge like a fused explosive. The internal fission was in direct contrast to his stern calm. Like a sniper's weapon with the safety in the firing position.

Storm recognized it as the same transformation he had gone through in Selim's home. Harry's customary restless impatience was gone. He was all tight calmness now, intensely focused. Storm watched him as much as the road, digesting the fact that Harry Bennett was the direct opposite of every other man she had ever known. Danger brought Harry into his element.

"Harry." She reached out and touched his arm. "Tell me what happened."

He swung the big car through another turn. "Give me a minute."

She withdrew her hand and went back to clutching the center console and the door. Harry drove in a pattern that could only be called random. Twice he spun through U-turns, racing back in the same direction he had come. He took turns very late, then spun and gunned and tracked hard. Finally he reversed into a drive screened by oleander, opened all the windows, listened intently, said, "Hang tight."

He opened his door, switched off the overhead light, slipped from the car, and melted with the shadows by the side of the drive. He carried the pistol down low by his thigh. He ducked into the bushes. Five minutes passed. Ten. The car's engine purred softly. As suddenly as he had evaporated, he reappeared. Harry's expression was so resolute he only *appeared* to be flesh and blood. At some deep level he was tempered and forged into a different element. One made for fire and peril.

He slipped back into the car, but did not fully shut his door. "I'm pretty sure we weren't followed. We'll just sit here for a while."

Storm waited.

Harry said, "I woke up to a warning."

Storm leaned against the opposite door. Whether to face him bodily or move further away, she could not say.

"A nightmare, a hunch. Call it what you want. All I can tell you is, I woke up and felt like I could smell cordite from guns that hadn't been fired yet." He slipped the gun's safety on, then rubbed the pistol up and down his pants leg. "You live with danger long enough, you develop a sense of how it smells. Or tastes. Both, I guess. Guys who pull long-term combat duty, they grow eyes in the back of their heads. You test the wind all the time. I figured we were safe there in the church for a couple of days. This morning I woke up knowing I was wrong."

She licked her lips.

Harry squinted at the sun rising above the eastern roof. "I dreamed Sean whispered my name."

"That would sure get me up and moving."

"The old man had that danger sense."

"You knew him better than I did."

"Different, maybe. Not better. That was why we argued."

"When?"

"The last time I saw him. Sean had promised to bankroll my op. We met at the church after evening service. It was often someplace like that. The only time I went by the shop was very late or very early."

"He didn't want to publicly reveal anybody from his confidential list."

Harry used the hand not holding the pistol to wave that away. Whatever. "When I showed up at church that night, Sean told me he had a bad feeling about the project. The Caribbean nations had been making noises about shutting down sal-vagers working the region. Sean felt in his gut they were looking for somebody to use as an example. He couldn't invest in something that might put me at risk."

"So you fought."

"It was the biggest haul I'd ever gone after. Two tons of minted doubloons. I had already spent four years on the search, fitting the pieces together." Harry fitted the gun into his belt, put the car into gear, said, "I called him a coward."

HARRY FOLLOWED STORM'S DIRECTIONS through the silent business district. The eight-lane highway rounded a man-made lake, then became mired in stoplights and strip malls and big-box superstores. Harry kept a constant watch in all directions, racing around slower traffic and gunning through lights. When the airport overpass loomed ahead of them, silver black and empty, Storm said, "Sean wrote me a letter. He left it with Richard."

He started to tell her that it needed to wait. But in truth he was beginning to wonder if maybe his senses were still prison honed and he had read the morning wrong. "Say again?"

"I spent yesterday reading and rereading it. And researching why those particular items in the vault might be important."

The overpass was only two years old, almost always empty, and already crumbling. The tires thrummed up the incline, spinning loose concrete against the car's underbody. Harry said, "Did you tell Emma?"

"She was with you all day, remember?"

"This is important, Storm. Emma needs to know this. Her boss—"

"The letter didn't come out and say directly that Sean knew somebody was out to kill him. And even if he did, Emma's boss wouldn't believe us."

"You don't know that."

Only when he glanced over did he realize she was fighting for control. Storm managed, "What he wrote was so beautiful."

"Can you tell me—"

His question was broken off by a sledgehammer striking the side of his head.

Only it wasn't a hammer. It just felt like one.

Maybe the driver of the other car saw Harry turn toward Storm. Perhaps fate merely handed them a low blow. The result was the same. Harry was totally focused on Storm when the attackers slammed into the Bentley and rocked his head against the car door.

The attack was timed to perfection. At the highest point, the overpass tilted downward and swept through a right-hand curve. At that juncture, a section of the railing had crumbled with the bridge's outer edge. The rails were temporarily replaced by wooden barriers painted with red danger slashes and topped by flashing lights. Some of the steel stanchions where the new railing would be attached were already in place. They glinted in the rising sun like hungry teeth. A scaffolding was suspended to the curve's outer edge, ready for the workers to fit in the railing. Harry noticed all this in the same adrenaline instant.

If he'd been driving any other car, the attackers would have rammed them straight through the temporary barriers and into a ninety-foot drop. But the Bentley was not just any car.

The Bentley Continental Flying Spur weighed in at a trace over six thousand pounds, about the same as a medium-sized truck. The Bentley also sat very close to the ground, on a wheelbase not much different from the Lincoln Town Car.

The attackers drove a Honda. It had probably once been a hot street model, with juiced engine and wide tires and flames down the sides. But the flames were mostly rust and the engine sputtered more than throbbed.

Their car bounced off the Bentley like a volley-ball.

Harry and danger were old acquaintances. Not friends. It was more of a love-hate relationship. But one thing was absolutely true about every instant that danger struck. Time never moved slower than in that instant.

The driver shouted something at the guy in the passenger seat. Both were young, no more than twenty. Latino blood was Harry's guess. The driver wore a do-rag, the passenger an Orioles cap pointed backward. Both were shirtless. Their shoulders and necks were heavily tattooed. The driver swung the wheel. The driver telegraphed the next move as clearly as if he'd semaphored out the open window. At the same moment, the passenger snarled something at Harry and thrust a snub-nosed machine pistol out the window.

"Down! Get down!"

Harry tapped the brake. They clearly expected him to slow, because the shooter was already swiveling in his seat, using the Honda's forward motion to draw them into position for one long spray of bullets.

Only Harry did not hit the brakes hard. He just touched the pedal once, long enough to change the angle. As Storm ducked into the foot well, Harry slammed his foot down on the gas. The Bentley roared and caught the Honda just behind the passenger door.

The Honda's rear tires shrilled and smoked. Harry kept his foot on the gas, driving the Honda into a spin.

The first bullets were high and wide. They splintered the right-hand corner of the windshield and tore the ceiling upholstery. Storm screamed.

"Stay down!"

Storm held to her fetal position, tight against the floor, covered now with glass fragments. Harry turned slightly to the left, away from the Honda. The smaller car continued its slow spin, like a revolving door set on smoking tires. The passenger let off a longer burst. It took out both side windows and rattled the rear fender as the Bentley rushed past and took them on to safety.

Or so Harry thought.

Harry did not consciously see the new threat until after he had responded to it. His was an automatic reaction, like a hand jerked from a flame, only this particular comeback was danger honed.

The shooter had set himself up perfectly. A new segment of steel barrier, including the railing, shone mirror sharp, reflecting the rising sun straight back into Harry's eyes. The little tan man stood on the scaffolding with his thighs leaning against the new steel. He held to a pro's stance, the long-bore hunting rifle balanced against a scaffolding pillar and one elbow braced on his chest.

The natural response would be to hammer the gas and turn hard into the curve. Away from the rifle. Only that would have given the shooter all the time in the world. His prey then had to drive straight past his lair. Which was why the shooter was showing himself. So that Harry would make the turn and draw the Bentley right across his field of fire.

Only Harry threw them *toward* the danger. Harry jammed the pedal to the floor and bellowed in time to the engine.

The muzzle flashed. But with three tons of roaring metal bearing straight at him, the shooter flinched. The high-velocity bullet hit the point where the windshield joined with the car's roof. It opened the top like a can opener. The rearview mirror dropped down on Storm.

The Bentley flew forward at ninety-six miles an hour. Harry knew because of the laser display that had flashed into view when his speed hit eighty, shining the readout onto the fractured windshield like an auto cue.

The tan man flung himself to one side. The same instant, Harry spun the wheel. The car responded like it gripped the concrete with tigers' claws, turning so they slammed the passenger door into the gleaming new barrier.

Harry was already accelerating away when they hit. The barrier shrieked like a woman, or so it seemed to Harry. Perhaps it was just Storm giving off some highly justified steam. The bolts tore out of the barrier's lower segment. Harry fought the wheel and watched the lower rail fall off and bang noisily through the scaffolding.

Harry kept his foot on the pedal, steering away from the barrier. The tires gripped and spun and gripped again. He pulled the pistol free of his belt, thumbed the safety, extended his arm out wide, and blasted away. He couldn't see the shooter, but he found a target almost as good. A new Harley Softail leaned where the scaffolding met the highway. Harry took aim at the gas tank as the car shuddered and finally tore away from the crumpled barrier. The Harley went up with a very satisfying boom.

As they accelerated away, the steering wheel shimmied and bucked so badly Harry dropped the empty gun and took a two-handed grip. The smell of burning oil rose from under the crumpled hood. Harry kept his foot down solid against the floorboard long after they left the overpass and were out of range. Finally, as they pulled into the airport entrance, he managed to unlock his muscles.

He looked at the figure still crouched in the foot well. "You can get up now."

EIGHTEEN

HARRY'S CELL PHONE RANG JUST as their flight was called. Emma said, "Sorry it's taken a while. I just got your messages."

His voice sounded breathless to his own ears. Like he'd just run a hard mile. Or was still taking incoming fire. "I've been trying to reach you for an hour, girl."

"Something came up. I hitched a ride to DC with Hakim's people. Where are you?"

"Boarding our flight to Reagan National." Harry stepped from the line and waved Storm onto the plane. "Who is Hakim?"

"My contact with Interpol."

Harry decided that had to wait. He gave Emma a swift rundown of the attack, then asked, "What happened to the agents guarding Storm?"

A tight sigh. "Dauer pulled them off."

Harry started to ask why, then decided the more important question was, "You're still on our side, right?"

"I want to be. Very much."

He felt a warm glow add itself to the already powerful mix. "That's got to count for something."

"Where's the Bentley?"

"Airport short-term lot, second floor, east bay. Bring a wrecker."

"How is Storm handling it?"

"She's got a lot of the old man in her. I thought for a while she was going to fall apart. But she's settled like a pro. She still gets the tremors every now and then. They come, she hangs tight, they go. Then she's right back into researching the treasure."

"In other words, she's working on something that may already have resulted in three deaths and two further attacks. While the assailant is still at large."

"Unless I hit him. Which I doubt. Yeah, that pretty much sums things up at this end."

"You don't sound worried."

Truth be told, Harry Bennett felt like the world had been etched with crystal clarity. He had almost forgotten the feeling, when all of life was brought to a higher state. Relearning the thrill, scenting treasure on the wind.

Strangely enough, he wanted to share that with

Emma. But as he walked forward and handed his boarding pass to the attendant, all he said into the phone was, "Storm needs your help with something."

Harry outlined what Storm had told him upon their arrival at the airport. Emma replied, "I'll see what I can do."

"All anybody can ask."

"I can't come to the funeral. Tell Storm I'm sorry. But I have to write a report and deliver it personally."

Harry dropped into the seat next to Storm. "You've got more trouble with that guy Dauer?"

Storm looked up at the man's name.

Emma replied carefully, "I can't protect you anymore, Harry."

"I hear you."

"I may not even be able to protect myself."

HARRY SHUT THE PHONE JUST as the flight attendant started her pre-flight announcements. He used the time to study Storm. The lady was so much like the old man it took Harry's breath away. Ninety minutes after taking a heavy shelling, she was so intent upon her work that the air about her crackled with condensed power.

Sean's old Bible was open in her lap. He knew it was Sean's because the page was bordered by his cryptic writing. One passage had been circled, underlined, annotated. Harry leaned close enough to see that the page belonged to the book of Matthew. The handwriting had been done with such vehemence that the page had been ripped and taped back together. No surprise there. Nothing about Sean's life had been done in half measure.

Harry's mind skipped across the electric sea of his thoughts. He knew what Sean would tell him. That maybe the reason their opponents, whoever they were, stayed on the hunt was not because of the treasure at all. The Turk, Selim, had told them straight out that Sean had been searching for the people attacking his company. Maybe all the enemy wanted was to chop off this last loose end, just in case Sean had told his granddaughter whatever he had managed to discover.

But Harry thought otherwise.

Sixteen years in the treasure business had left Harry certain that no mystery was buried alone. If the quest was simple, the treasure was already dug up and gone. Every major haul he had come across had required what the modern types called lateral thinking. Follow whatever thread was poking out, and just see where it led.

Hunting secrets buried under centuries of intrigue and storms and battle had also left Harry Bennett comfortable in trusting his gut. Sorting through the lies and the deception, searching for the one true nugget that led to the golden hoard, never forgetting why he was there in the first place. Any good treasure dog developed a sixth sense for what was real. And right now, this very minute, Harry was certain at the core of his being that they were closing in on the find of a lifetime.

And in some bizarre, convoluted way that only a treasure dog could happily live with, Harry Bennett was certain the quest for treasure was tied to Sean's investigation of a book that Harry had never bothered to open. Not once. Ever.

When the plane took off, Storm sighed her way out of the work. Harry watched her take a two-fisted hold and pull her hair back away from her face, tightening the skin until the bones stood out in stark angles. Just like old Sean. Harry shivered twice, once from seeing his best friend appear before his eyes, and again from how the old man had trusted him with this very fine lady. Despite everything that should have blown them apart forever.

Storm said, "I need to run something by you. I'm hoping if I lay it out, it'll make things clear for me. Which they aren't. Yet."

"Remember who you're talking to here. I never expect life to deliver me a straight path to treasure."

He could see she was rocked by that last word. Which was good for another grin. The lady wasn't quite ready to say it yet. Just like old Sean. Wanting the whole package tied up in a neat little bow and set in his hands before he ever spoke the word aloud. Treasure.

Storm pulled out a sheaf of handwritten notes but didn't actually look at them while she gave him some background. Harry did his best to stow his grin away, back where he hid a little boy's pleasure over playing bang-bang with the bad guys and driving away in a gut-shot Bentley. He shook his head clear of that recollection and did his best to focus. He'd heard most of what she was saying before. But not with the fragrance of gold drifting in the air.

The original Solomon's Temple was destroyed by the Babylonians in 586 BC, when the Judeans were taken into captivity. Building the Second Temple started seventy years later, when Zerubbabel brought a group of survivors back from Babylon. Then in 19 BC Herod the Great tore down that structure and rebuilt it from the ground up. Herod wanted the temple renamed after himself. But the priests were disgusted with Herod and his lifestyle and his loyalty to the Roman overlords. They continued to call it the Second Temple, using the excuse that the temple sacrifices went on unabated throughout this rebuilding process.

Seventy years later, the underground Jewish army revolted against Rome. They steadily pushed the Romans out of one province after another and finally retook Jerusalem in AD 66. Then the Roman general Vespasian landed sixty thousand Roman troops at Caesarea, and his son Titus brought two Africa legions to Joppa. Even with the new battalions, it took them eight years to defeat the Judean army. When Jerusalem finally fell, Titus ordered the entire city leveled and every male crucified. The Romans claimed the Second Temple caught fire by accident, but Judean accounts say that when the embers cooled the Romans returned and salted the earth.

Storm reached into her pocket and came up with a phone. She opened it to reveal a miniature keypad, then unfolded a color screen. "Titus returned to Rome in glory. They built the triumphant arch in his honor. Here's a drawing of the arch."

"Now that is one cool phone."

"Pay attention, Harry. This is important." She explained the book with the fore-edged drawing. "The drawing is an exact duplicate of the arch. I checked online." She drew up another photo and explained how the book had contained a second fore-edged illustration. "Only there isn't a second arch. I wondered if maybe one had been built somewhere in Israel and later destroyed. But there's no mention in any of the archeological findings."

"So you've got a drawing that's maybe a thousand years old of an arch that doesn't exist?"

She took her time stowing her phone away. "You've heard of the digs at Qumran?"

"Sure. Where they found all those amphorae filled with old scrolls."

"All but one of the Qumran scrolls were on vellum. That lone scroll had a list etched into copper. They've been arguing about this Copper Scroll for years. The thinking is, the scroll contained a list of the treasures inside the Second Temple. But none of the Copper Scroll treasures were among those taken by the Romans. And no one has ever been able to explain how these other treasures might have escaped from Jerusalem before the Romans broke the siege."

Storm took another two-fisted hold on her hair and tugged fiercely. Like if she pulled hard enough she could draw the world into tighter focus. "You remember what the bishop was holding in the Dürer painting?"

Harry shut his eyes and recalled the night. Or tried to. From where he sat, that particular event seemed years away. The image that remained far clearer was how his former best friend had reappeared when Storm had pulled her features taut. Strong, vibrant, and singularly intent. "A panel, right?"

"It's called a triptych." She reached into her purse and pulled out a velvet pouch. As she untied the leather drawstring, she described hearing from Claudia about her father's theft of Sean's treasures. And as a child finding the triptych hidden at the base of a safe she wasn't supposed to know about. And realizing the instant she laid eyes upon the canvas that it was the exact same item. "See how the edge is serrated into little steps and lined

194

with gold? I've never seen another one like this."

The panels were ivory, so stained with age they had turned the color of toffee. "I don't get it. Sean hunted down a painting because he wanted to confirm something about a stolen triptych?"

Storm stroked the panel's exterior as she spoke. Harry doubted she was even aware of her actions. "Sean was looking for what he had lost. His son stole the panels. Sean hoped the painting would show what the panels revealed. But the panels in the painting were indistinct. The only way I knew it was this one was because of how the two outer panels were framed in gold and carved so they would fit together neatly."

She opened the two outer panels. "This is what Sean was hoping to find."

Harry felt the image take grip of his gut and clench down so hard he could scarcely manage, "Oh man oh man oh man."

He felt Storm shiver against his arm. "It's real. Isn't it. The treasure."

The central panel showed an exact replica of the image Harry had last seen in the Guildhall vault. A headland or promontory with waves crashing down. Harry traced his finger along the outer edge and felt the current zing up and explode in his brain.

Storm said, "Selim claimed Dürer's letters spoke of painting the Bishop of Cyprus."

Harry cleared his throat. "Treasure dogs have

hunted over Cyprus for a thousand years and more. This headland doesn't exist."

"What does that mean?"

"That we'll just have to look harder."

Storm had him hold the triptych so she could shoot it with that fancy camera phone of hers. Which was more difficult than it sounded, since Harry's hands had developed a pretty severe case of palsy. She stowed the triptych back in the pouch and the pouch back in her purse. Then she brought out Sean's tattered Bible and pulled an envelope from the back flap.

She studied him a long moment, and then handed it over. "Here."

Harry looked from her face to the envelope and back again. "This is from Sean?"

"Read it," Storm said. "He talks about you."

NINETEEN

THE OLD-TOWN ALEXANDRIA CHURCH JUST down from Syrrell's headquarters was three-quarters full. The pianist who played as they entered was a student on a Juilliard scholarship funded by Sean Syrrell. The first Storm knew of this was when the pastor informed the congregation. Beside her in the front pew, Claudia's eyes widened in mutual surprise. Which was typical of Sean. He had kept nothing hidden quite so well as his good deeds.

Storm found considerable comfort from Harry's presence one row back. He had not said much since reading Sean's letter. Which had suited Storm fine. They had checked into an airport hotel, showered and changed, and taken a taxi straight to the church. Claudia had already been seated when Storm entered. Her aunt had not spoken as Storm slipped into the pew, just gripped her hand with the one not holding her tissue. She held it still.

Storm had debated showing Harry the letter. Only now, in the church's subdued atmosphere, was she sure she had done the right thing. When they stood for the first hymn, Storm glanced back. Harry stared at the coffin with a cavernous expression. She was getting to know this man. Down deep, below the strength and the pirate's grin, was someone as lonely as she.

Beside her, Claudia wept softly. During the tribute and the choir's songs, Storm's mind turned repeatedly to Harry Bennett and Sean's letter. She did not wonder about her lack of physical attraction for Harry. Her record in the male-female department was abysmal. She'd pretty much given up after realizing the last three men she'd almost convinced herself she cared about were all bottom-feeders. What gave her that special buzz was knowing she could trust Harry. A man this strong and worldly considered her a friend. An ally in this, their mutual mission. Of course she had shown him the letter.

She bowed her head at the pastor's request but did not hear the prayer. Instead, she felt so close to Sean she heard him speak the words he had written for her. Two paragraphs from a man whose normal correspondence was a single sentence long.

My dear Storm,

If you've made it this far, you've decided to share my quest. The illuminated chain book came into my possession the week you were born and started me on this search. For years I feared I had lost touch with the prize, after your father stole the triptych. Then nine weeks ago I heard about the painting by Dürer, the same day I realized we were under attack. I can only hope either the painting or the London researcher will confirm what I have long suspected. I bequeath to you these clues, along with all my remaining assets and my plea that you take great care. If Harry Bennett contacts you, I urge you to trust him. He is a better man than he knows, a knight seeking a chalice he has not yet managed to name.

You have always struck me as a better version of myself, filled with passion and drive and intelligence and a hunger to rise beyond the prison of your heritage. I hope you someday discover the same joy I have known in hunting out mysteries of the soul. I also pray you manage to achieve more than my own life-time of prideful acts, angry misdeeds, and impossible goals.

Yours ever,
Sean

AFTER THE GRAVESIDE SERVICE, CLAUDIA waited for the crowd to give them a private space and said, "We need to talk."

Storm had been about to say the same thing. "All right."

"Ride with me." When Harry approached, she added, "Alone, Storm."

Inside the limo, Claudia demanded quietly, "Who *is* that man?"

"I told you at the exhibition. Harry Bennett was one of Sean's closest friends. Sean asked him to contact me. He's saved my life."

Claudia leaned forward and asked the driver, "Can you turn on your radio or something?"

"Sure thing, Ms. Syrrell."

Claudia grimaced as she unwound the charcoal grey scarf from around her neck, as though easing out of a noose. "What is this I've heard of you handling a Dürer?"

"It's true."

"Why did I need to learn about this from another dealer?"

"I've tried to contact you daily. It's not the sort of news I'm going to leave on a voice mail. While we're on that subject, why haven't you called me back?"

"I haven't slept, I haven't eaten. That's how busy it's been. How was the exhibition?"

"Frantic. Let's back up. You're so busy you don't even call when I leave a message warning you might be in danger of being killed?"

"We've had this discussion before. Sean died of a heart attack."

"Interesting how you're the only one to believe that."

"Keep your voice down. I want you to tell me about this painting."

"First I need to ask you something."

"You're *negotiating* with me?"

"You're the one who's been out of touch."

Claudia sighed. "So ask."

"Tell me what Sean planned to do after New York."

Claudia turned and stared out the window. Sunshine adorned old-town Alexandria with a springtime glow. "The last three times Sean and I talked, we argued. That last one in New York was the worst. It had been building for weeks. He was planning a trip to Istanbul. Via Toronto. Which makes no sense at all. We needed him *here*. Keeping us afloat. Things were *desperate*. I said he should send you. Close the Palm Beach office and use you as our roving emissary."

"What did he say?"

"That timing was everything. Whatever that meant." Claudia dabbed her eyes with a crumpled handkerchief. "I've always considered myself a pretty calm sort of person. But Daddy could drive me up the wall with one look."

"Don't sell Syrrell's, Claudia. Please."

Her aunt had clearly been waiting for that. "Storm, there is nothing left to *keep*."

The limo driver pulled up in front of Syrrell's headquarters. Storm declared, "Then there is no painting to discuss."

"What is that supposed to mean?"

"That's exactly what I'd like to know. As in, how far would you go to protect your own job?"

"Excuse me. I am protecting Syrrell's."

"Have you been aware of any threat against you since all this started?"

"Other than my life's work being on the line?" Claudia shoved her door open, blind to how she almost knocked over the limo driver. "Where do you get off taking that insinuating tone with me?"

Storm watched her aunt drill a hole through the well-wishers and disappear inside Syrrell's. When Harry opened her door, she said, "Claudia hasn't been attacked."

Harry said, "It doesn't mean what you're worried about. Not if the treasure was the target, and Claudia isn't connected. You're the one with the cash and the notebooks and the quest."

Storm found enough comfort in that to rise from

the limo. Harry went on, "Emma called. It's all set up. Two hours."

"Great." Storm asked the limo driver, "How long are you booked for?"

"Open-ended, Ms. Syrrell."

"Pull down to the end of the block and wait, please. I need you to take us downtown." She started up the walk. "Come on, Harry. Let's get this over with."

SYRRELL'S OCCUPIED A FEDERALIST HOME on South Union Street, just up from what had been the Revolutionary War harbor. The house was erected between 1745 and 1760 by one of the Colonial government's principal financiers. It was Georgian in design, square and stalwart, built of local stone and fired brick. The rear garden still contained boxwoods planted over 250 years ago.

The main floor and principal showrooms were so jammed Storm felt no room for memories, save one. Directly opposite the entry, occupying a high alcove, was the same item that had greeted Storm the first time she had stepped through those doors. The jeweled cabinet had been built in the early sixteenth century for Pope Sixtus V. It stood thirteen feet and was shaped like a baroque chapel. The nineteen drawers and doll-sized compartments were hidden behind mosaic panels of alabaster and semiprecious stones. An etching of that cabinet formed the company logo. The thought that the cabinet and the house that contained it would soon be sold drove her through the crowd, past the velvet-rope barrier, and up the main stairs.

The house's middle floor contained the company offices, and the top floor held Sean's apartment. What had been the family parlor was now used for conferences and as a private showroom. Claudia's and Sean's offices occupied the two rear corner rooms. Storm entered Sean's office, padded across the antique Isfahan carpet, and stepped behind his desk. She could still smell the old man.

Harry pointed at the Steinway that dominated the room's other side. "I never knew he had a piano in here. He always met me, you know, outside. Usually down in Palm Beach, a couple of times in the Carib, never here." He took in the oiled paneling, the crystal chandelier, the shadows where Sean's few favorite paintings had once hung. "Nice."

"Sean only played after the shop closed and everybody went home."

"Everybody but you."

She opened the top right drawer, pulled out his calendar, and turned to the previous week. "This is very strange."

Harry crossed the room.

She pointed to the one appointment on the day after his expected return from New York, with a

Professor Morgenthal at Georgetown University. "That's his handwriting."

"So?"

"You know how secretive he was. Appointments Sean made were scrawled so nobody else could read them." Storm turned to other weeks. "Look at the difference between meetings scheduled by others and those he put in himself. Booking just one appointment makes no sense. Sean's days were crammed."

Harry pondered that. "Let's say he went to New York knowing he wasn't coming back."

Storm swallowed hard.

"But he sets out this one appointment, clear as day. Why?"

Storm turned and left the room.

Her own office had originally been the house pantry. In the eighteenth century, the pantry had contained items often used in barter when money was not available—tobacco, sugar, molasses, and liquor. The single narrow window was cross-barred, and the door was bound with iron. Before Storm's arrival it had been used as a storeroom for treasures in transit—those sold and not yet shipped, or going for outside analysis, or awaiting final provenance. Storm slipped behind her desk, gave the Potomac's sparkling waters a glance, and switched on her computer. Sean had arranged for her to maintain status as a postgrad with access to the Georgetown University system. She logged in and told Harry, "This shouldn't take long."

But Harry's attention was snagged by a photo on the wall. "Get a load of this."

The frame held the cover of the first catalogue Storm had put together. A lovely young woman held a chain that wound around her otherwise naked form, the chain so long she was modestly cloaked. The chain was 14 kt. gold and studded with doubloons. Storm asked, "Yours?"

"Old East Indian trader we found off Sumatra." Harry tapped the glass. "Sailors made chains of all their prize money because the Crown classed any valuable worn on the body as personal jewelry and wasn't taxed."

"I remember Sean telling me that. He didn't say it was your find."

"No. He wouldn't."

Storm printed two recent articles by Professor Morgenthal, one of which contained a picture. She then drew the phone from her pocket and plugged it into the computer's USB port. She scrolled through her stored photographs, selected four, and printed them as well. "Okay. I've got what I need."

Harry followed her down the stairs. "I'm never much for funerals and even less for glad-handing. I'll be waiting for you on the front porch."

Storm did not argue. As she entered the front room, Claudia glared at her, then turned away. Storm moved slowly through the crush, greeting

205

those she genuinely cared for and enduring the rest. Hearing other people speak of Sean with the ancient exasperation of true friends pierced deep. Storm took her time, allowing the crowd to shift her about, drawing her along, until she entered the rear showroom and found the person she had been seeking.

The solitary name in Sean's calendar, the woman Storm had been researching upstairs, had positioned herself by the back window. From there she could survey all three main rooms. Evelyn Morgenthal was an angry stump of a woman. She responded to someone's comment with a terse whip, not taking her eyes off Storm's approach. "My condolences, Ms. Syrrell."

"We need to talk, Professor Morgenthal."

Dark eyes held a fiercely intelligent light and no welcome whatsoever. "Your grandfather was a singular man, Ms. Syrrell. Unique. I doubt seriously the relationship we held is transferable."

"We have evidence that Sean was murdered."

The woman possessed a slight lilt to her words, a foreign tongue learned as a child and heavily overlaid with her Americanization. "Never did I consider Sean's death a simple act of fate."

"Did it ever occur to you that the appointment my grandfather made with you was intended for me all along?"

The professor rewarded Storm with a sharp nod of approval. "My office. Three hours."

TWENTY

EMMA ARRIVED EARLY ENOUGH TO grab a parking spot on Constitution, three blocks from the White House. A half hour from now, she could sell it for serious cash. She rubbed eyes grainy from lack of sleep. Some agents she knew bragged about going forty-eight, even seventy-two hours without sleep and staying alert, totally in the green. If she didn't get a minimum of four hours the day felt slightly out of whack, like she'd entered a global hall of mirrors.

Then again, given what was about to go down, her mental state might be in perfect harmony with the day ahead.

That morning, Emma had been wakened at four by two phone calls. She had checked the readout and answered neither. The first had been from Jack Dauer. The message he had left blasted her for taking Harry Bennett along on the central Florida run, then ordered her to report in person ASAP. The second had been from the two junior agents she had assigned to cover Storm. The message had been terse in the extreme, five words long. Dauer had called them off. Nothing more had been required. Emma had risen from bed knowing the juncture had been reached.

Seated in her car, watching the DC traffic con-

207

geal, Emma placed a call. When her former boss answered, she said simply, "It's me."

Tip MacFarland's response was just as swift. "Girl, I can*not* help you."

"Just the same, can we meet?"

"Where are you?"

"Parked outside."

"My office. Five minutes."

Emma shut her phone and turned to the man seated next to her. Hakim Sundera. Everything about him was precise, economical, tight. She said, "I wish I could be certain this was the right move."

"You made your choice when you flew up with us, Ms. Webb. Perhaps before." His gaze was dark, liquid, fathomless. "To hesitate now is only to lose what advantage you might hold."

She rose from the car and crossed the street. Homeland Security's main location was out near American University. But a number of senior power players worked three blocks from the White House in a building that had formerly housed US Customs. She climbed the front stairs, pushed through the brass-framed doors, signed in, took the elevator to the fourth floor, and entered a Byzantine maze. Midlevel staffers and below possessed offices with no names, only acronyms. HAZ-4AL, WAF-SR3—the signs had gone up since her assignment to Miami. She had no idea what they meant. Nor would she ask. Ignorance was the clearest signal that she did not belong. She found her destination only because her last job before heading south had been to move Tip MacFarland over from Treasury.

Her former mentor's outer office was empty. The desk Emma would have occupied if she hadn't made the switch to Miami appeared to be unmanned. MacFarland said through the open door, "I warned you. Twice."

Emma walked in and shut the door. "I'm back in DC less than six hours and I hate this place already. It was either take the assignment or quit."

"The only reason somebody as junior as you got that assignment was, everybody else knew Dauer would run his usual slash-and-burn show." Tip MacFarland was a DC survivor. But unlike most of his ilk, he was also fair-minded and direct with his subordinates. Sometimes brutally so. "I would've found you another slot."

Emma set the report she'd worked on since Dauer's wake-up call on MacFarland's desk. "You'd been promising me a new posting for two years."

"Word is, they popped a few corks over at fibby headquarters when Dauer left for Florida."

"He's jeopardizing our case."

"Correction. He's messing with *your* case. Jack Dauer's agenda is rolling along just fine."

"You don't know the evidence I've—"

"Dauer isn't after truth. He's after the next rung.

Jack Dauer has wasted a lot of good people on his climb." MacFarland had the build of a Boston cop, which was exactly what his father and grandfather had been. At six-four, he was big boned, redheaded with a touch of early frost. His smile was easy, but rarely reached his pale blue eyes. "Then there's the matter of your other move."

"I needed to find a balance against Dauer."

"But Interpol, Emma."

"They offered. I accepted."

"Now you're totally off the reservation. Your supervisor, what's his name?"

"Sundera. Hakim Sundera."

"What is he, Jordanian?"

"Syrian."

MacFarland rolled his eyes. "If that guy wrote you up for a presidential citation, Dauer could use it to blow his nose and nobody around here would say a word."

"Hakim is a good man, and my case is real."

"I don't want to hear about it, Agent Webb."

Emma hefted the plastic visitor's chair and carried it around MacFarland's desk. She planted herself tight in his private space. "For once you're going to shut up and listen."

Tip MacFarland had been head of the Department of Treasury's OFAC, Office of Foreign Asset Control. Plum job, high status, next in line for deputy director of intel. He left to head Homeland Security's new task force on international counterfeiting rings, specifically targeting criminal gangs sponsored by rogue states who had churned out more than half a billion in bogus hundred-dollar bills. MacFarland made the move because he believed in the work and its urgency. But nobody rose as high as MacFarland without a highly developed sense of self-preservation.

When Emma finished summarizing her case, MacFarland told her, "If they had a wall for careers sacrificed on the altar of good intentions, they'd already be polishing your plaque."

"Sean Syrrell was murdered. His company was the victim of major fraud. A professional assassin with international ties has been brought in from overseas. The granddaughter's life is under threat. These are facts."

"What I know is, Dauer will bury you and whatever evidence you've managed to scrape together. These interagency task forces are just cats and dogs locked in a bureaucratic cage. Washington goes through phases. Today's catchword is holistic. They want these agencies to set aside their warrior mentalities and take a holistic attitude to problems. But the feebs are sitting this tune out. Their current buzzword is *whack*. As in, to divide. You can whack up turf but you can't whack up credit."

"None of what you've said changes the truth." Emma took a single sheet of paper from her purse and placed it in front of him. "Sign this."

The page was printed on departmental stationery and officially assigned Emma temporary duty with Interpol. MacFarland read the page, glanced at her, and made as though he was going to argue. Instead he sighed and reached for his pen. "You've got one chance to salvage your career. Come up with a prize so big they can't ignore you. Find that or don't come back at all."

THE LIMO LET STORM AND Harry off at the border of the National Mall. The original Smithsonian building, known as the Castle, had been designed by James Renwick, the architect responsible for Saint Patrick's Cathedral in New York. The Castle was constructed of red Maryland sandstone in what was politely called the Norman style, a combination of Romanesque, Gothic, and a very large architectural ego. The Specialist Collection of the Smithsonian archives had been temporarily relocated to the Castle. Temporary was a bureaucratic term for almost forever.

"Remind me again," Harry said. "What are you after here?"

"I need to look through unsorted archives bequeathed to the Smithsonian by one of their staff archeologists. It's related to something I found among Sean's things in the vault. I'll tell you about it if what I think I remember turns out to be right. But raw field data is normally off-limits to outsiders. Which is why I got you to ask Emma for help."

"You plan to waltz in and find something they missed?"

"Oh, they found it all right. They just don't know it yet."

For the first time in the Smithsonian's history, its president had recently been fired for mismanagement. The instant Storm and Harry entered the front doors, the result was evident. Instead of the standard stone-faced federal greeting, the woman at the front desk said brightly, "Can I help you?"

Storm glanced at the name Emma had passed to Harry and said, "I'm here to see Lance Crowder."

"Ms. Syrrell?"

"That's right."

A man whose slender build only accented his bulging gut hustled across the marble foyer. "I understand you have a scholar's card?"

"Yes." For her first Christmas with the company, Sean had arranged for her to be granted privileges as an accredited Smithsonian researcher. "Here you are."

"Great." He checked the card, then asked Harry, "Are you with Ms. Syrrell?"

"I'll just wait out here."

"Right. Wear the visitor's pass at all times, Ms. Syrrell. Okay. This way." They passed through doors controlled electronically by the receptionist and entered a Formica maze. "Normally we don't allow anyone outside the system the sort of access you're after. But a call from Treasury combined with a scholar's card, that's a first. I guess you've heard about the recent upheaval."

Storm had lived in Washington long enough to catch the unspoken request. "I'll be happy to ask my superiors to put in a word."

"I've got to tell you, it wouldn't hurt. We're walking a tightrope over here. Those guys you saw me talking with, they're GAO. Everybody around here is shaking." He opened the doors leading to concrete stairs and started down. "I'm hearing rumors of reassignments to Guam."

Three flights down, they entered the subbasement archival library. Streams of fluorescent lighting almost hid the battery of pipes and wiring, all painted government green. Corridors lined with metal shelves marched into oblivion. Most of the oblong tables she passed were occupied with scholars lost in their dusty realms, peering through magnifying glasses, labeling bagged finds, tapping on keyboards.

Storm had often wondered whether she could have fit into the academic mold. Spend years delving into some obscure find, write an article read by a learned few, preserve treasures in the public eye, scorn money. And never, ever talk price. She studied the men and women they passed, and decided that she would have loved the research, tolerated the students, and hated the life.

The archivist led Storm to a table empty save for a trio of cardboard cartons. "I don't need to tell you that everything has to be put back where you find it."

"No."

He hesitated, then lowered his voice and said, "I've got kids in school."

Storm gave him what he was after. "I owe you."

WHEN EMMA RETURNED TO THE car, she found that Hakim had moved over behind the wheel. He watched her slip into the passenger seat with those liquid dark eyes. And waited.

Emma handed him the page her former boss had signed. "Tip MacFarland is an honest man and a solid boss. But he's also a survivor. And ambitious. He has a highly tuned sense of when it's time to cut and run."

Hakim folded the sheet and stowed it in his pocket. He started the car. "I received a call while you were inside. They have just found the Turkish dealer, Arkut. Two shots, small caliber, one to the heart and another to the head. He was left in the trunk of a car at the Palm Beach airport. Near where they found Arkut's bullet-ridden Bentley."

Emma used both fists to squeeze her temples. She felt trapped inside the amber of other people's plans. "Dauer is going to make Harry for the murder."

"No doubt Mr. Bennett's prints will be all over

the Bentley. Along with Ms. Syrrell's." Hakim said nothing more until they pulled up in front of another nondescript Washington office building. He parked at the curb, cut the motor, and said, "Make the call."

"DAUER."

"Sir, it's Agent Webb, phoning as per your—"

"I contacted you nine hours ago, Agent Webb. This delay is either a gross dereliction or flagrant insubordination."

"Sorry, sir."

"Where have you been?"

"Homeland Security, sir."

"You're in *Washington*? On whose say-so?"

"I tracked Ms. Syrrell, sir. And reported to my superiors."

"*I* am your superior, Webb. Who have you been speaking with?"

"Director MacFarland, sir."

"MacFarland has no jurisdiction in this matter."

"No, sir. He just requested a sitrep."

"Which should have been passed by me first!"

Emma gave Dauer what all of their team did when he turned up the heat. She went mono-chrome. Dull, toneless, terse. Tight inside her skull. "I'll make every effort to stay in touch, sir."

"Don't tell me you passed your report to MacFarland."

"I felt it was my duty, sir."

"What about our two suspects? You managed to lose them yet?"

"Storm Syrrell and Harry Bennett attended the funeral of Sean Syrrell. They then headed to the Smithsonian. Next they have a meeting scheduled at Georgetown University."

"Okay, Webb. While you've been gallivanting off the reservation, there have been some major developments. Arkut's body was found in the trunk of a car in the Palm Beach airport parking garage. Where did your pair fly to DC from?"

"The same airport, sir."

"Were you with them?"

"I just explained, sir, I flew in early to present my report—"

"Which means Bennett and Syrrell were unsupervised and in range. So here's the deal. I've met with the people who matter. We're moving against the two of them."

"Sir, did you share my report with your superiors?"

"No, Agent Webb. There was no need to bother anybody with your half-baked theories. The facts are plain as day. Syrrell's has run three illegal schemes in the past ten months. The granddaughter has wreaked all the havoc one girl is going to get away with on my watch."

"Sir, my report specifically lays out evidence suggesting Syrrell's was the repeated victim of carefully aimed attacks."

"You've been corrupted by them. Syrrell's is a major player. We have only identified the tip of a massive illegal operation."

"I inspected the company records going back six years. Ditto for the banks. I found nothing—"

"You didn't look hard enough. They laundered funds and dealt in stolen goods. We knew this going in. The only question has been, who are they working for. Which you were assigned to determine. How far have you gotten with that detail?"

"Sir, I no longer believe our premise fits the evidence."

"Nowhere, is the answer. Okay, Webb. Let's cut to the chase here. What exactly is the motive for somebody laying out this elaborate fraud and perpetrating these two attacks?"

"Actually, sir, there has been a third incident—"

"Oh, give me a break."

Emma gripped the door handle. Her hand went pale and bloodless. "I'm not sure who is behind the attacks, either on the persons or the company. Yet."

"They've got you hook, line, and sinker. What's more, your attitude is jeopardizing our case. We've decided there's too much risk of losing the suspects. You're hereby ordered to arrest Storm Syrrell and her accomplice."

TWENTY-ONE

INTERPOL OCCUPIED THE TOP FLOOR in a typical Washington monolith. The building also contained consulates of nations requiring heightened vigilance. The people who shared the elevator were silent, careful. The Interpol receptionist saluted Hakim, noted Emma's ID, and buzzed them through a bulletproof barrier. They entered a windowless bull pen staffed by a dozen different nations.

Hakim led her into the corner office, shut the door, pointed her into a chair, and said, "In some ways, our situations are not so far apart. I too have enemies within my own government who would rather see me fail."

"I'm still not clear on exactly what your mission is."

He walked behind his desk. "The same as you, Agent Webb. To arrest the criminals and to protect the innocent."

She dragged out the word. "Okay."

He unlocked his top drawer and withdrew a manila folder. "We have both reached uncomfortable junctures, you and I. We must choose between who we are taught to call enemies, and what the evidence is telling us."

He opened the folder and passed the first page across the desk. "You are hereby granted a temporary appointment with Interpol."

"Dauer will use this to have me fired."

"He may." Hakim's jacket fit as snugly as a handcrafted holster and was made from some smooth material, possibly silk. On Hakim it looked natural. "On the other hand, Agent Webb, this may actually be the break we have both been looking for. To find the perpetrators, we must understand their motives. Someone considers this affair so vital that they have brought in an international assassin. Such an assassin, repeatedly risking his life to take out two insignificant locals, is not logical."

Emma's mind was snagged by the word *assassin*. Hakim had given it a subtle shift, as though drawn from a heritage beyond her comprehension. She said, "They're after treasure?"

"Consider what I am saying. This assassin is a professional, which means he survives by being swift and unseen. Yet now he repeatedly risks being uncovered. And for what? No single treasure justifies the intensity of these attacks."

"You have something."

"Just one more small piece in the puzzle, Agent Webb." He traded her signed document for the next page from his file. "Just one more mystery to be solved."

The page was lined in a thick black frame. At the top of the sheet, below the Interpol symbol, a word was repeated in six different languages.

Alert.

Beneath that were four photographs of the same man. Two were standard mug shots. Two others were taken from surveillance cameras.

"Whatever is driving these assaults, Agent Webb, is far greater than we are seeing."

A single paragraph was translated six times: *This individual is on the international watch list. Notify Interpol immediately. Considered armed and extremely dangerous.*

Emma said, "They don't give his name."

"Go protect your two charges, Agent Webb." Hakim lifted her signed document. "As soon as Jack Dauer learns of your transfer to Interpol, he will send others to arrest Storm Syrrell and Harry Bennett. They must be beyond his reach before that happens. Then come straight back. We have important work to do."

THE DIGNIFIED DEMEANOR OF GEORGETOWN University's Healey Hall vanished the instant Storm and Harry stepped through the main doors. The charmless interior was dictated by too many students and too few dollars. Linoleum and fluorescent lighting tracked them down a scarred hallway and into a battered elevator. They took the elevator to the sixth floor, as high as it would go, then traversed a long corridor and found another elevator fronted by a dusty out-of-order sign. They climbed the final two flights into the tower, where a stone landing adorned a stubby hallway. Storm knocked on the peaked oak door. It creaked open. "Professor Morgenthal?"

Evelyn Morgenthal's office, in the building's turret, was crammed with documents and books. The woman sat in a padded chair yet remained half-hidden behind her oversized desk. She shut a folder, rolled up a scroll, set both in her desk drawer, and squinted at Harry. "Sean always came alone."

"Harry Bennett was my grandfather's friend. Now he's mine."

"He looks like a salvager to me. A treasure hound. My work is with artifacts. The legacy of lost civilizations. Invaluable testimonies to what was, and what was not, a part of their culture." She stabbed the air with a child's hand. "That man and his ilk are the enemy of all I hold dear. They find, they sell, they pocket their filthy lucre and smile as yet another fragment of our past is lost to some rich man's mantle."

Storm took the lone seat across the desk from the professor. "And yet you helped my grandfather. Sean was passionate about legacy. But he was also fanatical about profit. So what made it acceptable to work with Sean?"

Professor Morgenthal kept her hostility aimed at Harry, who took up station by the exit.

"Here's what I think," Storm said. "Sean made some discoveries that could only have been claimed as unique. But unlike a lot of other dealers, he was never a man in a hurry. He could keep his treasures out of sight for years. I think Sean worked out an agreement with you. If he came across something really special, he'd give you time to research it, write it up, make your presentation, collect your kudos."

Reluctantly the professor's gaze swiveled over. "You checked my publications."

"Just your two most recent articles. I didn't have much time."

Dark eyes held a fiercely intelligent light. "My husband has Parkinson's. The university medical system only covers the basics. Taking care of him costs a great deal and also makes travel impossible."

"But to maintain your stature in the professional community, you have to keep coming up with new finds. Which Sean supplied. The question we have to determine is, would you be willing to work with me on the same basis." Storm reached for her purse and drew out the pages she had printed off that morning. She set them facedown on the edge of the professor's desk. "Sean believed he had found some link between several artifacts and the location of treasures from the Second Temple. He asked you to research the Copper Scroll. How am I doing so far?"

Professor Morgenthal remained silent, her gaze locked on the unseen photographs.

Storm offered the professor the first sheet. "Perhaps you'd tell us what this is."

Evelyn Morgenthal inspected the page. She drew a magnifying glass from her drawer, swiveled the light in tight, leaned closer. "This is from a triptych?"

"Yes."

"Is it intact?"

"Yes."

"You have the other panels?"

Storm remained silent.

"This is the seal of Empress Constantia, mother of Constantine. The emperor Constantine converted to Christianity and brought the Roman empire with him. His mother, a believer since before her son was born, was a great one for furthering Christianity's reach." She tapped the page with one finger. "But this seal is shaped as a standard, such as a kingdom or provincial capital might use . . ."

The professor leaned closer still.

"What is it?"

"Perhaps nothing. I'll need to check this thoroughly."

Storm leaned forward. "Let's pretend we're actually on the same side here."

Professor Morgenthal set down her glass and studied Storm for a long moment. "In the fourth century, Salamis, the capital of Cyprus, was destroyed by earthquake. Empress Constantia traveled there on her return from a pilgrimage to Jerusalem. She sponsored the city's rebuilding, and ordered the Roman navy to sail in provisions to keep the population alive through the next planting season, as they had lost almost all the island's crops."

Harry murmured, "Cyprus."

"Legend has it, the island rulers wanted to rename their city and nation in her honor, but Constantia refused. It has been said they adopted her standard instead. But there has never been any evidence to that effect."

"Until now," Storm said.

"Which panel have you just shown me?"

"The right."

"The triptych's center panel is the most important," Morgenthal said. "The other two are always related in some way, but not so crucial."

Storm kept her hands planted on the pages. "Tell us about the Copper Scroll."

"The arguments still rage. But a growing number of experts, myself included, accept that the scroll is a record of treasures from the Second Temple. We feel this argument over the contents masks the true mystery."

Storm supplied, "And that mystery is, why the scroll was outside Jerusalem at all."

Morgenthal asked, "May I see what else you have?"

Storm handed over the next photograph. "Where does Cyprus fit in?"

The professor was too intent upon the picture to

respond. Harry supplied, "Cyprus is only a hundred miles off the coast of Lebanon. If ships were smuggling items through hostile waters, it'd be the perfect refuge."

Morgenthal nodded reluctant approval. "The island was considered docile by their Roman masters. They garrisoned the port, they guarded the copper mines, and they left the rest of the island very loosely manned. The island held strong Jewish and Christian communities."

Harry added, "Which adds weight to the possibility that the treasures might have been taken there. The people fleeing Jerusalem needed a safe haven. One they could reach fast and where they'd find people they could trust."

Morgenthal's gaze swiveled up once more. "Cyprus was also base for the second Jewish revolt."

"What revolt was that?"

"In AD 116, Jews from throughout the Roman empire gathered in Cyprus. A smaller force, probably made up of Jews who had spread through North Africa, came together in Alexandria. The plan was brutally simple. They defeated the Roman garrisons on Cyprus, both at Salamis and Kyrenia."

Storm said, "Having temple treasures located there would have added a special impetus to their rebellion."

"They began preparing and equipping an army to

retake the homeland," Morgenthal went on. "And they might have succeeded. Only the Romans vividly recalled the Jews' fighting ability from fifty years earlier, when they had managed to conquer Jerusalem, at least temporarily. So Rome sent their finest general, a young man by the name of Hadrian, who responded with a level of brutality that earned him a reputation throughout the empire. By the time he was done, two hundred and fifty thousand Cypriots were dead, and the burgeoning Christian and Jewish communities were erased."

Morgenthal rose from her chair and began pacing between her desk and the rear window. Behind her, the sun shone upon a springtime vista of college lawns and redbrick buildings and tree-tops and sparkling Potomac waters. "Paul and Barnabus traveled to Salamis on one of their earliest missionary journeys and converted the Roman consul, making Cyprus the first nation on earth to be ruled by a Christian. Remember, the earliest followers of Jesus were almost all Jews. But major schisms between the synagogue leaders and these Jewish Christians began around the time of Jerusalem's destruction, because these Christians refused to take part in the city's final defense. But we know they were actively involved in the second Jewish uprising. When the rebellion was crushed, Jews and Christians alike were slaughtered. Whatever secrets they might have held were lost forever."

Storm handed over the final page. "Not entirely."

Morgenthal returned to her desk. "What is this?"

"An etching from a fore-edged book. An illuminated Gospel of John. In both Latin and Greek."

"But this . . ."

"Had to be from the tenth century or later."

She clambered into her chair and reached for her magnifying glass. "A second triumphant arch has never been found. Or even mentioned."

Harry asked, "Is there any way a secret might have somehow been kept, or at least part of it, until around the tenth century, and then lost entirely?"

"Oh, most definitely." She continued to inspect the photograph through her glass. "Cyprus was struck by plague precisely at that point in time. The Black Death wiped out virtually the entire population. When King Richard the Lionhearted landed, he found Cyprus to be almost empty of human inhabitants. After he deeded the island to the Lusignan princes, they brought in subjects from all over the Mediterranean to repopulate the island. Holders of any such secret could have certainly been lost to the plague."

Harry's phone went off. He slipped out the door. Storm said, "I need a list of the treasures mentioned on the Copper Scroll."

The professor pulled the computer keypad in front of her, typed briefly, and the printer began whirring. She pulled out the printed sheet and asked, "May I see the triptych's third panel?"

Storm leaned forward. "How did the treasures get out of Jerusalem?"

Morgenthal straightened into as lofty a pose as her diminutive stature allowed. "I am months away from being ready to release my findings. Years, perhaps."

Harry stepped back into the room. "Storm. We have to go."

"In a minute."

"Now. Something's come up. Emma's downstairs."

Morgenthal's ire strengthened. "You bring another stranger into my life?"

Storm rose from her chair because Harry's hand was now on her arm. "The Romans had the city surrounded. The siege lasted over two years. When they finally conquered Jerusalem, they burned it to the ground. Sean must have asked you the same question."

Morgenthal's gaze tracked the unseen printout in Storm's hand. "There is no conclusive evidence. Nothing definite has turned up, not in two thousand years of searching. But the only logical answer lies in linking two men."

"Their names."

Harry's phone rang again. "Storm. Now."

Morgenthal shaped the words into bullets. "Titus Flavius Josephus, and Yochanan Ben Zachai."

Storm handed over the photograph.

Morgenthal studied the page, then demanded, "What is this?"

"I don't know. But I am going to find out."

TWENTY-TWO

WHEN STORM AND HARRY PILED into the car waiting by the Georgetown hall's entrance, Emma Webb said simply, "You have to leave. Immediately."

Harry responded with the same calm he had displayed under attack. "Leave town?"

"I had something a little farther in mind." Emma gunned the motor. "Where are your things?"

"The Marriott Courtyard out by National."

She burned rubber around the curve and raced through the Georgetown gates. "Did you register under your own names?"

"No reason not to," Harry replied. "At the time."

She hit an open stretch of road and punched the car hard. Storm turned in her seat so she could watch Harry in the backseat. His calm, pin-point focus was all the alert she needed. "What's going on?"

Emma hit sixty across the Key Bridge. She slowed to merge with traffic, swung onto the parkway, and jammed the metal hard. The charmless high-rises of Rosslyn swept by in a blur. "Say you had to disappear. You've got one chance to go to the heart of the matter and work things through. Where would you head?"

Storm recalled, "Sean was planning a trip to Toronto and Istanbul."

Emma did all but stand the car on two wheels to make the hotel entrance. She pulled under the front awning and slammed on the brakes hard enough to rock them all. "You have thirty seconds and not an instant longer. No, wait. Give me your credit card, I'll check you out."

Emma was already back in the car when they returned downstairs. She handed Storm her card and the hotel receipt. "The desk clerk stiffed you for the night's full charges. I flashed the badge but it didn't help."

"Will you tell us what's wrong?"

"Soon." Emma appeared grim but calm, not so much tense as extremely focused. "Right now we need to work on your final destination. Toronto's out. The extradition between Canada and the United States is so tight they'll meet you with a warrant at plane side."

Storm said, "Extradition?"

Harry leaned back in his seat. Glanced out the side window. He might have laughed.

Emma speared him through the rearview mirror. "Something about this strikes you as funny?"

He smiled at Storm. "Answer the lady's question while you still have time."

Storm took a breath. She could hardly believe she was saying the words. "Istanbul first. Then Cyprus."

"Forget traveling on to Cyprus for now," Harry said. "I'll handle that bit."

Emma asked, "You both have your passports?"

Storm replied, "I always carry mine." Harry just smiled.

Emma opened her phone, punched speed dial, said simply, "Istanbul. Roger. Both of them."

Storm said to Harry, "What is going on?"

Harry held up one finger. Wait.

Emma shut the phone and focused on the road for a time, grinding something so hard it clenched the muscles in her cheeks. Finally she said, "Jack Dauer is a menace who wields power like he's firing a Taser. He's also a lousy investigator. And he's got you in his sights."

Harry said, "You've given this a lot of thought."

"Jack Dauer is very territorial. He's got a rep for monopolizing all credit, all info. Everything he digs up goes straight to the feebs and nowhere else."

Harry settled down far enough to put his head on the headrest. The sunlight poured through the rear window, tightening his gaze to merry slits. "So you went to Interpol."

Storm demanded, "What is so *funny*?"

"Something's happened, hasn't it, Emma."

Emma merely pressed harder on the gas. Drilling them down I-295 to the Capital Beltway.

"She's had to declare where she stands," Harry said. "And she's come down on our side. Haven't you?"

"I've been ordered to arrest you both."

Storm demanded, "For what?"

Harry said, "It doesn't really matter all that much."

"Selim Arkut has been murdered. Dauer wants to hold you responsible." Emma gunned around a slow-moving truck. The tires' thunder almost smothered her words. "You've got to take the next flight out. Get good and lost before Dauer catches wind you're gone."

Storm said, "Jack Dauer is insane."

"You won't get any argument from me on that point." She fished in her pocket and came out with a card, which she gave to Storm. "That's got all my numbers: home and cell and Interpol. Tell me when you arrive. I'll try and catch up with you."

Her phone rang just as she pulled onto the Dulles Access Highway. She opened it and said, "Webb." She handed the phone over her shoulder. "Make yourself useful back there."

"Aye, aye, ma'am."

She passed back her purse. "Pen and paper in the side pocket. And wipe that grin off your face while you're at it."

"Sure thing."

Watching Harry scribble away, Storm said to Emma, "We made some interesting finds today."

"I need to hear all about it. But not now, okay? I'm scheduled to fly out with Hakim tomorrow, something he wants us to check out together. Soon as we're done, I'll try and catch up with you."

Harry slapped the phone shut and announced, "Air France to Paris. Three hours layover. Tickets to Istanbul and hotel info will be waiting for us at the information desk. Under the highly original name of Smith."

Emma entered the short-term lot and pulled into a yellow-banded emergency-vehicle space. "This is as far as I go. Get through passport control as fast as you can."

As they clustered by the trunk, Storm reached into her purse and came out with the velvet pouch. "Can you keep this safe for me?"

Harry said, "Good thinking."

"It's very valuable. You can look at it if you want. It's called a—"

"Right now, the name doesn't matter. I'll set up a lockbox at my bank, the Georgetown branch of Wells Fargo, and leave the key and instructions with the branch manager."

Emma stowed the triptych away, then looked Storm square in the eye and said, "Before we first met in your grandfather's shop, I already knew you were as genuine as they came."

Storm was still digesting that latest item when Harry stepped between them and said to Emma, "I never thought I'd ever say this to a cop. But you've just moved to the tippy top of my list."

Emma's face twisted as though she was trying to smile and keep from weeping at the same time. "Tough guys don't say tippy top."

"Maybe not." Harry gripped the woman and held her so tight Storm heard the breath whoosh from Emma's body. "They don't hug cops either."

He released her and turned to Storm. "Back in the game, lady. We're off and running strong."

TWENTY-THREE

HARRY BOARDED THE PLANE BEHIND Storm and trooped all the way to the last row, the only two seats they'd had available in moo class. Harry didn't mind. Especially not after Storm slipped into her seat, watched the other passengers settle, and shivered when the Air France flight attendant started his preflight announcements in French. She gave him a look that was part Sean in feminine guise and part wide-eyed wonder. Then she leaned over and kissed his cheek. Same place she'd smooched him back in her kitchen, just north of his jawline. She said, "I'm glad Sean chose you and I'm glad you came."

Harry didn't say anything, basically because he had no idea how to respond. Storm apparently didn't mind his silence. She settled back and was asleep before the plane left the ground.

Harry stared out the side window, his thoughts drifting with the clouds. He found himself recalling early days, back after his parents had died and he got to play shuffle ball inside the

Pennsylvania system. His last foster mom had been a woman named Agnes who'd packed as many as seven foster kids into her double-wide. Harry had always assumed the county kept her on their list because she never turned down a kid or kicked one out. To Agnes, they were all just so many sheep. Even the wolves.

Agnes's greatest talent was dispensing hopelessness. She stained her charges with small driblets of poison. Her favorite comment was, "You don't stand a chance."

Which was why, at fifteen, Harry had robbed a bank.

It wasn't like he'd spent months planning it out. Truth be told, Harry didn't even know what was going down until he was standing there on the sidewalk. He'd been chasing a buddy with this water pistol shaped like a .45 Magnum. At least, it looked enough like a Magnum that when he stuck it in the teller's face, her trembling fingers spilled as many bills on the floor as she managed to stuff into the Burger King bag.

Harry had watched enough television to know what came next. The bank had cameras in every corner, and naturally Harry hadn't thought to cover his face. He didn't even bother to run. Instead, he sauntered out the bank's front doors and slipped into a fancy steak house down the street, a place he knew from standing outside the kitchen and devouring odors of char-grilled steak and delivery truck fumes. Harry passed the maître d' a bunch of tens and asked for a table by the window. He feasted on shrimp cocktail and a fillet well done while cop cars screamed into flanking position and a train of uniforms ran in and out of the bank.

Even then, Harry was blessed with an overdose of dumb luck.

The cops never thought to check downtown's fanciest restaurant for a teenage bank robber. Harry tipped the waiter fifty bucks and asked if the place had a rear entrance.

He reached the end of the alley and realized he had no idea what came next. Then he spotted the doorman in the double-breasted coat and the matching top hat standing outside the city's top hotel.

In for a twenty, Harry thought to himself, and pushed through the revolving doors.

He managed to enjoy three nights of room service and Egyptian cotton sheets before the cops finally wised up. They actually laughed as they cuffed him.

The judge thought it was mildly hilarious as well. He rewarded Harry with three years in juvie.

Put a kid in Day-Glo orange and rubber sandals, and adults all see just one thing: trouble. By his eighteenth birthday, Harry had earned a rep for being less than a stellar example of the juvie system. He was given two choices: sign up for the men's dance school, or take a two-year stint in the state pen.

Harry went navy because the one jailer he almost trusted said they had the best food and the safest berths. Harry figured, how hard could it be?

The answer was, extremely. On account of two items Harry had failed to factor into the equation. The first was the Gulf War. The second was that Harry found himself volunteering for the Seals. A decision he still to this day cannot understand.

MIDWAY ACROSS THE ATLANTIC, THE whole deal became almost too much for Storm to hold inside. To release it fully meant giving in to a scream of pure pleasure. That was how good it felt.

Harry asked, "You cold?"

"No. I'm fine."

Harry reached under his seat, came up with a blanket, and pulled it from its plastic pouch. "Here, put this around you."

She had dozed through the flight's initial hours and woke not refreshed but rather able to balance the solemn lump of pain and loss from the funeral against the flight and the world and the mystery ahead. She let Harry slip the blanket around her. Like a brother might do for his little sister. Like they'd known each other for years.

"I've got something to show you." She reached for her purse. As she drew out her phone, her fingers touched the envelope holding Sean's letter.

For an instant, she felt the old man intensely close, like he had managed to squeeze into a seat between the two of them. Storm opened the phone, scrolled through the photographs, then swiveled the screen so that it faced Harry. "This is the chalice Sean left me."

Harry squinted over the screen. "Interesting shape. Looks old."

"It is."

"Shame about the lack of markings."

"There is one." Storm scrolled to the next photograph. "This was inscribed on the interior of the base."

Harry bent closer. "Are those letters?"

"Ancient Hebrew. It's what I was searching out in the Smithsonian. And this is what I found."

Harry studied the last photograph set into her phone's memory. "Looks like the same markings to me."

"Identical. This set was carved into the face of a royal coffin." She closed the phone and stowed it away. "The Smithsonian archeologist who discovered the coffin died while working on a dig they thought might be the lost city of Herodium. His assistant wrote up the preliminary report I read in the Smithsonian's journal. The dig was on the border of the Judean Desert, inside the West Bank. The archeologist was killed in one of the uprisings, which is why the Smithsonian blocked the assistant from returning and finishing their work.

Herod the Great basically built Herodium City from scratch."

Harry took two waters from a passing flight attendant and handed one over. "This is the same king who rebuilt the Second Temple."

"Exactly. The markings you just saw are the name 'Herod,' carved into a sarcophagus of pink Jerusalem limestone. The name was surrounded by an expertly carved floral motif. Exactly what you'd expect to see on a king's coffin."

"And the chalice?"

"I've been examining the drawing of the arch that doesn't exist. I've found three chalices."

"Show me."

She reopened her phone and found the picture. Harry leaned in so close the screen's illumination carved his face into a craven image. His face was not so much grim as hungry. "Herod didn't rebuild the temple out of the goodness of his heart. He was a cruel despot, loathed by his own people. Herod was obsessed with greatness. He was just the sort of man who would carve his name inside a temple chalice. Like donors putting a plaque on the wall of a church to make sure everybody knows about their donation."

Harry shut the phone. Handed it back. Took a long pull from his water.

"This is real, Harry."

"I'm not doubting that for a second. But like I told you, people have hunted the Second Temple treasures for five hundred years. Longer. And salvagers have scoured the Med for centuries, hunting the headland carved into your triptych. If that design represented anything along the Cypriot coast, it'd have been found a long time ago."

"There were earthquakes. Morgenthal just said the capital was destroyed by one—what was it called?"

"Salamis."

"Couldn't these promontories have been demolished by a big quake?"

In reply, Harry gave her the sort of grin that would have worried her on another man. "This is some high, isn't it."

"You're saying I could be right?"

"Hey, I'm just your basic treasure dog. I've bet my chips on a lot less than this."

TWENTY-FOUR

RICHARD ELLIS HAD LONG CONSIDERED himself a pastor without a home. Coming as it did from the number-two guy at the biggest church in one of America's richest cities, some people might have called that a little twisted. But working this place was sort of like living inside a diamond-studded cocoon. Richard had never been comfortable with the distance wealth put between himself and real life. Which was why he was happy staying relegated to the church's basement operations. And also why he had been so drawn to Sean Syrrell. The man had been as avaricious as a pirate.

Sean had never been held by the trappings of wealth. For Sean, money was just part of what it took to obtain the next prize. Given his surroundings, Richard had considered this a healthy disregard. He had found himself willing to overlook the man's shortcomings, which in Sean's case would have filled the National Archives. Memories of the man still brought him to a boil. Even though his heart limped from the loss.

Richard was the last to leave the church's activity building. He could have let the custodian lock up the place. But it was as good an excuse as any to hold back and let the crowds swirl away, chattering as they did over his latest gaffe. Tonight had supposedly been his night off, but the AA leader had phoned in sick. Which meant that Richard had been there to greet a reformed alcoholic who had arrived completely smashed. Richard's tirade had drawn an audience from two floors up. The man had departed a good deal more sober than he had arrived.

Richard locked the doors and turned toward the night. He was becoming more angry more often these days. It happened every spring around this time, in the run-up to the anniversary of his wife's death. He had met Sean for the first time this very same week. Sean had snapped at him on the way out of church and Richard had blasted back. Then he'd been forced to explain why. Every spring that followed, Sean had made it a point to come down and treat Richard to a fine meal. Which made for another reason he missed the most irritating man Richard had ever known.

Then he saw the shadow flitter between the palms.

He didn't know who the shadow belonged to and he didn't care. What he did know was that the local newspaper was still headlining Palm Beach's version of the OK Corral. Richard had seen enough of the city's underbelly to have a healthy respect for shadows that flittered. He ran.

Richard's passion was long-distance running. He had done the Boston Marathon five times, and twice finished within an hour of the leader. Which was why, when he dropped his briefcase and jinked right before heading back across the lot, he thought if he could just make the front lawn he'd be safe. Few people could catch him in open-field running.

He almost made it. The oleander border that would have granted him shadows of his own was three paces away when the night became a fist and slammed him hard from behind.

Only after he hit the earth did he realize he had also heard a bang.

He fell on his side. It was an immensely uncomfortable position. Almost as uncomfortable as his inability to draw a decent breath.

The shadows did not fully coalesce. Instead, the

moon overhead simply vanished, and in its place came a shape. Small and fast and strong. Richard felt hands grip his jacket and flip him onto his back. Which was the first time he actually felt pain.

A dark voice spoke with an accent so strong Richard could not make out the words. Not that it mattered.

Hands lifted and shook him hard enough for the pain to make him focus. The voice spoke more slowly, spacing out the words. "The woman Syrrell. Where has she gone?"

Richard blinked. Of course the night spoke with an uncommon accent. It made all the sense in the world.

The man shook him again. But this time the pain could not reach him. To his right he had noticed another change to the gathering night. One that thrilled him so much he let go of the pain and everything else that held him down.

He knew with a certainty beyond all his dimming senses that his wife was standing and waiting for him.

He was shaken again. Hard. Richard knew this only because what was left of his vision passed through more tremors. He felt nothing at all.

He opened his mouth and tried to say, *Into your hands I commend my spirit.* Perhaps he actually spoke the words. It no longer mattered. Nothing earthly did.

TWENTY-FIVE

STORM WOKE TO THE SOUND of throbbing. She opened her eyes to brilliant sunlight. The throbbing noise came from just outside her windows. A boat passed by, momentarily cutting off the sunlight. Storm swung her feet to the floor and rubbed her eyes. The boat passed. Sunlight sparkled off the water that began just beyond her hotel windows. She padded to the bathroom, passing beneath a domed ceiling. She washed her face and returned to the bedroom. The water and the sunlight and the boats were all still there.

She picked up the phone and hit O. A voice came on and said, "*Effindim.*"

She stared out the window at another passing boat. "Harry Bennett's room."

A pause, then, "Please?"

She remembered then. "Sorry. Mr. Smith."

The line clicked, the phone rang, and Harry picked up like his hand was poised over the phone.

"We're really here, aren't we."

"How did you sleep?"

"So well I don't know what day it is."

"You've been out almost fourteen hours."

They had arrived at Charles de Gaulle Airport just after eleven in the morning. As promised, a packet had been awaiting them at the Air France information desk. In it were two economy class tickets to Istanbul and the name of a hotel. Harry had noticed her expression and asked what was the matter.

Storm had replied, "The tickets are one-way."

Harry had put it down as bureaucratic penny-pinching. But as Storm dressed, she found herself recalling that moment, and the sensation of holding a pass to some new and unnamed destiny from which there was no return.

After breakfast they walked down to the village harbor and boarded the ferry to central Istanbul. Storm sat on one of five long benches that ran the length of the boat's upper deck. The wind was both hot from the sun and chilled by the water. Harry stood by the bow reading a newspaper, swaying easily as a passing trawler rocked their ferry, totally in his element. Dark eyes observed her every move, but she did not feel threatened. A pair of hawkers plied the ferry passengers with tulip glasses of tea and sweetmeats. Their hotel gleamed on the retreating shore, a miniature palace built by an eighteenth-century emir. Their ferry passed beneath the first bridge spanning from the hills of Europe to the hills of Asia, a simple link that defied three thousand years of war and distrust and lies. Storm wrapped her arms about her middle and whispered a name to herself, trying to make it real.

Istanbul.

● ● ●

THE FERRY ROUNDED SERAGLIO POINT and entered the Golden Horn, an inlet of the Bosphorous Sea that divided Istanbul and formed a natural harbor at the city's heart. Harry folded the *International Herald Tribune* and stowed it in his pocket. An article about North Cyprus had caught his eye, one of those odd little human-interest items that might pay off down the line.

Harry gripped the railing as the boat thrummed into reverse and backwash rocked the boat. They were surrounded by minarets and bridges and a constant rush of people and vehicles. Harry had been to Istanbul times beyond count. Everybody traveling beyond the borders of safety needed a haven, a place to recoup and refit. Istanbul was perfect. The city offered everything, if you knew where to look and had cash at the ready. Danger was a natural part of this place, a heady spirit over-laid on the sunlit day.

The city had changed a lot since his last visit, and not changed at all. A ban on donkey carts meant traffic moved faster along narrow streets originally designed for Roman soldiers. Harry spotted a lot more women decked out in black body veils. Turkey's current government was drawn from the religious right, the first since Ataturk had wrested Turkey from the disinte-grating Ottoman rule and founded the Middle East's strongest democracy. The Islamists drew much of their support from the nation's poor. Harry had heard they offered Istanbul widows a small stipend to don these head-to-toe black tents. The result was a subtle threat to the city's more cultured women and their singular independence.

He skirted the edge of the quayside market, the stalls stinking of smoked fish and mussels in buckets of seawater. Harry liked how Storm didn't need to be told to stick close. They passed the first of the bridges crossing the Golden Horn, where fishing poles bobbed like a forest of willows in the sultry breeze. He headed away from the water, taking the pedestrian bridge across ten lanes of Oriental mayhem. Harry stopped in front of the train station, built as a mock pasha's palace in Constantinople's heyday.

Harry said, "The bazaar's only a mile away, but it's all uphill. On the other hand, the taxis are hot and they don't have AC."

She took a double lock on his left hand. "Let's walk."

"I need to be free to move fast. You know. In case."

She dropped his hand. "Sorry."

"But when this is over, you want to resume that position, you absolutely have my permission."

Storm realized he was joking and produced a tiny smile. "I won't let you down, Harry."

"Girl, if there is one thing I'm sure of, it's that. Okay, let's move out."

The street they took was steep enough for the sidewalk to be fashioned as broad steps. Tiny shops selling everything from hardware to wedding dresses spread their wares onto the crumbling stone. Pedestrians either picked their way between the hawkers or joined the traffic. A dim haze clung to the city's numerous hills. The air was rich with the odors of roasting lamb and diesel and charcoal and mountains of spices and baking bread. To their left rose the walls of Suleiman the Magnificent's palace. A muezzin called the midmorning prayer, his sonorous moan taken up by a hundred other amplified voices. The city took little notice, just one more item amid the daily din.

He took Storm through the Covered Bazaar, mostly so he could watch her reaction. The gold quarter sparkled in the cool air, every window an Aladdin's cave. The floors were ancient mosaic, the high ceiling a series of ribbed domes. The branching avenues were tunnels filled with colors and hawkers who chanted their constant welcome. The crowd was thick but fluid. They made good time.

They emerged by the eastern gate, traversed the tree-lined path, and entered the pedestrian district. The stores were large and their displays elegant. The shoppers were drawn from the Turkish elite. They stopped before a window holding a silk carpet twenty-five feet wide, the color of caramel smoke. Spotlights shimmered upon solid gold threads. A sign at the base said the carpet had been a gift from Suleiman the Magnificent to the Egyptian emir.

The air-conditioned interior was a series of interconnecting rooms, partitioned by single granite steps and veils of interlocking spotlights. Storm took her time inspecting the wares on display, until a stylish woman approached and asked if she could be of service.

"I'm here to see Mehmet Ozman."

The woman blinked. "But Mr. Mehmet is not here."

"Could you tell me where we could find him? Mr. Ozman was probably expecting my grandfather, but he . . ." She stopped because the woman had vanished. She turned to Harry in confusion. Harry shrugged.

The saleswoman returned, this time led by a slender young man with spiked hair, a black stovepipe suit, and an attitude that angled his chin toward the ceiling. "Yes, you are here wanting something?"

"My name is Storm Syrrell. My grandfather—"

"Is dead." He wore a dress shirt minus cuff links so that the cuffs flopped when he waved his arm. "Yes. Of course we know all this."

"I'm sorry, you are—"

"Rolfy Ozman. This is my store now."

"Your father has—"

"Uncle. My uncle. He is a sick old man. You have business, perhaps?"

"Your uncle and my grandfather did business together for many years."

"This is important to me?" The delicate chin lifted higher still. "So now you come here why, maybe you are looking for a loan?"

"No, of course not. I'd just like to ask—"

"You want I should call the police?"

Harry said, "No cops."

"Listen to your smart friend. Go back to America and take your questions with you."

"My grandfather and your uncle were friends."

"I don't care. It is over. Phht. Yesterday's news. Like your company, yes? Go see the ruins of Istanbul. You will find so many ruins. You will feel at home. Now good-bye."

Storm held her ground. "Your uncle may know something vital about how Sean—"

"Syrrell's is finished, yes? Doors closed, so sorry. You have no business, nothing to sell. I have nothing here for people with no money. This is a real gallery. We have real clients." He wheeled about, tossing his cuff over his shoulder. "No information for beggars here. Bye-bye."

STORM APPEARED TO STROLL AS they left the elegant walking district and entered the lower-priced sprawl stretching from the hilltop to the Bosphorus. Salesmen in front of carpet stores and jewelry shops beckoned with the same chorus: Pretty lady, come see, we have beautiful things,

251

pretty lady, for you special price. Storm gave no sign she heard any of it. Harry walked a half pace behind her, waiting for the explosion.

When she reached a T-junction, she stopped. A bus smoked past, inches from her nose. Storm didn't blink.

Harry gripped her arm. "What say we back up a pace and maybe find a little shade for that over-heated brain of yours."

She allowed herself to be pulled over in front of a pastry shop. "The nephew didn't need to speak with us like that."

"No, Storm. He didn't."

"We've been doing business with his company for years."

Harry tasted the air, found no hint of rage. "Maybe he's just trying to put the past behind him."

"So he shows us the door. Why be angry?"

"So maybe he's afraid."

"Of what? He said it himself. Syrrell's is fin-ished."

"I thought you'd be furious."

"We don't have time for that." She snapped into focus. "Call Emma. Tell her what happened. See if her contacts at Interpol can locate the uncle."

TWENTY-SIX

EMMA WEBB SNAPPED HER PHONE shut and stowed it in her purse. She pressed her sunglasses tighter against the bridge of her nose. Her hand slipped down to apply thumb and forefinger to the corners of her mouth, holding tight until she was certain the smile was well hidden. The one that had almost erupted into laughter while Harry was still on the phone. She could do nothing about the funny little quivers disturbing the space below her rib cage. It had to be jet lag.

Emma crossed the Nice airport arrivals hall, back to where Hakim stood speaking in fluent French with a local police officer. He asked, "Trouble?"

"Harry and Storm need to locate somebody. Storm thinks it could be critical."

Hakim spoke to the policeman, who sketched a tight bow in Emma's direction and backed off. Emma related what Harry had told her. Most of it, anyway.

Hakim's reply was instantaneous. "They are blown."

"Harry wonders if maybe the guy was just trying to avoid paying any debts his uncle might have racked up with Syrrell's. Storm thinks otherwise."

"The woman is correct." Hakim's tone brooked no doubt. "Business at this level is done with courtesy. Particularly in that region. Even enemies are treated with respect. Especially in public. Honor is everything. They have done business before, yes?"

"With the uncle, not the nephew."

Hakim waved that aside as unimportant. "More is at work here than a whiff of former obligations. I will inform our driver that departure must wait until I speak with Istanbul. Would you be so kind as to buy me a water for the journey?"

"Sure thing." Emma walked to the café and ordered a double espresso and two bottles of water. The Nice airport was a palace of light and gentle French chatter. Even the flight announcements sounded enchanting. Emma had never been anywhere in France outside of Paris. Before this morning, visiting the Côte d'Azur had been just another item on the long list headed "Sometime." As in, one day she would get around to something more than work.

Standing in a golden French midmorning, staring out forty-foot windows at palms and Mercedes taxis and a world from her dreams, probably had a little to do with why she thought again of Harry Bennett and let her smile slip out.

The waiter set her coffee on the bar and must have thought the smile was for him. He gave her liquid French eyes and scoped her from bar to hairline and back. Emma had known medical exams that were less thorough. The bartender said,

"You wish to see the Riviera with me? I can show you many secret things."

"Hey, that's a super offer and I'm really tempted, but I'm here to do business with those police officers over by the door. You understand police?"

The waiter sniffed an extremely Gallic response and flipped the dish towel off his shoulder to slap the espresso machine.

"Yeah, that's what I thought." Emma picked up the thimble-sized cup, turned her back to the bar, and recalled the conversation with Harry Bennett.

After passing on news of the confrontation and Storm's request, Harry had finished with "You really in Monte Carlo?"

"Outskirts. Hakim thinks we might have found something important, don't ask me what."

Harry had made a sound intensely like a growl. "Should I be jealous?"

"Excuse me?"

"Here I was, thinking maybe, I don't know . . ."

Emma astonished herself, how much she wanted to have him finish that thought. When he remained silent, she prodded, "This from the man holding hands with the lollipop in Istanbul."

"Number one, Storm is no lollipop. Number two, old Harry's got his eye on bigger game."

"Thanks a lot. Give me a second to decide which I like less, being big, or being a game."

"I didn't mean, big as in hefty."

"Wait, I got it. You meant tough. As in, old shoe leather."

"You're saying I should stop while I'm in reverse."

"Before you drive straight off that cliff behind you."

"I'm a little out of practice."

She had clenched her teeth to hold in a retort about Harry's jail time. When she remained silent, he asked, "Maybe you'll give me a chance to polish my act?"

"In your dreams, sailor."

"Please tell me that's just a cop's way of saying yes."

Emma broke all her own rules. She said what she thought, using the low voice she'd almost forgotten about. "You know what? I'd really like for us to find some time together."

Harry gave that a respectful beat, then said, "This place is way too hot to be giving me a case of the shivers."

Which was sort of funny, since she had been thinking the exact same thing.

THE RENAULT WAITING FOR THEM at curbside could only have been an unmarked cop car. The blue was a shade that nobody except a government official would ever dream of buying. The driver ushered them both into the rear seat, started his supercharged motor, and zoomed away. Hakim addressed the driver in French, then said to Emma, "We should be there in just under an hour."

"Where are we headed?"

"Grasse. A lovely city. Heart of the perfume industry. Alas, we shall have no chance to view the valleys of lavender and thyme. Our destination is far less scenic."

"Your French is fluent?"

"French, Arabic, English, a Lebanese hill dialect my mother made me learn. I loathed it. A barbaric tongue."

It was the most he had ever spoken of himself. "You're Syrian, right?"

"My father. So officially, yes, though I only lived there two years. My mother is Marionite. You have heard of this perhaps?"

"The name, sure."

"Marionites were some of the earliest Christians. A few remain as hill tribes above the Bekaa Valley. Our territory once extended as far south as the Golan Heights. Now we are dispersed all over the world. My mother's parents worked in Beirut when the Lebanese civil war broke out. They died in the early fighting."

"I'm so sorry."

"Thank you. My mother was sent to live with relatives in Damascus. She fell in love with a Syrian Muslim. You must understand, the Syrians were deeply involved in the same civil war that had killed my grandparents. My mother's act was unthinkable. She was banished from her family. My parents lived in Damascus for a time, with my father's family. But this too was difficult, so they fled, first to France and then to Canada. Now they are in Jordan." Hakim flattened his moustache. "It is a familiar story in the Middle East. Our Bedu past breeds a common restlessness. We have always been migrants."

His story was fascinating enough to take her mind off the road, at least until a tight curve jammed her into Hakim's side. "And I thought I was an aggressive driver."

"He is probably showing off."

"Tell him it's a wasted effort."

"He is French. He would only drive faster. You have been to France before?"

"Paris. As a student."

He gave an airy wave to the yawning drop and the Mediterranean beyond. "This road is known as the Corniche. It was originally laid by the Romans, who used Nice as one of their ports. Here the Alps begin very close to the sea. We are going to a natural plateau region. Plenty of sunshine, a long growing season, water pouring off the mountains beyond, small tight valleys that form natural hothouses for growing flowers and herbs that create the aromas to make a woman more alluring."

Emma spotted the driver giving her a tight grin through the rearview mirror. "Keep your eyes on the road, bub."

"He claims not to speak English. Which may mean he speaks it perfectly, but was ordered simply to repeat back to his superiors whatever we say."

"I thought we were on the same side."

"Like our esteemed allies in Washington, yes?" Hakim slipped a pair of sunglasses from his pocket. "We are invited here because the local authorities need something. What exactly, I am not sure."

They powered through countless switchbacks in tightly controlled four-wheeled skids. The road had no barrier between them and the abyss except occasional painted stone markers.

Hakim said, "After the second World War, international conventions and public shaming forced the French to close their South American penal colonies. They reopened a prison originally built by the Romans as a fortress."

They turned off the main road, onto a narrow lane the color of the surrounding ochre hills. The driver whipped around a turn and the world dropped away. Thirty miles to the south, the Mediterranean sparkled and beckoned, bordered by a necklace of beaches and seaside towns and verdant green hills. Their road, carved from a cliff face, swept them away from the sea and into a vista of dry alpine peaks. The rising heat separated the mountains from the earth, such that they rested upon clouds of shimmering dust, their summits melting into the chalk blue Provençal sky.

Hakim appeared as unconcerned with the view as with their speed. "The practice of tattooing prison rage has been imported from America. But here it is done with French flair. Each prison has its own signature. The symbol for our destination is a burning rose. The next valley north is used for growing wild roses. I am told you can smell their fragrance when the wind is right."

A final turn revealed an earthen bridge set upon a ridgeline. The road narrowed further, to where the tires seemed ready to fall away on either side. At the far end, a lone mountain had been flattened, as though mashed flat with a giant's hand. Upon it was set a fortress from beyond time.

Even Hakim slid forward in his seat for a clearer view. "Legend has it that eight thousand Roman slaves lost their lives levelling that peak and building this road."

The prison's outer walls were built of dry cut stone. Emma found it impossible to tell where the old stone ended and the new stone began. The yellow dust turned every surface the same pale and hopeless shade.

Hakim said, "The prisoners call this place *La Parfumerie*. The perfume factory."

The driver radioed ahead. A claxon sounded from the fortress wall and massive steel doors slid back. They entered a confine beneath dual guard towers. The driver pulled into a parking space and pointed them toward a door. As Emma rose from the car, he winked at her and said, "Have a nice day."

THEY PASSED THROUGH TWO SECURITY portals and entered the prison's admin wing. Guards coming off duty barked their words, their faces taut. A subaltern approached, saluted smartly, and addressed Hakim in rapid-fire French. They were led to a narrow antechamber between the main guardroom and the commandant's office. All the guards she could see wore uniforms of police blue cut in a distinct military style, with caps fitted into their shoulder lapels, cloth badges of rank, and then trouser legs tucked into polished leather boots. Emma stepped to the window as Hakim's phone rang. The view was of hills baking under a porcelain sky.

Hakim shut his phone, joined her at the window, and handed Emma a slip of paper. "Tell them that Mehmut Ozman can be found at this place now."

She read, "Ciragan Palace."

"Harry Bennett has been in Istanbul before?"

Emma reached for her phone. "That's the impression I have."

"He will know this place. Tell them to hurry."

She had time for a few terse words with Harry before the door opened. A battle-hardened officer entered the room, lantern-jawed, grey hair cut to nubs, eyes of cold smoke. He inspected them both, then spoke in French. Hakim responded. The officer had a remarkably soft voice, toneless and flat. Behind them, the guardroom banter had vanished.

Hakim said, "Colonel Bretin speaks some English, but would prefer that I translate."

"I can wait here if you like."

The colonel addressed her directly, his accent so thick it shellacked the words. "You have seen this man?"

"For a millisecond only. There and gone in a flash."

The colonel's implacable gaze swiveled to Hakim, who translated. Emma went on, "But I've interviewed the eyewitness to one murder in London and two further attempts in Florida. That is, assuming your guy is our guy."

When Bretin reached out his hand, the subaltern had the file ready. He checked the contents, then handed Emma the folder.

One look at the mug shots was enough. "That's him."

Bretin asked directly, "You are certain?"

"No question. Who is he?"

"Yes. That is what we also wish to know." The colonel indicated the door. "Please. Come."

They were joined by two guards who carried long batons at the ready. They descended stone stairs, passed through another checkpoint, and were buzzed into the prison yard.

The cells had been built up the interior fortress walls, five stories of rough stone and bars. The cells faced inward, overlooking a broad exercise yard. The yard was rimmed by guard towers with downward-slanted mirrored windows. A wedge had been cut from the interior square by walls of steel mesh. The colonel led them across the main yard to a metal door. At their approach a claxon sounded and the door ground open. They entered the miniature yard, tighter than the walls were high. The heat was as vicious as the stench. The only sound was the door grinding shut behind them.

The colonel's voice matched the prison's atmosphere, all force and emotion concealed beneath a brutal exterior. He stood to Emma's left, Hakim to her right. The effect was a sibilant stereo. Bretin pointed to a narrow steel-plated door and spoke. Hakim translated, "This leads to the prison's oldest section, known as *Les Bains*. The narrow pits were once used as baths by the Roman soldiers. Now they are the punishment block. Do you wish to see inside?"

"Not a chance."

"The exterior wall faces east by south. In the summer, inmates must hunch away from that wall because the stones will blister the skin. They stay there twenty-three and a half hours each day, panting like dogs and dreaming of the Côte d'Azur, where people sit in umbrella-shaded cafés and watch the naked bodies glisten upon the beaches."

Emma stepped back to where a steel pillar offered a narrow slit of shade. "Is there a point to this?"

The colonel refused to be hurried. "At midafternoon a special claxon sounds. Every prisoner who has been inside *Les Bains* freezes for a moment. These prisoners know what it means to wait in desperation for that sound. They are granted thirty minutes in this exercise yard. There is no light inside *Les Bains*. There is no air. In the high summer, even the hardest prisoners are known to weep aloud as they are dragged inside."

The colonel marched to the precise center of the courtyard. He stood at attention, defying the sun and the heat. The yard was so silent his soft voice carried perfectly. "On this particular day, there were only two prisoners in *Les Bains*. One had murdered three generations of his family. He is a huge man and brutalizes the other prisoners. The other is your man." The colonel pointed to the corner by the fortress wall. "When the prisoners are brought out, the murderer crouches there. The afternoon shadows block that corner. The mass murderer does not move. Do you understand?"

"He was terrified of the little guy."

"This is true of all the prisoners. Your man was known here as the Asp, after the only reptile who kills without warning and for pleasure. You must

264

understand, this prison is intended only for the most dangerous criminals in France. Your man should not have been here at all. An eight-year sentence for two counts of involuntary manslaughter. His car struck another vehicle carrying a mother and daughter, pushing them over a cliff. He had an alcohol blood level that was only three points above the legal limit. He was originally assigned to a low-security prison outside Carmague. But he was sent here after murdering three inmates."

Emma said, "Almost like he planned it."

The colonel nodded, perhaps in approval. "He murdered another two here last month. A mistral blew that day. The mistral blows high and hot off the Sahara. It sucks the moisture from the body. The noise of it rushing through these tight valleys is like a huge drum beating constantly. A helicopter blasted up from the valley floor. Its approach was masked by the wind. The chopper angled its rotations so that dust clouds rose in the whirlwind. A rope dropped. Your man climbed into the loop. Everything happened so fast, it took a moment for the guards to react. Finally my men fired, but the chopper was heavily armored. Your man was protected from sight by the dust. The chopper rose far enough to lift him over the walls. Then it dropped. Down and down to the valley floor. We are fairly certain they escaped on motorcycles, your man and the two pilots."

"We've tied him to a motorcycle theft and murder in Florida."

"So." He waved a hand. The same claxon sounded, the door ground back open. Emma told herself there was no logical reason why air was easier to find on this side of the wire-mesh wall.

They crossed the baking yard, passed through the security door, and climbed the guardroom stairs. The subaltern served coffee in a conference room as the commandant passed out two copies of the file. "The helicopter was stolen from a local construction company and found abandoned on the valley floor." The colonel motioned for them to turn the page. Hakim translated as he read, "An arrest record for one Leon Cresceau, Romanian. Occupation given as professional bodyguard. Unemployed at the time of his arrest."

The commandant said through Hakim, "Just before he arrived here, we finally heard back from the Romanian authorities. Leon Cresceau does not exist."

Emma asked, "You checked his prints?"

"He does not exist on any system."

"So we have no leads on a guy with no name," Emma said. "Excuse me for asking, but why are we here?"

The commandant spoke, and for the first time Hakim smiled. *"C'est vrai?"*

"What is it?"

"It appears the colonel has contacted the *avocat*

266

who represented Leon in the manslaughter trial. The colonel might have insinuated that Leon was back in custody and asking for him."

"Leon's attorney is here?"

"In the conference room next door." Hakim rose to his feet. "The colonel is hoping that we might be able to apply pressure."

TWENTY-SEVEN

THE CIRAGAN PALACE WAS A combination of historical grandeur and modern money. The former emir's palace had been extended along the Bosphorus shoreline and now housed a five-star hotel run by the Kempinski Group. A majordomo led them along the lavish forecourt and out onto the patio. "You say Monsieur Ozman is expecting you?"

"Is there a problem?"

"The monsieur, he is a favorite guest. But he never receives anyone." The majordomo wore a summer-weight tux and a pasha's authority. He pointed them to a halt. "You will please to wait here."

He strode beneath the canvas tent covering the indoor-outdoor patio to a table overlooking the pool and the sea. He bowed and spoke to the lone gentleman seated by the railing. The old man's eyes were hidden behind sunglasses and he might well have been asleep. The majordomo spoke a second time. The old man shifted in surprise. The majordomo maintained his bow as he pointed back toward them. The old man peered at them so long Storm feared he was going to order them away.

Instead, the old man extended his arm for the majordomo to help him to his feet. He fumbled slightly, reaching for the cane that the majordomo handed him. With the cane on one side and the majordomo on the other, he remained steeply bent and twisted slightly to one side. Even so, his smile was warm and his voice warmer as Storm approached his table. "There is no question in my mind who you must be."

"Mr. Ozman?"

"Please, please. The child of my dear friend Sean Syrrell must call me Mehmet."

MEHMET OZMAN WAS A COURTLY gentleman even when cloaked in the shadows of mourning. He refused to discuss business until they had been served a lavish *mezze,* a Turkish delight of minia-ture delicacies—smoked salmon wrapped about feta cheese, fresh grilled artichoke hearts, mousse of local snapper, stuffed grape leaves, flakes of roasted lamb, marinated and roasted chicken, hot flatbread, a salad of mint and shallots and coriander, on and on it came until there was no room on the table and more plates were deposited on a trolley parked between Storm and Harry. Tea was served in Limoges china cups. Three servants hovered in constant expectation. Every time she finished one miniature portion, they swept away her plate and brought another. When she finally refused anything more, Mehmet said, "Sean called me to say you might be in touch. I told him sadly there was nothing an old man like myself could offer the young."

"Your nephew ordered me not to make contact."

"Rolfy is overly protective. He fears for my heart. I have little to do with people these days. I wake, I come here, I sit while the hours pass, I go home. Just another day lost of meaning, just another lonely old man."

Storm said, "I'm here because we think, well, we're pretty certain, that Sean was murdered."

An unseen string pulled his hand up, and then dropped it. His ability to give more of a response had been robbed from him.

"But Sean was your friend."

"Young lady, I understand the destruction of loss. I appreciate your desire to search and to understand. I know there are whispers in the night that eat away your soul. I pray you are able to find a life again."

Jet lag and regret formed a force as oppressive as the day's heat. Storm feared the visit was wasted effort. But she had to try. "Could I please ask what happened to you?"

"Of course I don't mind telling. Why should I? I live with it all the time." He made an ancient's attempt at pouring tea, and nodded acceptance when Storm took the pot from him. "We were in France on vacation. Côte d'Azur. My daughter's favorite place in the entire world. I left them to visit a new client in Paris. A major dealer seeking to open ties with Istanbul. Yves Boucaud." He lifted his grief-ravaged face and pleaded with Storm. "How could I have refused?"

Storm recognized the man's need for forgiveness, even from a stranger. "I would have gone."

"Would you?"

"Definitely. It's who we are."

"Your grandfather said the same."

"What happened?"

"An accident. A drunk driver. A professional bodyguard, of all people. Someone who should have known better. My wife's car went off a cliff, into a ravine. They say there was no pain. At least for my darling wife and daughter, there was no pain."

"So you gave the company to your nephew."

"I could not go on. It was my work that killed them."

"That is not true." But the gloom was too deafening for the old man to pay any attention to such comments. Storm changed the subject. "Did my grandfather ask you about all this?"

"Of course. I could refuse him nothing. He has been my friend since the very early days. A trusted ally."

Storm took a breath. "I am sorry. I know I don't have any right to ask you this. All I know is, my grandfather considered something about this connection important enough to plan a visit to Istanbul. I'd appreciate any details you could possibly share."

"Sean said nothing to me about traveling here himself. Only that you might come." A pause, then, "He asked me about Leon."

"Excuse me?"

"The bodyguard. The destroyer of lives. I forget his last name. He was Romanian."

Storm heard Harry's chair scrape across the marble portico as he drew himself closer. She asked, "You saw him?"

"Of course. How could I not attend the trial? He was drunk. Did I already say that? The judge sentenced him to eight years. Two counts of manslaughter. Of course, it was three counts, but what was I to say?"

"What did he look like?"

"He is still imprisoned in France. Does it matter so much?"

"Maybe. It could matter a lot."

"Leon was a wraith. An insignificant phantom. You could look at him for hours and not see him. He could make himself so small, so . . ."

"Like a silent little tan rodent."

The old man stared at Harry. "But how could you know such a thing?"

271

"Right now, we're just guessing." Storm was already rising to her feet. "If we discover something definite, you'll be the first to know. You have my word on it."

THE ADVOCATE WAS A PRECISE gentleman with a distinctly patrician air. He was seated at a narrow metal table in a windowless chamber reserved for meetings between lawyers and prisoners. The advocate blinked as the three of them filed into the room, followed by a massive guard who shut and locked the door, then filled the doorway with his bulk. Emma took position next to the colonel against the rear wall. The lawyer asked the colonel a question.

Hakim slipped into the chair opposite the advocate and translated, "Monsieur Monnier asks if he is under arrest."

"Not whether his client is joining us," Emma said. "Interesting."

The lawyer switched to perfect if heavily accented English. "I did not ask, mademoiselle, because your little parade suggests my client has not been, in fact, recaptured at all." He extended a hand, revealing a gold Cartier watch and matching cuff link. "May I see your IDs?"

When Hakim and Emma handed them over, he smiled. "I must say, Mademoiselle Webb, Interpol is recruiting from a far more refined stable these days."

Emma despised him already. "I am seconded from American intelligence."

"Are you indeed. One obviously adept at harassing innocent people. Now if you'll excuse me, this little charade has pulled me from some very pressing issues. I have real clients with real needs."

Hakim said, "Not just yet."

"Pardon me?"

"We require answers to a few questions."

Emma slipped to the corner across from the door. She wanted to observe Hakim in action. He wore another tailored jacket, this one the color of sand. His tie was woven silk, a few shades darker than his jacket. Hakim's movements were economical, sparse, drawn from a well so deep he remained unaffected by the room and the lawyer's disdain.

Across from him, the lawyer was all affected motion. He shot his cuffs, adjusted his tie, smoothed a lapel. Even clearing his throat held the theatrical quality of standing before a jury. The lawyer replied, "That is quite impossible."

"One or two questions only."

"Out of the question. How dare you even propose such a thing."

"The matters are of crucial importance."

"You are suggesting I break the law, not to mention my code of professional ethics?" The advocate had the coloring of a silver fox, one dressed by Lanvin. "I regret I have no choice but to inform your superiors. Who shall condemn you most severely."

"Even so, I must request your assistance."

The language was far more refined than Emma was used to, the mannerisms much more genteel. But the scene played out the same. An officer braced, an attorney blustered and played the law like his own personal violin. Emma decided she preferred the American way—less foppishness, more volume.

The lawyer set both hands upon the table. "I am leaving."

"I regret, sir, that you are not."

This time the anger was real. "Your actions are scandalous!"

"You are being held on the prevention of terrorism acts. They were instituted by President de Gaulle during the Algerian crisis. As they have been in effect for more than sixty years, you are no doubt aware of what happens now. A magistrate will be called in. You will be formally arraigned. Your rights are hereby suspended."

"You are spinning absurdities! I defended a client on involuntary manslaughter charges!"

"Who escaped from this very prison, and has since been involved in murders both in England and the United States."

"Even if true, which I doubt, this has nothing to do with me."

Hakim leaned back in his seat. "You are a distinguished member of your profession. As you yourself said, you have any number of clients. It is therefore very interesting that you would choose to represent an unemployed immigrant who clearly had no way to cover your expenses. And did so in a court several hundred kilometers from your own city."

The attorney removed an ironed white handkerchief from his lapel pocket. "It was at the behest of a valued client."

"I need that client's name."

The attorney dabbed at the perspiration on his forehead. "Impossible."

"Then this has become a matter of criminal complicity. You will be detained here while extradition papers are prepared. This being a case of such high priority, your transfer to the American prison system will be by government jet."

The lawyer went utterly still.

"The jet will be supplied by a branch of the American government represented by this agent, who has taken considerable offense to your comment about stables. As, sir, did I. Your route to the American federal prison will be somewhat circuitous." Hakim swiveled in his chair. "Did I say that correctly, circuitous?"

Emma said, "Works for me."

"I have no direct experience in these matters, sir. But I understand the stopovers are in places that will make this prison seem like the Hotel du Cap." He paused, then, "A name, good sir. Tell us who paid for your defense of this assassin, and we will let you go."

AFTER ANOTHER FRUITLESS TWO HOURS, the colonel walked them personally back to the car baking in the forecourt. He spoke to Hakim, who translated, "He can only hold the advocate for thirty-six hours. The magistrate will arrive on schedule, establish that the advocate was within his rights to refuse our request, and that our evidence is not strong enough to extradite. I fear the colonel may be formally rebuked, but I hope that by claiming he acted upon my orders, he will not be brought up on charges."

Emma offered the commandant her hand. "Sorry we couldn't be of help, sir. In any case, I owe you. Big time."

The colonel bowed over her hand and massacred the words, "I am fully recompensed, mademoiselle. *Bonne chance.*"

TWENTY-EIGHT

WHEN THE TAXI LEFT THE road running along the Bosphorus and the city rose up around them, Storm opened her phone and accessed her grandfather's notebook. She heard Harry discuss their destination with the driver, but paid little attention. The taxi deposited them by a hillside manor whose interior courtyard was a graveyard for lost dreams. The palace's former grandeur was now reduced to old bones. Harry led her to a corner table set upon the raised patio that ran around three sides of the courtyard. He settled into the chair next to hers. Concern creased Harry's features. Funny how a guy showing he cared could bring that burning sensation to her eyes.

Harry asked, "Think maybe you should take a break?"

"Not yet." She set the notes she had made in the taxi on the table before her, took a hard breath, and dialed the first number. Claudia had said Sean was planning a trip, first to Toronto, then here. Storm had found seven Toronto-based antique companies listed in Sean's notebook. As each number was answered, she said she was working for a major client who wished to remain confidential, and then she asked for the name on Sean's list. No one but the owner would do.

Storm hit pay dirt with the fifth call. The saleswoman's response carried the quality of a well-trained lie, claiming the former owner had retired the previous winter and was no longer available to anyone, for any reason. He had no contact with the firm. The new managing director would be in shortly. Storm asked for his name but did not recognize it. She asked the saleswoman to spell it and wrote it on the side of her sheet.

She found a listing for the owner's home number in Sean's notebook. She dialed the number and once again came face-to-face with the living dead.

This time a stroke had felled his beloved wife. Very sudden. Storm drew a slow and jagged circle around the name as the man described how his wife had been his partner in the business and in life. She asked, "Who runs your business now?"

"My daughter's second husband. I suppose I should call him a stepson. But I never have cared for him."

"Your daughter divorced?"

"Just last year. If you ask me, this new fellow is all flash and fancy airs. But she wouldn't listen to me. She never did."

Storm checked the name given to her by the saleswoman. "His name is Victor Dupree?"

"That is correct. From Montreal. Why?"

"Just bringing my notes up to date," Storm replied, underlining the name three times.

"The children loathe him. My granddaughter wants to come live with me."

"Let her."

"Her mother would never allow it."

"Listen. This guy . . ."

"Yes?"

Storm rose from the table and stepped back into the patio's deepest shadows. One pace for every carefully measured word. "Go to Victor. Tell him either he lets—What's your granddaughter's name?"

"Christina. She goes by Chrissy."

"Either Chrissy comes to live with you, or you'll retake control of the business. You could do that, couldn't you?"

"He and my daughter made me sign over all rights."

"But you could go to a lawyer and raise a stink. Meet with your daughter, just the two of you. Tell her the loneliness is getting to you. You miss the action."

"I do, you know. At the time, with the loss it seemed the right thing to do. Now I wander about this old place like a ghost."

"Tell that to your daughter. Suggest having Chrissy live with you is the only alternative worth discussing. Soon as she has a chat with her Victor, she'll come around."

A pause, then, "You sound very definite."

"Let's just say I have some extremely serious suspicions. If I'm right, you need to get Chrissy out of that house."

"What about Daniel?"

"He's your grandson? How old is he?"

"Sixteen. Chrissy is four years younger."

"The boy's probably lost in teenage land. Worry about the girl."

"You won't recall, but we met once. It was soon after you started in the company. Your grandfather pointed you out. Of course I had heard about the problem between Sean and your father. Sean confessed that he had not wanted to bring you in. But he saw a certain spark in you. Something very rare."

"He never told me that."

"No, Sean wouldn't. But he always had an eye for hidden treasure."

"EMMA, IT'S HARRY."

"Where are you?"

"Old-town Istanbul. Standing in the street outside a villa they've turned into a restaurant. Safe. What about you?"

"Checking into a hotel in Cannes."

"Must be nice."

"We've just spent the day in a prison so bad it would have made your place in Barbados look like a Four Seasons."

Here he was, joking about his felony count with a cop. "Don't bet on it."

"Where's Storm?"

"Corner table, hunched over this little phone that opens into a computer, wired into the Web." He decided there was no need to add how Storm looked, which was pretty much undone. "You doing okay?"

"To be honest, I'm a little shook up."

"Yeah, prison will do that. Emma, we've found something that can't wait."

But Harry barely got started, relating what Mehmet Ozman had told them, before Emma stopped him with "I need to get Hakim in on this."

"Emma—"

"Hold it right there, Harry. This could be important." Thirty seconds later she came back on the line. "Hakim and I are going upstairs to his room; we'll call you back."

"I've got a new number." They had stopped by a phone shop and equipped him with one that reached Europe-wide. He read her the number, then asked, "Are you coming down?"

She responded with public formality. "That depends on other people. But I hope so."

"It'll be good to see you, Emma."

"Roger that. We're headed for the elevators now. We'll be back to you soon."

Harry passed back through the manor's ancient entryway. The portal was large enough for a carriage drawn by six matching steeds to have once pranced through. The villa stood on the Golden Hind, the sequence of hills that had once made up the heart of Constantinople. It had been built by the first minister to Suleiman the Magnificent and was flanked on one side by the Aga Sophia mosque and on the other by the Topkapi Palace stables. The restaurant sprawled about what had once been a formal courtyard. The stonework was flecked with lichen and the wall paintings were reduced to mere shadows. The central fountain's stone sculpture was worn down to nubs and the courtyard's mosaic was pitted and almost lost to weeds. Even the waiters seemed drawn from a bygone era, ancient crones who drifted about and did not speak even when taking orders.

Storm did not merely occupy the restaurant's corner table. She had staked her flag and claimed the space as her own. She sat hunched over the little phone, open now to the larger screen, and tapped on the keypad. She'd made sheets of notes on the pad Harry had bought at a bookshop next to the phone store. A map and tourist guide to Cyprus lay open on the chair to the right. Another chair to her left held a tulip glass of tea and an untouched sandwich. Harry didn't care whether she ate. They had stuffed their faces with Mehmet. Harry had ordered the food because he wanted her to know he was there and concerned.

It was hard for a woman as vibrantly alive as Storm to appear wraithlike. But when they'd left the palace and headed back into Istanbul, she had grown as ethereal as smoke. Just drifting on the seat next to him. Lost to the certainty that her aunt and oldest friend was doing business with the people who had murdered Sean.

Harry walked up to her table and said, "Emma wants to get me and Hakim on the phone."

Storm looked up, but Harry had the impression she didn't really see him at all. He went on, "He'll want to take this to the next level. Which means either we trust him, or I insist that only Emma handles your names."

She had the list ready for him. It covered two

pages. "You decide. I'll e-mail the names and addresses as soon as you say."

"Storm, you still can't be sure Claudia is in cahoots—"

"Don't. Please. This is too much to be a coincidence. Claudia is in this up to her eyeballs."

"Okay, yes, she's negotiating the sale of the company, and they've offered her a job. But that doesn't mean—"

"She said it herself. This company is her *life*. If she's blind to what's going on it's because she wants to stay blind."

Harry set his hand on her shoulder. Left it there until his phone rang. Then he walked back across the courtyard before opening the phone. "I'm here."

"Harry, I'd like to introduce Hakim Sundera," Emma said.

"Very nice to speak with you at last, Mr. Bennett."

Harry said, "I've got to know if we can have a total trust between us. I'm not just talking about facts related to whatever you're after. I'm talking about treasure. Because I'm pretty sure it's out there." Harry passed through the portals and parked himself on the alley's opposite wall, where the shadows hid him but he still had a clear view of Storm. "This stage of the game, you normally shut everybody out who's not absolutely essential. Not bring in a new player."

Emma took her time responding. "I've brought in Hakim because I think he is just that. Essential."

"Mr. Bennett, I assure you—"

"I go by Harry."

"Harry. Nothing you tell me will be passed further. Nothing will be put in any report. Not until your search is over, or you give me permission."

Emma said, "I trust Hakim enough to place my professional career in his hands."

"I guess that works." Harry sketched out their meeting with Mehmet Ozman at the palace hotel. Then waited. Making it a test, see how far this guy could take it.

"Let us for the moment refer to our attacker as Leon. Counting Sean, our foes have possibly eliminated three different antiques dealers. And you think each shop has become a front."

"And they form a pattern."

"They identify a prey. They attack. But they do not take over. They replace the original owner with a puppet. Someone who has the name but lets them direct matters according to a hidden agenda. Harry, could you please tell me why Ms. Syrrell is not part of this conversation?"

But Emma had already made the connection. "The relative who's handling the sale of Syrrell's."

"Storm's aunt Claudia. She and Storm were superclose. The evidence points at Claudia either knowing, which Storm doubts, or letting herself be used by Sean's murderers. Storm is cut to pieces."

Hakim asked, "When did Storm receive news of the company's sale?"

"First at the Palm Beach exhibition, then again at Sean's funeral. Claudia told Storm both times she doesn't know who the buyer is, only the lawyers handling the transaction. Claudia claims it's either sell the company or go bankrupt."

Hakim said, "It is good that Ms. Syrrell trusts you, Harry. Very good for her to have a trusted ally at the moment when she is weakest. Emma, perhaps we should tell Harry what has happened at our end."

Emma related the international alert for a man with no name, the prison, Leon, the escape, their confrontation with the French lawyer. "Hakim pushed hard as he could. But the attorney didn't give. Not a peep."

Hakim said, "The commandant can only hold the advocate for thirty-six hours. The morning after tomorrow, the magistrate will arrive on his regular rounds. The advocate will be the first case on his docket. Anything else and the commandant would be open to charges. He has a letter signed by Interpol, formally requesting that the advocate be held for extradition. But in thirty-six and one-half hours, the advocate walks free."

Harry mashed the phone to his ear, as though the compression would make the man easier to read. Try as he might, he couldn't detect any hint of gold fever. That was what treasure dogs called getting close to the score. Gold fever bit like acid into a crew's nerves. Guys who had been friends for life suddenly turned on one another like coyotes over a kill. Harry liked this guy's formal diction, the precise way he laid things out. Harry said, "The enemy is bound to know we know. Speed is everything."

Hakim asked, "Do you or Ms. Syrrell have any idea what we should do now?"

Harry found himself liking this guy more with each turn. "That is the absolute first time I've ever heard a cop asking a civvie for advice."

"We at Interpol are specialists in liaising, Harry. We seek to aid others at reaching their prize of a solid arrest and a successful conviction. Why should it be any different with you? Of course I ask your advice."

"I can see why Emma likes you, sir."

"Please, call me Hakim."

"Storm has prepared a list of all the dealers in her grandfather's book. She'll pass it on, but only if you won't delegate the job. This is top-secret stuff. You need to contact them and see who else has been attacked. Once you've made the calls, we want your word the list will be destroyed and you'll pass on just the dealers who are part of this daisy chain."

Emma said, "I'll do it."

Hakim said, "No. I want you to join them.

Tomorrow. I will do this, Harry. And then I will personally destroy Ms. Syrrell's list."

Harry steeled himself against the sudden flutter at gut level. Getting the quivers over a cop joining their crew, that was definitely one for the books. "There's something else. Before the accident that killed his wife and daughter Mehmet Ozman had been on his way to Paris to see a guy. Yves Boucaud." Harry spelled it out. "The deal was powerful enough to drag Mehmet away from his family while they were on vacation. Storm thinks it might be worth checking this guy out, see if there's a link."

"Harry, I really must speak with Ms. Syrrell directly. I have several urgent questions."

"I'll pass it on."

There was a pause, like the world needed to take a very difficult breath. Hakim said, "Emma, perhaps you should tell him what you have just learned."

"I've had a call from a contact with the Palm Beach police. Richard Ellis was shot and killed last night. They're putting it down to a robbery gone bad."

"You know that's not true."

"We passed on what we suspect. But without evidence that ties these events together in a fashion the prosecutor can follow, we're just shouting into the wind."

Harry grimaced over the loss of a man he wished

he had come to know better. One more connection to his late best friend gone for good. Leaving him to carry the news to Storm.

Hakim gave them a moment for shared remorse, then asked, "Is there anything else you need?"

"Absolutely," Harry replied. "A gun and a way out of town."

TWENTY-NINE

EMMA SAT ON HER HOTEL room's narrow balcony. Actually, two of the chair's legs were inside the French doors, so she had room to put her feet on the railing and stretch her legs out fully. Her room faced south. Somewhere out there, the Riviera beckoned. All she could see was a postage-stamp garden, a miniature pool, the hotel parking lot, and red-tiled roofs marching down the hillside. Emma had napped and showered and eaten a meal with Hakim. Hakim had suggested they sit at one of the sidewalk tables so they could enjoy the air. The food had been nice. Then Hakim received two phone calls. Now the meal sat in Emma's stomach like a lump of French concrete.

A copy of the *International Herald Tribune* lay by her feet open but unread. Emma had bought it at a newsstand down the road, something to fill the wait. But her eyes skipped over the words, searching for a headline that existed only in her brain.

The house across the street had louvered shutters painted red to match the barrel-tile roof. A parrot sat on a swing inside a gilded cage and squawked words in French. The smell of green peppers frying in olive oil drifted in the still air. There was a knock on her door. Emma rose from her chair, shut the balcony doors, and crossed the room.

Hakim stood in the hallway. "We are ready."

She followed him into the room next to hers. The bed had been pushed to one side, making room for three chairs pulled around the desk. "This is Remy. He is half French and half Californian."

The slender young man had spiked dark hair and nervous hands. He did not look up from the array of electronic equipment. The laptop's screen showed a pair of audio readouts. He picked up a headset connected to the computer and spoke into the mike. "Test, test, one, two." The volume level jerked the readout into the red zone. Remy tapped a couple of keys, repeated the test, and said, "Okay, we're good to go."

Two chairs were drawn up beside Remy's. Emma said, "I think better on my feet."

"Sorry, the headset cord won't reach."

Emma needed to focus exclusively on the man at the other end of the line. She picked up the chair closest to the open French doors and turned it to face the sunset. When she'd seated herself she realized the smell of frying peppers had followed her.

Hakim slipped into the third chair. He handed Emma her cell phone, which was now connected to the techie's equipment. "Your phone has rung twice since we turned it back on. Jack Dauer both times."

Emma did not reply. There was nothing to say. Hakim had received word that Dauer had issued a formal complaint to Treasury, seeking her dismissal. He also intended to bring her up on criminal charges for willfully obstructing a federal case and aiding the flight of two suspects.

Then Hakim had a call from his contacts in Paris, relaying news about the man Mehmet Ozman had gone to visit, the day his family had died. News that had widened the hole blown by the message about Dauer. A double-barreled barrage to her universe.

Hakim handed her the headset. "All we need is enough to suggest obstruction."

Emma said, "I still can't believe Dauer has gone this far."

Hakim leaned in closer, ensuring she actually heard what he was saying. "We are not after implicating anyone. We just want to free you from the threat of being withdrawn from the case. A couple of minutes, nothing more. When we have enough, I'll signal you. Then mention the Parisian's name so that we can officially register his response."

"Where's the file?"

Hakim handed it over. "Remy?"

"Green across the board."

She dialed Jack Dauer's number from memory. The voice mail kicked in instantly, suggesting Dauer was on another call. An impersonal voice repeated Dauer's number and nothing else. Emma said, "This is Emma Webb returning your call. I can be reached for the next twenty minutes or so."

She clicked off. Emma set the phone on top of the file's cover. She made two fists, mashed down on her thighs, and worked at breathing.

Hakim said, "This man Leon reminds me of something from our past. Most Syrians are Sunni Muslim, the majority sect in Islam. My father was Shia. The divisions between Sunni and Shia are very deep, very old, and very bitter. The Wahabists, you have heard of them, yes? They are the ultraconservative Sunni sect that spawned Osama bin Laden. Wahabist clerics have recently declared Shias to be demonic. The Shias have their own extremists. A thousand years ago, a break-off sect called Ismailis . . ." Hakim caught her look. "What is it?"

"You shift from now to ten centuries back like it's just around the corner."

"To the Arab mind, it is closer than that. It is *now*. Here. In this room. Alive today. As I was saying, the Ismailis were the minority of a minority and remain so today. They ruled a cluster of mountain fiefdoms in Iran, eastern Iraq, India, and Nepal. Marco Polo visited there. These Ismaili fiefdoms exported professional killers. They were sold as slaves to wealthy pashas and rulers about the Islamic world. Palaces were traded for these men, lifetime treaties, trading routes, entire fiefdoms. Several became generals and sovereigns. One even ruled Egypt for a time. They called themselves *aishishin*, men without law. From their name comes the word *assassin*."

Emma's phone rang, but she made no move to pick it up. "You're saying this deal is bigger than what's happening to me in the here and now."

Hakim nodded once. "Answer the phone."

EMMA OPENED HER PHONE AND waited. Remy whispered, "Rolling."

"This is Emma Webb."

Jack Dauer snarled, "Just exactly where do you get off? You think a couple of letters signed by people with no connection to this case are going to save you?"

"I have been seconded to Interpol, sir."

"Wrong, Webb. You have disregarded a direct order from your superior. In case you haven't heard, I'm bringing you up on criminal charges. Something you've basically been begging me to do from the start of this investigation." He gave her a minute to respond. When he got nothing but silence, the phone's temperature hiked another notch. "Where are you, Webb?"

"France. We have tracked down several new leads—"

"Don't give me that. Where are the suspects I sent you to arrest?"

"Storm Syrrell and Harry Bennett are no longer suspects."

"That is not for you to determine. *I* am running this show. *I* decide who is under suspicion. And I did *not* authorize you to travel to *France*!"

Dauer's words worked on Emma's internal control like a steel rasp, filing off the lid she normally kept clamped shut. She felt the rage and the memories well up, hidden images shooting through her brain, brilliant as grenade blasts. She saw the moment her father had suggested she had some deep-seated mental problem for wanting to become a federal agent. Then she flashed to the first time her mother had called her job an obsession. She remembered the night of her rehearsal dinner, when her fiancé sprung the news that he loved her but hated her cop's attitude, like they were two completely different things and he could use the ultimatum of breaking off their wedding to force her to abandon her dreams.

Her control snapped with an audible bang.

Emma said, "I'm curious about one thing, Jack. I've handed you some major evidence and you've blocked me at every turn. So I'm asking. Just exactly whose side are you on?"

Hakim motioned to her. Enough.

"Clamp down on that attitude, Webb. You're already in over your head."

"Everybody puts you down as just an extreme version of the fibbie attitude, going for the glory, stealing all the credit. But now I'm wondering if there's more."

"You have *no* right addressing your superior—"

Emma turned toward the wall so as to block out Hakim's urgent signals. "Just so you know, Jack, I'm recording this conversation and I'm talking to you in front of witnesses. What I need to know is, have you been put in place to make sure we never get too far? Did Washington appoint you because they knew you'd obstruct any *real* investigation? Was your job to railroad the inquiry, deliver the verdict, hand over a couple of minor scapegoats, and hide any facts that could make trouble for your superiors?"

"Wait . . . you're recording?"

"Why does that bother you, Jack? Suddenly grown a conscience? Maybe you'd like to retract some of your garbage and play like we're on the same team?" She swatted Hakim's hand away from her shoulder. "Here's something for you to start with. A name, Jack. Yves Boucaud. Ring any alarm bells?"

"Consider your career officially terminated. I am personally issuing a warrant for your arrest. Aiding and—"

"You were never after the truth, were you, Jack. You were *chosen* to make sure we never linked that name to your case. You were brought in to *hide* the agency's involvement with this man. Well, Jack, here's some news for you. I'm going straight to the attorney general of the United States. And I'm going to inform him that Agent Jack Dauer's obstruction of this investigation has resulted in the murder of six people in four countries. Remember that name, Jack. Yves Boucaud. Because my guess is, this is going to turn into the FBI's very own Iran-Contra affair."

She snapped the phone shut and slammed it down on the folder. Panted her way out of the rage. She never got angry. Never lost control. When her heaving chest stilled somewhat, she turned in her chair and met Hakim's gaze full-on. "You got a problem?"

"No," he said quietly. "No problem."

"Good. There's more where that came from." She turned to face the techie. "I want you to get ready to play that conversation back over my phone. No, don't look at Hakim. I'm talking here. You've got thirty seconds."

She faced the wall and dialed a number from memory. Waited through two rings and about five dozen rapid breaths.

"MacFarland."

"Tip, it's Emma."

"Oh, man. You okay, lady?"

She almost lost it. She had no shield against MacFarland's unexpected concern except cold rage. "Don't ask stupid questions. Are you recording?"

A pause, then, "I am now."

"I want you to pay very careful attention, Tip. I am going to play back a conversation. And then I am going to tell you what we have learned. And I am taping our conversation, so there is a clear record of your hearing everything I've got to say. You are going to listen very carefully, and then you are going to your superiors. You're going to do this, Tip, because if you let me down I am going to go first to an attorney in the private sector. I'm going to wrap this up in a neat little file, and I'm going to make two copies, and I'm going to deliver one to the attorney general and the other to the *Washington Post*. Do you follow?"

He spoke with the slow motion of grinding gears. "I hear you."

Emma said to the techie, "Okay, roll."

When the recording of the conversation with Dauer was done, Emma gave the rest to Tip fast and cold—the prison break, the unnamed attacker with the false Romanian documents, the French attorney, the murder of Mehmet Ozman's family, the nephew put in place. "The day his wife and daughter were murdered, Mehmet Ozman was traveling to Paris to see one Yves Boucaud. We tracked that name through the Paris authorities. Yves Boucaud is an international financier. He has no record. But get this, Tip. When Interpol ran his name through their own system, they found a link to the Justice Department."

"Don't tell me."

"The FBI has a top-secret seal on his file. Which suggests they are being intentionally blind to an international conspiracy to murder, extort, and subvert the course of justice."

It was Tip's turn to huff through a couple of very hard breaths. "When I told you to go find yourself a major prize, I didn't mean you needed to bring down the US government."

"You've got twenty-four hours. Then I go public."

"No, Emma. Calm down. That's not enough time."

"You're not the one who's got a wrecking ball aimed at her career. Not to mention a warrant. A *warrant*, Tip. For my *arrest*."

"I'll take care of that. But I need more time. Where can I reach you?"

She gave him her two cell-phone numbers. Hakim slipped something into her hand holding the file. She did not realize her vision had blurred until she could not read the numbers on the card. She swiped at her face. "You need to be in touch with my superior here at Interpol. Hakim Sundera. I may be off the map for a while. You want more time, I have to trust you to get Dauer off my tail."

"I told you I'd take care of it. Give me two weeks."

"Five days, Tip. Five. Then you can hear all

about this on CNN." She slapped the phone shut. Stripped off the headset. Forced herself to her feet. Said to the two men watching her, "That's how we do it in the good old US of A."

THIRTY

VERY EARLY THE NEXT MORNING, Hakim insisted upon accompanying Emma to the Nice airport. After she had checked in, they took a table at the airport café and Emma had the finest croissant and cappuccino she had ever tasted. Hakim gave that minimalist smile of his, barely creasing the edges around his mouth and eyes. "There are some things which the French do really quite well."

She studied the imperial palms beyond the taxi stand, the beautiful people loading into waiting limos, the mountains, the dawn light. "Someday I'm going to come back here and see it all for real. Someday soon."

Hakim used his thumb and forefinger to press the coffee's froth from his moustache. "You were most impressive yesterday."

"I didn't exactly follow orders."

"You did your job. That is what is most important."

"Is it?"

"We share the same objectives, Agent Webb."

"Emma." She caught his look. Two smiles in one morning. A record. "I bet you are a superb boss."

"Something I would like you to keep in mind."

That was a direction she had no interest in taking. Not after a semi-sleepless night, jerking awake after repeatedly dreaming her way through the conversations she'd had, totally losing it in transatlantic phone calls to her superiors. Over and over and over. "How did you track down the information on Yves Boucaud so fast?"

"I did nothing except make one phone call. What I said to Harry Bennett was the truth. Interpol has no place for action heroes. No stars. No headline grabbers. Our director general is an American who spent decades in the Washington intelligence services. He loathed the infighting, the way they battled with local police forces, scrabbling like dogs over bones. His objective is very simple. To protect and to serve."

Hakim finished his coffee, then used his napkin with a surgeon's precision. "Let us say you successfully conclude this case. You would gain all the attention, because we take none. You return to a stellar position at Treasury or at Homeland Security."

She was pierced by a desire so strong her heart missed a very painful beat. "Fat chance."

Hakim contradicted her with a moment's silence. "So you return, taking all the credit with you. And one day you receive a call. Perhaps from me, perhaps from another Interpol officer who uses my name. What would you do?"

"Star service. Top of the pile."

"Precisely."

She tried to clear the burning from her throat, but it only seemed to shove it up behind her eyes. "I've never wanted to do anything else with my life but this."

In response, Hakim rose and hefted her suit bag. He badged the officers handling the security checkpoint and waited while her bag was scoped. The passage leading to the planes was ribbed with Riviera sunlight. Hakim said, "There is one other item we must discuss. Something I require your help with."

"Name it."

Hakim led her to a window just down from her gate. He set down her case. "I have had my associates check on Harry Bennett. He has been at the forefront of several discoveries. Treasures whose appearances have become true international events. This was prior to his being arrested for bringing up almost a ton of gold doubloons inside Barbados waters without a license."

"He claims he was in international waters and was framed. I believe him."

"For the moment, that is irrelevant. What we need to accept is, if the prize is big enough, Harry Bennett will take whatever risk is necessary. And for a prize as large as the hidden treasures from the Second Temple of Jerusalem, Harry Bennett might be capable of anything at all."

Emma did not have anything to say. Swallowing was hard enough.

"Trafficking in salvaged treasures found within international waters is a crime covered by international treaty."

"I'm aware of that."

Hakim's gaze had magnified to where the airport's clamor was filtered down to a faint whisper. "When I said that I or my colleagues would call upon you for assistance, Agent Webb, I was speaking about a very real tomorrow."

AFTER AN EARLY BREAKFAST, HARRY shepherded Storm down to the Bodrum Harbor and bought two tickets for the ferry to Rhodes. Storm waited until they were crossing the gangplank to say, "Last time I checked, the Greek islands are in the opposite direction from Cyprus."

"I was planning to tell you yesterday," Harry replied. "But the way things were, I figured your brain could use a night off."

Hakim had arranged for them to fly from Istanbul to the coastal village of Bodrum. Harry had been there once before, just after he'd gone full-time into salvage work. In the nineteen years since then, Bodrum had grown from an idyllic fishing village to a tourist mecca. They had spent the night in a portside hotel, dined by room service, and slept with the connecting doors opened between their rooms. Twice Harry had awakened to the sound of a strong woman using her pillow to stifle her sobs.

This morning Storm looked fragile but intact. They took a pair of seats on the ferry's top deck and stowed their bags under the bench. Storm pulled out Sean's tattered Bible, opened her phone, and began tapping the little keys. She would turn to a page marked by a slip of paper, lean over a passage, then type. When she noticed Harry watching, she said, "Sean had these verses he fought with. I'm making a list of them." She tapped a passage almost obliterated by Sean's angry scrawl. "I don't understand what he was after. I don't understand why they were so important. All I can say is, even accepting the mystery has given me some very real peace."

"You want, I could take a walk around the boat, give you some space."

"No, Harry. I'm very glad you're here."

So he stayed where he was, warmed by the day and by the lady beside him. If following Sean's tread along this spiritual quest helped Storm reknit the fabric of her heart, then Harry was all for it.

Forty-five minutes later, Harry watched the sailors cast off the mooring ropes. The motors drummed under his feet as the ferry pulled away from the harbor wall. Storm must have noticed how he breathed easier, for she said, "You were worried we'd been followed?"

"Not really. But it's good to be away, just the

same." Their ferry was an ancient vessel whose ulcerous wounds wept rust. He watched as they passed the harbor's encircling arms and said, "Outward bound again. That's what skippers of the old sailing vessels used to write in their logbooks when they left safe harbor and entered the deep. Outward bound."

"How long will the trip take?"

"Three hours. This was Hakim's suggestion. Rhodes is the closest major Greek island to the Turkish coast. We're just trying to cover our tracks a little. Emma will meet us there with a plane."

Storm stowed away the book and her computer. "We need to talk."

Harry watched her bundle her hair away from her eyes with a rubber band, then shuck off her pullover and stow it away. The lady was getting down to business. "Fire away."

"There's so much I don't know. And even more I can't figure out."

"Rule one in the treasure business. You'll never have all the answers. Comes a point, you lay your money on the table. If there was a sure-fire answer, somebody else would have already found it."

"What's rule two?"

"Leave with the loot in your pocket and the skin still on your back."

"I like that one better."

"I'd like to hear you actually say what it is we're after."

Storm took a breath. "Treasures from Herod's Second Temple in Jerusalem. Treasures that didn't show up on the triumphant arch of Titus in Rome, but are on the Copper Scroll. The evidence suggests that they were secreted away on Cyprus."

"Okay, good. So here's what we do. From now on, we assume we're right. We lay out the trail the best we can. And set aside the doubt. It just makes us stumble."

She gave that a moment. "I can do that."

Harry leaned back, crossed his arms, stretched out his legs. "So tell."

"Okay. I've been checking out the two men Professor Morgenthal mentioned in Washington. The first was Titus Flavius Josephus. He was born a Pharisee, a scribe. This made him ideal as a historian, which is what he became for the Romans. Before that happened, he was a general in the first Jewish rebellion."

She fished through her shoulder bag and pulled out a sheaf of folded notes. She flattened them in her lap. But Harry had the impression they were there more for reassurance than because she needed to check her facts. "In the year AD 39, the Emperor Caligula declared himself a god. He ordered his statues to be erected in every temple throughout the Roman empire. All sacrifices were to be made in his name. From that point, it was only a matter of time. The first Jewish revolt finally erupted in AD 66 in Caesarea and spread like wildfire. But the Jews were far from unified. In his history, Josephus mentions a number of sects or divisions. But only three are important to us. The Zealots, the Temple priests, and the Pharisees."

Across the calm Aegean waters, a farmer plowed a field on the Turkish headland. Gulls squawked and fought in the dust clouds that drifted in the windless morning. The sound of a guitar and Moroccan drums floated up from the stern. Harry tasted a clove cigarette's pungent odor through the diesel and the salt.

"The Zealots were determined to go down fighting, but others wanted to surrender. While the Romans began laying siege to Jerusalem, civil war broke out inside the city. The Zealots came out in complete control. The die was cast. The city would fight to the last man.

"At least initially, Josephus must have sided with the Zealots. After all, they made him a general of the Jewish forces in Galilee. But there's no hard evidence that he ever became one, or if he did, that he stayed one. In his history, written years later, he introduces himself as the son of Matthias, an ethnic Hebrew, a priest and Pharisee from Jerusalem. Nothing about being a Zealot. In AD 68 he surrendered to the Romans, and in AD 69 he was granted an audience with Vespasian. Something happened, because in AD 71, as the siege of Jerusalem began, Josephus was a close confidant of the Roman general. Vespasian actually sent Josephus into the city as his personal emissary, to negotiate a surrender. The Zealots responded by burning the city's remaining food supply. They intended for the city to fight until every able-bodied Jew was killed. I think Josephus saw this coming and was absolutely against it. I think he tried to save the city and as many of his people as he could."

"But he failed," Harry said.

"He failed and the Romans destroyed the city. Which brings us to the other man Professor Morgenthal mentioned, Yochanan Ben Zakai. He was known as a *tannaim*, a sage of the Torah, the first five books of the Jewish Bible." Storm stopped and looked at him. "At this point it becomes only a tiny bit of fact inside a whole world of speculation."

"You're on a roll," Harry said. "Go for it."

"In the years leading up to the revolt, a real battle raged between the Pharisees, who saw themselves as guardians of Jewish law, and the Sadduccees, the priests who dominated the temple council, which was called the Sanhedrin. The Pharisees accused these other temple priests of living inside the pocket of their Roman masters. They accused the temple's high priests of bribing Rome for their appointments with money from the temple coffers. I'm guessing these Sadduccees were on the side of those wanting to surrender.

Whether the Zealots killed the priests is anybody's guess. But we know this. The Roman accounts do not mention any priests being there when they torched the temple. And we know something else. In the middle of this siege, Yochanan Ben Zakai got out."

Storm waited.

Harry caught it then. "He escaped from Jerusalem?"

"The only man on record to do so. Supposedly his students smuggled him out as a corpse. But there were thousands of bodies rotting in the streets. Josephus writes of this. It gets even weirder. Not long after his escape, Ben Zakai has an audience with General Vespasian. In this audience, he predicts that Vespasian will be named emperor of Rome. Vespasian is so taken with this that he lets Ben Zakai establish a new center of Jewish law in Yavneh. After the temple was destroyed, Ben Zakai set up a council that replaced temple sacrifices with prayer, the study of the Torah, and observance of the *mitzvot*, or commandments. He saw this as the means by which the Jewish people could maintain their unity wherever they were exiled, even without the temple."

"Hang on a second. How did he get to meet the Roman general?"

Storm nodded with her entire upper body, a slow rocking in confirmation. "I haven't found an explanation for that anywhere."

"Josephus set it up."

"I think so."

"It had to be. They were both, what did you call them?"

"Pharisees."

"Okay, so Josephus offers to enter the city and negotiate for his new friend, Vespasian. Supposedly he fails. Next thing we know, this other guy shows up and has an interview with Caesar."

"He doesn't become emperor until later, but the rest is on target."

Inside Harry's brain, the energy hummed a constant rush, like a waterfall, quiet and easy until it went over the edge and careened into space and fell in a blistering roar that caused the air to tremble. Harry had worried that he'd lost that rush for good. He released his breath and the words one at a time. "Josephus did a deal on the side while he was in the city, not to get out this other guy, but to rescue the temple treasures. The guy smuggled the temple treasures out with him. He took the ones he could get his hands on and skipped town."

"That's what I think."

"Cyprus would be the perfect place to stash the goods. They'd be looking for a place that was close at hand, but safe."

"And it was a different Roman province. One totally at peace. Thousands of Jews who survived the rebellion fled there." Storm continued her rocking motion, like she was feeding off Harry's tension, releasing it the only way that didn't interrupt the flow. "But there's more, Harry. Remember what I said. To the Pharisees, the Torah, the law, was most important. The last thing they'd want is for a new high priest to use these treasures to restart a temple sect."

Harry started rocking as well, just keeping time. "So they were hidden from Jews as well."

"That's what I'm thinking. It explains why the Copper Scroll was found in an Essene village, an outcast sect, a group that had already rebelled against the problems in Jerusalem."

"But they didn't want to risk putting the treasures there as well. Too close to the battle."

"The Romans forced almost all the Jews who didn't die in the battle to leave Israel."

"So where do we head in Cyprus? This is vital, Storm. The island's been cut in half for over thirty years. The south is Greek and is entering the European Union. The north is a rogue state. North Cyprus is recognized only by Turkey. Fifty thousand Turkish troops are stationed there. We need to know which side to hunt."

"I've been working on that. One possibility stands out. At the end of the first century, a lot of Christian believers were Jewish, some authorities say as many as two-thirds. But these Jews were being excluded from local Jewish communities. They were seen as another outlaw sect.

They created conflict just when the Jewish nation was under dire threat. They threatened to dissolve the bonds of Jewish blood, because Christians were specifically instructed to treat all believers in Jesus as brethren. Twenty years later those Jewish Christians were officially excommunicated from all synagogues throughout the Roman empire. But in the period we're talking about, a number of these Jewish Christians were also Pharisees. Paul of Tarsus, author of over half the New Testament, was one himself."

Harry chewed it over while Storm rocked and waited. He said, "Christian Jews on Cyprus."

"That's what I'm thinking."

"I like it."

"Do you?"

"Yes, Storm. I like it a lot. So where do we go?"

"North," she replied. "The first Christian settlements were all in the north."

THIRTY-ONE

ENTERING RHODES HARBOR WAS LIKE joining a carnival built around a movie set. The village was a glimmering white jewel nestled in flowering scrub and mountains and the Aegean Sea. Houses were sculpted from whitewashed stone. The port was filled with brightly painted fishing boats. The rocky beaches to either side of the harbor were packed. The long road fronting the quayside was a riot of noise and color and people.

Even so, the first face Harry latched onto was Emma's.

"There she is!" But it was doubtful Storm heard him, as the noise on the ship had risen to match that from the shoreline. Storm smiled at him, a lovely sight, especially as the plum-shaded rims to her eyes were hidden behind her Ray-Bans. She mouthed to him, "Go."

Harry was first down the gangplank. But when he made it through the crowd to where Emma stood, he turned uncertain. First-date nerves. At thirty-nine. "You look great, lady."

She wore khaki shorts revealing legs as fine as the rest of her. "Where's our girl?"

"Taking her time."

Emma's hands seemed to have a life all their own. They fumbled with the strap to her purse, then scrambled up her neck and started to touch the air between them. Harry stepped across the chasm, suddenly at ease. Just swept her up and filled the space inside her arms. He felt the strength in her embrace, the soft cheek that met his own, the warmth to her breath as she whispered in his ear, "Harry, Harry. What are we doing?"

THEY LET THE IMPATIENT, LAUGHING, jostling tide carry them along the port. They took a taxi to the airport, a single north-south strip fronted by a pair of whitewashed buildings. As soon as Emma rose from the taxi, a twin-engined Beechcraft started its engines. Harry followed the two ladies up the stairs, nodded to the pilot, settled into his seat, watched the pilot heft up the stairs, lock the door, then return to his seat. As they rolled toward the runway, Harry said, "I'm liking this guy Hakim more and more."

The Beechcraft was an international workhorse, known throughout the world for its range, ease of handling, steady ride, and payload. The twin turbos pushed them across the miles. The pilot promised they would be landing in Larnaca in less than three hours. Harry checked his watch and smiled. They just might make it.

Emma said, "You've got something in mind."

Harry was seated next to Emma, close enough to feel the lady's heat. And tension. During the ride to the airport, she had remained tight within herself. As the plane had taxied and taken off, Harry had caught her shooting him coplike stares, intended to peel back the superficial and reveal the hidden core. Which was no real surprise. The lady was caught up in a situation that probably hadn't been covered in the Treasury Department rule book. She had every reason to be on edge.

Harry said, "I've got some things to tell you. And Storm's got more. But before we start, you need to give me your word that nothing we say will go any further. There comes a point when you commit to the hunt. And that point is now."

Emma's tension radiated out in full force. "What have we been doing so far?"

"Researching. Fitting the pieces together. We've known there's something worth finding. Old Sean didn't attract this sort of attention because he was a gnarly soul."

"Our evidence suggests Sean Syrrell's murder was attached to something far larger than one possible find."

"I'm not disputing that. But right here, right now, we are talking treasure. Storm has some leads. We're going to chase them down. And my gut tells me we've got a chance to grab the gold ring. So now we're working according to salvage rules. And the first of these is, secrecy is everything."

Emma said, "Hakim can help us."

"He might. Then again, he might turn us in." Harry raised his hand to both ladies' protest. "All we can say for certain is, Hakim is not here."

Emma said to Storm, "Hakim needs to speak with you. Today."

"Tomorrow," Harry corrected. "We're going to be kinda busy from the minute we set down."

Storm said to Harry, "I know. Nothing about where we are."

"You can tell him we're on Cyprus. Seeing as how this is his plane, I think he's already got that square covered."

Emma said, "He's helping us because this work

313

is related to a case with potentially vital conse-
quences."

Storm said, "Nobody is forgetting about the case
or the murders, Emma. Not for an instant."

Emma turned to the window. Storm started to
say something more, but Harry shook his head.
Outside Emma's window a cloud drifted between
them and the blue-blue sea. Harry said, "I need
your word that everything we say, everything we
do, everywhere we go, stays among us three."

Emma turned back and said, "If it gets to a point
where I can't live with that, I'll tell you."

Harry said to Storm, "Works for me."

Harry gave Emma a running account of what
Storm had related so far. He took his time, finding
genuine pleasure as Emma became absorbed in his
tale. Toward the end, Storm settled back in her seat
and listened as well. Harry waited for her to come
in with corrections. He knew he was leaving some
things out and not getting all the words right. But
Storm just sat across from him and listened, a
smile flickering in and out, sunlight playing
between the clouds that had gathered over the past
few days.

When he was done, Storm said, "You make it
sound real."

"I'm just giving her what you gave me."

"I don't mean that. The way you say it . . ."

Emma finished, "You're a pro talking about a
find waiting at the other end of the trail."

Storm said, "Okay. Time for round two." She gathered her pages, forming them like a line of paper soldiers on the table between them. "Back at Georgetown, the professor said none of the items on the Titus arch were on the Copper Scroll. So what I've been doing is making a list of all the things that appear on this second arch, the one from the fore-edged book. All of them appear either in the Copper Scroll or the Second Temple treasures listed by Josephus."

Harry's gut started its tight quivers again. "Every one?"

"Yes. Nineteen treasures in all."

Emma asked, "Excuse me for asking. But what exactly is the Copper Scroll?"

Storm had a page of notes at the ready. "It was discovered by Lancaster Hardy, an archeologist from Cambridge, working at Qumran in the late forties. The text was stamped or carved on thin sheets of copper that were then joined together into two scrolls. At least, only two have been found so far. The scrolls were heavily oxidized and could not be unrolled, so the archeologists worked for five years, sawing the scrolls into twenty-three strips that could be flattened and read. There was some trouble deciphering the text, because almost all Hebrew from the biblical era comes from religious texts, and the Copper Scroll deals with treasure. There was also some Hebrew from a later era, what is now called the pre-Mishnaic or pre-Rabbinical

Hebrew, and mixed into this were also some letters and words in Greek. None of the Greek has been translated, but experts believe it came from a lost dialect, possibly an island tongue."

Harry muttered, "Island Greek."

"Josephus's description of temple treasures appears in his multi-volume history and nowhere else. His list has been disputed for two thousand years. None of the items he describes were either on the Titus arch or listed in the annals of Roman treasures from Judea. The same arguments have raged over the items listed on the Copper Scroll since its discovery."

Storm took a long breath. "Okay, the items from the Copper Scroll first. A chest of silver that weighs seventeen talents. Golden vessels of offering. A golden urn that contains a golden scroll. Golden vessels for aloe and incense. I'd say the chalice I left with you in Washington is one of those. Then there are temple trumpets, three of them. Two incense shovels. All gold."

Emma's hand slipped across the hand rest and took hold of Harry's. He jerked slightly at the unexpected touch. He checked her from the corner of his eye, and decided she wasn't really aware of what she'd just done. But he knew.

Storm finished, "And lastly there is a menorah, possibly more than one."

Harry protested, "The menorah forms a central point on the Titus arch."

Emma asked, "Menorah?"

Storm replied to Harry, "I've checked on that." Then to Emma, "A menorah is a candlestick formed like a tree with curved branches. The menorah on the Titus arch looks to be the size of the soldier carrying it."

Emma asked weakly, "Gold?"

"Solid." Maybe it was the fact she had spent days working through this. Or maybe it was just the professional edge. But Storm seemed unaffected by what she was saying. "In Solomon's Temple, the menorah stood at the south wall of the Holy of Holies. This was tended daily by the High Priest, so that the chamber was always filled with light. Josephus does not give the number of menorahs in the Second Temple, but he uses the plural. More than one."

Harry said, "What else."

"A platter for the show bread. Solid gold." Storm looked up. "This is where it gets interesting."

Emma had shifted over so that her shoulder and her arm were in tight contact with Harry. "What's it been up to now?"

Harry liked how he could keep his voice easy. "The lady sure knows how to make an entrance."

"The last three items," Storm said. "The breastplate, the crown, and the golden vine.

"The breastplate first, the *chosen ha-mispat*. This was worn by the High Priest. According to Josephus, he wore two or three sets of robes, depending upon the ceremony or the festival. Over that came the ephod, the waistcoat. The breastplate went on top, and was inset with twelve jewels in three rows of four. Each jewel was inscribed with a name of one of the tribes. The breastplate itself was solid gold and connected to the ephod by two gold buckles. There was also a gold chain that went around the priest's neck."

"Which meant it was heavy enough to need double support," Harry said.

"Next, the crown. Also worn by the High Priest when he entered the Holy of Holies. It was solid gold and shaped in three tiers. The crown also had a gold forehead plate, upon which was inscribed the name of God.

"And finally, the vine. This was something new. Josephus describes this in great length. He actually states this was Herod's idea. The vine itself was a golden rod that ran across the top of the main temple doors. The rod was five inches thick, if my calculations are right, so I'm assuming that, even though it may have been made of real gold, the rod was probably a pipe, with a hollow core."

Harry repeated, "Across the main temple doors."

"That's right," Storm said. "Both of them."

"How big is that?"

"Forty feet."

"A solid-gold pipe forty feet long."

"According to Josephus, it became a practice of Jews coming to Jerusalem from wherever they had been scattered to buy a golden leaf and have it attached to the rod, or vine. This symbolized their being rejoined to the family of Israel. Paul also refers to that in the New Testament, as Christians are grafted onto the vine."

She stopped. Folded her notes. Stowed them and the phone away. Waited.

Emma said, "What comes next?"

"I've located the positions of the first three Christian settlements. We need to check those out. And then something else, a long shot. I found a mention in the Smithsonian archives of an article from a Cyprus English language newspaper. The newspaper doesn't have a Web site. I need to go to their offices and check their back copies."

"Where's the paper?"

"Lefkosa. The Turkish side."

"How do we get there?"

Harry said, "I've been working on that."

THIRTY-TWO

HARRY HAD FIGURED THEY WOULD need to hit the island's northern side sooner or later. And do so quietly. He had visited the place twice while on salvage ops in the eastern Med. The southern side, the Greek side, was a European nation in the making. Investment capital was flooding in, as well as waves of tourists from all over Europe.

North Cyprus, on the other hand, was the Wild West of the Med.

What had actually caused the island's partition depended on who was talking. Harry had heard both sides and figured there was enough blame to spread around, with plenty left over for Britain, Turkey, Greece, and the United Nations. The latest began some forty years ago, when the mainland Greek government made threatening moves and Turkey responded by landing seventy thousand troops on the island's northern shores. As the military pushed south, almost two hundred thousand Greek Cypriots fled in their path. Bloody reprisals began in the island's southern half against Turkish families who had lived there for centuries. In the north, many Greeks who refused to leave their homes were never heard from again.

Forty years later, North Cyprus remained a pariah state, shunned by the UN and officially recognized only by Turkey. Adding fuel to the flames, North Cyprus had opened its doors to emigration from Turkey, drawing fifty thousand new inhabitants from the poorest farming villages of Anatolia. These families occupied farms whose titles still belonged to Greek families.

Recently there had been an even more volatile set of newcomers. Smugglers operating throughout the Arab world saw North Cyprus as a safe haven. They invested in new houses and apartments erected on Greek-owned land. Every time a new Middle East crisis brewed, speedboats crisscrossed the Mediterranean, ferrying families and goods and guns.

As soon as Harry told the taxi driver at Larnaca Airport what he had in mind, the three of them had an ally. The driver was short and severely bow-legged. His shock of white hair was startlingly bright against darkly tanned skin. Harry had been hoping for an older guy. He figured someone who had lived through the troubles might be more sympathetic.

The idea had come to him while reading the *International Herald Tribune* article on the Bosphorus ferry. What they needed was a way over the border without being noticed. At the time, Harry hadn't been thinking specifically about the assassin. He was just using a treasure dog's love of guile.

The driver's English was limited to a few words and a lot of hand gestures. He pointed to the women's shorts and said, "No good for Agios Mamas."

Harry asked, "You ladies pack any long pants?"

"It's hot," Storm protested.

"It'll be dark in a few hours. Things will cool off."

But the driver wasn't done. He flattened his hands down both sides of his face, then formed a knot below his chin. Harry interpreted, "And you'll need head scarves."

The driver took them around the outskirts of Larnaca and stopped at a market for locals. He personally selected two brightly colored scarves and bartered on their behalf.

When Harry then said he needed three backpacks, the driver gave him a knowing squint. "You no come back?"

"You have a problem with that?"

"My family is from Salamis. You know?"

"In the north."

"Yes. Now city's name is Famagusta. My father, he stay to . . ." The driver stood as if holding a rifle at parade rest.

Harry supplied, "He stayed to guard your home."

"Home, land, sheep. Many sheep. We farm sheep, olives. My father . . ." The driver blew on his fingers. Dust in the wind. "Never word. Nothing."

"I'm sorry."

The driver motioned with his chin to where the women returned from changing in a café restroom, carrying a sack of drinks and sandwiches. "Your friends, now they are ready."

"Maybe you should come too."

"When land is ours, yes. Land, farm, sheep. Now, is nothing." The driver handed Harry two long candles he had purchased in the market. "You light these for me, yes? In church. One for father and one for family."

"I'd be honored."

The driver clapped him on the shoulder. "Is good."

Harry handed a backpack to each of the women. "Take only what you can carry. We'll replace the rest later."

The drive to the border took another forty minutes. The road paralleled the Trodos Mountains. Storm sat in front and constantly shifted about, watching the mountains, the driver, the road, the broad central plain they traversed. Heading north.

The *Tribune*'s article had stated that after thirty years of padlocks and steel shutters and graffiti, the Church of Agios Mamas was to reopen. For two weeks.

The most famous church in Cyprus was over one thousand six hundred years old. The church itself had long been an icon, revered as a place of prayer and miraculous healings. But for the past thirty years the Turkish army had used it as a grain warehouse.

Three years earlier, a Greek Cypriot had flown a hot-air balloon up next to the border and shot the church through a bazooka lens. Photographs of the decrepit weed-strewn building had been cut from the local magazine, mailed to displaced friends and relatives, and posted on thousands of walls around the world. The church was home to more than the remains of Cyprus's patron saint. It symbolized all that had been lost in the island's division.

The island's situation was grave and growing ever more entrenched. One of Kofi Annan's last efforts before retiring as UN secretary-general had been to broker a peace accord. Annan had wanted to make a reunified Cyprus the jewel in his legacy's crown. He had failed. Turkish Cyprus had voted in favor, but the Greek Cypriots had turned Annan's proposal down flat. The Greeks wanted their land back. They wanted a unified island under a single government ruled by a Greek majority. They wanted the fifty thousand Turkish immigrants to be expelled. Until then, they were determined to use their growing power within the European Union to keep Turkish Cyprus isolated. Shunned. Banned from the worlds of finance and tourism and politics and progress.

Recently North Cyprus had elected a new government. This new government wanted to renegotiate. As a symbol of good faith, the new Turkish Cypriot government cleaned up the church and erected a temporary border crossing.

Up to now, rules governing the border changed from week to week, sometimes hour to hour. The Greek side instituted some change, and the Turks retaliated. One day, visas went from being free to costing five hundred dollars. The next, visa applications went from a few verbal questions to running twenty pages. The following week, only non-Cypriots could pass. Then only EU citizens. Or Cypriots could cross to the other side only once a year. Or only for a week, a day, or sunrise to sunset, or they could remain only within the confines of Nicosia.

Not everyone within the new North Cyprus regime was in favor of change. A lot of people made a lot of money from the status quo. These opponents couldn't stop the event, but they could make it as difficult as possible. The church and the border crossing would reopen for just three days. No vehicles were permitted to cross. All visitors were required to walk the five miles from the border to the church. Journalists and photographers were forbidden.

Harry knew they had arrived because the traffic simply congealed. People began pulling to the side of the road—buses, campers, farm tractors pulling trailers piled high with people. They passed dozens of people in wheelchairs. Hundreds.

"Ladies, scarves." Harry handed out the packs, asked the driver, "You'll take care of the suitcases?"

"Is no problem." He accepted the payment, shook Harry's hand, waved to the ladies, and was gone.

They were close enough to the front for Harry to watch the system collapse. The border was a pair of barbed-wire fences thirty feet high, with fifty yards of no-man's-land between the Greek and Turkish sides. When the Greek soldiers lifted the bright yellow barriers, the crowd surged forward. At the procession's head walked a row of black-robed orthodox priests. Each priest held an icon, a framed portrait of some bearded saint. As they approached the Turkish side they lifted the icons over their heads. The Turkish soldiers cranked open the gates, then shouted and gestured for the oncoming crowd to split in two and head for the pair of grey trailers set up as temporary customs sheds.

The priests kept moving straight ahead.

The soldiers shouted and gestured angrily. The crowd kept coming. The soldiers raised their weapons. Taking that as some kind of signal, many within the crowd raised up icons of their own. Thousands of icons, their heavy gold frames glinting in the sun. The people who weren't carrying icons held bunches of candles. No one spoke. They simply kept moving.

Beside Harry, Emma took a long, tense breath.

An officer stood on the back of a jeep and shouted something. The soldiers backed off, moving to the side of the road. The people surged forward.

When they made it past the barrier and were into North Cyprus, Emma said quietly, "This was your big idea?"

"I guess I didn't totally think it through," Harry said.

Emma started to say something more, but Storm said, "We're in and there's no record. Harry did right."

Emma looked at the younger woman but said nothing more.

A mile farther on, Harry took over pushing a wheelchair because the old guy wheeling his wife looked totally done in. Harry's head was growing so hot he was about ready to ask for one of the lady's scarves. The sun burned through his shirt and evaporated the sweat almost before it formed. What the old lady in the chair thought of the heat, dressed as she was in head-to-toe black, she didn't say. She sat with her gnarled fingers curled around her own personal icon, milky eyes fixed on the horizon. Her husband's gaze was as tightly locked as his wife's. A dozen or so tall white candles emerged from one coat pocket.

Emma asked Harry, "Want me to take your pack?"

"I'm good."

"You are, you know. Better than you give yourself credit for."

Storm glanced over and smiled. After that, Harry didn't mind the sun so much.

As they crested a rise, Harry took time to look behind. The road was packed, far as he could see, by a silent tide of people. In the far distance, people continued to pass through the border.

As they approached the church, something remarkable happened. The road became rimmed by Turkish Cypriots. So many people they managed to gently shoulder the Turkish soldiers to the background.

An old man stepped forward and murmured words as he handed the woman in the wheelchair a plastic cup of water. For the first time since the procession had entered North Cyprus, the woman's gaze shifted from the church just ahead. Her eyes followed the old man back to the side of the road, then she turned and looked at her husband.

A pair of middle-aged North Cypriot women stepped forward and pressed flowers into their hands—the old couple, then Storm, then Emma. One of the women smiled and patted Harry's hand where it held the wheelchair. On and on the greetings came, a soft defiance against two regimes who had forgotten how the vast majority of Cypriots had lived in harmony for centuries.

The Greeks responded with gifts of their own. They parceled out their loads of candles, until by the time Harry pushed the wheelchair through the church entrance, every set of hands he saw held either flowers or candles or both.

At his word, Storm and Emma remained in the growing throng outside the church. Harry pushed the wheelchair inside and swiftly checked the place out. As expected, the church revealed nothing of any use. Faint shadows of ancient mosaics covered the walls and floors, but the decorations had long since been scraped off and sold on the black market. He lit the taxi driver's candles, set them on the stand, and returned to the ladies just as the priests began the service.

They slipped away as soon as dusk hid them. The road into Turkish Cyprus was strewn with buses and parked cars and taxis waiting for return fares, much the same as on the Greek side, only dingier. Storm and Emma clutched each other as they followed him, stunned to silence by a combination of the church service and sheer exhaustion. Harry found a taxi driver who agreed to take them to Lefkosa, as the Turkish side of the divided capital was now known. Before starting off, they all turned and gave the church another long look— Harry, the ladies, and the driver.

Black fields stretched out beneath an almost full moon. A farmhouse in the vague distance cast a dim glow. Departing cars marked the road with headlights. The only other earthbound illumination came from the church, which was rimmed by candles. Thousands of candles. The church windows glowed like lanterns. The surrounding meadow was a sea of flickering lights. As he slipped into the taxi, Harry heard the crowd begin to sing again. There was an ancient cadence to the melody, one that carried the weight of centuries. Their taxi trundled off the verge and headed away, into the night.

THIRTY-THREE

THE NEXT MORNING, STORM LISTENED to Emma's soft breathing in the bed next to her own and recalled life in Palm Beach. Five-thirty in the morning was as close to Gothic as Palm Beach ever came. Mist often blanketed the predawn waterfront. The yachts docked along billionaires' row were vague etchings of wealth sketched from impossible dreams. Storm usually ran six miles, less if the humidity clogged her lungs. She often took it slow on her return down Worth Avenue, using parked cars as stretching rails and stopping for a bagel and coffee at her favorite side-street deli. She'd window shop with her breakfast, the street quiet enough for her dreams to thrive. The passage back to her shop and apartment were flanked by personal favorites. Chopard, the French jeweler, stood to her left, Bottega Veneta to her right. Across the street beckoned Hermès and Jimmy Choo. A girl could do a lot worse for neighbors. That morning she reflected on the utter strangeness of having a lifelong dream finally fulfilled, journeying through danger and mystery, searching for treasure. Yet here she lay, still bone weary after a full night's sleep, yearning for the life she had left behind.

A man's heavy tread marched down the hotel hallway and stopped in front of their door. Storm had not realized that Emma was awake until the woman slipped from bed and moved to the door in one fluid motion. One hand held a pistol down by the trailing edge of her Redskins T-shirt. "Yes?"

"It's me."

Emma unlatched the door, the pistol glinting in the light filtering through the hotel room drapes. Harry stood holding a tray with coffee and toast. He took in her thigh-length nightshirt and gun and smirked. "I believe I've had that very poster on my wall."

Emma slipped the pistol back under her pillow as Harry stepped inside, shut the door, and deposited the tray on the table between their beds. "When you're ready, there's a place down the street where we can rent a car. I thought I'd go check out Salamis while you hit the newspaper archives."

"Thirty minutes," Emma said.

"I'll see you ladies downstairs."

When he was gone, Storm accepted a cup from Emma and said, "I've been lying here missing the way things used to be."

"That makes two of us." When Emma drained her cup, the cords of her neck stood out in taut precision. "Okay if I take the bathroom first?"

THE TRIP TO SALAMIS WAS probably pointless, but needed to be done. Harry liked how Storm had seen him off, no unnecessary instructions, no reminders of things he'd never forget, just off and go. He was less pleased with Emma's response—the guarded words, the tension. Not to mention the gun and the gaze to match.

Which was why he wanted to make this trip alone.

Once out of Lefkosa's snarl, the road ran straight and flat and hot under a milky Mediterranean sky. The map called the baking plains the Mesarya. To his left, the Kyrenia mountains ran high and sharp, carving out a patch of sky. Harry found himself recalling mornings on the sea. He had always been an early starter. The seas were often calmest then, the water clearer. He loved the early morning dives, when the light still wasn't strong enough to filter down below about thirty feet. He loved to stop at the point of liquid twilight and float in the blissful nothingness. He had made some of his biggest hauls while the rest of the world was still dragging itself out of bed.

Soon as Harry pulled into a Salamis parking lot, he knew the trip was useless, at least as far as finding clues to the treasure. Storm's findings had been reasonably precise. The early Christians had been relegated to a forest outside the city walls. They formed a separate community, away from the Roman and Greek temple cults that dominated Salamis. They supported themselves as woodcutters and suppliers of charcoal and pine resin, which was used as an early antiseptic. They were excluded from most city activities, and persecuted on occasion. The forest was still there, but had been reshaped into a city park. Families picnicked and kids played and dogs barked. There was no way Harry was going to walk through a city park and come up with a prize.

Still, he spent a couple of hours scoping out the ruins. Salamis had been almost completely destroyed by the earthquake of AD 332, and the peninsula that had formed its harbor area had disappeared beneath the waves. When Constantine's mother arrived ten months later and offered royal support, the survivors had chosen to rebuild three miles farther inland. Harry walked the ruins, reveling in the silence and the timeless quality of a billion buried secrets. Part of what made him a good salvager was loving the tales attached to the prizes, like the nine-tenths of an iceberg that remained hidden from almost everyone else.

A rock bounced down the coliseum wall, making him start. Sean suddenly seemed impossibly close. The brusque old man stumped alongside Harry in his impatient gait, as though angry his aging body could no longer keep up with his mind. Just as he had walked that last night, leading Harry into the church, trying to cut off Harry's argument by entering hallowed ground. Only Harry had been too hot to pay any attention to such niceties, and he had lifted the church's roof with his angry blast. But Harry was paying full attention now. And the hairs on the nape of his neck rose with the certainty that he no longer walked alone.

The Roman road ran arrow straight from the submerged port to the Coliseum. Overhead the wind drifted through the pines. It was a remarkably natural sensation, walking through ruins seventeen centuries old, communing with the dead. Sean's voice seemed as clear as the murmuring trees and the waves lapping the bitter shoreline. Harry didn't mind that he couldn't make out a single word of what old Sean said. The meaning came through anyway, written on the ancient stones and the floating clouds and the deep hush of days beyond count. It was all tied together, threads woven on the loom of mystery. Death and life, treasure and love. All of it.

By the time Harry returned to the car and headed back to Lefkosa, he knew exactly what needed doing.

LEFKOSA REMINDED EMMA OF MEXICO. She had vacationed once in Acapulco. She had loathed the other tourists' frantic laughter almost as much as she had the tequila. She'd started walking the city, delving into the regions beyond the reach of tourist dollars. The second day of her self-guided tour, she'd been stopped by a couple of *federales* who spoke passable English. They had found it hilarious, this Anglo agent walking the city's backstreets, searching for she knew not what. So they'd let her play "ride along," and that night she'd helped subdue a bank robber. After that, they'd basically adopted her. She'd gone to both their homes for cookouts. A relative had taught her how to dive in Acapulco Bay. At the end of her holiday, three carloads had come to see her off.

Lefkosa held a dusty down-at-heel air, like the areas leading from the glitzy Mexican beaches back inland toward the barrios. Only Lefkosa contained no resort area. It sat at the base of the island's northern mountain range, on a flat, hot plain beneath a sky turned milky with dust. To her left she could just make out the official border crossing. The car rental agent had told them the border had been closed for two weeks. No reason why, no timetable for reopening. She stared at the towering gate with its banners and flags. Beside it, razor wire glinted around the rooftop of an abandoned building with bricked-up windows, now a part of the no-go zone.

Storm said, "Harry Bennett is a good man."

Emma stared at her. "Talk about out of the blue."

"Oh, right. Stand there and tell me you haven't been thinking about him."

Emma kept walking.

"He's got his eye on you, girl."

"What about you two? He obviously thinks the world of you."

"The feeling is mutual." Storm said to the street ahead, "One moment I feel like I've known Harry all my life. Then he does something, and I don't think I know him at all."

"I don't follow."

"Most people see trouble coming and then *run*. Harry goes into attack mode. The man I think I know disappears and somebody else takes his place. A primeval warrior. Barely tamed."

"Your knight in shining armor."

Storm stopped and looked at her. "That's how it feels."

Emma pulled her forward. "Harry is a treasure hunter. A deep-sea salvage man. I'm . . ."

"You're lonely."

Emma wanted to deny it. But the lie would not emerge. "What about you?"

Storm shook her head. "There's a difference between being alone and feeling lonely. I'm a pro at this game."

"What, you're saying nothing is ever going to break through and get to you?"

"Someday I'll tell you about my early home life. I've tried men. My scars run too deep to ever give them a decent chance."

They passed a café filled with men, only men. Hookahs bubbled. Dice rattled across a backgammon board. The café froze as all the men watched them pass. Emma gave the men five seconds of heat, then changed the subject with "Tell me again what we need from the newspaper."

"The Smithsonian maintains an archival record

of archeological finds around the world. I spotted a mention of a mausoleum discovered beneath the ruins of what may have been a fourth-century church. The mausoleum walls had carvings the author called curious. Vines and treasures and a shield he could not identify." Storm pointed at the newspaper's faded logo on the structure dominating the next block. "The source they quoted was this paper. The discoverer was an amateur archeologist, a former British commandant who had retired here."

"When was this?"

"Winter of '75."

"So, around the time of the partition." Emma had her foot on the newspaper office's front step when her phone rang. She fished the phone from her purse and checked the readout. She didn't recognize the number, but the area code was downtown DC. She passed through the door Storm held open for her and said, "This is Webb."

"Agent Webb, this is Evan Raines."

"Hold on." She cupped the phone. "I have to take this."

"When you're done, find me in the archives."

Emma nodded and headed back toward the sunlight. "Go ahead."

"Do you know who I am?"

"Yes, sir." Evan Raines ran the FBI's National Security Branch. Since his remit covered the

Intelligence Directorate, he was Jack Dauer's direct superior, only removed by six levels. The National Security director also ruled over the Counterterrorism Division, Counterintel, and Weapons of Mass Destruction. The fact that Evan Raines personally placed this call was a very big deal.

Raines said, "That makes things easier. We need to talk."

"I'm listening."

"Off-the-record."

"Absolutely not."

"As your superior—"

"You're wasting your breath and my time. Anything you say is official and will be passed on to my partner in Interpol. If you can't handle that we have nothing to discuss."

"Your partner."

"That is affirmative, sir."

He sighed. "I'll be back to you in ten."

"Make it twenty." Only when she cut the connection did Emma realize her heart was racing.

The newspaper receptionist was a slender man in his twenties who directed Emma up three floors to the archives. She found Storm seated at a long, scarred table surrounded by stacks of yellowed newsprint. The papers had become compressed over time until they looked ironed flat. Storm said, "Can you believe it? They don't even have microfiche."

"I just got a call from the FBI. I need to check in with Interpol, then talk to the FBI again."

"Take your time. I'm fine here."

"Hakim is going to want to know when you will talk with him."

Storm's attention had already returned to the pages spread out before her. "Tell him tonight."

"I'll be downstairs by the front entrance."

Emma coded in Hakim's number as she descended the stairs. Hakim answered with "Where are you?"

"I've had to give Harry my word I won't discuss any details of where we go or what we find. Not with you, not with anybody."

The contrast to her American superiors was jarring. No argument, no verbal shoving. Just, "Harry Bennett knows you are an intelligence officer, yet he relies on you to keep your word. That level of trust is remarkable."

She didn't have time for the burning lump that filled her heart cavity. "Evan Raines just called me."

Hakim digested that, then, "Deputy Director Raines has a reputation for being extremely honest and outspoken. It is said these are the reasons why he will never be made director. Assigning him to speak with you sends a clear message."

"What should I do?"

Hakim's smile filtered through the system. "Your American hardball approach has worked well so far. They have responded in less than two days. Raines has phoned you in the middle of the night his time, which suggests they have just reached a decision and feel the matter is so pressing they do not have a moment to lose. I would advise you to continue in the same vein."

"Are you sure?"

"The harder you push, the faster they must react, and the more we might learn. Good luck."

"AGENT WEBB? EVAN RAINES. WHERE are you now?"

"I'm not at liberty to say, sir."

"That's hardly the proper way to begin our dialogue."

"With all due respect, sir, your picking up the phone doesn't change a thing."

He didn't take that well. "I'm trying hard as I know how to make amends, Webb. I suggest you limber up and bend a little."

Emma did not respond.

"Look, we all know Jack Dauer made a serious error in judgment."

"I want a formal written apology, one that censures Dauer."

"Let's be reasonable—"

"Your letter must state categorically that any charges leveled against me are bogus."

"Dauer did not formally charge you with anything, Webb."

Emma did not need to pretend at heat. "I thought you were supposed to be stand-up, *Raines*. But here you are, feeding me that same old fibbie drivel."

"Dauer warned me you made a habit of getting out of line."

"Try treating me with the respect I deserve. In the meantime, your letter must include a full commendation, and state that I and I alone was responsible for bringing to light the *real* issues at stake in this case."

"I haven't seen any such conclusive evidence."

"And you won't. Not unless I hold a letter that counteracts any downcheck Jack Dauer even *implies* in his report."

Raines mulled that over. "I'll need to get back to you."

"I'm not done. Matter of fact, I haven't even started. I want contact details for Yves Boucaud. And the full reasons why you have been protecting him. In writing."

Raines actually laughed out loud.

"You think Interpol won't track him down? Here's your big chance, Raines. Prove us wrong. Show the world how the fibbies can be team players." When he didn't respond, Emma added, "Otherwise I'll break this case without you, and in my official report I'll give full details as to how the fibbies went out of their way to shield a murderer and a possible terrorist."

"That is absolutely not true."

"Then prove it."

"If I give you my word I'll do my best to make both these things happen, will you retract your threat to go public?"

"Absolutely. For another three days."

"We're not adversaries, Agent Webb. No matter what you may now be thinking."

"Show me."

THIRTY-FOUR

HARRY FOUND THE LADIES WAITING for him in the hotel lobby. The vast chamber echoed a refrain from the era of waxed moustaches and stiff crinoline and gin sipped on sunset verandas. The potted plants were dusty, the furniture lumpy, the walls decked out with campaign flags and animal heads. Storm asked, "What did you find?"

"Nothing. Nada." Harry slumped into the neighboring seat and motioned to where Emma sat clamped up tight, arms wrapped around her middle, chewing on something attached to the inside of her cheek. "What's with her?"

"She's been like that since she got a call from Washington this morning."

Emma did not look over. Storm's face, however, looked illuminated from within. Harry asked, "You found something?"

"Maybe."

"Looks to me like it's a lot more definite than that."

"There's a problem."

"Hey. This is the treasure business. Problems come with the territory."

She laid out her notes. "Colonel Braitheswaite. Commandant of the Fifteenth Hampshire Foot, whatever that is. Amateur archeologist. According to the Cyprus *Times*, he loved nothing more than puttering around ruins."

Harry could feel the tension radiating off Emma, strong as heat. He had no choice but to turn his back to the lady. One thing at a time. "So the colonel's a putterer."

"There were two articles. One about the colonel, who had retired on Cyprus after running the British bases here. The article described how he refused to leave North Cyprus after the partition. How he was happy here and felt safe and could still get his marmalade from Harrods."

"Local propaganda," Harry interpreted.

"Pretty much. The other was by the colonel himself. Describing the monastery and how he'd been around it several times over the years. Then on his last trip, he found the entrance to the mausoleum and got inside. He'd planned to go back and take pictures, but that next week the uprising started and the Turkish army landed."

"So there's this one amateur putterer who saw this thing one time."

"Yes."

"So far so good."

"It gets better." She used her notes as something to anchor her hands and keep them from crawling with the excitement that lifted her voice to one notch below music. "The colonel describes a vine carved into the crypt walls. One that ran the entire way around all four walls."

"A vine."

"Unlike anything he had ever seen before. There were also mosaics, some in excellent condition. A Menorah. A chest. Three shovels crossed like blades. And a shield that resembled the old Byzantine royal emblems, but with a crest he had never seen before."

Harry found it necessary to clamp down hard on his own internal fusion power source. "Now give me the bad."

"He never got back inside the crypt," Storm replied. "Because the Turks turned the area surrounding the ruins into a military compound. Six months later, the colonel suffered a stroke. Three weeks after that, he was gone. I found his obit."

Harry leaned back. Thinking.

Storm watched him. "Pretty bad, huh."

"Where is this place?"

She had a map ready. "The region is called Guzelyurt. Around the peninsula from Kyrenia. Between these two villages here, Yayla and Akdeniz."

Harry rose to his feet. "Time to relocate, ladies. Kyrenia is calling."

THEY STOPPED AT A KYRENIA real-estate agency advertising weekly rentals. The agent was only too happy to show them a former shepherd's cottage in Bellapais, a village perched on the hills above Kyrenia Harbor. The agent took the details of Emma's passport and credit card, accepted Storm's cash payment, showed them around the place, and departed. They shopped for basics at a local market, enjoying a trace of normality. Emma gradually emerged from her tight shell, even going so far as smiling in response to Harry's antics.

When they returned to the cottage, Storm insisted they go off on their own. What she wanted more than anything else was a chance to be alone. As they departed, Emma appeared flushed— radiant and tense and strong and fractured.

Storm ate a solitary meal of local cheese and salad and bread. Then she took her cell phone out to the minuscule veranda and dialed the number Emma had left. When Hakim answered, she said, "Mr. Sundera, this is Storm Syrrell."

"Thank you for speaking with me, Ms. Syrrell. Would you mind if I recorded our conversation?"

"Do I have a choice?"

Hakim's accent sounded tempered by a gentle nature. "I am not your American authorities, Ms. Syrrell. I do not consider you either a threat or a suspect. You are an ally. An important one. Of course you have a choice."

There was more than gentle politeness behind his response. This man reminded her of some of Sean's favorite clients, people who held lifetime passions down deep, whose money had neither corrupted nor changed the core of them. "In that case, be my guest."

"Thank you. One moment, please. Very well, we are ready at this end."

"How many people are listening?"

"Just myself and a technician. I have no gift for technology. I would ask that you tell me about the art market. What has changed in the past few years."

The cottage was perched on a natural ledge overlooking the Bay of Kyrenia and the section of Mediterranean known locally as the Akdeniz. Clouds clustered around the peaks behind her. The descending sun laced the far western edges with brilliant hues. "We could spend days on that topic and get nowhere."

"Pretend there is no time. A swift discussion, then I am gone. One thing. Maybe two. The biggest differences."

Storm tried to focus. Not to identify the most relevant items. She could have done that sleepwalking. But she needed to place the words in an order that would make sense to this man. "Okay, two things. First, the money. Despite the overall economic situation, prices within the art and treasures markets are rising faster than ever before. What was last year's ceiling is today's cellar."

"Why is this, do you think?"

"Partly because of the new investors. In the seventies and eighties it was the Arabs with their petrodollars. Now it's the Chinese and the Russians. But the market itself has gone through a drastic change. Real estate and stocks and bonds are all uncertain investments. Rich collectors see this as the time for a boom in the art and treasures market. But the amount of genuine articles available is limited. And there are a lot of dollars out there. Even some of the world's largest museums are finding themselves priced out of the market."

"This is very clear. I thank you for putting this in terms I can understand. What is part two?"

"There are fewer dealers who really count. The agencies and shops and auction houses that once handled midlevel items have no product to handle. But whatever trapped these players in the middle range remains the same—bad credit, bad rep, not enough smarts to predict what will rise or fall, low funding level, poor client contacts, patchy expertise. So these middle-tier people are getting frozen out."

"Like Syrrell's?"

"We're more high-end than most. And we were doing okay in a tough market, until the scandals hit."

The setting sun cleared the cloud's lowest edge, turning the ancient harbor and the surrounding waters a pure and timeless gold. Her internal illumination struck just as hard. "That's what it is."

"Excuse me?"

"What this guy is after. It's not about cornering a portion of the market. He's after untraceable transfers. In and out of countries, completely beyond the reach of bank controls. It's perfect."

"Could we perhaps return to my question about—"

"Perfect," Storm repeated. "Who can say how much a piece is worth in this crazy market? Ten million, twenty million, who cares? So he sells the item . . ."

Hakim gave her a moment, as though pushing to catch up. Then, "You were saying, Ms. Syrrell?"

Her mind raced ahead. She was trained for this, the best provenance expert Syrrell's ever had, a specialist in half truths and mysteries hidden beneath centuries. That wasn't bragging. It was fact. "He's setting up a string of dealers and maybe a few auction houses, all in different countries. Which would make it incredibly hard to track the flow of money, right? *He's going to sell the pieces to himself.* On and on, a daisy chain around the globe. His name doesn't appear on any ownership documents. Who's to know? He keeps inflating the price, laundering money every time."

Storm heard his hesitation, and knew with the

same piercing quality that Hakim was tempted to lie. And if not lie, then deflect. But when he spoke, it was to say, "I asked you for honesty, Ms. Syrrell. I did not expect brilliance as well."

To her right, the wind drummed through the tree limbs, making cymbals of parched leaves. A gull flew overhead, turned to a golden blade by the setting sun. The gull gave one operatic call and swept away, leaving the sky empty of all but her dreams. "You've known this all along."

"Suspected. The international banking industry is becoming increasingly well patrolled. But certain groups need money. Large amounts of untraceable cash."

"We've got to stop him."

"With your help, Ms. Syrrell, I am certain we are going to do precisely that."

THIRTY-FIVE

THE ORIGINAL ROMAN PORT HAD been located to the northeast of Kyrenia's present harbor. In AD 120 Hadrian, the same general who had crushed the Jewish rebellion, extended the rock promontory out and around the deepwater basin, in case he needed to recall his ships in winter storms and put down another revolt. Fifteen thousand Cypriot Jews who had survived Hadrian's initial slaughter died building the breakwater. The old harbor was now used by the local fishing fleet. Everything was exactly as Storm had found in her research. A modern road had been laid over the original track leading inland from the port to the island's second Christian community, Chrysova.

The community had been built around a rock quarry. Harry and Emma found the stone pit the Christians had worked, but nothing else. A tiny museum held little besides confirmation of all that Storm had uncovered. The quarry was about 220 yards long and about 110 yards deep. Steps carved into the quarry face had been worn to dangerous nubs by the ensuing two thousand years. Harry slipped under the warning rope and made a careful descent. He walked the base, searching for a carving or inscription that had managed to survive the twenty centuries. But his hunt was futile. When he returned to ground level, they found where the church had once stood, a meager square of stones about the size of a modern-day living room.

Back at the harbor, Harry asked if Emma would mind a detour. "It doesn't have anything to do with our search. But I'd sure like to have a look."

"Tell you what. Why don't we declare ourselves a night off."

"I like that idea. I like it a lot."

"Let me check on Storm and I'm yours."

Harry bit down on the words that popped into his mind, which were *I wish*. He waited until she snapped the phone shut and stowed it back in her purse. Then he reached out and took her hand.

Emma looked down, then up at him. Harry met her gaze and waited. She sighed her way to his side and said simply, "Lead on."

The Kyrenia fort marked the beachhead between the original Roman garrison and the modern town. The initial fort had been rebuilt and enlarged by one set of rulers after another. A series of poorly translated placards gave a brief rundown as they climbed to the inner keep. The Romans had been followed by the Byzantines. They had lasted the longest, ruling from the fourth to the twelfth century. After that, King Richard the Lionhearted used the island as his staging point for the conquest of the Holy Land. He sold the island twice, first to the Knights Templars, who failed to pay him. Richard then resold Cyprus to Guy de Lusignan, former king of Jerusalem, after Lusignan was defeated by the Ottoman general Saladin. Two hundred years later, the Lusignan kingdom was conquered by Venetian merchant princes, who in turn were defeated first by the Egyptian Marmeluke kings and finally by the armies of Istanbul. The island remained under Ottoman control from 1570 until 1878, when Britain took control by force and by treaty, intending to make the island a fortress against Russian aggression in the eastern Med. After decades of revolt, the island finally won its independence in 1954, but had a constitution imposed upon it that satisfied nobody, and in the minds of many, resulted in its current divided status.

The former royal chambers held a museum for the oldest boat ever recovered, a merchant vessel that had plied the Aegean over twenty-five centuries ago. They walked a raised platform around a glass cage sixty feet long. The ship was the color of dried mud, old bones stuck together with time, encased in an air-conditioned sarcophagus. Harry felt the air spark with the joy of a major find, even one that wasn't his. The other chambers held the ship's cargo, raised with the vessel from the mud outside the Kyrenia harbor walls. Harry stopped before a display of shoulder-high clay jars. "These amphorae were used for over two thousand years. They made for great storage. The narrow end was designed so they could be stacked in a ship and fitted to the vessel's curved bottom. Brilliant concept."

Emma watched him with the same intensity, but her former tension was absent. "You really know your stuff."

"I got my start with these babies. The insides were insulated. Resin was used for jugs carrying wine, wax for those holding oil. On land they were held in three-legged iron stands or terra-cotta holders. I once found an amphora and holder both painted with dancing nymphs, probably used in a wealthy household for lamp oil. Sold it to an Athens museum. Tore me up to let the thing go."

"You sold it through Sean?"

He led her up into the light and across the inner courtyard. The sun was blocked by the western keep, casting the courtyard into shadows made more brilliant by the wall of light overhead. "Sean came four years later, when I brought up my first treasure off Sumatra. A sixteenth-century Chinese junk hauling porcelain down to the island kings. Porcelain, jade, and gold are the treasure dog's favorite loot. They're the only three items known to man that aren't corroded by salt water. Sean saved my bacon."

"Saved you how?"

"Three-quarters of all salvage operations are sucker work. As in, the local government is the sucker and the treasure dog is the suckee. Government bureaucrats are nothing but leeches in suits. Sean personally negotiated a deal for me with the local politicos."

They descended the hill to Kyrenia Harbor. The tourist vessels were painted in bright colors, matched by the myriad flags fluttering in the sultry breeze. The stone walls lining the harbor were burnt ochre by the sunset. They selected a restaurant whose three tiers of waterfront tables extended from a medieval trading house. They let the owner order for them, then Emma asked, "What got you into treasure work?"

"I guess you could say it was a case of finding the only job I'd ever be decent at. My street radar is very very good. Growing up in a foster home with future murderers for roommates meant either I honed my radar or I was marmalade. This is all-important in the treasure business. You've got to have a gut honed for danger, and for knowing which trail to follow."

"You were in the Gulf. I read that in your military records."

"My feelings about my navy stint are pretty mixed. On the one hand, it got me out of what the county officials called juvenile care. On the other, I learned a whole different way to shuck and jive. After the first Gulf blowup was over, I stood duty on the fleet patrolling the region. We took our shore leave on Bahrain, which a lot of the guys hated. Me, I got to know some of the local fishermen. One day, they started complaining about something that caught their nets. Too deep for any of them to find out what it was. I offered to go down for a look-see. I found this old vessel. At the time I didn't have a clue what it was. Now I figure it for a dhow. Some of them went to two hundred feet long, traveled as far as Sri Lanka to the east and islands off the Cape Horn down south. I spotted this old treasure chest off the rear, what must have been the lieutenant's cabin. Couldn't decide what to do with it. If I hauled it up, they'd cut my throat for sure. Those Gulf fishermen are all half pirates to begin with. I figured they knew what it was all along, and were just waiting for some wet-behind-the-ears yokel to haul it up for them. So I swam back and told 'em it was just coral. Things went bad in a jiffy."

"They attacked you?"

"Sort of. They left me stranded on this atoll a mile and a half off the shore. Then off in the distance I heard the nasty sound of all the fleet's anchor chains being hauled in. Then came the big blast from the admiral's boat, and off they chug. Leaving poor Harry standing there looking at thirty days in the brig for going AWOL."

"Did you go back for the chest?"

"I tried. Got my papers nine months later, took off straight for Bahrain. Spent two weeks diving the area. Couldn't find the wreck. Last time I ever left a treasure without putting down a tracker."

"But you'd found your calling."

"Only job I ever want. Only thing I'm good at. I've worked salvage ops all over the world. Five in the Med, in Malta and Egypt and in Libya and two off Greece. Florida coast twice, once with Mel Fisher's group and the other with Bob Marx. Manila. Malaccan Straits. Hong Kong. Singapore."

When Harry stopped, Emma quietly added, "Barbados."

He squinted over the harbor. "I heard about this wreck my first year out. One of the last Spanish treasure galleons lost in the New World. Worked on the research for years. A lot of other dogs had tried and failed. But I had this idea that was taking me in a different direction. Winds and currents and politics, basically. I never liked the work like Storm does. I'm your basic point-and-shoot kinda guy. I did the research because I didn't have anyone else to trust with it."

"But you found it."

"I took the details to Sean. He tried to warn me off. I went down anyway." He looked down at the table. "They nabbed my boat, took just about everything I owned. Including the wreck. Which was right where I said it would be. In international waters."

"If it's any consolation, Harry, I believe you."

"Back in America, they've got all these special names for being inside the joint. You say the word, prison, it means one thing. Jail is something else entirely. Then there's the farm, work release, county lockup, the federal system, whatever. Where I was, things stayed a lot more basic. There was one jail for the whole island. Place called Glendairy. There was another place for women, I heard the name but I don't remember."

"It was awful, wasn't it."

Harry felt his face grow so tight the skin around his mouth and eyes probably looked seared. "I have nightmares."

Emma pushed her plate aside, reached over, and snagged his hand with both of hers.

Harry looked down. The strength of those

smooth-skinned hands radiated through him. "I wake up inside the dream. I'm just another bum, cadging drinks from one of the bars where me and my mates used to meet and laugh and pretend we were all going to be kings one day. In the dream my strength is long gone, my money, my good name. I laugh with them though I don't understand what they say. And I pretend I don't see the disgust in their eyes, or feel the shame that burns me."

Emma traced the hair over his wrist, her fingers slipping up to his elbow, then back again. "You've been out of prison, what, a couple of weeks. You get hooked up with a beautiful young lady. Storm is wounded herself, and she's come to rely on you totally. It'd be so easy for you to . . ." Emma shook her head. "Never mind."

Starlings swooped about the water and the moored boats, shrilling what was only a song to them. Every restaurant played a different music, from Turkish salsa to Snoop Dogg. The muezzin's cry melted into the sunset tune.

Harry said, "I met a woman the first time I went into Barbados for supplies. I went back. Several times. The last time, the cops were waiting for me. They based their claim that I was diving inside their waters by how they arrested me at her front door."

He looked at her. Straight on. Open as he knew how. "Then Sean sprung me. I still had 366 days on my sentence. But he did it, and the lawyer working for him was the one who told me Sean had been killed. Sean's last request was, take care of Storm. And that's exactly what I aim to do."

Emma met his gaze, the fading dusk magnifying the golden tint to her eyes. "I keep waiting for a buccaneer's line. And you keep surprising me."

Harry told her what he had decided on the Salamis road. "There's a thousand reasons why it won't work between us. So I've decided to toss away the salvager's standard line, which is to sing you the myths. It makes for a pretty tune, but it doesn't last. I'm going to give you the truth, Emma. Much as you want. Whenever you ask."

Emma leaned forward, coming in so close he could smell the mint and the coriander on her breath. See the pain in her features. "What are you *doing* to me?"

He stood, dropped some bills on the table, said, "Let's walk."

THEY WALKED OUT TO THE BREAKWATER to the ancient lighthouse, a cone of pitted rock shaped like a giant's torch. Somehow Emma seemed smaller, walking up close to him. Or perhaps it was how she was more relaxed than ever before. She molded to him, holding his hand and also gripping his upper arm. She said, "There ought to be a different word for the colors here. Especially the hour after sunset."

Harry felt her head ease over to rest upon his

shoulder. He buried his face in her hair, taking in the flavor of her in one huge draft. "You have my permission to make one up."

She walked slightly tilted, so that she could curve to him from ankle to hair. Even so, she trod the rocky path with the grace of a cat. "Cypriot blue."

"I like it."

"A thousand different hues. A painter's palette, all in one color." The wind whipped her hair into his face. "Sorry."

"I don't mind."

They reached the end and turned back. The harbor mouth wore the restaurant's gay lights like a necklace, one that swayed in the evening breeze. "Sunsets last a long time here."

"Not long enough. We could go right through to tomorrow, and it'd still be over too soon."

The twilight magic was strong enough for Harry to remember without pain, even without the need to acknowledge his recent black hole. Instead, he looked back and saw another dusk, heading home from a day of diving, after finding treasure scattered across the Caribbean floor. He recalled the weary grins, the taunting laughter of a crew who for that night, that sweet hour, knew in silent communion that theirs was an impossible quest. Because even on the best evening of the best day of the best find, the hunger never went away. It was the myth as much as the find that attracted a good treasure dog. But no one ever admitted it, except on a perfect evening, with a beautiful lady sharing a warm sunset breeze. A lady who turned to him then and said simply, "Kiss me, Harry."

THIRTY-SIX

HARRY SAW EMMA INTO A taxi and headed off alone. He told her that he had something he had to get done, and he didn't want their time to be ended by a return to the gritty edge. Not that he didn't trust her or know she could handle things. Emma must have understood, or was simply too filled with the night to press. Because she kissed him again, a lingering good-bye that melted his words. He stood on the sidewalk a long time after the taxi pulled away, smelling her perfume and the scent of her hair, feeling her arms and her strength. Waiting until the sensations had dimmed enough for him to put them away. Tuck them into that carefully guarded compartment. The one that had stayed empty for far too long.

He drifted along a road that was little more than an alley yet bound on both sides by every variety of shop. The people were poor, the city was just one crumbling step above squalid, yet there were thousands of these little stores. He could outfit an expedition along this one road, all from shops smaller than a walk-in closet. He took his time, buying items that had often been useful in bygone days. A coil of lightweight rope, a pair of high-impact flashlights, a mountaineer's hammer, a knife with a carbon-steel blade, a Swiss-army pocket knife, a professional backpack to replace the cheap one he had bought in Larnaca, a box of energy bars, and just-add-water meals. He loitered and he dickered and he kept shooting glances back behind him. Not because he expected to be followed. Because he needed to refocus. Be ready. For whatever. If not now, when the danger came. Because it would. Harry had no illusions about that. None whatever.

His destination was midway between the harbor and the castle, where his alley joined with a more upscale tourist avenue. The shop occupied two angles of the transition zone and had a banner that read OMDURMAN CAFE, ULTRA HI-SPEED. The windows were taped over with fly-blown posters of warriors in armor and women in fur bikinis, both wielding light sabers and watched over by bearded magicians.

The guy behind the counter had deep acne scars and an abdomen twice the size of his slumping shoulders, as though he had spent so long on his stool all his weight had shifted south and congealed. Harry leaned over the counter and shouted what he wanted against the roar of acid rock.

The guy didn't even blink. "You got money?"

Harry showed him a fifty. "One now, another when I get what I'm after."

"I know just the man you want."

"He's here?"

"Every night he has leave, he is here. Same time, same channel."

"Go talk to the guy and see if he's interested in a little business."

"He owes me big-time. He is interested." The guy held out his hand. "You pay, Joe."

"Sorry, Abdul. First you chat, then I hand you the bill."

The guy shrugged and shifted his weight off the stool. He walked through the double row of computers and leaned over the corner station. He shouted into the ear of a gamer who didn't glance up from the screen.

The proprietor's gut jiggled as he returned up the central aisle. "The money. Now."

Harry handed him the fifty. "What's his name?"

"Turgay."

"You sure he speaks English?"

The proprietor was already settling his bulk back onto his stool. "You go talk, you see."

Light from the street filtered through a second set of inward-facing posters. Walking down the central aisle was like swimming through reddish soup. About half the computer terminals were in use. The players all wore headsets and chattered as fast as they typed. Nobody paid Harry any attention. They were lost in their worlds of swarming gremlins and universal war. The atmosphere buzzed with tension and fatigue. The computers were high-end, the flatscreens big as television panels. The walls were bare, the floor grimy. The only clock these players worried about was the one counting out their cash. This was definitely not a place where tourists came to check their e-mails.

The guy in the corner was the same as the others, only with shorter hair. "You Turgay?"

"Hang tight, my man. Be with you in a jiff."

At least the proprietor had been right about the language. "You're stationed at the military compound outside Yayla?"

"Been there a thousand years. Or six months. Take your pick." His fingers blurred over the keypad. "Can't talk now. Ten minutes max."

Harry reached over and switched off the computer. "For five hundred bucks, my man, you will listen now."

THIRTY-SEVEN

THE DRIVE FROM KYRENIA TO the military base outside Yayla took just under two hours, a long time to cover forty-seven miles. The first half of the trip wasn't bad, a straight stretch following the cities along the coast—Kyrenia, Aylos, Elea, Incesu, Alsancuk, Karsiyaka. The North Cyprus coastline was a mixture of the sublime and the wretched. The two were so intertwined it was easy to miss one or the other entirely. The rocky shoreline sprouted more cranes than trees. Beyond the highway, where the coast began its rise to the staggeringly steep peaks, ancient villages nestled pearl-like in arid meadows. Out to sea, fishing boats dug furrows through the sun-splashed waters.

Just before Gecitkoy the road turned inward, narrowed, started to climb, then narrowed some more. They passed through a valley tight as a chasm, with a river flickering far below. The road was paved, but scarcely broader than a farm track. Though there was no traffic, Harry kept it in first gear.

Emma finally asked, "What are you doing?"

"Being careful."

"You're going five miles an hour."

Storm spoke from the backseat. "Slow is fine by me."

"If you don't like heights, stop and let me drive."

"Roll down your window."

Emma did as he asked, but didn't like it. "The dust is worse than the heat up here."

Harry didn't answer because he was too busy listening.

"Let's get a move on here. Pedal to the metal."

Harry thought he'd heard something. He slowed further.

She crossed her arms and huffed, "I met a driver in France. We need to get him down here to give you some lessons."

"Quiet." There it was again. The rumble, the thud, the high-pitched squeal.

Harry slammed the car into a tiny pocket carved from the cliff face. There was nothing to suggest it was meant for cars. The road had no markings at all. Emma's door shredded as the rock bit into the metal.

"Harry—"

Fifty feet ahead of them, a truck bellowed around the hairpin bend. The massive locomotive carried a full load of building stones. The brakes of all four wheels smoldered. It thundered past, shaking the earth, shrieking with metallic pain. Then it was gone. The day returned to hot emptiness.

Storm said, "You go just as slow as you want."

Emma's voice shook. "How did you know?"

"I didn't." He had no interest in saying anything more. He needed to focus on the next bend. But he also knew Emma was seriously spooked, the professional who had just made a bad call. "I've been on a hundred roads like this. You haven't. It's that simple."

The road climbed through one series of peaks after another, finally leveling off as it entered a vast highland plateau. The road broadened and Harry accelerated around slow-moving farm traffic. They passed stone-walled groves of olives and fruit trees. Many of the carts they passed were pulled by donkeys. A young woman in country

Muslim black used a staff to halt traffic as her goats crossed the road. A mile or so to either side, the flatland gave over to rising slopes covered with vineyards.

The Turkish army compound reminded Harry of a Soviet depot he had come across in Mozambique, only neater. The Soviets had been gone for five years, which was why Harry had been inside at all. The Soviets had brought money to the ruling faction and trouble to everybody else. When the Soviets left, their puppet regime fell. The new Mozambique government had been desperate for hard currency, even if it meant issuing an offshore salvage license to a treasure dog. They had even given Harry use of the Soviet compound, a weed-infested and derelict station two miles from the port. Following a pair of severe earthquakes and a recent typhoon, Mozambique had been desperate for dry warehouses and solid buildings. Yet the compound's forty walled acres of paved roads, empty barracks, assembly halls, machine shops, even a generator plant, had all stood empty. That was how much they had loathed their so-called benefactors.

The Turkish compound was military neat. Even the street curbs were whitewashed. Ditto the rocks lining the guardhouse walk, the rifle-range target supports, the metal stanchions supporting the razor wire fence. The entrance was flanked by eight flagpoles, a massive red banner with gold printing, and a billboard bearing the image of an impossibly brave soldier. Harry pulled into the visitor's lot and parked so that a tall bronze statue shaded their spot. "Our man's not out front like he promised."

Emma got out and studied her damaged door. "I'm beginning to believe in the paranormal."

But Harry didn't want to go back there again. He asked across the hood, "Something you said back at the DC airport, how you trusted Storm before you met her. I've been wondering about that."

Emma turned in a slow circle, studying the terrain, before replying, "I'd been with the task force about two months. Still finding my way, learning to duck whenever Jack Dauer took aim. There's a long learning curve in the agency business. You fight for an assignment to somebody who knows the business. If they like you, and if they're not superpossessive of their knowledge, they mentor you. In return, you schlep coffee. So there I was, two months into my first operation outside the Washington zoo. One morning this evidence just lands in our lap. All packaged and tied up with a nice blue bow. And I'm not kidding. The evidence arrived in a Venetian water-stained box."

Storm opened her door. "I love how you two are suddenly talking like I've disappeared."

Emma said, "You don't want me telling him about it?"

Storm turned away. "Whatever."

She watched Storm walk away, then continued, "There was this dealer by the name of Duksejian operating out of Manhattan. He'd buy a midlevel not too expensive Impressionist. Storm caught him doing it with Chagall. But not a *major* Chagall. We're talking in the range of five hundred grand."

"Is that all."

"When a museum-quality Chagall goes for six to eight mil, five hundred thou is not big bucks. Anyway, he'd buy the item at public auction. And like a lot of dealers, he'd hold it a while. Maybe in his home, maybe in the office at his shop. Set it where people could see it. It was for sale but not for sale. He was attached to it. He treasured it. Then after a while, he let the people who'd admired it know he was ready to let it go. Usually when he'd found another favorite piece. It happens all the time."

A pair of roach coaches stood across the street from the main entrance. Off-duty soldiers loitered beneath their awnings, eating the Turkish version of fast food. The smell of roasting lamb drifted in the heat. Farther along the dusty block stood a single café. Two trucks painted military green trundled past. A dog barked in the distance. Harry asked, "This is a crime?"

"Remember, Jack Dauer was setting up a task force to look at fraud inside the art world. And he had targeted Syrrell's as a major suspect. So what happens but Sean's granddaughter hands us this box of evidence. Related to a fraud we knew nothing about. One that implicated this Manhattan dealer, who as far as we knew was squeaky clean."

"Dauer must have loved it."

"We're talking low-altitude orbit. Which only gets worse when he realizes the fraud is real and he's been upstaged. Storm's evidence revealed how Duksejian used his contacts in Eastern Europe to find talented artists. There are a lot of gifted people over there, and except for a tight handful, most artists are starving. Duksejian offered to sponsor them as immigrants into America. But for a price."

"They worked off their voyage as forgers."

"As *his* forgers. Duksejian was very careful. He hired only artists who didn't speak a word of English. He shacked them in a tiny Florida town just north of the Everglades. He had an experienced forger he'd hired from prison to act as instructor. The deal was, they painted an even dozen forgeries. Then they were given papers. But not for the United States. For Argentina. He set them up in Buenos Aires with a small apartment and enough cash to keep them quiet."

"This guy was smart."

"When the story broke, dealers fanned the air with their certificates of authenticity. Turns out, Duksejian took the *original* work, which he owned, to European experts who were only too happy to offer provenance. Which he copied as meticulously as the artwork."

Harry watched Storm's reluctant approach. "I don't get it. Dauer gets this gift-wrapped and still treats Storm like a suspect?"

"Dauer thinks Sean Syrrell caught wind that he was being investigated and had Storm work this up to take the heat off."

Harry asked Storm, "How did you discover this forger?"

"I'm good at my job." There was a note of tight defiance in her answer. "The provenance was too perfect. You expect a second-tier painting, even from somebody this well-known, to have a few holes. I started checking, and things began unraveling. Then the same Chagall came up for auction in Yokohama, identical to the painting in our front window. And Chagall was never known for doing multiple versions. Which meant one had to be a fake. To my surprise, it turned out both were. When I showed Sean what I'd learned, he told me to tell you guys."

"He had Dauer's name?"

"Name, address, the works. Sean reimbursed the defrauded museum almost a million dollars from his own pocket. Five months later, we discovered that some silver plate we had handled was stolen. Sean made good on that one too. It pretty much wiped him out."

Harry straightened. "Here comes our man."

Emma turned and inspected the man hustling across the compound. "Are you sure about this guy?"

Harry could see the soldier's sweat from fifty feet. "Absolutely not."

THE MAN HARRY HAD LAST seen in the Kyrenia Internet café wore an officer's uniform that was lighter weight and better tailored than the sentries'. Turgay saluted the guard, waited for the barrier to lift, then hustled over. "You have the money?"

Harry riffled through the five hundred dollars. "You have our passes?"

"I must have it now." The guy smelled of fear.

"The deal's the same as yesterday. One hundred now. The rest when we're done."

"How do I know you will pay?"

"What's got you sweating, Turgay?"

"Inside the fence I am Lieutenant Sayed. Come now." But when both ladies started forward, he held up his hand. "Two, only two."

"Two, three, ten, what's the difference?"

Emma said, "I'll hang out here." When Harry started to object, she said, "May be good to keep us a back door outside the reach of the goons."

Turgay's forehead creased. "What is she saying?"

"Nothing. Let's roll."

Past the barrier, Turgay said, "The commandant

wishes to see you. He will have questions. You have answers?"

"Absolutely." Harry asked Storm, "You have your Smithsonian ID?"

"In my purse."

"Get it out. Okay, Lieutenant. We're ready."

"My money." When Harry slipped him the top bill, he said, "They must be very good, your answers."

THE COMMANDANT WAS A SKINNY weasel who started lying before he opened his mouth. His smile was a lie framed by a Mussolini-era moustache. The guy's uniform was another lie, and the medals on his chest only made the lie worse. Harry knew soldiers. This man was not one. He was a bureaucrat who specialized in not staying bought.

Turgay translated, "The commandant wishes you good welcome."

"Great. We don't want to take up his precious time."

"The commandant invites you for tea. It is coming."

The commandant's handshake was too cold to be wet. He spoke in a brittle singsong, his eyes never still. "The commandant asks for your passports."

Harry fished his out of his pocket. "Give the guy your Smithsonian ID." To Turgay, "Make sure the commandant understands the lady here is a famous archeologist."

The commandant and the lieutenant both departed. The office stank of stale cigarette smoke. A window AC rattled busily but produced no coolness that Harry could detect. Storm rubbed the hand the commandant had shaken down her pant leg. "Ick."

An aide brought in a tray holding two tulip glasses of tea. His hand trembled slightly as he deposited the glasses on the table between their chairs. Harry sighed an echo to the word his brain kept shouting: *trouble.* "How much money do you have on you?"

"Six, seven hundred."

"Let me have it."

She reached into her purse. "We already paid the lieutenant to get us in."

Harry took the money and set all but two bills in the middle of the commandant's desk. He weighted it down with an ashtray made from the casing to an armor-piercing shell. "Take a look around. We are as *in* as we ever need to be."

THIRTY-EIGHT

THE COMMANDANT CAME BACK INTO his office and pretended to search his desk for something. He left once more and did not return. The money remained planted under the ashtray. Harry did not know whether to take this as a good sign or not, until the lieutenant entered, handed back their IDs, and said, "I take you now."

Everyone they passed showed a careful determination not to even see them. The back of the lieutenant's shirt was black with sweat. When they were out in the sunlight and walking the track away from the main entrance, Harry asked, "How much did the commandant take from you?"

"All but one hundred. I'm restricted to base for six months." He gave Harry the stink eye. "You make too much trouble for too little money."

The base was shaped like a rough triangle, with the main gates at the pinnacle. The border to Harry's left was formed by a copse of hardwoods. Through the trunks he saw a flicker of blue, where the cliff dropped away and the sky joined with the sea. They passed the officers' quarters, a trio of barracks, squads drilling and snapping rifles to their shoulders, trundling military vehicles, all the bits of a life Harry missed not at all. Where the road curved right and inland, the lieutenant took an unmarked path that aimed straight at the trees. Harry waited until he could see the ruins to say, "Okay, we'll take it from here. Stay here in the shade. We won't be long."

The lieutenant made sure they were unseen. "I want more."

"Look—"

He chopped the air. "Forget the deal. I owe much money."

Harry stepped in close enough for his bulk to

shadow the lieutenant. "You stay here. You stay alert. You take us back to the front gate. We make it out, you get another two."

Harry turned away. "Let's go, Storm."

When they were well into the trees, she asked, "Are we safe?"

"He's got two hundred good reasons to make sure. But we need to hurry."

The monastery was perched on a promontory that pushed seaward until they were surrounded on three sides by the Med. The monastery was not directly on the cliff's edge, but not far off either. Harry walked over to the ledge. One glance was enough to explain why this region had seen no tourism. There was no beach whatsoever. The rock face fell sheer to the sea, a drop of seven or eight hundred feet. The cliff face extended to his left until it faded into a bluish grey horizon. To his right, the cliff joined the mountains forming the island's northern spine. The peaks marched east-ward and melted with the heat and the dust. Harry turned back to the ruins. Something about the setting bothered him. He gave it a few minutes, but came up with nothing.

Storm jumped at the sound of repeated bangs. "What's that?"

"Rifle range. Let's get to work."

A single Corinthian column marked the entrance to a dusty enclosure. The interior walls were bitten down to shoulder-high chunks. The lower halves of narrow windows framed white-capped waves. The wind rustled and moaned about the ruins. Harry made a slow sweep. "Touch of paint, a good cleaning, and we could move right in."

The monastery ruins were a series of interlocking rooms that revolved around a central courtyard. The monks' chapel was the largest chamber and contained space for what once had been a door to the outside. Harry had twice gone after early religious relics. Some of the oldest monasteries had developed from religious communes. There was probably some fancy name for them, but commune worked for him. Families lived together and shared everything. They made up the core group. But there was also outreach. But new believers and their families weren't just invited in. Harry had read how this interim period could last anywhere up to three years. During that period, newcomers could enter the church but nowhere else. It wasn't until the fifth or sixth century that most of these original communities turned celibate. And even then, many kept to the habit of opening their daily services to outsiders. So these old chapels had their own entrance.

Harry asked, "Did the colonel say where the crypt was located?"

"Not a word."

Harry headed for the front of the chapel. The nave was marked by an oblong stone frame the size of a dinner table. The sanctuary faced east, back away from the sea. The front wall was three-sided and rose to cup the lower remains of windows. The view was over mountains rising out of the sea. Harry could think of worse ways to start the day than this view. He turned away and started kicking the earth floor.

"What are you doing?"

"Most tombs are located under the altar. So the dead remain part of the service, and they're prayed over by the brethren. Why don't you work your way around the left walls."

Harry found the mausoleum by tripping over the lid.

A lid that should not have been there.

"Now this is interesting."

"What?" She stepped over beside him.

Harry kicked the metal plate. "Give me a hand with this thing."

The steel lid was three feet square and over half an inch thick and weighed a ton. No way could they ever actually lift it. Harry found a length of rusting pipe and Storm grabbed a tree limb. Together they managed to shift it about a foot. Harry pulled one of the flashlights from his pack and shone it down the hole. Far in the distance gleamed a rocky base. "What do you know."

Storm broke her limb and Harry's pipe bent like a question mark. The lid still covered more than half the opening. Harry drew the coiled rope from his pack and knotted it around one corner of the lid.

"Walk over there and keep tension on the rope."

He made sure the rope didn't slip until Storm was in place. Then he joined her. "We're not going to pull straight back. If we do the rope will slip off. We walk to our right."

"Unscrew the lid."

"That's the idea. Ready? Okay, pull."

Harry had to refit the rope three times before the lid was over far enough for them to slip past. He looped the rope around one stumpy outcrop growing from the nave, tested it, then said, "Don't rely on this thing unless you have to."

Storm peered into the dark. "Does Cyprus have snakes?"

"I guess that means I'll go first."

The opening was scarcely broader than Harry's shoulders and descended at an angle somewhere between stairs and a rock ladder. He made sure he had a fresh grip with the hand not holding the flashlight before each step. The chapel floor was maybe five feet thick. When his head finally cleared the ledge, he saw he was descending a rock outcropping carved from one wall.

"Shine your light over my shoulder. No, lay down and extend your arm in here. Yeah, that's it." Harry slipped his own light into his pocket and kept going. "Okay, I'm down."

"What have you found?"

He retrieved his light and flashed it about the chamber. "Come down and see for yourself."

Harry kept his light on Storm's next step and his other hand extended toward her leading leg. She slipped down lightly beside him. "You go right, I'll take left."

The chamber's side walls were lined by floor-to-ceiling tiers. The room was fifty feet long and thirty wide, the stone ceiling curved into a high arch. The rear of the chamber held a dozen stone coffins. The shelves were filled with a jumble of bones.

The front of the chamber held a smaller replica of the main chapel's nave—same stubby legs of a vanished stone table, same curved front wall facing east. Harry knew the place would have been used as a second chapel, both for funerals and for night-time prayer vigils. The early folk had not kept bereavement at arm's length. Death was too close.

Storm traced her hand over the scarred front wall and moaned.

"It's not so bad."

"Don't you dare patronize me."

"I'm serious."

Storm's light made an angry sweep of the room. "There's nothing here!" Her voice echoed through the looted chamber. "They took *everything*."

"Pretty much." Harry walked to the back and peered into the stone coffins. They were all empty. "I figure these coffins were for bishops and the shelves held the common folk. The bishops were probably buried in their robes, maybe with a cross or a ring, and the coffin lids were carved. Which is why they've been looted."

She dropped to her hands and knees and ran her fingers over the stone floor. "I can see shadows where the mosaics used to be."

Harry walked over and squatted beside her. "Here's what I think probably happened. The commandant heard about the crypt. My guess is one of his enlisted men got caught pilfering. So he came in and did a professional job on the remains. Probably made a killing."

"Which may be how Sean wound up with the chalice."

"Makes sense." Harry's light played across walls where the rocks were scarred with fresh chisel marks. "The monks probably had a secret compartment in the stone altar there at the front. They could have brought the chalice out for special occasions, maybe a once-in-a-lifetime thing, like when they inducted a new bishop. That commandant might actually have done us a favor."

Storm's head raised in stages as his words sunk in. "What?"

"Think about it. We've got a peeved British colonel with no ax to grind except a desire to get back here for another look. And nobody else knew about this place, from the sound of things. So the commandant loots this place, finds the chalice, Sean buys it off some black-market dealer, and look where we wind up."

"You're saying the treasure is still here?"

"Maybe. For sure the commandant didn't get it. Otherwise he'd be poolside in Aruba."

"What do we do?"

Harry rose to his feet. "Let's go see if the lieutenant stayed bought long enough to get us out of here."

WHEN THEY EMERGED FROM THE trees, the lieutenant was nowhere to be found. The road was empty, the rifle range silent. Even the wind seemed to have been defeated by the day. They walked a barren road, past silent buildings.

They rounded the commandant's office. The main gates were fronted by a traffic circle holding a half dozen flagpoles. The flags hung limp, hot, defeated.

On the other side of the traffic circle stood a squad of armed soldiers. The commandant and the lieutenant stood in the gatehouse's shade.

Harry said, "If he stops us, I'll argue. You run."

"There's no way I'm leaving you."

"Do like I'm telling you." At a signal from the lieutenant, the soldiers started forward. "Here we go. Watch for my signal."

But there was no chance of her running anywhere. A phalanx of soldiers remained by the barrier while the rest split and came around both sides of the circle. The commandant walked forward with his lieutenant in tow. The lieutenant's uniform was more sweat than cloth. "The commandant asks if you found what you sought."

"Just more rocks and weeds."

"The commandant asks if you care to join him for more tea."

"Hey, you know we'd love to stay and chat." Harry pointed to where Emma stood by the main barrier, her arms crossed, her legs planted, her stance shouting anger. "But the federal agent over there needs to return and make her report."

Storm corrected, "Interpol."

"Whatever."

The lieutenant stiffened. The commandant snipped off a quick question. The lieutenant translated. Both men turned and looked at Emma.

The commandant asked the lieutenant, "Interpol?"

Harry said, "You tell him whatever it is you need to, get us through those gates, meet me at the café tonight and you'll still have your cash." He raised his voice and said, "The commandant here wants to see your badge!"

Emma had them ready. She flipped both open and raised them over her head, one in each hand. "Tell him to take his pick!"

The lieutenant asked, "Is it true, she is agent?"

"The American government and Interpol both wanted to make sure this *extremely important* lady with me here had a proper welcome. Please tell the commandant we're grateful for his hospitality. But we're walking out those gates right now." He took hold of Storm's arm. "Let's go."

Harry felt the itch of two dozen soldiers taking aim at his back. They walked around the barrier's tip, on the entrance's side opposite the guardhouse. Storm puffed tight little breaths but stayed steady, even when the soldiers fronting the barrier shouted something, whether for Harry to stop or for the commandant to give orders, he had no idea. "Keep moving."

Emma came around to Storm's other side and walked in lockstep back to the car. Not saying a word. Just moving with them. A stroll across the lot. Into the car. Harry had a little trouble getting the keys into the ignition and the car in gear. But he managed. The soldiers watched but did not move.

None of them drew a decent breath until they rounded the first corner.

THIRTY-NINE

BACK IN KYRENIA, HARRY WORKED out two shopping lists. He took the longer for himself and left with Storm, a fistful of Sean's money, and a plan to rendezvous in two hours. They had just started down the line of shops fronting the main harbor road when Storm's phone rang.

"Hello, Storm. It's me." Claudia sounded beyond drained, as if the life had been sucked out of her days ago and she just kept going, a husk without the energy to lie down and quit. "What is that noise?"

"You caught me on a street." Storm stepped into the entrance to a block of apartments and cupped the phone. "What's going on?"

"A lot. Where are you?"

Storm hesitated a long moment, then decided: "Outside Paris." By about fifteen hundred miles.

"You've found a job in France?"

"Actually, I'm looking for a possible new find."

"Who for?"

Storm had to shout against the roar of passing motorbikes. "Me."

"You're opening up your own shop?"

"Thinking about it."

"With what?"

"I have the Dürer, remember?"

"One painting doesn't make a shop, no matter how special. Why not use it as an entré into a big house?"

"What do you have against my going into the business for myself, Claudia?"

"I'm concerned about your future. That's all."

"Is that why you called?"

"No." The silence thundered louder than the road. Then, "I've sold Syrrell's."

"Don't."

"It's done, Storm. The papers are signed. I wanted you to hear it from me."

"Who will run things?"

This pause was the hardest of all to bear. Claudia finally replied, "That's still under negotiation."

Storm realized the afternoon light had become somewhat blurred. "Traitor."

THEIR PREPARATIONS TOOK THEM THROUGH the rest of the day and well into the night. But Cyprus ran by Mediterranean time, which meant none of the shops Harry needed to hit closed before midnight. Emma endured the Kyrenia rental agent's scathing comments and traded in the damaged car for a Suzuki four-wheel drive. They all returned to the cottage well and truly spent. They ate a cold supper on the patio. Overhead the clouds clustered about the peaks, while below them the lights of Kyrenia sparked a promise of what lay ahead.

After dinner Storm hugged Harry good night and declared, "You're the best."

"You did okay back there yourself."

She hugged him harder still. "Only because you were there."

Emma fitted herself into the space Storm left vacant. She held him less tightly, but more completely. When Storm could be heard moving about inside the cottage, she asked, "Do you think there will ever be a time for us?"

"Count on it."

She kissed him, then moved back far enough to

inspect him with star-flecked eyes. Her tongue touched her lips, like she was tasting him. She kissed him again. Then slipped away.

The next morning, Harry started an hour or so earlier than he would have liked, drawn awake by a thousand urgent tasks. He rose and brewed a pot and took his mug out front. Their supplies were crammed into the back of the Suzuki. He heard the women stirring and returned to the kitchen. "One small backpack each. Dress for a hot day. Bring extra layers for warmth, in case."

Storm did not look over. "You told us that already."

"Twice," Emma said.

They left twenty minutes later. They went to the fishing port and parked down from a shop advertising Jet Skis for rent. Harry didn't go looking for a boat because he didn't want the hassle. This close to smuggling routes, boats were carefully monitored. Jet Skis were considered tourist toys. Even so, the only way they obtained two for an overnight adventure was by flashing money. "We'll need two sets of diving gear. Tanks, fins, suits, spearguns, weight belts. And sleds to carry the stuff around."

"One of the ladies does not join you?"

"They'll switch around. We need to keep one person up top, remember?"

"You are going to much trouble for this privacy." The guy was both young and darkly handsome, and possessed an easy manner from feasting on tourist dollars and women. "Why you not come on my diving tour? We take nice boat. I know many beautiful places only I can show you."

"It's our vacation and we like to do things our way."

"Sure, sure, I understand. You want private beach. Do private things."

Harry heard Emma's chair creak and figured she was about three seconds from handing this guy his head, one tiny piece at a time. "How much?"

They dickered over price for a while, then longer over the deposit, which wound up being almost enough to buy the two Jet Skis outright. They slipped across the street and tucked themselves well back in a harbor restaurant, lone Westerners surrounded by rattling backgammon dice and bubbling hookahs and men. They ate a shank of lamb and rice and salad and sketched plans on the paper tablecloth until the dockhand came to say their Jet Skis were ready.

They loaded the gear onto the sleds and lashed it tight with bungee cords. Jet Ski sleds were built both to haul and to act as dive platforms, and were remarkably stable so long as they remained attached to a machine. The shop owner stood and watched and did not lift a finger to help. "You have dived the Med before?"

"Many times."

"Is very lovely, the waters here. Very romantic. I have favorite place." He made solemn eyes at Storm. "I show you, make the other lady happy."

Harry covered the ladies' growl by revving his engine. "See you tomorrow."

The sleds dragged heavy against the Jet Skis' desire to kick in and fly. The wind was light, the waves a gentle onshore wash. Harry increased the speed at a gradual pace, pulling past the fort and the main Kyrenia harbor, watching to make sure Storm could handle the other machine. The city sprawled across the seafront lowlands, the cranes marking where new tourist developments began to scale the first ridges. High overhead, the tallest peak was crowned by the remnants of Hilarion Castle, one of three mountain fortresses built by King Richard the Lionhearted. They left the tourist mania behind, passing small seaside villages and exchanging waves with coastal fishermen. The engines churned, the spray flew. Emma tightened her grip about his waist, her warmth a sharp contrast to the water's chill. The sun baked them with sea salt for spice.

They rounded Cape Korucam, with its medieval stone lighthouse and emerald pastures, shepherds watching them from the point. The mountains closed in, spilling in timeless grace down to the sea, their crowns lost to clouds. The hills marched in stolid certainty into the lavender distance, joining finally with the sea and the sky. Harry moved in closer to shore, the cliffs a looming wall blocking the east.

He knew they had arrived because the ledge upon which the monastery sat was a solitary hook of rock, extending at a jagged angle from the main cliff face. Harry pulled a bit farther offshore, checked the current to ensure they were safe for a dive, then cut his engine. After two hours of whining engines, the silence was achingly strong.

Emma slipped back a notch. It seemed to Harry that the lady might have been a bit reluctant to release her grip. He patted her arm, unable to come up with words quite as fine as that sentiment. She seemed to understand, because she kissed the sun-splashed back of his neck before finally letting go.

Storm called over, "I saw that."

Emma said, "Stick around, you might learn something."

Harry said, "I wish."

Storm's quip was cut off by a ringing from Emma's backpack. Emma said, "I don't believe it."

"The military base up on the cliff must have its own cell-phone tower," Harry said.

Storm asked, "Do you have to answer?"

Emma slipped agilely onto the sled. She pulled the phone from her pack, checked the readout, and hit the button. "Agent Webb."

"Business," Harry said.

Storm sighed.

Emma's tone went steel hard. "What I need to hear from you, sir, is the history and whereabouts for Yves Boucaud."

Storm turned in her seat. As intent now as Emma.

Harry swung one leg over the center console. He kept a hand on the controls, balanced against any movement from Emma. Waves lapped against the windward side of his Jet Ski. The woman's face grew as hard as the cliffs overhead.

Emma fumbled inside the backpack and came up with pad and pen. The light was Aegean clear, a luminosity so brilliant Harry saw what he had missed up until then. Emma Webb was in fact two people. There was a woman strong enough to be soft with him. And this other person. A federal agent. Hard and cold and utterly professional. He studied her with the sadness of knowing she was locked into a world from which he was forever barred.

Emma cut the connection. The wraparound shades clung to a face more stone than flesh. "Washington's come through. I need to let Hakim know."

Storm asked, "Can you tell us first?"

Harry replied, "No. Make the call."

"Thanks."

He watched her so intently he only half heard her side of the conversation. Her tone held him, though, clipped and terse, chopping each word off with a sniper's precision. The question Harry had to work through was, could he handle having less than 100 percent of this lady? Because he was certain there would always be places she went without him.

He gripped the Jet Ski's rubber handle and looked over the side, down into the waiting depths. Down into his world. He looked back to the sled. As Emma talked about the bad guys, she left his world behind. Harry knew this would be a lifelong pattern. It left him a little sad, but not much. Because he felt what was really happening was a whole lot bigger than just one shift in his perception. Like he'd taken some giant leap of his own. Adding another mystery to the world.

Finally Emma shut the phone, put away her notepad, zipped up the backpack, said, "Okay. Here's what we know. Yves Boucaud was born Robert Montalband in Marseilles to *pied noir* parents. *Pied noir* translates as blackfoot. It was intended as a semiderogatory way of describing Europeans cast out of Algeria after France lost the civil war, but the families apparently use it to describe themselves to this day, and with pride. They are very close-knit. Some are involved with crime lords inside the Arab world. Ten years ago, Boucaud became a principal conduit for clandestine arms shipments to US allies. In the lead-up to the second Gulf war, Boucaud was the largest supplier to Kurdish rebels in north Iraq."

Storm asked, "Why the name change?"

"You see that sometimes. Maybe he stiffed the wrong partner. Or maybe he moved up in the world and wanted to break from his past. In any case, the US recently discovered that our boy had started using his ally status to sell arms wherever he could find a buyer. The US government has been playing it low-key, hoping threats would bring him around and allow them to avoid a major publicity nightmare."

Harry said, "He's fronting for terrorists."

Emma shrugged a maybe. "As of yesterday, Homeland Security has officially put Boucaud on their watch list and has frozen any further business."

Storm said, "That's it?"

"My guy claims they have no concrete evidence to take it any further."

"In other words, they still aren't looking very hard."

Emma did not respond.

Harry let the water lap against the hulls for a time, then said, "Let's get wet."

STORM HELPED THEM SUIT UP and fit on the tanks. She declined Harry's offer for her first-ever diving lesson, said she'd be happy to snorkel when they were done. She watched them slip over the sled's edge and gave it a full twenty minutes. Harry had lashed the two Jet Skis together so

Storm could easily hold them both offshore. She waited until their air bubbles had shifted so far south of the boat that she could no longer make them out from the waves and the sun. Then she shifted to the other machine, climbed onto the sled, and reached into Emma's backpack.

Emma's notepad and pen were in the same side pocket as her phone and the Interpol badge. Storm scouted about, half expecting to see Emma rise from the waves and hurtle accusations. But she was alone on the calm waters, save for a distant boat and a pair of gulls floating overhead. Storm opened the Interpol ID, the leather wallet so new it creaked. Emma looked out at her with a steel-hard gaze, the total pro. Storm ran her finger down the edge of the cover. The night before, in the darkness of their shared bedroom, Storm had asked her how it felt to be a federal agent. Emma had replied sleepily that it was the best job in the world, but only if you could put up with the sexist hassles, the lack of stick-around men, and parents who urge you to get psychiatric help. For some reason, Storm had felt sad for them both.

Right then, she wished for a bit more of Emma's hard-core strength.

Storm put down the wallet and opened Emma's notebook to the last page. Yves Boucaud's telephone number stood out clearly because it was the only thing not written in Emma's personal shorthand. Storm unzipped the backpack's other pocket and drew out her own cell phone. The signal was down to a single bar. Storm dialed the number.

After three rings, a man's voice came on. "Speak now."

The shock of hearing the voice behind Sean's murder felt as sharp as an ice dagger. "My name is Storm Syrrell. I am calling to ask you for a job."

She slapped the phone shut and clenched both hands between her thighs, rocking slightly until the body tremors eased.

FORTY

WHEN HARRY AND EMMA RETURNED to the surface, the evidence of a good dive was clear on both their faces. Harry helped Emma out of the water, then set his speargun on the sled and clambered up to sit beside her. He unhooked the line of fish from his weight belt and connected it to the Jet Ski's footpad so the fish remained in the water. He eased off her tanks and her weight belt, then stabilized the sled while she took off her wetsuit and slipped shorts over her bikini. They talked in low tones about the water, the fish, the coral, the sea, the light. Not shutting Storm out. Just reveling in the intimacy of an experience that was all theirs.

Harry fed them all energy bars and water. He asked Storm if she wanted to go out, but didn't press. Storm had the impression he was waiting for something, particularly after he picked up the small binoculars he'd bought in town and played them over the cliffs looming to the east. Emma combed out her hair, slipped on a sweatshirt, then leaned back on the sled and sighed with genuine contentment.

Later, Storm decided. I'll tell them later.

Emma said, "I could learn to love this."

"Glad to hear it," Harry said, not taking his eyes off the cliffs.

Emma smiled his way. "Looking for anything in particular?"

Harry seemed to take that as his cue. He lowered the glasses and said to Storm, "Tell us about these hills."

Storm had left her notes back at the cottage but did not need them to respond. "The mountains of northwest Cyprus were the world's first major source of copper. King Aurelius, leader of Cyprus during the rule of Nefertiti, empress of Egypt, was known to have paid all his tributes in copper talents, mined from those hills. The island became rich off the export of copper, which became one of the cornerstones of the first and second Bronze Ages."

Emma said, "Okay, I'm impressed."

"Enkomi was the island's first capital and was located near Salamis, away from the eyes of people coming to buy their treasure. Then the Phoenicians invaded and captured the island. They moved the capital near where Lefkosa is now."

Harry asked, "Any mention of earthquakes in the mining area?"

"No, but I didn't check that specifically."

Emma said, "They'd talk about cities being destroyed."

"Maybe. Then again, maybe there wasn't any to mention." Harry pointed to the sharp line of peaks rising from the sea to their left. "Hills struck by earthquakes tend to be rounded. These mountains have been fashioned by eons of wind and rain."

"What are you saying?"

Harry replied, "Tell me what you saw down there."

Emma sat up on the packs. "Coral. Fish. Seaweed."

"You saw a ledge, right? The bottom comes flat off the cliffs there, straight out to here, and then it drops off to infinity and beyond. A classic eastern Mediterranean island configuration."

"So?"

"It's been bothering me since I got my first look off the cliffs by the monastery." Harry turned to Storm. "What brought us here? I don't mean the treasure. I mean the first clue we had of its being here at all."

"The three-fingered design from the triptych."

"Exactly."

Emma said, "You've lost me."

"Hand me your notepad." Harry flipped to an empty page and related his and Storm's findings as

396

he drew. "This is what we saw. Three stubby peninsulas sticking out to sea. The central one is squared off at the tip. Waves are crashing around the outside."

Emma said to the page, "So maybe an earthquake sheered it all off."

"That's what I came here hoping we'd find." Harry handed back the notebook and pen. "But I don't think that's what happened. If an earthquake sheered off a face that high, you could spot the rubble from the surface."

Storm said, "You're telling us we got it wrong."

"No. I'm saying it's not *here*." Harry stabbed the water with a forefinger.

"All this for nothing," Emma said.

"No. Absolutely not. The treasure is real and we're closing in. I can smell it." Harry hefted the binoculars and studied the cliff again. "But I can't get around to solving this riddle until our watchers take off."

Emma sat up straight. "I don't see anybody."

"That boat on the horizon. They've been shadowing us since before we made our dive. So far, all they've seen is three people doing exactly what we said we'd do." Harry unleashed the Jet Skis. "So let's go find us a secluded beach, and maybe they'll leave us to get down to the real work."

EMMA CONTINUED TO RIDE BEHIND Harry as they motored south by west, following the line of cliffs around a gradual curve. The man was all muscle yet lacked the buffed quality of most men she knew. She found herself drawn to his raw strength, so completely different from the standard Washington male.

As the sun gentled into the sea, clouds gathered like skyborne sheep about the cliffs overhead. They rode around a headland to discover a cluster of perhaps fifty miniature peaks rising from the sea, rocky islands huddled in three tight clumps just offshore. Five miles before the islets began, the cliffs made a tight curve inward. A shelf of sand rose from the sea and nestled into the rocky overhang. Harry stopped fifty yards offshore and jumped into the water with snorkel and fins, making sure the bottom was safe. At his signal, Emma and Storm ran the Jet Skis slowly forward and beached them on the shore.

Harry stood on one of the rocks planted in the sand and gave the ladies a quick dousing from one of the five-gallon fresh-water containers. Just enough to get the worst of the salt off their skin. He used a ladle on himself, then turned to making dinner. They dined on fresh-speared fish and freeze-dried vegetables and pilau rice, with two energy bars each for dessert. The sunset was blocked by towering cliffs that formed a gentle sweep out in both directions. As happened every night since they'd been on the island, the clouds condensed about the peaks. Harry fed the fire from an endless supply of driftwood. Emma sat on a rock just beyond the fire's reach and listened to the waves whisper about conflicting desires.

Storm's cell phone began ringing. Emma watched her fumble in the pack, grip her phone with both hands, clench her eyes tight, then raise the phone and say, "What?"

The metallic edge to her voice lifted Harry's head. "Storm?"

She turned her back to them both and said coldly, "That is not the question you need to be asking."

Emma asked, "Who is it?"

Storm said to her phone, "You need to realize the kind of resources the woman who tracked you down would bring to the table. And then decide whether you want her on your side."

The fire crackled. The waves lapped the shore. Storm said, "No. Not a chance. If you're interested, you meet me here, Monsieur Boucaud. We decide on a way we can trust . . . Oh, please. As if you haven't been chasing us since Palm Beach."

Emma covered the distance between them in a pair of giant leaps, only to be met by a stiff-armed rejection. Storm went on, "Think about it. The old man *fired* me. I was left totally out in the cold. Why should I feel loyalty to a guy who kicked me out?"

Harry moved up close enough for Emma to feel his heat.

Storm said, "You know perfectly well where we are. You want to talk, you've got forty-eight hours. Otherwise I'll see if the authorities . . . No. Forget that. No threats. Because you *are* interested. If you weren't, you wouldn't have called."

She slapped the phone shut. The shudder that wracked her left her crouching so low her hair smoldered in the fire. She didn't seem to notice.

"Step back," Harry said, taking her arm. "That's it. Okay, unlock. Give me the phone. Good girl. Unlock. Relax. It's over."

But Emma wasn't about to let it go. "Let me get this straight. You went through my purse and got Boucaud's number?"

Storm let Harry guide her over and settle her onto a rock. "I had to do it."

When Storm swiveled away, Emma followed. "Just exactly how did you *have* to go through my things?"

"How long has the FBI known about this guy?"

"I'm asking the questions here."

"Four months, isn't that what you said? If they had done something four months ago, Sean would still be alive!"

The pain was so raw in Storm's voice, Emma found herself calming. "They didn't roll because they didn't have a case."

"You said it yourself. Arresting him still isn't their priority. So how long do they give him this time? Who does he get to kill next?"

"You should have discussed it with me."

"What for? So you could take it up with a committee?"

"I don't work like that and you know it."

Storm didn't respond.

"You're putting yourself out there as bait."

"No, Emma. I'm *making things happen*. Your job is to *do* something with it."

Harry walked away from them both. He scrunched through the sand, down to the shoreline. The clouds surrounding the peaks blocked out the stars. The sea was inky black and very still. Harry stood staring out at nothing.

Emma called over, "Don't you have the slightest bit of concern here?"

Harry replied to the night, "I know what old Sean would say."

Storm's head popped up. "What?"

"Sean would say, the vine from above the temple doors is the key. A gold pipe five inches in diameter and forty feet long, let's assume it's hollow because if it isn't we're in serious trouble. Even hollow, if it's got gold leaves soldered along its length, the thing is going to weigh two, maybe three hundred pounds. I'm guessing they folded it six or seven times, got it down to the height of a man. I can lift it. But I can't carry it anywhere alone."

Emma knew she was defeated, but went down fighting. "Did you even hear what we've said?"

401

Harry turned toward them. The fire carved his features into battle-hardened lines. "Storm did what she felt she had to. That doesn't change a thing. We were under life-or-death pressure long before she picked up the phone."

He pointed toward the night. "We're tracking one of the greatest prizes the world has ever known. If it's there, we're going to have to move fast. And get it right the first time."

FORTY-ONE

THEY LEFT THE BEACH IN the darkest hour. The fire had burned down to sullen embers, but still had enough heat for Harry to make a buccaneer's brew. He dumped three handfuls of coffee and one of sugar into boiling water, then left the pot to cool and settle. Harry scooped three mugs from the pot and sipped his while loading the sleds. The coffee tasted furry and gave a proper jolt to the day ahead.

Emma joined him loading the sleds. They moved in a natural rhythm, an economy of motion, like they'd been working together for years. Like they were meant to be together.

Storm was groggy but steady. She helped Emma fit the straps around the oversized load her Jet Ski would be carrying, not asking why Harry insisted on leaving the second sled empty. Storm handed each of them four energy bars.

Harry devoured one and stowed the rest away for later. He pushed Storm's Jet Ski out to waist depth, waited for Emma to power up the second Jet Ski, then slipped on behind her. He fit his arms around her waist, feeling the woman's supple strength. They kept the motors purring at a low and easy pace. The thrumming rose through Harry's spine and accelerated his heart. Emma took one hand off the controls and rested it on his knee. Harry found it a struggle to focus on what lay ahead.

The Jet Skis sliced through water so calm they might have been riding on air. They rounded the rocky promontory and entered deeper waters. A gentle swell lifted beneath them, riding in easy rhythms.

When they were just off the monastery peak, Harry signaled for them to cut power. He pulled Storm's Jet Ski in close. There was no need for a line, the water was that calm. "Here's what's going to happen. Emma is going to take me in alone, then come back out here to wait with you. I'll make the top in about an hour, maybe less. Another hour to scout the church."

Emma said, "Hold it right there, sport."

"If I find something, I'll signal. You bring Emma in, I'll drop the rope, she'll come up and help."

Emma replied, "You never said anything about going up there alone."

Harry went on, "If Emma comes up, lash the Jet

Skis together, but have your knife ready to cut loose if things go bad."

"We're not leaving without you," Storm said.

Emma said, "It's not going to get to that point, because he's not leaving here without *me*."

Harry touched her arm. Looked at her. The first faint grey hint of dawn showed a woman ready to do battle. "I'll move faster and quieter alone. If there's anything, trouble or otherwise, you'll be the first to know." He applied a trace more pressure, stilling her protest. "That's how it's going to be, Emma."

The woman was used to taking orders. Which, given her strength, was remarkable. She stifled her arguments and sat there, simmering.

The minutes stretched out long and slow. Storm shivered as a predawn mist floated in, hugging the waters. Harry slipped off his sweatshirt and draped it around her shoulders. He'd be warm soon enough. "It's time."

Storm reached over and hugged his neck. Emma started the motor and they pulled away. The sea was gone now, lost beneath the drifting mist. Harry carried his grin with him.

The cliffs looked monstrous in the dim light, and only loomed larger as they closed in. Harry said, "See the tight corner there? Looks like a tear in the rock?"

"I see it."

"Aim straight for the cleft."

He slipped off the saddle and scooted onto the sled. He squatted and checked the gear in his backpack one last time. He pulled on the driving gloves he'd bought in the market, flexed his fingers. There'd once been a time when the skin of his hands had been tough enough to handle rocks without protection. Not anymore.

Emma glanced back. "Harry, why is your safety rope still in your pack?"

"Keep your voice down."

"Answer the question, Harry."

"I checked out the crevice yesterday afternoon. I think the fissure runs all the way to the top."

"And? Tell me you're not scaling that wall without roping up."

"Emma. Please. Pipe down."

She did, but it only made her heat more intense as she hissed, "What is this, some kind of macho stunt you're pulling?"

"Two things. First, if I use the hammer, they might hear me. Sound carries. If I give them a reason to look over the edge, I'll be one of those little rubber duckies in the carnival shooting booth."

"I'm going to be sick."

"And two, it'll only slow me down. I want to be off that rise before the sun crests the eastern hills."

"Don't . . ." Emma stopped. And sighed.

Harry was so grateful she'd held it inside he leaned forward and kissed her soundly. He settled back on the sled and reached for the oncoming rock. "Slow and steady. That's it. Okay."

He stepped into the cleft and began climbing, easy as you please. Fred Astaire, step back and give a guy some room.

She powered away from the wash drenching the lower rocks. And called softly, "Harry, come back in one piece. Please."

TENDRILS OF MIST BOILED UP, blanketing her vision as Emma drove slowly out to where Storm waited on the second Jet Ski. Storm refused to meet her eye as Emma tied the machines together. Two ladies with their hair up, waiting to see who scored the first hit. Emma slipped onto the sled and reached into her backpack. "I need to report developments to Hakim."

"Developments," Storm muttered. But the word was soft enough for Emma to pretend not to have heard. She slipped back into her saddle and dialed. When Hakim answered, she said, "We might have a situation here."

Storm huffed softly. *Situation.*

The conversation took all of three minutes, mostly because Emma couldn't take her eyes off the rocks. When she shut the phone, Storm demanded, "Well?"

"Hakim can't officially help you with Boucaud."

"That's it? No official slap on the wrist for breaking protocol?"

"North Cyprus is not a recognized nation-state. Interpol has no official connection to anybody on the ground. Those were his exact words. Along with wishing us all good hunting." Emma slipped back onto the sled and stowed her cell phone. "Where did Harry put the binoculars?"

"I have them." But when Emma reached over, Storm did not let go. "Does that mean you're not going to help me?"

"Don't talk silly. I don't like the way you did it. But you might have been right to call him."

Storm released the binoculars.

"Nothing was happening. The fibbies don't have a case. Even if they started focusing on Boucaud today, it could be months before they build a connection that would stand up in court. Maybe longer."

Storm's voice was little-girl small. "So are we still friends?"

Without stopping her scan of the cliffs, Emma reached across with the hand not holding the binoculars and gripped Storm's hand. "I can't find him."

HARRY ARRIVED AT THE TOP just as the mist rose from dew-covered grass to cluster about the copse of trees bordering the cliffs. He sat there a minute, puffing hard, a little proud he'd made it. He checked his watch. Fifty-three minutes from waterline to ridge. When his heart stopped threatening to leap from his chest, he started off. Head down, legs pumping, a loose-limbed lope that scooted him along the cliff's edge. The Jet Skis were two tiny specks floating in the fogbound sea. Harry gave them a quick wave, saw nothing in response, figured the mist and the light made it hard for them to see anything.

The trees followed the ridge about thirty feet in from the cliffs. Harry scouted constantly, but saw no movement. The military base appeared totally asleep. Which was impossible, of course. There were bound to be sentries on duty. But if there was ever a moment for a sleepy guard to grab a quick snooze, it was now. Not even the birds were chirping. Which was fine by him.

He stepped into the monastery and moved directly to the chapel. His plan was simple. Go through the place room by room, searching for another hole. Because Harry was certain there was no reason to go back down in that crypt.

What Harry had noticed his first minute down in the crypt were the chip marks. He'd counted a half dozen divots in the stone floor, triangular holes formed by someone using a pick. Which meant the commandant had ordered his men to search for a way through to another chamber. They'd done a far more thorough job than Harry could in a few silent minutes.

Which probably also meant they had checked out the rest of the monastery.

Harry intended to do a quick scope, see if there was something they might have missed, which he doubted. Then put his *real* plan into action.

Because he was certain that the treasure was linked to this place. He figured the records did not mention earthquakes in this region because there hadn't been any. All the surrounding peaks were riddled with holes, man-made caves, ancient copper digs, the sort of opening that would have vanished in a heartbeat if the earth had given a single good shake.

Which meant one of two things. Either the image they had found described a different place entirely, which Harry was convinced was wrong. Or the image did not describe the coastline at all. Perhaps it was a carving meant to mark a secret access. Perhaps something lost to time and weather and war. But Harry would have wagered a secret hoard that the image had been misread for centuries.

So Harry planned on finding a good, safe anchor for his line, then he was going back over the edge. And search the cliff face *below* the monastery. For the sealed opening. The one the commandant hadn't thought to scope out.

This was the sort of idea that the ladies might have called harebrained, as in, how stupid was he, swinging around a cliff, suspended below a Turkish army base, looking for a cave? Was he nuts? So Harry had decided to keep that part of his plan to himself.

He started his search at the nave, just to get his bearings on where the crypt began and ended. His adrenaline rush kept the blood singing, almost a fizz in his ears. He felt light enough to flitter over the ruins. Harry Bennett was back in the game.

Then he turned and saw the sunrise.

What he saw was so intensely mind-boggling he feared he'd gotten caught in some dawn mirage, a figment of his adrenaline-drenched brain.

Which was when he dropped his gaze down to where his hands gripped the stone frame of the central window.

And saw the second sign.

HARRY SCOOTED BACK TO THE cliffs, so loopy over what he'd just discovered that his feet scarcely disturbed the weeds. The mist was almost completely gone now. Below him the sea gleamed sapphire blue. He dug the rope from his pack and knotted it to the base of the two strongest tree trunks growing close to the ledge. He slipped the rope through the hooks and slung it about his frame, forming a rudimentary rappelling harness. His fingers fumbled like a first timer's, like he was trying to do the drill with somebody else's hands.

He stepped to the cliff's edge and made sure the rope lay snug and unseen on the grass. He glanced down and felt the moment congeal around a sudden lump of fear. He hadn't rappelled in years. He hadn't liked it then and this was way worse.

Alone and a little shaky from the adrenaline flood, betting his life that the trees and this rope would hold through the descent. The worst moment was the first, turning his back to the sea, trying not to think of the seven-hundred-foot drop and the rocky teeth eager to chew his bones if he fell.

Harry forced himself to steady and took a regulation hold on the rope—left hand in front of his body and right behind. Another hard breath. Then he leaned backward over the ledge, half sitting himself into the harness, and dropped.

The rope ran through his hands and around his lower frame. Harry huffed hard with each step. His knees were rattling like dice. He kept his eyes on the rock face and skipped downward.

Not needing to look for a sealed opening in the cliff below the monastery turned out to be a very good thing.

Because right then a head popped out over the precipice.

Harry froze and crouched in tight to the rocks. Just his luck there was a sentry awake enough to see the trees shiver under Harry's weight. Which was the only way Harry could figure the sentry had found him.

The sentry stood about a hundred yards to the right of where Harry's rope was anchored. A voice drifted down.

Harry stepped up the pace, tripping down the stone wall. He felt the rope begin to burn through

411

his gloves and his clothes. It made quick zipping sounds, pushing him to move faster still.

The head reappeared, along with three others. The men were all shouting.

Harry raced down, pushing out with both feet, just barely off total free fall. His gloves were smoking and his hamstrings were shrieking. The harder he pushed off, the faster he slammed back. His knees struck his chest with each impact.

One head disappeared, probably the guy bright enough to figure all they had to do was race over and cut his line. Another soldier unlimbered his pistol and took a two-fisted aim.

Harry huffed and kicked off again. The rope sizzled. A clip of rock flew off the wall in front of his face. From above came a booming echo.

Harry did not hesitate. The next time he hit the rock face, he kicked harder still, released the rope, and turned in midair.

The water looked blue as polished steel plate and a million miles down.

He flew, kicking his legs, so as to bring his boots down below his body. The rope whizzed free, its tune one shriek above a whistle.

He hit and went deep. When he came up, Emma's Jet Ski was racking toward him.

She leaned her body into the turn, whipping about, slamming the sled into his outstretched hands. Harry gripped and rolled and screamed, "*Go! Go! Go!*"

FORTY-TWO

THEY SCOOTED AROUND THE HEADLAND and entered tourist mania just as two marine patrol boats thundered past, heading no doubt for the point where some nut just dove from a military-restricted cliff. They left their Jet Skis in a small cove dominated by a new hotel resort. They just lined the machines up with a half dozen hotel rentals, next to the Sunfish and the sailboards. Emma watched Harry work his magic with the lifeguard. He paid a hefty sum to have the guy refill the gas tanks, repressure their dive tanks, and store their gear in the waterfront shed. They washed off the sea salt in the hotel's beachside changing rooms. Once they were dressed in fresh clothes, Harry led them to the front drive and loaded them into a taxi. On the way back to the center of Kyrenia, he started going through the list of supplies they needed.

Storm interrupted him with "I've got a few questions."

Emma said, "I'll give that a big affirmative."

Storm went on, "A thirty-second explanation shouted from one Jet Ski to another is not going to cut the mustard."

Harry jutted his chin in the taxi driver's direction and said, "Let's take this one step at a time."

He settled back in his seat and dozed. When they

arrived in Kyrenia he negotiated another three days' rental from the Jet Ski shop. Then he walked back to where the ladies were storing their first purchases into the rented Suzuki. Harry slipped into the Suzuki's backseat and said, "You know where to find me."

He settled into a prone position, cradled his head in his arm, and started snoring softly. Bang and gone.

Emma said, "Apparently getting shot at takes a lot out of the guy."

They returned from their shopping excursion to find Harry still asleep. He had obviously awakened at some point, however, because a map lay unfolded on the driver's seat with a circle drawn around a village in the middle of the mountainous headland between Kyrenia and the Yayla military base. The village of Korucam sat at the end of a tiny winding road. One way in, one out. Nothing around it except bare grey map. Emma and Storm stowed the rest of their purchases in the rear and set off.

Korucam was a curious sort of place. There was a neatness not found in most North Cyprus towns. Every house looked planted. All were painted with the same off-white stucco, all had red varnished doors and clay-tiled roofs, all had curious oval cutouts atop their chimneys. The men wore beards and funny black caps.

"Marionites," Harry said, popping up in the

backseat. His hand scratched over his stubble as he rubbed the sleep from his face. "Old-timey Christians from the hills above Beirut. You find these villages all over the Med, mostly in hidden valleys like this one. They fled the Ottomans about seven hundred years ago. Very tightly knit."

Emma recalled Hakim's description after their flight to France and asked, "How are you feeling?"

Harry gave his face a hard rub. "Ready to rock and roll."

Harry leaned in between them and pointed out the way ahead. Emma kept being surprised by this guy. He cased the area like a pro with twenty years on the force. They drove through the town on the only lane heading toward the mountains. They stopped each time they hit a lonely rise, so Harry could study the trails ahead through binoculars. Taking his time. Walking himself up the mountain.

Emma asked, "Are you sure you know which mountain we should aim for?"

"Yes." He pointed at a medium-sized peak, one of dozens. "See that dark vein running sideways like a partly open zipper? I spotted that from the monastery. It lies just above our cave."

When the asphalt petered out, Emma slipped the Suzuki into four-wheel drive and continued along a rutted goat path. Harry stayed close enough to breathe soft directions into her ear, which she found both nice and disconcerting. The final ascent was so steep Emma feared they were going to topple over backward. Storm moved to the front of her seat, gripping the console with both hands. They popped up over a ledge and bounced to a halt. In front of them, the trail narrowed to a foot-path and grew even steeper.

Storm gave Harry a narrow-eyed focus as they emerged from the jeep. "I'm not moving a step farther until I get some answers."

"Gather round, ladies." Harry began sketching in the dust covering the hood. "Here's what we knew before setting out. Three stubby peninsulas, always drawn with waves crashing around the out-side."

"And a hole in the top of the middle one," Storm finished.

"Right. Only these lines aren't waves. And the peninsulas don't stick into the sea." Harry pointed to where the peaks rose in the harsh afternoon light. "Every afternoon the clouds come rolling in. An hour after sunrise, the heat burns the clouds away. What I saw at dawn was, the top of every mountain was cut off. Standing there in the monastery chapel, looking out what was left of their front window, I saw these three stubby peaks. And the clouds were streaked by the sun rising *behind* them."

"Streaked like waves," Storm said.

"Those monks sat in the chapel and stared out windows every dawn, and watched the hidden cave take shape in the sky." Harry slung his pack. "Let's hit the trail."

The track was so steep Emma occasionally used her hands to pull herself forward. Gradually the slope gentled somewhat, and they passed a herd of goats. The bells sounded like chimes in the rarified air. Then the slope steepened once more, and they left the animals behind.

Ahead of them, Harry appeared to skip from rock to rock. Storm came up beside Emma and panted, "Is that man actually humming?"

Which was exactly what Harry was doing. The guy was just legging off, leaving them in the dust. Humming.

Storm looked a little stunned by the climb and by the altitude. But still able to grin. "How can you not love the guy?"

Very easily was the answer, if logic played any part. Which, truth be told, it didn't. Not just then. Not fresh from an assault on a foreign military base, one that ended in gunfire. Granted, it had been pistol shots at maximum range. But still.

Yet here she was. Climbing a hill in the same nation that had probably put out an all-points alert. In the company of a treasure dog. And thinking about the future. Together. Wondering what it might be like, to hive off from the Washington bureaucratic mayhem every now and then, clear her mind with a little adventuring. Join a certain salvage expert for a few weeks of exploration and treasure. Then return to the day-to-day life. Restored in her soul. Just like now.

Which was what had left her legs weak and her lungs struggling to find a decent breath.

Up ahead the trail appeared to crest another plateau. She figured her legs just might hold out that long.

Then the world just dropped away.

Emma was so shocked by the sudden change in scenery she fell to her knees. Storm made the final rise and gasped so hard she started coughing. Harry was instantly beside Emma, gripping her arm. He helped her sit and kept hold of her arm. "Steady. Take a deep breath. That's good. Scope out the clouds. Don't look down."

But Emma couldn't help it. She'd never seen anything like that drop. The steep pasture simply came up a final rise, and ended. On the other side, the world was *gone*. Like a giant had slammed an ax into the mountain and left a precipice that dropped away to forever.

"The good news is, the spot we're after is on this side of the chasm. We'll take a breather, then rope up."

Storm said, "I know that tone. There's bad news coming."

"Here. Have some more water."

Emma drank. "Okay. Hit me."

Harry said, "The trail follows the chasm's leading edge."

Both girls moaned. Emma finally asked, "How far?"

Harry rose to his feet. "Until the other side drops away, too."

IF ANYONE HAD EVER ASKED her if she could survive such a trek, which no sane person would ever attempt, Emma would have replied, "Not if I were drugged, blindfolded, and stretchered across."

Yet here she was, last in line, walking a dirt track maybe twenty inches wide.

And nothing but empty air and swooping drops to either side.

She could see Storm's legs trembling from ten feet away. Emma was surprised to discover she had enough breath to say, "Steady."

"Almost there," Harry called back. "Another thirty feet. Less."

The drop was spectacular. Their path ran atop a limestone precipice carved by eons of wind and rain. Emma made it by focusing down so tightly on the next step that the yawning drops to either side blurred somewhat—not a lot, but enough.

She only knew they'd made it when Harry said, "You ladies can go ahead and faint now."

Storm just went down, like the big hand in the sky had suddenly let go of her strings. Emma teetered forward a couple more steps, intent on making it to where he stood grinning. "I'm a pro. Pros don't weep from sheer terror. It's in the manual."

Harry's arms had never felt so good. "You're tops in my book. Both of you."

She listened to the steady thumping of his heart and felt her own nerves ease. "Weren't you the tiniest bit scared?"

"Right out of my size sixteens."

She struck his chest. "Liar."

Storm teetered over. Harry made room in his arms for her as well. Storm tucked in her elbows, put her hands up under her chin, and made herself munchkin small. "Will you carry me back?"

"I figure we'll all be floating on the way home." Harry took a huge breath. "Smell that?"

Emma sniffed. She tasted sage, eucalyptus, wildflowers, creosote, dust, all the flavors of highland desert. "What?"

Harry lowered his head until his breath teased her ear. His whisper sent shivers through her entire frame.

"Gold."

FORTY-THREE

T HE HILLS FORMED A U–SHAPED enclosure around their highland ledge. Harry and the ladies rested on a shelf that jutted out from about two-thirds up the peak. A narrow lip of rock extended from the wall across from where they had just entered, sweeping around the rim. Harry studied the way ahead, trying to hide his impatient two-step. Emma passed Storm the water bottle and said to Harry, "Oh, go ahead before you explode."

"I'll be right back."

Storm watched him almost skip across the ledge, round the corner, and disappear. "How does he do it?"

"I doubt he even saw the drop."

Harry came swinging back around the bend. "There's no cave."

Storm cried, "Are you *kidding* me?"

"Calm down."

"We came up here for *nothing*?" Storm reached toward Emma. "Pass me your gun."

"We came here for a lot. Ease up a notch and come give me a hand."

But Storm was not really done until her stomping fit carried her too close to the edge and she stared straight down. "Oooh."

Harry was instantly there, gripping her arm. "Steady. We're almost there."

"I never knew I hated heights until right now."

"It's not far." He led her back to the wall and retied the rope around both the ladies. "Grab the rocks. Eyes on the wall. One step at a time."

There were actually two outcroppings, both about eight inches wide. One at chin height, the other Emma did not dare to look down at. They rounded the rim, one baby step at a time. Then, "This is it."

This time, Harry did not let either lady go down. They stood upon a second ledge, this one oval and eight feet wide. He guided them to the verge and faced them almost directly west. "Take a good look."

Beside Emma, Storm moaned.

"This is important. Okay. There's the military base, the flags, the front gates, the statue. Follow the cliffs around, see where the trees thicken, there's the monastery."

Emma thought her gut was completely numb from what she'd just been through. But looking out and down was good for another wingless swoop. She swallowed hard and made herself focus. The monastery was a tiny square of pebbles, set in a postage stamp of green. "I see it."

"So do I." Storm walked back to stand in front of the rock face. "But there's no cave."

"No."

"So this must be the wrong place."

"This is it. The dark indentation over your head there was what I saw from below." He pointed at the cliff face above them. "I've been aiming for this point where it splits like a zipper coming open. Which is right here."

"But there's just an empty ledge!"

Harry walked back to the edge and dropped to his knees. "It's got to be here somewhere."

"What?"

"We'll know when we find it. Start looking."

Storm and Emma exchanged a look. Emma said, "Don't ask me."

Harry started brushing the earth. When he had exposed one segment of rock, he moved over a fraction and started again. "Look around and tell me what you see."

"Mountains."

"Mountains and *caves*. Hundreds of caves."

Emma had been so spooked by the climb she'd missed that entirely. But Harry was right. The surrounding mountains were riddled with caves. Like a hive of giant rock-eating worms had spent centuries going to town. "So?"

"So how come we're directed to the only place in sight with *no cave*?" Harry slid over another fraction. "Storm, take the rock face. Emma, start on the floor over by where we just came in. Work your way toward me." He scrambled in his pack, came up with a T-shirt, handed it to Emma. "Protect your hands."

Vines grew up the left side of the cliff, emerging from a crack where the ledge met the face. Storm pulled a sweatshirt from her pack, tucked her hands in the sleeves, and started clearing the rock.

Emma said, "Tell me what we're looking for."

"Something unnatural. Something man-made." Harry brushed clear another area, the clean bit covering maybe a couple of square yards now. The dirt formed too thin a covering to permit much in the way of weeds or grass. Harry's hands worked in a steady sweeping motion, hurried yet gentle. Like he'd done this a thousand times before. Emma knelt where they had arrived and began.

There was a skill to this work, along with dogged determination. She mimicked Harry's actions. Sweeping, blowing, inspecting, moving, doing it all again.

"Hang on a second."

Both ladies turned around.

Harry started working at a feverish pace. Muttering between blows over the dust, "Oh boy oh boy oh boy oh boy."

Harry blew and rushed and blew. Then stopped and leaned back. "This is better than Christmas."

A crude fish symbol was carved into the rock face. The head pointed out over the cliffs.

Harry said, "I saw a smaller version of this cut into the chapel's window frame. It was pointed directly at this ledge."

Emma said, "And you're telling us about this *now*?"

He traced a finger around it, as though making sure it was real. "I wasn't certain that it meant anything until this moment."

Storm said, "So it's a sign. Find this and . . . What?"

Harry's finger slipped into a shallow indentation at the tail. He bent over, blew, inspected it, and asked, "Can I have your pen?"

Emma did not realize her hands were shaking

until she had trouble unzipping the pack's side pouch.

"Thanks." Harry fitted the pen into the hole and used it to swab out more dirt. He ran his finger out in a straight line, beyond the head of the fish, hunting. And stopped. He leaned forward and began clearing a second hole. "Do you have a second pen?"

"No."

Storm stepped away and came back with a straight section of vine. "Will this do?"

"Great." The branch was thicker than the hole, so Harry had to jam it in. He lay down prone on the earth and leveled the pen with one hand, the vine with the other.

He crawled back. Motioned to the ladies. "Tell me what you see."

Storm said, "You first."

Emma also lay prone and lined up the two implements like oversized rifle sights. "Oh, wow."

Out in the lavender distance, where the afternoon sunlight joined the sea with the cliffs and the cliffs with the sky, rose the rocky islands they had seen from their seaside campsite. In the middle of the closest cluster rose a conical peak, almost like a minivolcano.

The sights pointed straight at the peak.

THEY RACED THE DWINDLING LIGHT back down the hill. Harry did not push them to move faster only because both women were on the verge of dropping. Returning over the precipice went marginally better than the ascent, but not much. Fear as much as fatigue kept the ladies stumbling and their lungs gasping for their next high-altitude breath. So Harry kept the pace easier than he wanted and murmured things not even he heard very clearly.

They lit the final segment of path by flashlight. When they reached the Suzuki 4WD, Harry pretended not to see how they dribbled water down their fronts, trying to gasp and drink at the same time. He fed them the last two energy bars and loaded their gear and resisted the urge to do a wild highland jig around the car.

The car remained utterly silent on the ride back to the cottage. It was a risk returning there. But the only other places open to them this time of night would be hotels, and going there would heighten the threat of being located by the growing number of wrong people. When they parked in front of the cottage, Harry started to run through the hundred things that needed saying and doing before the next dawn. But he watched them drag their packs along the walk, their shoulders slumped, and knew he was just going to have to wait. He followed them inside and entered the kitchen.

Storm lay on the living room floor, spread-eagle. She moaned with the pure pleasure of not needing to go anywhere, at least for a few moments. Emma asked, "First bath?"

Storm used one finger to wave her forward.

The cottage was filled with the sound of a ringing phone.

Emma called from the back, "That's yours, Storm."

She groaned, rolled over, fished the phone from her pack, said, "What."

Storm listened a minute, then snapped the phone shut and sent it skittering across the floor. "Talk about hitting a girl when she's down."

Emma reappeared in the bedroom door. "Who was it?"

"Boucaud."

Harry froze in the process of chopping vegetables.

Emma said, "And?"

"Noon tomorrow. Saint Hilarion's castle."

Harry resisted the urge to stab his knife through the counter and shout his frustration at the night. He stood staring down at the pair of clenched fists. Just one thing after another, the whole world trying to stand between him and his treasure.

His treasure.

Storm made it to her feet and staggered over. She leaned in the kitchen door. Emma closed in behind her. "What do we do?"

Harry did not look up. "We'll do this thing. Then go for the treasure."

He tried to tell himself he had no choice in the matter. But his gut was screaming otherwise.

FORTY-FOUR

HARRY WOKE UP IN THE middle of the night with a raging thirst and burdened by a half-remembered dream. On his way to the kitchen, he found Storm in the living room. She was seated by the rear windows overlooking the slope and the city's lights and the ink-dark sea beyond. She held Sean's Bible. Not reading. Just sitting and staring at the night.

"Is everything okay?"

The lady remained as she was, her legs tucked up into her oversized T-shirt.

"Storm?"

She said softly, "Sean should be here. With us. For this."

Harry walked over and squatted on the stone floor beside her chair. "I'll tell you how it feels, finding you here. Like you're not letting him go. Not his business, not his Bible, not his search. It's his legacy and you're going to keep that alive."

"That's right," she said softly, "I am."

"In that case, I'm pretty sure Sean would tell you that he is not just here, but complete." He reached over and stroked her hair. "You're his girl, all right."

EMMA DRIFTED UP THROUGH CRYSTAL-CLEAR waters. In her dream Harry held her hand, but she could not see him. His presence offered an amazing sense of both comfort and exhilaration. He was sharing his world. It was the finest declaration of love she had ever known, all without saying a word. Light cascaded about her, a billion lances that shifted and flowed in orchestral precision. She paddled gently, knowing she had to surface, yet sad this incredible moment had to end.

She opened her eyes.

Storm snored quietly in the other bed. Emma rose and padded into the kitchen to find coffee simmering on the machine and a note propped on the pot. Outside her window, the morning light brushed the Kyrenia plain with a rich copper glow. The note repeated what Harry had said to them over dinner the night before, which was to get up and get ready. He was headed out to buy some last-minute supplies and then to scope out the castle. He'd return to the cottage at ten, and they needed to be ready to rock and roll.

Emma checked her watch. She set down her mug and went in search of her phone. Then Storm's. She rang Harry's number. When the recording popped on, she carried both phones into the bedroom. "Storm. Wake up."

"Not yet."

"Something's wrong."

Her head untangled from the pillow. "What?"

"Harry's fifteen minutes late."

It sounded silly, raising the alarm for a quarter of

an hour. But Storm flung back the covers. "Not Harry. Not today."

"Exactly."

Storm went into the bathroom and emerged wiping the water from her face. "You've checked your phone for messages?"

"And yours. Harry isn't answering."

When the phone chimed, she started so hard she almost dropped it. "Harry?"

"I'm in major-league trouble."

"Where are you?"

"The road to Saint Hilarion. I've been rammed by a cop car."

Emma said to Storm, "He's been in an accident."

"It was no accident. Here they come. They've got their guns drawn. Emma, I just want you to know how much—"

The phone went dead.

HARRY HADN'T SEEN THE POLICE CAR.

He had bought their supplies from several places on the outskirts of town, doing his best to get all they might need while avoiding anywhere they'd been before. Then he headed into the hills. Scoping out the Saint Hilarion Castle took longer than he'd expected. Yves Boucaud had chosen well, especially if it was to be the ambush Harry expected. Saint Hilarion's was the largest of the three castles built by King Richard the Lionhearted as a staging post for his assault on

Jerusalem. The ruins rose and fell along the ridge-line, covering several acres inside the outermost walls. Harry went through all the nooks and crannies, working out where he and Emma might station themselves, stomping all the while on his rising impatience.

He took the return too fast, especially for somebody already deep in planning his next step. But he was both running late and in full operational mode. Not to mention that the treasure's proximity left him oblivious to the here and now.

To Harry it seemed as though a flicker of sunlight coalesced into a hammer. The car whacked his door so hard it shoved him into the passenger seat. His seat belt parted and flipped across his face. That scratch was what hurt the most, at least initially.

He rose in stages, brushing the shards of side-window glass from his chest, glad to find his body still in working order.

Which was when he saw the three cops emerging from their car.

Dialing Emma was an automatic response. Harry didn't see cops. He saw doom. His instantaneous reaction was to reach out and touch the lady one final time.

The cops walked toward him with guns out and aimed. Harry did not move. One hand held the phone to his ear. The other was raised beside his head. Open and empty.

"I just want you to know how much—" Harry didn't finish the sentence because the cop reached through his window and ripped the phone from his ear.

They couldn't get the driver's door open, so they pulled him out through the passenger side. Which was when he realized he might have cracked a rib.

They had him assume the position with hands planted on their car. He shifted his head enough to watch two of them search the car, pulling out his purchases, searching the trunk. They spent some time on the car radio, one cop guarding Harry with a cocked pistol. They pulled his arms behind him, fitted on the manacles, shoved him into the rear seat. Two of them took off, hoofing up in the direction of the castle. Harry watched them disappear through the rear window, knowing with utter certainty what it felt like to have a pro set them up.

FORTY-FIVE

HARRY BENNETT WAS BACK IN THE BOX.

This particular cage was concrete, while the isolation tank in Barbados had been rusting steel plate. But the mildew was the same. And the stench, a funky brew of sweat and heat and fear and bone-aching hopelessness.

From somewhere down an unseen corridor, Harry heard a moan. He opened his mouth, partly in sympathy, partly in a horrible exercise, like he needed to reacquaint himself with the darkest recesses of his own psyche.

The concrete cave was seven feet long and five wide. The ceiling was so low his head scraped if he stood upright. A lamp inside a wire-mesh grid burned at eye level. The bed was a joke, a concrete slab jutting from the wall, so narrow he could not lie flat on his back without slipping off, and no way did he want to hit that floor. A single blanket. No pillow, just a slanted lump of concrete for his head. Harry wanted to tell himself he'd survived worse. But he knew it was a lie.

A ten-inch square was cut from the outside wall, another from the wall facing the hallway. Wire mesh covered both. Now and then a puff of hot afternoon air filtered through.

The cop had driven him back along the road toward the interior. Harry had feared that the cop was delivering him to the Turkish military base. But when they emerged from the mountains, the cop took the turn toward Famigusta, the provincial capital. Harry had leaned against the door, breathing like he'd run a mile. The cop had grinned in the rearview mirror. Harry didn't need to understand the man's words. He knew the cops had plenty of tricks of their own in store.

The cop pulled up in front of a squat municipal building. Harry saw a guy walking past with a briefcase and another in robes and figured the one building saw duty as the provincial courthouse, police station, and lockup. The cop pulled Harry through a side entrance that led straight to the rear jail cells. His induction took all of three seconds, a terse exchange between the cop holding his arm and the guy behind the counter. Harry asked for a telephone call and got whacked for his trouble. They dragged him back and dumped him on the slimy floor.

Harry eased himself down on the cement bunk and gingerly rubbed the side of his knee where the police car had rammed his door. His cheek hurt where the seat belt had scratched him. He was breathing easier, so he decided his rib was only bruised. A single bit of good news in a truly awful day.

Harry felt the weight of the heat bear down with casual brutality. He recalled how liberated he had felt the previous day, and was vaguely ashamed of himself. Like he had momentarily forgotten a vital lesson, one deeply ingrained by the Barbados jail. That failure was a pattern he would follow for the rest of his life. He rubbed his face, trying to scrub away the sensation that he had been wrong to let himself hope again. Pretend that he was normal. That he could shape his own dreams. Find a woman and love her. Claim a treasure. Claim a future for his own.

"HAKIM SPEAKING."

"Do you know who this is?"

434

"Of course."

"I'm breaking my word with this call. What's worse, I'm breaking the trust of a very good man." A shaky breath, then, "But I can't stand here and let him die."

THE HOURS PASSED INTO A heat-sodden dusk. The guy in the cell down the hall kept up his soft moaning. The wire-mesh window in the outside wall became etched with the day's final light. The bulb burned relentlessly inside the ceiling cage. But in his heart, where it mattered, everything was going dark. Harry knew the sensation. The nightmare crept out from the recesses of his past and slithered to sit beside him on the cement bunk. Close enough to whisper straight into his brain.

His mind's eye became filled with dread images. The cops would let him cook here a while, then take him out and work on him. Then they'd shackle him and hand him over to the Turkish commandant. The soldiers would drag him into a building set deep inside the base. Surrounded by acres of soldiers so scared their hands shook when they served tea in the commandant's office. They'd lock Harry into that place, and they'd work on him some more. Long and hard and slow. And nobody in that compound would hear a thing.

Eventually Storm and Emma would come for him. Harry was certain of that. Sooner or later the commandant would let him go. And Harry would shuffle out, toothless and weary. Ready to take his place outside whatever bar would have him. Cadging drinks. Pretending not to notice the disgust in the eyes of other salvagers. Guys like he used to be.

STORM MADE THE CALL ON her own phone, tersely apologizing to Boucaud for not making the rendezvous, and requesting a second chance. The man's response was so strident the words did not truly register. Storm shut her phone and sat cradling it with both hands.

Emma said, "We don't know if Boucaud actually showed up. It could all have been a ruse."

"This is supposed to make me feel better, thinking maybe my making that phone call had a hand in getting Harry jailed?"

"Did you ever think maybe Boucaud expected to land all three of us in that prison instead of just Harry?"

Storm didn't respond. She sat in the passenger seat, rocking slightly, her hands clenched between her knees.

They were seated in their latest rental, watching the night close in. The dashboard clock was the loudest Emma had ever heard, a tinny ratcheting sound, like it was built to remind them of every lost minute. Emma said, "When I started out as a federal agent, I took an oath. I don't recall every word. But I'm pretty sure there was something in it about not committing a series of felonies in a foreign land."

Storm's gaze never left the barbed-wire fence gleaming in the yellow streetlights. "That's why you're not coming."

"Have you ever driven one of those things before?"

"Have you?"

Emma bit her lip. "Something I heard my first day of training. Scope the terrain. Know where you're going and what you'll find when you get there. The unknown can kill you. What if—"

"No time for that." Storm ended the conversation by opening her door. If she waited any longer, the fear would freeze her up solid. "You stay here until I come out those gates. Then leave."

The quarry office was a pair of grey steel trailers set on stone foundations just inside the main gate. Storm climbed the stairs and entered, her legs as weak as they had been coming off the mountain. A lone guy sat behind a desk in the front office. She walked up and announced, "I'm here for the truck."

Storm couldn't tell if the man behind the desk understood her. She pointed out the window at the vehicle stationed at their side of the lot. "Keys. For that."

He held out his hand. "Passport."

She reached into her purse and set a pile of bills on the desk. "Will that do?"

• • •

STORM STALLED THE TRUCK TWICE leaving the lot. The guard emerged to shout something up at her. When she finally rolled onto the street, the guard shook his head, waved in disgust, and went back inside.

Famigusta looked exactly like the poor provincial capital that it was. The region was almost entirely agricultural, the rocky cliff line cutting off any hope of beachfront development. With all routes to the wealthier Greek Cyprus cut off, Famigusta had spent the last thirty years in dusty neglect. The night only accented the city's flaws. Storm passed rusting produce warehouses, driving streets that were utterly empty by nine o'clock at night. The only sign of newness came as she approached the city center, where a few brightly lit shopfronts gleamed inside crumbling facades. The truck jounced hard, the engine throbbing so loud she could hear nothing save her own pounding fear. The hood went on forever. She felt like she was seated twenty feet off the ground. The wheels made a high-pitched whine. She kept the truck in second, as shifting gears was a workout she did not want to repeat too often.

The municipal building was just where Hakim had described to Emma, which eased Storm's panic a fraction. A lot was riding on Hakim getting all the details right. A man's life, for one. Storm rumbled straight past, not wanting to risk a U-turn in front of the police station. Two blocks later, she cut back through an alley so tight she scraped a fire escape with one side mirror and might have dislodged an AC unit with the other. She took another left and returned to the municipal building from behind. As she struggled to put the truck into neutral, she spotted a wrecked Suzuki parked at the far end of the fenced-in municipal lot.

This time, seeing that Hakim had gotten another item right only accelerated Storm's terror.

EMMA FOLLOWED STORM AT A distance, listening to the truck's rumble echo off the surrounding buildings. The alley behind the municipal building was utterly silent. Emma parked in the empty lot to the building's north, which granted her views both of the front entrance and Storm, all without leaving the comfort of her latest rental. They had signed for this particular car using Storm's passport, since Emma's was still with the harbor Jet Ski operator. Not to mention that the severely dented Suzuki parked inside the municipal lot had been rented in Emma's name. The largest car on the rental company's lot had been a four-door Peugeot sedan. It was painted the color of a dirty cream puff and drove like a well-padded tank.

The front of the municipal building was very colonial. The four steps descending to the street were broad as patios. The colonnaded porch held an outdoor waiting area and a glass-fronted guard station and was completely empty. Even the guard station was vacant.

Emma watched Storm emerge from the truck and walk over to stand beneath the rear wall. Storm called up. Emma rolled down her window in time to hear someone answer. She was fairly certain the voice belonged to Harry.

Then a car rolled up and parked across the street from the front entrance. Emma ducked and hissed through the side window, "Storm!"

HARRY LAY ON THE CONCRETE bunk listening to something drip. He had no idea where the sound came from. His cage didn't have a sink, just a pair of buckets by the steel door. He could hear insects crawling on the floor. He lay with his outer arm tucked across his body to keep from falling off and told himself none of it mattered. Or at least, it wouldn't matter for long.

He had a sudden image, back to the moment it had all gone wrong. Back to that night in the church, when he had called his best friend a coward and a cheat. Lying there on the concrete slab, Harry finally realized why Sean had met him inside that church. It wasn't to cool Harry down, like he'd always assumed. Harry lay there and sweated from the coming pain, and finally understood that Sean had wanted to share the best of himself. The old man knew he was reaching the end of the line. He couldn't name the date, but he knew the hunters were out there. So he had tried to both protect his friend and offer what he considered the best part of himself.

Only Harry had remained too blind and too proud and too stubborn, right to the end.

So whatever words Sean might have been willing to share, if Harry had ever been willing to ask, had gone unspoken. The gift ungiven. Because that was the way Harry had wanted it.

Harry lay on his back and wondered what he might have to offer anyone. Some tiny fragment of himself worth passing on. There at the last minute, spoken in the final breath, a shred of lasting meaning to a life lived for little more than the next good haul.

Which was when he heard an angel call his name.

FORTY-SIX

FROM THE BACK, THE MUNICIPAL building looked like a giant pillbox. The ground floor was windowless. The second floor was rimmed by tiny little squares, denoting the prison block. Just as Hakim had described.

Storm stood in shadows as dark as the dread that almost choked her. The three streetlights lining the alley and the municipal lot were all out. "Harry?"

There was nothing but silence in response. She raised her voice and called again.

"Storm?"

She clenched her fists in the effort required to keep from wailing. "Where are you?"

"Here! I'm here!"

But where was that? Shadows flitted over several of the little squares at once, which meant more than one prisoner had heard the exchange. Storm felt submerged in sweat. She needed an oxygen mask just to stay upright. "I can't tell which one is you!"

She heard a sharp crash. Then another, followed by a loud pop. The little square at the building's right-hand corner went dark.

"Is that you?"

"Yes."

"Stay right there!"

She heard Emma call her name. But there was no time to stop. An instant's hesitation would leave her weeping in terror.

Which was why she did not realize she had just told Harry to stay where he was, locked inside a prison cell, until she got back in the truck, found reverse, and started revving the motor.

EMMA STARTED TO CLIMB FROM the car. But she was in clear view of the vehicle parked in front of the municipal building. It was part SUV and part pickup. The yellow streetlight made it impossible to make out the vehicle's color. But the vehicle had a squarish ugliness that was uniquely military.

And the driver's door was painted with a red star.

Emma hated the chains of indecision that held her. For the first time in her professional career, she wished for a superior on site to issue marching orders. She should warn Storm, but what of Harry?

Then a shadow flittered from the vehicle. The man was small, slender, and impossibly swift. He molded so naturally with the gloom he might as well have cast the shadows out before him, netting the dark, dragging it along with him.

Emma started her motor, slammed the car into drive, and rammed the gas pedal into the carpet.

Out of the corner of her eye she saw Storm's giant truck belch a lungful of smoke and gradually gain momentum. In reverse.

THE TRUCK WAS BUILT FOR hauling stones down from the mountain limestone mines to the beach-front tourist developments. Clearly the designers had not intended for their twelve-wheelers to need ramming speed in reverse. Even so, once it got going, the truck built up a gut-wrenching level of thrust. The only problem was, Storm could not see where she was headed. The lid of the hold completely blocked her rear window. She scouted one side mirror, then the other, back and forth, while the truck roared and belched and rumbled and flew.

She had only the vaguest idea of anything beyond step one. Her own personal "mission impossible" was to spring Harry. After that, well, everything was just left up to Emma.

Only at that very moment, Storm saw Emma peel the Peugeot away in a swirl of smoke and tires. Headed for the exit.

Storm shouted her friend's name. Then the wall loomed up, completely filling her vision. She had time for one final glimpse through the side mirror, taking aim straight at the lone dark square. Then she straightened in her seat, pressed her head hard into the seat rest, and braced herself tightly, both hands on the wheel, both feet ramming the gas pedal into the floorboards.

And gave off a truly magnificent scream.

EMMA FELT BETTER THAN GOOD, finally having a target for her rage. It was *wonderful*. She hammered the pedal down so hard it probably mashed straight through the cheesy carpet and floorboard, connecting her straight to the engine block. The motor shrilled, the tires spun, and she catapulted forward.

She really hadn't given her aim much thought, other than stopping the tan man from making it through the building's front doors. The guy flitted up the stairs, fast as a bat on steroids. Which left her with no alternative, really. Except to follow.

The Peugeot's suspension was built to cushion its passengers over bumpy French lanes. Even so, smacking the patio-sized steps bounced her head off the ceiling. Emma gave the vacant guard station a flitting glance, and had a sudden notion that the place was empty on purpose. Everybody drawn away by an official crisis, sent far off enough to let this guy do his job and escape unseen.

The little man reached the front doors and turned. His startled expression was captured by her bouncing headlights, a wide-eyed viper trapped between the entrance and oblivion. Which was good enough for her to yell, "Hi there, Leon!"

He flung open the door and leapt through.

Emma didn't have any choice, really. She followed Leon right through the doors.

The glass shattered and the wooden door frame came to rest on the car's splintered windshield. She thought she saw Leon lying inert in front of the car, but her vision was marred by dust and the windshield's hairline fractures.

Then the building erupted a second time.

She imagined a near strike from a shoulder-fired missile would feel about the same. A distant *whump,* then the building sort of lifted on its foundations. One solid jolt, then nothing.

Somewhere ahead of her, an alarm started clanging.

Emma coughed through the dust and said to no one in particular, "Gee, ya think?"

Taking the alarm as her cue, she slapped the car into reverse. The tires spun, sending up a spray of glass and debris. The car rocked but did not move. She lifted her foot off the gas and tried drive. The glass tinkled as it flew like spray off a speedboat. She tried reverse again, and this time just let the tires scream and smoke. Abruptly the car broke free, bouncing over the door frame. Emma launched into a gut-swooping ride backward down the front steps.

Straight into the side of the military vehicle.

She heard a loud bang, which she took as the only starting gun she would ever need.

Emma rammed the car into drive. In her rearview mirror, she saw the military vehicle cant steeply toward her as she wrenched away. She realized she had blown one of its tires. Inside the cab a single head flopped and slumped forward. She turned her attention to the road and smoked her way into a sharp left.

And came within a hairsbreadth of slamming into a dump truck that came roaring around the side of the building.

The yellow behemoth was almost buried beneath its load of debris. A massive dust cloud billowed in its wake. And there on top of the bricks and mortar and rubble, gripping the cab's railing with one hand and waving the other over his head, rode Harry Bennett.

Emma would have laughed out loud if her throat hadn't chosen that moment to throttle off her breath.

FORTY-SEVEN

THE TRUCK DRILLED THROUGH THE empty roads like a locomotive. A spume of dust blew off the back, blanketing Emma's vision. Even so, Emma remained grimly attached to the truck's bumper. Every now and then she flicked the windshield wipers. Only the one on her side worked. Occasionally a rock rattled across her roof. Three miles outside town, she watched as Harry leaned over the side and shouted in Storm's window. The truck shuddered to a halt. Storm leapt down from the cab and hurried over to Emma's car. Harry grinned and blew Emma a very dusty kiss as he slipped behind the truck's wheel.

Storm slid into the passenger seat and pointed ahead. "Harry says get in front and head for the Kyrenia road. He's got an idea."

As they started off, Storm stuck her head out the window. "I don't hear any sirens."

"They'll be coming." Emma kept accelerating so long as the truck remained a looming, roaring beast in her rearview mirror. When the distance grew to where she could see the dust boiling off the truck, she eased off.

Storm said, "Where did you go back there?"

"I spotted our friend Leon. He was going after Harry. I chased him into the building." She caught Storm's look. "What?"

"You entered the police station."

"Courthouse. But yeah."

"In your car. This from the lady who couldn't commit a felony."

"I was in hot pursuit."

"Oh. Is that what you call it. And what happened to your rear end?"

"That was an accident. Sort of. I did a number on the commandant's car."

Storm grinned. "I know what Harry would say. This just keeps getting better."

The road entered the hills and narrowed. When the hills closed tightly, Harry flashed the truck's lights and gave his horn a blast. When Emma stopped, he came trotting up and said, "Pull around the next hairpin and wait for me."

Three hundred yards later, Emma rounded a bend so tight she feared Harry's truck wouldn't make it. He blinked his lights and stopped the truck where the road jinked back on itself. She turned and watched the truck rumble and grind. The rear began to rise, dumping its load of municipal rubble. The debris completely blocked the road from cliff face to drop-off.

He left the dump truck as it was, climbed down from the cab, and flung the keys into the crevasse. He ran back, climbed into the rear seat, and said, "I'm hoping I'll find the right words to thank you ladies once we're truly out of this."

FORTY-EIGHT

Harry?"

He swam up through impossible depths. A hand took hold of his shoulder and shook him gently. "It's time, Harry. You need to wake up."

The words warmed like sunlight, caressing from his ears to his heart. He murmured, "I could lie here forever."

"You were the one who said we had to make an early start." Emma helped him sit upright. "You also said no fire, so all we've got is water and energy bars."

Harry rose to his feet, taking it in careful stages. He was whipped, bruised, battered, and about as tired as he'd ever been in his life. So were the ladies. More than the flashlight's glimmer carved new caverns into Emma's cheeks and around her eyes. He chewed the energy bar and willed his body to shake off the fatigue. He needed to be totally ready for what lay ahead. "What's the matter with Storm?"

Emma glanced over to where Storm stood between the Jet Skis, silhouetted by the night. She searched for words and settled on "We missed out on Boucaud."

Harry nodded. He had almost forgotten the guy. His brain only had room for one clear thought. He finished his breakfast, drained the mug of water.

"Thanks, Emma. For everything. Most especially for right now. Thanks."

It was a futile clump of words, for she merely gripped his arm, then handed him a flashlight and said, "I'll start packing up."

They had dumped the car outside the resort's perimeter fence and sauntered through arm in arm, just three weary tourists returning from a night of revelry. They smiled and laughed for the guard. Harry made himself into a drunken clown, pantomiming a roll in the sand. The guard made a pretense of checking their names on his clipboard. But he spoke no English, and the three of them kept up a good-natured banter as he waved them through. They held to the smiles and light chatter, walking hand in hand down to the shore.

Harry broke the lock on the lifeguard's shed with his boot. They loaded the sleds and pulled the Jet Skis into waist-deep water, out past the reach of the shoreline lights, then motored out, taking it slow. They spent what was left of the night on the same beach as before.

Harry filled his mug from the water canister and walked over to where Storm stood. The tight sliver of moon revealed features etched by fear, excitement, apprehension, loss, and sheer exhaustion. Harry thought she had never looked more beautiful. "I'm really sorry about messing up your rendezvous."

She jerked at that final word. "What?"

"With Boucaud."

Her look was beyond despondent. "We did what we had to, Harry. That's all that keeps me going."

"We won't let him get away with this."

"He already has."

"No, Storm. You're wrong." He gave it as long as he felt he could, then said, "I need to say this. The words aren't much, but they're all I have. Thanks, Storm. You are one amazing woman."

He could see her struggle, as though searching for words that had been lost to the night. Harry knew exactly how she felt. He drained his mug and called, "Let's saddle up."

THEY PASSED THE LAST HEADLANDS between their seafront campsite and the islands just as dawn's first faint wash illuminated their world. Harry had not wanted to navigate the rock-strewn waters in the dark. Everything but the three sleeping bags and what food and water Harry could carry in his backpack had been left behind, in a small cave.

When they approached the first cluster of islets, he signaled for the women to hold well back. Emma cut her throttle. Harry leaned over and puttered forward at a walking pace.

The islands started close to shore, then rose to their highest point a mile and a half to sea. Their destination was in the outermost group, neither the highest nor the most readily accessible. The island cluster stank of seaweed and guano. Harry saw no sign of human presence. The water remained clear of fog, perhaps due to the heavy clouds gathering overhead.

From a distance of five hundred yards, the island looked like an ice cream cone that had been mashed hard into the rocky base. The pedestal was a flat rock about a hundred yards to a side, canted slightly so that the morning waves lapped over the low end.

Harry ran aground twice during his final approach. Both times he put the Jet Ski into neutral, found footing on the underwater rock, and shoved himself free.

When he finally arrived, he pulled the machine up onto the ledge, then turned and waved. Storm kept her face close to the water's surface, calling soft warnings. Emma made the approach without once becoming stuck.

There was a rhythm to it now, a sense of shared commitment so strong that words were unnecessary. Storm hunted about the base on her hands and knees, searching as much by feel as with her eyes. Emma took one hammer and worked higher up, moving counterclockwise around the base. There was no need for Harry to tell either woman to take great care walking on the water-slick rock. He started climbing, his ascent timed to plinks from Emma's hammer.

The cone was canted slightly to the north and

ringed by ridges at semiregular stations, like a fossilized beehive. Harry reckoned it was two hundred feet in diameter and twice as high. He decided to climb the north face, the most difficult angle, for the simple reason that nothing about this search had been easy. This side was the position least likely to be found by accident. The slant wasn't critical, just enough to make his climb a little tougher.

His plan was simple. Scale the summit, hammer in a pair of hooks, set his rope in place, then work his way back down, swinging around the entire peak before descending the next step.

That is, unless he got it lucky on the ascent.

Which was exactly what happened.

The rock was so blackened by salt and seawater, Harry was actually past the sign before his mental alarm started clanging.

He eased back a notch, wiped one hand over the rock's surface. Then he used the same hand to swipe at his eyes. Making sure it wasn't a figment or an illusion or a dream to balance out his nightmares in the cage.

The sign stayed right where it was. A stone fish rudely carved into the face, about two-thirds of the way up.

"Emma!"

"Yo."

"Come give me a hand."

"I'm not done."

Harry took a deep breath. Filled his lungs with the iodine stench of rotting seaweed and the strong flavor of sea. And the special taste of gold.

He called down, "Yes, you are."

FORTY-NINE

HARRY ATTACKED THE ROCK FACE with all his might. Emma worked one side of the fish, he the other. He tried to keep the carving intact, though as his frustration grew he was tempted to batter it into oblivion. They kept firm grips upon the rock face, because Harry had serious doubts that the hooks holding his support line would hold. He had not found any pitons in Kyrenia. So he had bought the longest nails he could find, hammered them partway in, then bent them so he had something to knot the rope around. It was there for an emergency only. And to hold him when his fingers cramped and he had to take a moment's break. Like now.

He said, "I think maybe I've found a seam."

Emma shifted over a notch. "Like a natural rock seam, or one between stones?"

"I can't tell yet. If it's our spot, the stones were wedged in there supertight." He ran his hand over the face. "Of course, there's a real good chance we've got it totally wrong and we're wearing ourselves out for nothing."

"This is the right island and this is the right

place. I took aim through the sights, the same as you." She patted the fish, now framed by raw chip marks. "And this baby is set into the only flat space on the whole hill."

Storm called up from below, "Why don't you two go get a room and let a girl do some real work?"

Harry hammered until his shoulder threatened to fall off, then shifted to his other hand. Overhead, the morning never got a solid start. Clouds rolled in with the sunrise. The longer he worked, the thicker and gloomier grew the overcast. A stiff wind pushed in from the northeast, jamming the covering ever closer to earth.

Then it happened.

One minute he was pounding solid rock. His neck and shoulder and arm and fingers all shrieked for him to stop. The next, the rock just fell away. Into nothing.

Harry's pain vanished instantly. He levered his hammer into the hole, wrenched with all his might, and another stone fell away. "Got your flashlight?"

Emma was already sliding her hammer into her belt. She flicked on the light and shined it through the widening hole.

"Will somebody up there tell me what's going on?"

Harry drew his head back out of the hole, looked down, and said, "We're in."

• • •

STORM REMAINED AT THE BASE. The line she held was cinched around a Jet Ski's steering console. Emma sat on the opening's ledge, ready to pull up the line and drop whatever Harry found down to Storm.

Harry slid his other leg over, ready to descend. "I should have brought another rope."

"Shoulda, woulda, coulda. Ready?"

"I've been ready for this all my life."

Even so, Harry took his time, raking his light over the interior walls, mapping his way down. "Okay, here we go."

Emma kept tension on the rope now lashed to his waist. But her position was too precarious for him to use her as a mainstay unless there was an emergency. Thankfully the interior wall was uneven enough to offer a multitude of handholds.

About midway down, Harry jerked at a low booming sound. "What was that?"

Emma's voice rolled about the stone interior. "Thunder."

The first flecks of rain struck his upturned face. "You okay?"

"Don't worry about me, Harry."

Another dozen handholds into his descent, the rain was steady and drenching. The rocks he held grew increasingly slick. He took as firm a hold as he could manage, pulled the flashlight from his pocket, and took a long look down. "Emma!"

"Here!"

"I'm about twenty feet from the bottom. The interior face is slick like glass. There looks to be a sandy bottom. I'm going to jump."

"Is it safe?"

"Better than falling. Give me slack."

When the rope loosened, Harry released his grip and dropped.

The bottom was fine as silt. Harry rolled and came up on the rock wall.

"Harry!"

"I broke my light."

"Are you all right?"

"Yes, except I can't see anything."

Emma's light flashed on. "Here's mine. Ready?"

"Go."

The light fell, illuminating what Harry had seen up top. The chamber was shaped like a pipe about fifteen feet wide. He caught the light and studied the cave more closely. No shelves, no markings, nothing except the soft sand bottom.

He searched and searched, plowing furrows into the sand with his pick. The rain fell so heavy it filled the chamber with a constant sibilant rush.

Emma called, "Storm wants to know what's happening."

Harry lowered himself to his haunches. The weariness and the cold and the utter futility left him hollow.

It happened all the time in this game. Searching

and hunting and coming agonizingly close. Finally finding the key, the last remaining clue. Opening the door, expecting the big one, the lifetime find. Only to discover he'd been beaten out. By a century, by an hour. The result was the same. Harry shaped the words with his mouth, *it's empty*. But he didn't have the strength to make a sound.

Then he realized, "Something's not right."

"Harry?"

He stepped around the perimeter. Water kept falling. And *water kept moving out*. None was collecting in the bottom. The ground was muddy, but nothing more.

Harry dropped to his hands and knees and started chipping his way around the base. He plinked the stone over and over and over and . . .

Hit air.

This time he could use both hands to grip. He swung the pick so wildly he shouted through each chop.

The entire wall crumbled. One moment he was hitting immovable stone. The next he faced a narrow opening about three feet high. Harry crouched and shined his light through. And cried out loud.

"Harry!"

His light did a crazy dance over the glittering gold, the temple painting on the opposite wall. The golden pipe folded into a trunk-sized unit.

A woman kept shrieking his name.

Harry turned his face to the rain. Some of the drops on his face were frigid, others so hot they burned.

He said, "Get ready to haul up treasure!"

FIFTY

THEY SLIPPED THE TREASURE INTO the three sleeping bags and lashed them onto the sleds. Every time one sled or the other became stuck on the return journey, all three of them gathered and coaxed the sled over the obstacle. The rain fell and fell. Harry's vision was down to a few feet. The water's surface was clouded by dimples, another reason they got stuck so often. Harry forced himself to take it slow, even when his mind screamed with the urge to get away, get clear, get gone.

Harry's plan was simple in the extreme. Pull the sleds across the eighty miles to Turkey. Hug the shoreline until they found a truly desolate spot. Which Harry figured wouldn't be all that tough. The Anatolian coast was rugged, wild, and vastly underpopulated. All he needed was a place that would stay unnoticed for the two days it would take him to hire a larger vessel and return. Then he would put off for some isolated stretch of sea and wait for a seaplane with a trusted pilot.

Once they were beyond the rocks, they were under way. Harry was tempted to shout his plans across to the ladies. Suggest they work on a map and mark the spot with an X. But neither Storm nor Emma appeared much in the mood for laughs.

Not that he could blame them.

What Harry had not counted on was the tempest. The wind built to gale force. The rain felt a degree or so above freezing and struck them like ice bullets. They throttled back to one-third power. The sleds were so heavy they acted like sea anchors, dragging and tugging and fighting the waves. Their forward progress was slow and jerky. The Jet Ski motors weren't made for this kind of going, waves lashed and constantly yanked backward by the sleds' weight. Harry's greatest worry, even larger than the very real prospect of hypothermia, was that one of the Jet Skis would lose power. If a sled sank there was no way he could mark the place. But there was also no way for them to turn around. Other than Cyprus, if they ran with the wind the next nearest landfall was Lebanon, the last place on earth Harry wanted to land with a boatload of gold.

Every time the rain let up enough for him to get a decent look, the ladies were shivering harder. But stopping was no good. There was no place for them to take cover. Even if he lashed the two Jet Skis together, the waves could swamp them. His only hope was for a break in the weather. Until then, they had to just keep going.

Out of nowhere, a ghost ship appeared ahead of them. At least, that was how it first seemed to

Harry—a vague shadow etched in the rain and lashing wind. He figured it for a fishing boat. But then he saw the superstructure and was gripped by an old familiar dread. It was a patrol vessel. Of which country scarcely mattered.

He shouted, "Scramble left!"

Then a megaphone blasted through the storm, loud and clear enough for the man's voice to carry a familiar accent. "We have you in our sights, Mr. Bennett. Heave to."

FIFTY-ONE

THE VESSEL REMAINED BROADSIDE TO the storm, granting the winch operator calm seas off her lee side. Harry stayed on deck until both sleds and then the Jet Skis were safely on board. He watched the armed guards stow his treasure in the aft hold, lock the portal, then post a guard. Harry stayed well away from both the soldiers and the women. He needed time to seal his emotions in tight. And to scope out the situation, which Harry decided looked somewhere between grim and hopeless.

Hakim Sundera had brought an entire army. The ship was about 150 feet long, heavy at the beam, steady even in these seas. A pair of inflatable pursuit vessels were lashed to the aft holds. The foredeck held a pair of cannons on swivel bases. Harry spotted the NATO shield on some of the foulweather gear. The soldiers were pros. They treated Harry as both a guest and a suspect, keeping two armed men between him and the treasure at all times.

When he entered the pilot's cabin, Hakim Sundera greeted him with a towel and a steaming mug. Harry ignored both. He stepped over to where Emma cowered in the corner. She looked so miserable he wanted to crush her to his chest and say he'd do his best to make it all better. Which, given the circumstances, was not going to happen.

He had no choice but to face the facts. The treasure had been his for all of about three hours.

Harry said to Emma, "You gave me your word."

Storm replied softly, "She kept it."

He gaped. "You sold us out? *You?*"

"It was the only way to save you. Hakim located the prison where you were being held. He arranged for me to borrow that truck." Storm bore the look of having already been whipped bloody. She watched him in utter submission, her fractured gaze saying she had already called herself everything he could come up with and more. "But I had to agree to this."

When he started to turn away, Storm gripped his arm. "Sean didn't sacrifice his life to this for you to make a killing!"

Her fingers felt like a branding iron on his skin. "Let go of my arm."

She only held on more fiercely. "It's been staring

me in the face all along, but I only saw it last night. There were never two quests, Harry. They were always one and the same. That was why Sean wouldn't let go."

This time, when he jerked away, she released her hold. But her fractured voice and eyes held him fast. Storm said, "Sean was a man of treasure and a man of faith, and this quest took just such a man. Remember what I said that night in Kyrenia? I want to hold to his legacy. *All* of it, Harry. My grandfather was murdered by people who'd take these sacred relics and use them as just another weapon. If you put them on the market, they would become just another prize. Sean was after something much greater here!"

Harry turned and fled the pilot's station, chased by Storm's words: "Sean trusted us to do the same!"

HARRY SHOWERED AND SHAVED IN the crew's quarters. Hakim found him in the general mess, dressed in trainee sweats and chowing on meat loaf, potatoes, and regulation navy ketchup gravy.

Hakim recharged Harry's mug and slipped into the booth beside him. And waited.

Harry asked, "How did you track us?"

"I instructed Storm to phone a certain number, one that tied her to an ultra-secret GPS service. The service is used by intelligence agents on clandestine missions. It acts as a homing beacon, precise to half a meter." Hakim Sundera was not so much small as intensely compact. Even his gaze carried a tensile strength. "You must not condemn Storm, Harry. She is an extremely wise woman who made the right choice at a harrowing time. If she had not agreed to my terms, you would be most extremely dead by now."

Harry shoved his plate aside.

"Shall I tell you what is already in the process of happening?"

"As in, to my treasure?"

"A Professor Morgenthal at Georgetown University, whom I believe you have met, is making arrangements on your behalf. I cannot be involved in these negotiations, as officially I am not here. But I understand Professor Morgenthal is proving a very tough bargainer. Your treasure is to become the centerpiece of the renovated UN headquarters in New York. This renovation will not be completed for another six years. In the meantime, the treasure will be on exhibition at several major museums. To take part, the museums must come up with a substantial payment. In cash. Which you will all share. Your and Ms. Syrrell's names will feature prominently. Ms. Webb has refused the honor, for reasons I am sure—"

"It's my treasure."

Hakim sighed. "I will share a secret with you, Harry. Between friends. Once my role in all this is discovered, there are many among my own people who will call me a traitor. To give up this Jewish treasure is to relinquish a major bargaining tool. Which is why, I am certain, your attackers remained on your trail. The Israelis will work through the international courts and eventually their claims will be accepted. In the meantime, I chose the United Nations, a bastion of peace and not war, as the holder and the arbiter."

Hakim leaned over the table, closing the distance between them. "What Storm told you is the utter and brilliant truth, Harry. This find will become one of the beacons by which this century will be remembered. It may well prove the fulcrum through which lasting peace in the Middle East is finally established. Do you truly believe that such artifacts should ever appear on the open market? This is more than treasure, Harry. This is *hope.* Even I, an Arab and a Muslim, can recognize this. And so should you."

Harry slid from the booth and stood. "I'd be grateful if you'd drop me at your next port of call."

FIFTY-TWO

T HREE DAYS LATER, STORM UNLOCKED the doors to the shop in Palm Beach. She set down her bags and walked through the empty rooms, turning on all the lights as she went. Emma shut the front door, set down her case, and stood watching her. "Where it all started," Emma said.

Storm stepped behind the front room's main counter and asked, "Can I help you?"

"Absolutely," Emma replied. "I need a new heart. Mine is broken."

"We're a little low on stock right now. But I'll see what I can do. Soon as I pick up one for myself."

Emma walked to the dusty front window. "If I keep telling myself it would never have worked between me and Harry, do you think there's a chance I might someday believe it?"

Storm slowly wiped the countertop, clearing a tight circle of dust. "How long can you stay?"

"Long as it takes to know you're safe."

"Any word on Claudia?"

"Same response as yesterday. The lady has vanished. Soon as I hear anything different, you'll know."

They had spent two days in Washington, where Emma had been feted as the returning hero. Hakim's investigation had yielded four more shops Boucaud had taken over. Hakim had given Emma the details, then departed. Leaving Emma to accept all the credit as hers. International arrest warrants had been issued for one Yves Boucaud, others for a shadow known as Leon.

Storm had spent hours with the lawyers. Nobody knew precisely what to do about Syrrell's. Ownership was now held by an offshore corporation that suddenly had ceased to exist.

And Claudia was nowhere to be found.

And Jack Dauer had been invited to resign.

The FBI had egg all over their faces. Treasury was doing backflips. Emma was up for a major promotion, possibly being assigned her own task force.

Emma asked the window, "Decided what you're going to do?"

"This shop is mine if I want it. The title is now in my name, and I have eight months still paid up on the lease."

"You want it."

"I thought I did. But now . . ."

"Bite the bullet, Storm."

"I betrayed Harry and destroyed his dream. Now I'm supposed to use the blood money to make my own dreams real?"

Emma gave that the silence it deserved. Storm walked to the kitchen tucked beneath the stairwell, next to her downstairs office, and put on coffee. As she stood watching the pot brew, she said, "I was right, though. What I did and what I said. Sean combined the best of what he was, his faith and his passion for art treasure, and from this came his gift. It didn't make him perfect, but it made him a great man. There are a lot worse things for a girl to do with her life than follow her grandfather's example."

From the front room, she heard Emma say, "You've given this a lot of thought."

"Harry's the last of several men I've argued with who weren't actually there." She poured two cups and brought them back. "I'm out of milk."

"Black is fine." Emma accepted her cup. "Washington is asking again."

Storm sipped her cup. She preferred her coffee adorned with steamed milk and brown sugar and a sprinkle of chocolate if any was being offered. But the bitter brew suited the moment.

"They really want you there, Storm."

Their recovery of treasure dating from the Second Temple had created an international furor. The official unveiling was to take place in three days at the Smithsonian. The president and the UN secretary-general and the Israeli prime minister were all slated to speak.

Emma said, "You can't believe from how high these requests are coming."

"They want me so bad, fine. Find Harry."

"We're trying. Believe me."

"Tell them to try harder."

"He's vanished, Storm. We're talking completely off the map. It's like he stepped off the boat and melted into the storm."

The cup rattled against her teeth. "He can't be gone."

They shared the quiet with the dust and the shadows and the empty rooms. Emma asked, "You hungry?"

"I suppose I should be."

"I'll go grab us a couple of sandwiches. You want anything special?"

Storm waved the hand not holding the cup. Whatever.

After Emma departed, Storm remained where she was, staring out the front window. Through her entire adult life, her one goal had been to exceed her grandfather's expectations. Which was doubly tough, since almost nothing had satisfied the old man, and now he was gone from her forever. Just like Harry. She cradled her empty cup and tried to breathe around the rock of sorrow in her chest. She and men were such a losing proposition.

She picked up her suitcases and walked through the back room. She decoded the rear door's electronic lock and started up the stairs, thinking no further than how nice it would feel to shower off the trip.

When Sean had refitted the shop, he had effectively designed a shell within a shell. The shop was sheathed in steel plate and bulletproof glass. The stairs leading up to the apartment were narrow and claustrophobic, with reinforced doors at both ends. The upstairs door would not open until the other sighed shut on its pneumatic hinge. The upstairs door faced directly into the living room, across from the kitchen and her bedroom entrance. Storm opened the door to the same empty space, with one impossible difference.

On the room's one remaining item of furniture,

the lumpy sofa where Harry had slept, sprawled her aunt. Her hands and ankles and mouth were taped. Her eyes were closed. Her face looked lumpish, pale, utterly removed from Claudia's customary elegance.

The blow to her head came out of nowhere. The pain was so sharp it shattered her vision. Storm went down hard.

FIFTY-THREE

STORM AWOKE TO A SOUND from her childhood. She breathed the same sweet cloying odor that had permeated every room in their house. She sat with her eyes closed. Coming to terms with everything she had gotten wrong.

Her father collected pipes. Hundreds of them. His favorite traveling pipe was a hand-blown bong. The base was shaped like a yellow tulip. Her father liked to fill it with ice. The sound of sucking smoke through the melting ice was almost musical. Storm would have known that sound anywhere.

"You might as well open your eyes. I know you're awake."

Her first sight was of him standing by the open freezer door, unscrewing the bong's top so he could drop in more crushed ice.

The things a girl remembered about home.

Claudia said, "Are you all right?"

Storm's mouth felt gummed shut. Nodding threatened to dislodge the top of her skull.

Her father slammed the freezer door. "Oh, come on. Leon didn't hit you that hard."

They were seated in Storm's kitchen alcove on a pair of metal folding chairs. The chairs were set up to face the rear window. The shade was drawn tight and nailed to the counter. A laptop sat open on the counter beneath the window. Storm's wrists were tied to the chair's rear legs. Her ankles were taped to the front legs. More tape bound her waist. She glanced over. Claudia was lashed the same way. Tape ran around the crossties running between the chair's front and rear legs, and this was nailed into the floor.

Storm managed, "I'm so sorry."

Claudia's eyes filled. Her hair, normally so perfectly coiffed, was matted and mashed flat. "For what? I'm the one who didn't believe you and your threats."

"I thought it was you."

Her father choked over his smoke. "Her? My perfect little sister? Do something wrong?" He laughed wildly.

Claudia snapped, "This is your *daughter*."

Joseph Syrrell's pupils were tight pinholes, his hands never still. Meth, Storm decided. He'd started mixing and matching his highs about the time she left home. Her father snapped, "Way wrong. I lost this girl the day she went to work for

471

that man." He spat the words, his face constricted by the effort of releasing a genuine emotion for once. He rounded on Storm. "You just wouldn't leave the thing alone. This was supposed to be *my* time. *My* shop. Take back everything the old man stole from me."

Claudia said, "You're the only thief in this room."

"Oh. Right. Ask Storm why she stopped by my house the other day." He flicked the lighter, toked hard, and grinned around the mouthpiece. Blew out a long stream of smoke. "Cute move, by the way. Using the siren to spook me."

"The triptych was Sean's."

"Like I care."

"Whatever Boucaud has promised you, it's a lie. The whole deal has gone south. The authorities—"

"Save it." He set down the pipe and started tapping on the laptop's keyboard. His bulk blocked the screen from view. After a moment, he asked, "Can you see okay?"

"If you will move aside, I'll tell you."

The voice froze Storm's gut.

The face on the laptop screen smiled directly at her. "Storm Syrrell. We meet at last."

FIFTY-FOUR

EMMA LEFT THE DELI BOUNCING the sandwich bag off her leg. The afternoon light bathed an almost empty Palm Beach Island. Humidity now replaced tourists in this off-season town. Her fatigue was as heavy a burden as the heat. The past few days had been like living inside a fireworks display. So many explosions coming so fast, the clamor had been deafening. News of the discovery had broken before their flight landed. They had been met at Dulles by a barrage of mikes and lights and cameras and shouted questions. Emma had suspected Hakim had been behind the leak, but he was nowhere to be found.

Emma's reports on Boucaud and the art market scandal had brought turmoil to the halls of power. Emma had been pulled into one conference after another—Treasury, Homeland Security, a Senate subcommittee, even one meeting with senior White House staffers. Foiling an attempt to use the international art and treasures market to finance global terrorism was a major coup. Everyone wanted to be seen as taking part in the triumph.

Only now, walking the sweltering side street back to Worth Avenue, could she see beyond the moment. And be confronted yet again with all she had gained. And the far greater burden of all that was lost forever.

Then she saw the bike.

This one was a brilliant red two-wheeled rocket. Even the emblem looked fast; the gold letters ending in flames. The bike was massive, low to the ground, with a tiny windshield and stubby controls—everything drawn in tightly to help the driver withstand a g-force stronger than the space shuttle's liftoff. The bike was parked directly opposite the passage leading back to Storm's shop. A flame-red warning meant just for her.

Emma dropped the bag and ran, fumbling about in her purse for her gun. At the moment of sunlit blindness, a man stepped into her path. He was scarcely larger than an olive-skinned elf, and had eyes that burned with coal-dark rage. His hand was extended, almost in greeting. The single whiff from the perfume canister struck her face before she had even truly seen him. It was done so swiftly and smoothly she blocked his hand only after the mist clung to her skin and eyes.

Emma tried to raise her gun, only to discover she had no hands.

FIFTY-FIVE

STORM KNEW SHE WAS SOON going to die. This knowledge granted her the ability to split each moment into crystalline fractions. There were eons between each frantic heartbeat. Time to etch the man on the computer screen deep into her psyche. Time to hear Claudia's ragged breathing and know she was helpless to do anything about it. Time to watch her father take his leave from Boucaud and depart without glancing her way. Storm heard each precise tick of the clock above the stove. She felt the urgent need to get this one last thing totally right.

She said to Claudia, "I betrayed your trust by thinking what I did. I was totally wrong. I'm so sorry. I want you to know how much I love you."

"How utterly American," Yves Boucaud sneered from the screen. "This ridiculous need of yours to unload your emotions."

Claudia's tears dragged her mascara into dark trenches across her cheeks. "Why is he doing this?"

"I wrecked his plans."

"Only temporarily," Boucaud corrected. The computer gave his words a metallic drone, a deep and dead voice overlaid with a precise accent. "The authorities will scurry about for a time, then another crisis will arise and their attention will turn elsewhere. Then we will resume our work. There is nothing on paper to link me to anything. The plan is still an excellent one. I'll simply identify another conduit."

Claudia addressed the man on the computer for the first time. "What do you want from us?"

"Regrettably, your niece has stirred quite a fuss. Certain clients of mine insist upon knowing what else you have discovered."

"But I don't know anything, and neither does Storm."

"No. Probably not. I suppose they suspect this as well. But they still wish to observe as you both are interrogated. Thoroughly."

Boucaud was groomed in the manner of a polished ornament, gleaming and lifeless. His skin looked professionally tanned. Perfect silver-grey hair. But there was a certain brutal crudeness to his features. His nose was a battering ram, his lips overfull and the color of raw meat. Dark eyes were half hidden by puffy folds.

Claudia stammered, "I don't understand."

Storm said, "It was never just Syrrell's. We've uncovered six other dealers also under attack. Not to mention the treasure. We found it. What Sean was after. All of it."

"I confess that has also rather irked my colleagues. They very much wanted it for themselves. A symbol. A negotiating tool. Or both." He waved it aside. "It is all petty nonsense as far as I am concerned. Be that as it may, you have managed to irritate some very dangerous people. They insist upon vengeance."

There was a rumble from downstairs. A door slammed.

"Excellent," Boucaud said. "We can finally begin."

The stairway door opened. Emma was slumped over the shoulder of a man she completely dwarfed. Her hands dragged on the floor as he kicked the door shut and stepped into the kitchen.

The little tan man moved with remarkable ease. The only sign of the weight he carried was a heavy rasping breath. His gaze drifted over Storm, his eyes murderous.

"I can't tell you how much my colleague is looking forward to this." Boucaud switched to rapid-fire French: "Put Webb on the floor where she can watch. Bind her well and feed her the antidote. Do her last."

He must have seen the horror on both their faces, for he said, "You both speak French. How convenient. I fear my colleague's English is rather limited."

Claudia whispered shakily, "Who is that woman?"

"Emma Webb. Homeland Security."

"Why is she here?"

Boucaud replied, "To protect your troublesome niece. Isn't that delicious?"

The man they knew as Leon held a vaporizer spray under Emma's nose, puffed once, then slapped her face. Again. The tan man had a serious bruise on one cheek and surgical threads dangling from wounds on his forehead and one arm, no doubt the result of Emma's attack in Cyprus. Storm hoped Emma could focus enough to see she had at least scored the first hit.

Boucaud said, "She will watch her last and final

failure, then depart. I understand there are quite a number of her colleagues who will not mourn her passage." He said in French, "Very well. You may begin."

As Leon picked up the duct tape and ripped off three segments for their mouths, Claudia screamed, "Help! Oh please, somebody help us!"

Storm felt no need to remind her aunt how well the place was soundproofed. She stared at Emma. Wishing for a way to make things right. For once.

The gunfire was so rapid the shots sounded like a military drumroll. Which, in a way, it was.

The reinforced French windows splintered, the webbing extended from a series of neat holes. Then a shadow obliterated the sunlight, and Harry Bennett came crashing through.

He tucked and rolled and came up in one fluid motion. He straightened his arm, taking aim with a pistol that looked as big as a club. "Freeze, hotshot."

Leon instantly gripped Emma and pulled her in front of him. He twisted his body so he was fully shielded behind hers, this skinny little gnome holding Emma with one hand at her collar. Emma choked slightly as her wind was cut off. The guy reached into his pocket.

Boucaud screamed in French, "Do him! Do him!"

Harry shifted his aim a fraction to the left and blasted away.

The sound in the room's confines was murderous. Claudia screamed, or perhaps it was Storm.

Harry's gunshots shattered the cabinet beside Leon, sending shards of wood and tile ricocheting around the room. Leon flinched as measles-sized flecks of blood appeared on his face and neck. Emma recoiled under the barrage and twisted her head so the worst of the splinters buried into her hair. Harry moved as he fired, racing toward the assassin.

Leon roared and *threw* Emma at Harry.

Harry did the man thing. And caught her.

Leon was on him before Harry could release her. A blade sliced. Harry shouted far too high for a guy his size. Emma thumped onto the floor at his feet. The lady was all pro, drugged and dazed but still able to roll and grip by drawing her thighs up to her belly, anchoring Leon's legs.

Leon snarled his shrill rage as he swung the knife in a wide arc. Emma curled and ducked. Leon kicked her forehead. Emma slumped.

Harry's gun was on the floor and his shooting arm was drenched red. He hammered Leon with a straight left, hard enough to back him up a pace.

From the kitchen cabinet Boucaud kept screaming his commands, shrill as a woman.

Storm twisted and pulled with all her might. The tape binding her chair to the floor ripped free. She toppled her chair over. Leon flashed a silver arc, his knife came within a hairsbreadth of taking out Harry's throat. Harry backed away.

Storm was there, her one remaining weapon at the ready. When Leon took his next step, she lunged and caught his ankle with her mouth. She clenched down with all her might.

Leon roared and the knife swished. She actually heard it slice through the flesh of her shoulder. She bit deeper still, grinding down to the bone.

Harry stepped forward and pounded Leon straight between the eyes. The little man staggered but stayed aloft. Harry hit him again.

Leon went down hard.

Harry leaned over her, took a ragged breath, said, "You can let go and be sick now."

FIFTY-SIX

THEY WOUND UP IN FOUR adjoining rooms at the hospital in downtown Palm Beach. Claudia was under observation after having been fed a cocktail of drugs for three days. Emma recovered well from her mild concussion. Storm's shoulder took three hours of surgery and left her with her arm bound tightly to her chest. Harry was the only one who really worried them. But on the second day the doctors allowed the two ladies some unsupervised time.

Emma began with "I've got to leave for Washington in about half an hour. Until then, you're mine. The police are going to make certain nobody comes in. No matter how loud you scream."

Harry watched them through guarded eyes. "You're ganging up on me."

Storm used her good arm to raise his bed. "Answers. Good ones. Now."

Emma said, "Start with marching off the boat."

Harry pushed himself up a bit more erect. "About that."

"Yes?"

"I'll tell you. If you're sure you want to know."

"What's that supposed to mean?"

"You're a cop. You'll always be one. The question you need to ask yourself is, can you live with my kind of secrets."

She gave that a long moment. Then decided, "I have to, don't I?"

"I sure hope so."

Emma nodded slowly. Back and forth. "Tell us, Harry."

"I went back."

That brought them both up sharp. "Back where?"

"To the island."

Storm shrilled, "You went *back*? Are you *insane*?"

"I said what I did and acted like that for two reasons. First, I wanted Hakim and his boys to think I was totally fed up, so angry I couldn't talk, much less plan."

"That was an act?" Emma leaned in tight enough to cook him with her heat. "Do you have any idea what I've been through?"

"It was necessary. I also needed Boucaud to think there were only the two of you. If he thought there was the slightest chance I was going to show up, he'd have been more prepared. So I came into the US by boat from the Bahamas. I know it's total paranoia to think Boucaud could have been watching the borders. But I had to get this one *right*. I knew he wasn't going to hit you in Washington. The feds were swarming and the whole world had their eyes on you. So I camped out here, took a room in that overpriced guest-house down the street, and I waited."

"How long were you going to wait, Harry?"

"I figured he was coming sooner rather than later. But I was in for the duration."

Storm planted her face on the sheet by his hand. Shook her head back and forth. Clearing her eyes. "You gave Sean your word."

He let his hand settle into her hair. "Actually, you were the one I promised, lady. I told you I'd be there for you. Remember?"

Storm kept dragging her eyes back and forth over the sheet.

Emma said, "You mind if we back up to that first little item? About going back to North Cyprus? Alone?"

"With a pal."

"But without *us*."

"It had to be that way. We hired a speedboat in Rhodes. My buddy got me in diving range. I swam in. Swam out. We left. I flew to Freeport, boated here. End of story."

"No, it's not," Storm said. "Not by a long shot."

Emma agreed. "You risked your life, your future, *our* future. And for what?"

Harry said, "I love hearing you say that."

Her tone sharpened. "Answer the question, Harry."

He pointed at the closet. "Reach into the back pocket of my trousers. There's something in my handkerchief I want you to see."

Storm came back, opened the cloth, and let two coins spill onto the bed. They glinted rough and red in the light.

"Herodian gold. Stamped with Herod Antipas on one side and Pontius Pilate on the other." He drank in the sight of their two stunned faces. "It was pretty simple. Soon as I saw your faces that morning, I knew something was up. I mean, how did you know which police station to hit? The closest jail to where I got ambushed was Kyrenia. Somebody told you where to go. You couldn't just call the police and ask. Hakim had to have stepped in. So I took the coins from the chest and I buried them. Just in case."

Harry winced as he linked his hands behind his head. "Where should I send your shares?"

FIFTY-SEVEN

HARRY FLEW TO WASHINGTON IN a private jet. Emma met him planeside with a limo bearing diplomatic plates. Emma was a study in midnight blue—pumps, stockings, hairband, new suit by Givenchy. Harry knew because he saw the label. Emma gave him space to absorb it all—the early morning drive, the smooth slide through the nation's monuments. She only spoke once, when he asked how she arranged for all these perks.

Emma replied, "Haven't you heard? It's Harry Bennett Day."

The Smithsonian Museum's Art and Industries Building dressed up the Jefferson Drive stretch of the National Mall. The edifice was gaudy enough to outshine the carousel located just beyond its southern perimeter. The style was high Victorian. The brick exterior was adorned with peaks and turrets. The crowd stretched in accordion style through guarded ranks between the building and the road. Harry guessed there must have been a thousand or more people, at eight-thirty in the morning. It was a typical Washington throng. Tourists mingled with pin-striped bureaucrats whose plastic IDs were strung around their necks, reading the *Post*, sipping lattes, talking into their Bluetooths, too caught up in being important to even notice the fine June morning. They all stopped and watched, though, as Emma stepped from the limo, waved away the driver, and helped Harry maneuver himself upright.

"Can you manage?"

"Sure thing." He debated momentarily, then decided to leave the cane in the car. He probably needed it. But he was determined to make this trek on his own steam.

"Storm wanted to make sure I told you again how sorry she was not to be here. But Sean's memorial service is turning into a monster."

"I understand." Harry's bruises were at the stage where they looked worse than they felt. But the stab wounds pulled tight with each step. The one in his hip caused him to limp slightly, but he figured he could manage the distance. What bothered him the worst was where Leon had knifed him on the same rib bruised by the Turkish Cypriot cops. The doctors had wanted him to stay down another day or so. But the previous night Storm had told them what was planned for the next day, and Emma had sprung this little surprise. So here he was. Too excited to let his body hold him back another minute.

Emma had phoned him every day he'd been in the hospital. Sometimes twice. Once three times. She alternated between showing him the caring feminine side and being a tough-minded cop. Harry found he didn't mind the switch at all. He felt like she was intent on more than just clueing him in. She wanted to make him a part of her world. All of it. As much as he could handle.

Her reports on the ongoing investigations remained very upbeat. Leon's true identity remained a mystery. But it was only a matter of time. His fingerprints and DNA linked him to two other killings, one in Brussels and the other in Singapore. He was being held in a maximum-security federal prison in upstate Maryland.

The computer link Yves Boucaud had used proved marginally rewarding. The authorities had established a direct connection to the attorney's office in Marseilles: the same advocate who had refused to help Emma at the prison. The link was undoubtedly a cutout. But it was reason enough for the French authorities to place the lawyer in custody and sweat him thoroughly.

Arrest warrants had been issued for Boucaud, and all known assets had been seized. The current operators of his seven art dealerships were being questioned. Including Storm's father, who sang louder with every hour that further separated him from his last high. The art dealers who had either resigned or been shouldered out were taking up the reins once more. All, that is, but Claudia, who was uncertain whether she would ever reenter Syrrell's.

Harry and Emma walked past the crowds and the barriers. Emma buzzed the main entrance. The left-hand door opened to where it banged on the security pylon. "Yes?"

"I'm Agent Webb. You were called about me."

"ID?" He inspected it carefully. "Your guest is?"

"Harry Bennett."

The guard was ex-military and paid to play like human stone. Even so, his eyes glinted approval. "The man himself."

"Can we come in?"

"Sign in with the agent behind the desk. You armed?"

"No."

"You both have to turn in all phones and electronic gear. No pictures, no recordings of any kind."

"We were informed of procedures."

"Sure you were. But I've got to say it just the same."

"Come on, Harry."

"You've got twenty minutes before we open the doors."

Once they had signed in and passed through the security checkpoint, another agent led them down the central hall. Harry said, "In case I forget to say something later, I just want you to know how much this means."

She squeezed his hand. "I think I know."

The treasure was in the main ballroom. The building had been completed in 1881 and originally housed the National Museum. But its first function, before the museum opened, had been to host the inaugural ball of newly elected President James A. Garfield. The entire building had recently undergone major renovations. The ballroom positively sparkled.

Harry felt a bloom of heat rise from his core, so thick and powerful it totally erased his former aches. The moment, the chamber, held no space for anything except what stood straight ahead.

The cabinets formed a single long line down the center of the gallery. In between each case were drawings, models, photographs, historical overviews. The cases were plain in the extreme. The cubes of bulletproof glass were brilliantly illuminated.

The central case was forty-four feet long.

They had done a remarkable job straightening the vine. The places where it had been bent back upon itself were still visible, but only because Harry was looking. Harry was very glad they had decided to stretch it out again. The vine did not run straight and true. No vine would. Instead, it twisted upon itself, it curved and flowed, adorned along its entire length by grafted-on leaves of solid gold.

Sean walked the entire length of the room alongside Harry. Harry was as certain of that as he was that Storm had been right to share their quest with the world. These treasures belonged to humanity.

They stayed until the main doors opened and the

hordes arrived in a hurried rush of footfalls and conversation.

Harry had no interest in sharing his moment with anyone but Emma and his departed friend. She must have understood, for she moved up close and said, "Take my arm."

FIFTY-EIGHT

THE SAME PRIVATE JET FLEW them back to Palm Beach. As they left the terminal, Harry said, "The last time I came through here I was wearing a Bentley. Most of one, anyway."

First stop was Storm's apartment, where Storm greeted them both with a hug made clumsy by one arm still being in a sling. She then walked them around, showing off the progress she'd made in the cleaning and renovation. The kitchen cabinets Harry had shot up had been torn out and the stains had been worked from the hardwood floor. The movers had returned the furniture, and Storm talked about consignment items she had been offered, enough to reopen the shop. Harry spotted a few smudges of fingerprint powder in the bedroom as he showered and dressed in the suit Storm had laid out on the bed. Maybe one day he'd be able to enter here without seeing Leon's manic gaze, glaring at him through the veil of Emma's hair.

Emma drove them by the bank and accompanied

Storm inside. Harry sat in the car, reveling in a day he could only describe as complete. Emma emerged with a bank carry bag, which she settled on the backseat beside Storm. Storm looked like she was sheathed in smoke, a dynamite frock of blue grey silk that somehow managed to look utterly severe and alluring at the same time.

They rode to the church in silence. Harry stared out the side window as the line of Imperial palms flashed by, recalling another trip down this very same avenue, one far more heavily laden. He sighed contentedly, ready to finally put that to rest. As much as was humanly possible.

The church's parking lot was jammed, as were all the surrounding streets. Cars and limos and television vans lined the beachside highway for a mile or more in either direction. When the guard blocking the main drive tried to wave them away, Emma leaned forward and flashed her badge, saying, "The show can't start without us."

Douglas Kerr, the senior pastor, bounded out the rear doors before Emma cut the motor. He watched her pull the case from the rear seat and asked, "Is that it?"

"Yes."

The pastor was decked out in his most formal set of robes. The overmantle's gold embroidery glittered in the sunset. "We've still got a few minutes. We can wait in the chancellery."

As they entered the church, the pastor said,

"Your aunt sends her best. But she adamantly refuses to budge from the front pew."

"She's still pretty shook up," Storm said.

When they were inside the offices behind the main hall, Harry declared, "I'm with Claudia. I'd feel a lot better sitting this one out."

"Not a chance," Storm said.

"Sean wouldn't like the idea of me standing in front of his church."

"Sean wouldn't have it any other way," Storm replied.

"I feel like an enlisted man sneaking into the officers' mess wearing a stolen uniform."

"You look great, and I know the suit's not stolen because I've still got the receipt in my purse."

Emma's eyes glinted. "Don't tell me you're frightened by the thought of holding a little treasure."

Harry sighed his defeat. "Whatever."

Emma stepped forward. "Your tie's crooked." She fitted the knot in close to his collar. "There." She smoothed the lapels to his jacket. "You look totally edible."

There was a sharp rap on the door. An older man entered in a formal dark suit, a silk skullcap adorning his bald pate. "Ms. Syrrell?"

"That's me."

"Rubin Kleinman. Ambassador of Israel to the United States."

"Thank you for coming."

"On the contrary, Ms. Syrrell, it is I who am indebted for this invitation." He embodied diplomatic elegance from head to toe. Every move seemed measured against a lifetime of wielding power.

"You already know Emma Webb."

"Indeed so. An honor, Agent Webb." He turned to Harry. "And you must be Mr. Bennett. So glad to see you up and around again, sir."

"Thank you, Mr. Ambassador."

The man's polish was matched by an extremely intense gaze. "My government is interested to know if you might be willing to help us with another matter of missing artifacts, Mr. Bennett. We could possibly use the services of a resourceful man who also values discretion."

Harry's interest sparked. "It would sure make for a change, having a government play like I was on their side."

Emma added, "That's the first word that comes to mind when I think about Harry Bennett. Discreet."

The ambassador handed Harry a card. "Perhaps you would be so good as to contact me when this is behind us."

Storm stepped to the desk and slipped the chalice from the bank's carry sack. "You might like to have a look at this."

The ambassador's polished manner simply melted away. "May I?" His hands trembled as he turned the chalice over. He inspected the name inscribed in the base, then slipped a photograph from his jacket and compared the two inscriptions. "It is just as you said."

"I'm glad you agree."

He handed back the chalice, then made a mess of refolding the photograph. "You have not mentioned a price."

The pastor accepted the chalice from Storm and filled it with wafers. Storm knew he objected to their talking business in this setting. But Sean had never been one to isolate his work from his faith. Far from it.

When she was certain of her voice once more, she replied, "Sean trusted you." So much so that he had starred the man's name. There were only nine such entries in his notebook. "You may have the right of first refusal. The offer is to you personally. I will deal with no one else."

Before the diplomat could recover, the pastor said, "Mr. Ambassador, if you would be so kind as to take your seat."

Emma hugged Harry. "I'll see you outside."

Storm watched the two of them embrace and found herself filled with a sudden sense of completion. There was no logic to the moment. But the sensation of having arrived at Sean's goal was so overwhelming, she was forced to look away, afraid if she didn't she would lose control.

They entered the sanctuary to the sound of the

choir singing a Brahms liturgy. The chamber was bathed in harsh white television lights and the frenetic flash of countless cameras.

The sanctuary was lofty and grand and packed. The central aisle was crammed with folding chairs to handle the overflow. The upper loft was a mass of cameras and journalists and lights.

The pastor set Sean's battered Bible on the bronze stand. He directed Harry and Storm to stand at either side of him as he gave his opening benediction.

Sean would have hated the fuss. And loved it. Loved even more the fact that his passage had brought her here. To this place. With his final treasure taking center stage.

The pastor said, "We are gathered here to commemorate the loss of two dear friends, Reverend Richard Ellis and Sean Syrrell. Two friends unto death. United into eternity."

He turned and took the chalice from Harry. Lifting it high over his head, illuminated by far more than all the camera lights, he said, "Behold the bread of life."

Center Point Publishing
600 Brooks Road ● PO Box 1
Thorndike ME 04986-0001 USA

(207) 568-3717

US & Canada:
1 800 929-9108
www.centerpointlargeprint.com

DATE DUE